GULLIVER'S TRAVELS

RIVERSIDE EDITIONS

RIVERSIDE EDITIONS

UNDER THE GENERAL EDITORSHIP OF

Gordon N. Ray

Jonathan Swift

GULLIVER'S
TRAVELS

EDITED WITH AN INTRODUCTION AND NOTES BY

LOUIS A. LANDA

PRINCETON UNIVERSITY

HOUGHTON MIFFLIN COMPANY
Boston • The Riverside Press Cambridge

The Riverside Press

CAMBRIDGE · MASSACHUSETTS

PRINTED IN THE U.S.A.

CONTENTS

INTRODUCTION

Louis A. Landa

"I have observed," wrote Mr. Spectator in 1711, "that a reader seldom peruses a book with pleasure 'till he knows whether the writer of it be a black or fair man, of a mild or choleric disposition, married or a bachelor, with other particulars of the like nature, that conduce very much to the right understanding of an author." This insistence on the value of biography for the appreciation of literature applies with peculiar force to Jonathan Swift because he was one of the most *personal* of authors. What manner of man was he? Legends have swirled about him and facts have been so stubbornly resisted that the true lineaments of his complex and compelling personality have all too often been left obscure. Let us begin his story, not as custom decrees, with his birth, but, perversely, with his epitaph. He penned his own epitaph (a pleasant practice now sadly fallen into desuetude), intent on embodying in a few pungent phrases the essential aspect of his character, that special vision he had of himself and wished posterity to respect. Although Dr. Johnson once remarked that "in lapidary inscriptions a man is not upon oath," one feels the incontestable rightness of the commemorative words which Swift wrote into his will, with the request that they be inscribed in black marble, "in large letters, deeply cut, and strongly gilded."

"You remember how it goes," William Butler Yeats wrote. "It is almost finer in English than in Latin: 'He has gone where fierce indignation can lacerate his heart no more' [*Ubi Saeva Indignatio/ Ulterius/Cor Lacerare Nequit*]." But it is not these words alone, striking as they are, which made Yeats say that "Swift sleeps under the greatest epitaph in history." There is also a spirited Latin injunction to the wayfarer to imitate, if he can, what Swift did in behalf of liberty: *Abi Viator/Et Imitare Si Poteris/Strenuum Pro Virili/ Libertatis Vindicatorem. Libertatis*, we may be certain, in no narrow sense, as Professor Maurice Johnson has remarked in an excellent comment on Swift's epitaph. Swift had in mind a larger liberation, not merely political (though that would be included), but a freeing of the human mind from error and the human spirit from baseness. Now, we need not make him more noble than he was. His ideals doubtless were at times, as his enemies loudly insisted, the prey of crass circumstances; and when his deeper convictions were affronted, he could be relentless and hard. He was perhaps more apt to exercise than suffer the proud man's contumely. Nevertheless, his vision of himself, as suggested by the epitaph, is no misrepresentation. Many of his works and much of his career testify to an abiding concern for the plight of man. Fierce indignation did lacerate his heart as he observed the shackled human spirit. The *saeva indignatio* hints at the wrathful moralist, one utterly incapable of looking at the world with detachment. Any conception of Swift as a man of letters withdrawn from the world and registering his wrath, contempt, and despair merely in words is completely false. Like so many other literary geniuses of the eighteenth century, he was a man of action, anything but aloof from the stresses and strains of local and national life. His public career lasted for almost three decades, from 1710, when he was a prolific political journalist in England for a period of almost four years, to about 1739, when ill health and age had drained his energies. For over two decades following 1714, he was one of Ireland's great men, a zealous churchman in control of a great cathedral and a vigorous participant in the affairs of the nation. Swift was, in fact, a practical reformer, as ready with deeds as with his pen.

He would not have felt a dichotomy between the man of action and the satirist. Nor would he grant the validity of a later-day assessment of satire as something merely negative. To the great satirists of the period satire was an affirmative thing, with constructive intentions. It seemed to offer the best corrective to the vices and follies of man and society as no other literary mode could; and if Swift's ironic wit derives mainly from the bent of his mind and temperament, he was fortunately born in an age that cherished and nourished this quality. "The satirist," Henry Fielding once wrote, "is to be regarded as our physician, not our enemy." Although there was some vocal dissent from this view even in Swift's day, we owe to a later period the extreme conviction that the satirist is somehow an offensive person, at his worst a misanthrope, at his best a cynic, and in either case a man with little or no compassion and hope. The fierce, dark, and violent rhetoric of Swift's major satires, the mingling of acerbity, wit, gloom, and anguish, has often been disconcerting to critics and has unbalanced their judgments of him as a man. Thus Thackeray and other Victorians could view him as living constantly in a raging compound of madness, malignity, and misanthropy, a portrait curiously oblivious to that extensive portion of Swift's works in which comedy and intellectual play prevail, untouched by a darker note. Swift as a smiling satirist should be given his due, the author of the *Bickerstaff Papers* and of many witty poems, for example, one who would tickle mankind into good manners or laugh men out of their favorite follies. It is not easy to release Swift from the legend of the gloomy dean which has been so firmly established. His life, it has been said, "was a long disease, with its disappointments, its self-torture, its morbid recriminations." This is as false as it is theatrical. Philosophically, certainly, he was inclined to an astringent and realistic view of life (habitually expressed in comic terms), but that his personal existence was one of prolonged agony is nonsense.

It is true that Swift's letters in the 1730's show an increase in gloomy pronouncements, a result in good part of his bad health. He knew what it was to suffer from poor eyesight, giddiness, and nausea, the last two of these stemming from a malady which had afflicted him from his early years, Ménière's Syndrome. His correspondents hear much of his ill health in this decade. One of the most frequently quoted letters dates from July, 1740:

> I have been very miserable all night, and today extremely deaf and full of pain. I am so stupid and confounded, that I cannot express the mortification I am under both in body and mind. All I can say is, that I am not in torture, but I daily and hourly expect it. Pray let me know how your health is and your family. I hardly understand one word I write. I am sure my days will be very few; few and miserable they must be. I am, for those few days,
>
> > Yours entirely,
> > J. Swift.
>
> If I do not blunder, it is Saturday, July 26, 1740. If I live till Monday, I shall hope to see you, perhaps for the last time.

This is indeed the outcry of a wretched man, one of a number of such letters written to friends in Swift's later years. If gathered together by an assiduous critic predisposed to theatricalism, he could use them well in support of a theory of "agony and rage and self-torture." But the letter just quoted belongs to Swift's seventy-third year, and it, along with others in the 1730's, should be kept in their proper perspective. By 1735 Swift was approaching seventy, in an age when medical science could not bring either cure or relief to ills which now yield easily to treatment. Men had to live with their maladies, and endure them as well as they could. It is possible that Swift, who was no stoic, was more vocal than others on the subject of pain and misery or that he merely used, characteristically, unrestrained language. But granted that he did undergo in his later years a considerable agony of body and spirit, the point is that this has been excessively dramatized, made to represent the whole man, read back into his earlier years, and used crudely in interpreting his works.

"Good night, I hope I shall never see you again" — this is reported as Swift's manner in later years of bidding farewell to friends, to illustrate a presumed characteristic bitterness and an anguished wish for release by death. If he actually used this remark, if he used it seriously, clearly some weight would attach to it; but I should want to know to whom he used it and in what tone and spirit. It sounds very much like his usual banter, the transparent friendly insult and genial vituperation, which so often distinguishes his letters and his manner to friends who understood his ironic turn and his liking for the inverted compliment. His biographers have displayed a naïve susceptibility to such casual remarks and incidents, his supposed habit, to instance one more, of reading the Book of Job regularly on his birthday — a habit that he himself mentioned only once, on his seventy-first birthday. It has been said of Dr. Johnson that everyone thinks of him as an old man, a fate that not infrequently happens to writers who live beyond the allotted biblical span; and Swift too has suffered from being mirrored in the minds of later generations by selected details from his declining years. But there is another Swift, the man described (even in the 1730's) as a person of "infinite spirits" and "very good humour." There is the Swift who wrote delightful light verse, the punster, the genial, witty companion of Queen Anne's Lord Treasurer and her Secretary of State from 1710 to 1714, the Swift who was an eagerly sought guest at great houses, the Swift who had a genius for friendship with both sexes (to balance his competence in making, usually, the right enemies), and the Swift whose letters, squibs, poems, and daily activities give evidence of vitality, playfulness of mind, and many wholesome satisfactions. These aspects of the man should be taken into account, to bring the picture into proper proportions.

Biography and criticism have reciprocal influences; and the conception of Swift as a man has been greatly influenced by the criticism of *Gulliver's Travels*. The masterpiece became the man. One might enter a caveat against selecting a single work of an author who wrote many, over a period of forty years, and finding in that particular work a final explanation of his personality. But the range and the volume of Swift's work have to many critics seemed of little weight; and not even the whole of *Gulliver's Travels* has been thought necessary for a full understanding. The Fourth Book, with its contrasting pictures of Yahoo and Houyhnhnm, has been thought ample. Here the critics of the past (and a dwindling few of these times) found all they needed to construct the horrendous image of the man, though they have been adept at selecting precisely the right biographical fact or myth to enforce their conception, including his few scatalogical poems, whose purport they have abysmally failed to understand. We are more recently emerging into a period of sounder criticism and fuller comprehension of the man and his genius, but for almost two hundred

years most readers were prevented from viewing either Swift or
Gulliver's Travels in a perspective that did justice to either. The book
became an ethical or psychological case history, or both, of its author,
in which the presumed intolerable misanthropy of Part IV, its debase-
ment of humankind, showed — as Swift's first biographer maintained
— that Swift himself was the degenerate Yahoo he had so infamously
depicted as representative of man. Other commentators of the later
eighteenth century took a similar high moral line. A man who could
thus libel human nature must be reflecting, it seemed, his own moral
deformity and defiled imagination. Inevitably, and unconsciously, the
degraded nature of the author had a subtle influence on literary
judgment. The ethical culpability of the writer lent strength to the
view that the Fourth Voyage is an artistic failure, as though a Buddhist
should deny the literary worth of Dante's *Divine Comedy* or Milton's
Paradise Lost because they are doctrinally unsound. Yet it ought to
be said to the honor of the eighteenth-century commentators that they
paid the author of *Gulliver's Travels* the compliment of believing him
a sane man. It remained for the nineteenth-century critics to take
a new tack and elaborate a less defensible charge. Though they readily accepted the view that Part IV could be explained in terms of a
depraved author, they added that it might well be explained in terms
of a mad one. Early in the century Sir Walter Scott, repelled by
"this horrible outline of mankind degraded to a bestial state," thought
it must be the result of "the first impressions of . . . incipient mental
disease." The theory of malignancy was supplemented by the theory
of lunacy. It was then only a step to Thackeray's advice to his
audience, when he was lecturing on the eighteenth-century humorists,
that Part IV should not be read. Pass over it, he counselled his
hearers, and hoot its author for this portion of the book — "filthy in
word, filthy in thought, furious, raging, obscene." Similarly Edmund
Gosse, a product of the second half of the nineteenth century, whose
prolific criticism spanned the Victorian period and the first three
decades of the twentieth century, found evidence of a diseased brain
in the Fourth Voyage, which banished it from decent households.
It is not surprising that in our century the psychoanalysts have seized
on so attractive a subject as Swift; and now we find *Gulliver* explained
in terms of neuroses and complexes. Witness these words from *The
Psychoanalytic Review* (1942): *Gulliver's Travels* "may be viewed
as a neurotic phantasy with coprophilia as its main content." It
furnishes

> abundant evidence of the neurotic make up of the author and
> discloses in him a number of perverse trends indicative of fixation
> at the anal sadistic stage of libidinal development. Most con-
> spicuous among those perverse trends is that of coprophilia,

although the work furnishes evidence of numerous other related neurotic characteristics accompanying the general picture of psychosexual infantilism and emotional immaturity.

By a diligent search the psychoanalyst was able to discover "evidence" that the author was afflicted with a formidable variety of neurotic tendencies, including misogyny, mysophilia, mysophobia, voyeurism, exhibitionism, and compensatory potency reactions. This indeed is helpful! And it carries conviction in direct proportion to its help-fulness. If the psychoanalytic approach seems to have in it an element of absurdity, we should recognize that it is only a logical extension of the disordered-intellect theory of the nineteenth century, the chief difference being that the terminology has changed and that the psy-choanalyst frankly sees *Gulliver's Travels* as a case history, whereas many earlier critics were presumably making a literary appraisal.

Perhaps these crude and amateur attempts deserve little attention, yet they are a phenomenon that the serious reader of Swift can hardly ignore in the light of their recurrence and their effectiveness in per-petuating myths. And they sometimes come with persuasiveness and literary flavor, as in Aldous Huxley's essay on Swift in *Do What You Will* (1929), where Huxley arrives at an amazingly over-simplified explanation of Swift's genius: "Swift's greatness," he writes, "lies in the intensity, the almost insane violence, of that 'hatred of bowels' which is the essence of his misanthropy and which underlies the whole of his work." The critics who have relied on a theory of insanity or disordered intellect to explain Swift have vitiated their case by re-sorting to *ex post facto* reasoning. The failure of Swift's faculties towards the end of his life, some fifteen or sixteen years *after* the publication of *Gulliver's Travels*, has been seized upon to explain something the critics neither liked nor understood. It seemed to them valid to push his "insanity" back in time, to look retrospectively at the intolerable Fourth Voyage of *Gulliver*, and to infer that he must have been at least incipiently mad when he wrote it. Yet the same commentators who observe manifestations of a disordered in-tellect in Part IV have not thought to question the intellect behind the Third Voyage, which we now know was composed in point of time after the Fourth. These same commentators have nothing but praise for the vigor, the keenness, the sanity, and the humanity of the mind that produced the *Drapier's Letters*, the first of which Swift was writing only a month after completing a draft of Part IV of *Gulliver*.

This is not to deny that a central fact in Swift's life and his works is his pessimism. If we reject the extreme view that his life was com-pounded of bitter malignity, raging madness, and black misanthropy, or even the more moderate tradition that misery and gloom were pervasive in his daily existence, we still must grant that his pessimism was real and ample. The burning phrases of the epitaph, the fierce indignation and the lacerated heart, are not to be discounted, as I have already suggested. The problem is to explain his pessimism in less melodramatic terms and to substitute for mere speculation a due regard for the known facts of his life and for any other influences, intellectual and social ones, for example, which may be relevant. In the external aspects of his career, even when soberly examined, one can observe a pattern of frustration that took its toll of his spirits, or somehow left him scarred. His early years in Ireland, of which all too little is known, probably left no ineffaceable scars. Born in Ireland in 1667, a posthumous child in an Anglo-Irish family of little means, he nevertheless was fortunate enough to receive a good education through the aid of a relative. He first attended Kilkenny School, and then, aged 14, entered Trinity College, Dublin, where (as he later misleadingly said) "he was stopped of his degree for dullness and insufficiency." Actually, though his record was indifferent, he was graduated a Bachelor of Arts in 1686 and remained at Trinity College until early in 1689, when the disruptions of the Revolution of 1688 succeeded the disruptions of post-Cromwellian Ireland. Reflecting on this period much later, in his *Autobiographical Fragment* (c. 1727), he recalled the ill treatment of his relatives, the neglect of his studies, and his sunken spirits; yet his university days certainly did not sour his nature, and in the decade that followed 1689 the years were brighter. He passed a considerable portion of his time in England, in the household of Sir William Temple as the secretary of that distinguished Whig statesman and diplomat. Here, at Moor Park in Surrey, Swift moved in an atmosphere of culture and enlightenment; he read widely and fruitfully, and came to know several prominent men who later entered significantly into his life. Not least of all, it was here that he first met Esther Johnson, the Stella of his poems and his *Journal*. At Moor Park also his literary inclinations were nourished and stimulated, to result in *A Tale of a Tub* and *The Battle of the Books*.

In an interval in his residence with Temple, Swift took an important step. In 1694 he went into holy orders. There had been a rift with his patron, in what was at best a makeshift relationship, and his decision to enter orders resulted less from deep conviction that the Church was his mission in life than from the necessity of settling himself, an attitude that the eighteenth century did not find strange. He had been promised a good appointment. Instead he found himself, in what must have seemed banishment, relegated to the bleak northeastern coast of Ireland as a country vicar of three small run-down parishes, the chief of which was Kilroot. Here, in a diocese recently shaken by scandal, in which the bishop had been deprived and a number of clergymen excommunicated or suspended for such varied offenses as fornication, adultery, drunkenness, neglect of cures, and simony, Swift began his long clerical career of half a century, fully exposed to the spiritual and physical dry rot of the Anglican Establishment in Ireland. His parish churches were in decay; the temporalities of the Church had been alienated to laymen, and he had only a handful of parishioners to serve. In striking contrast to his own moribund benefices was the flourishing Presbyterian Kirk. The circumstances were highly appropriate for developing his detestation of nonconformity and his fear of its power; and we must recollect that his brilliant *Tale of a Tub*, with its satiric attack on religious dissent, dates from this period of Swift's career, when the experience of Ulster Presbyterianism was fresh enough to give a dark and bitter tinge to that work.

It was an inauspicious and barren beginning for the youthful clergyman, bound to leave lasting impressions. He was soon to suffer another disappointment. Leaving his desolate parishes behind, he returned to the household of Temple in 1696 with expectations of a good appointment in England, though not necessarily in the Church. But Temple's death in 1699 ended his hopes and once again he returned to Ireland, this time as domestic chaplain to the Earl of Berkeley, one of the Irish Lord Justices. Even now Swift thought that he had excellent prospects, preferment to a lucrative deanery, only to find that he was put off with three insignificant country parishes, united under the name of Laracor, and soon afterwards, perhaps as a conciliatory gesture, the prebend of Dunlavin in St. Patrick's Cathedral. Later in his career, as he looked retrospectively at these early frustrations, Swift remarked on them with some bitterness; but in 1700, at the age of 33, he had enough youthful buoyancy and ambition to look forward without undue brooding over past disappointments. In the next few years he solidified his position as a canon of St. Patrick's Cathedral and came to be looked upon as a rising clergyman in the Church of Ireland. At the same time he was maintaining his English connections. He published in 1701, in London, where he was then visiting, the first of his political pamphlets, *A Discourse of the Contests and Dissensions between the Nobles and the Commons in Athens and Rome*. Although this tract has some interest for Swift's political theory, it is more significant for personal reasons. By means of it he achieved influence and reputation with powerful leaders of the Whigs. Several of the Whig statesmen, among them Lord Somers, to whom the *Tale of a Tub* was later dedicated, had been impeached by the House of Commons. Taking advantage of the situation, Swift came to their defense, thus strengthening his friendly relations with the Whigs which had begun during his residence with Sir William Temple.

And with the Whigs in power in 1707, he became a logical emissary to represent the bishops of the Irish Church in a matter of moment — a plea to Queen Anne for remission of certain clerical taxes paid to the English Crown, the First Fruits and Twentieth Parts, imposts that fell heavily on the already impoverished Irish clergymen. The importance of this mission in Swift's life cannot be over-estimated. In a significant sense this was the beginning of his public career. He appeared in England to make his plea to the Whig leaders, and received encouragement from such powerful statesmen as Halifax, Somers, Pembroke, and Sunderland. But the most powerful of all, the Earl of Godolphin, the Lord Treasurer, he did not win over — for political reasons. Godolphin, and in fact the Whig government, wished the clergy of the Irish Establishment to support legislation in Ireland removing the Test Act, an act designed to preserve the exclusive political position of the Anglican Church in that country by excluding all except Anglican communicants from holding public offices. If the clergymen of Ireland lent their endeavors to this political manoeuvre, which was intended to ease the lot of the dissenters, Queen Anne's first minister indicated to Swift that he would influence the Queen to remit the First Fruits and Twentieth Parts. Swift's deepest convictions never received a more severe test. Throughout his life he believed that the Anglican Church as established by law should be *the* Church of England and Ireland, firmly protected against political encroachments from the dissenters, though he granted the nonconformists the right of conscience and the practice of their beliefs. He never forgot what had happened to the Anglican Establishment under the rule of Cromwell and the Puritans; and the removal of the Test Act he conceived to be a significant step towards returning dissenters to power. Much of the intensity of feeling against nonconformity in *A Tale of a Tub* and the *Argument Against Abolishing Christianity* derives from his fear that this might occur again. In this respect he was possibly more a man of the seventeenth than of the eighteenth century. In any case, at this critical moment in his career, his loyalty to the Church he served remained firm, at the expense of his personal fortune. He expected preferment from the Whigs, and had a right to expect it. But he never wavered in his rejection of the terms proposed by the Lord Treasurer. And in what unquestionably were acts of self-abnegation, he wrote several pamphlets opposing the policy of the Whig ministry and defining the true principles of a Church-of-England man as he conceived them. But the incident left him bitter and disappointed. At the same time it helps to explain why his enemies, who occasionally jibed without justice at his religious faith, never mocked at his devotion to the Church — a man, one of them declared, "whose affection to the Church was never doubted, tho' his Christi-

anity was ever question'd." In this period, from 1707 to 1710, Swift
grew familiar with the scheming methods of courts and statesmen
and with the pointless delays and manoeuvres that could envelop an
honorable project. Unquestionably some of the cynicism about the
political tribe so pervasive in his writing stems from these years. But
there were other experiences in these busy months, more satisfying
ones, as the widening of his friendships, which included Addison and
Steele, the publication of the *Bickerstaff Papers*, and the contributions
to *The Tatler*.

The late fall of 1710 proved a decisive point in Swift's career. It
brought his shift in political allegiance from Whig to Tory, something
his enemies never permitted him to forget though it was logical in all
of its aspects. He watched with more pleasure than concern the fall
of the Whig statesmen who had rebuffed him and the accession to
power of moderate Tories under the leadership of Robert Harley,
later the Earl of Oxford, destined to figure so prominently in Swift's
life. Early in October he was received by Harley, to whom he now
made his plea in behalf of the Irish clergy. Harley listened sympa-
thetically, promised his support, and, with a keen eye for the practical
uses of literary genius, turned Swift to political journalism in defense
of the new Tory ministry. What is more, in a mere two weeks the
Queen, at Harley's suggestion, acted favorably on Swift's mission, in
contrast to three years of futile effort under the Whigs. It was all
very gratifying; and he immediately wrote to Stella with obvious
pleasure that Queen Anne would soon inform the bishops in Ireland
and would take notice that "it was done upon a memorial from me."
"I believe," he added, "never any thing was compassed so soon, and
purely done by my personal credit with Mr. Harley." At this very
moment, by one of those minor ironies that are sometimes big with
consequences, the Irish bishops who had commissioned him decided
that he was not, after all, the appropriate person for the task. Before
word of his success reached Dublin, he was informed of their lack
of faith in his endeavors and their desire to work through other chan-
nels. Swift's reaction may easily be imagined! Then, to compound
the injury, when notification came from the throne, the bishops gave
formal thanks to the Queen, to Harley, and to the recently appointed
Lord Lieutenant of Ireland (who had played no part) without any
reference to Swift himself. It was a slight, deliberate, ungenerous, and
ungrateful, one that left him bitterly resentful and helps to explain
perhaps the contempt for bishops which later animated him. The
whole situation was hardly calculated to sweeten his nature. He had
nursed the project carefully over a period of years and seen it clearly
as something bound up with his personal ambitions and fortunes. For
almost three years the Whigs in England had kept him in suspense

with constant promises of advancement in the Church. It never came; and to this grievous frustration of personal hopes was added the intolerable and ungracious behavior of the bishops in Ireland.

There were, however, balms for his wounded feelings. His new political alignment, with the Tories, was congenial in its personal relationships and promising for his future. Moreover, it was based upon those very convictions and principles relating to church and state which had made his alliance with the Whigs an uneasy one. In November, 1710, he was made editor of *The Examiner*, a journal founded to defend the policies of Harley, Bolingbroke, and the Tory ministry. The position of power and trust he now occupied gave him a sense of exhilaration and released his energies. The years 1710 to 1713 represented for him a full tide of excitement and achievement. Political verses and pamphlets flowed from his pen. He struck out with consummate skill at Godolphin, at the Duke of Marlborough, the famous general and statesman, at the Duchess of Somerset (the Queen's confidante), at disgruntled Whigs and deists, at recalcitrant Tories and stubborn Scots. He found new friends — and inevitably in his position became himself a frequent political target. The friendship with those staunch Whigs, Addison and Steele, cooled, to be replaced by intimacy with authors inclined to the Tories, the poets Pope, Gay, and Prior, the dramatist Congreve, and the brilliant scientist and literary man who was physician to Queen Anne, John Arbuthnot. Swift moved about among the statesmen, court officials, titled aristocrats, and other dignitaries with aplomb and satisfaction, with a special sense that he was seeing history made, and with a special gusto for the incidents of each day. It is all zestily detailed in the *Journal to Stella*, that intimate revelation of his thoughts and actions mailed back to Ireland for the eyes of Esther Johnson. One gets from his letters and other writings in these years a vivid impression of unfolding dramatic events, events which swirled around him and are now part of the history of Queen Anne's final years — the undermining of the influence of the Duke and Duchess of Marlborough, the attempted assassination of Robert Harley, Jacobite intrigue, the secret negotiations to end the War of the Spanish Succession, and many lesser occurrences, all of which have as he presents them a dimension and color that coldly objective history does not attain because Swift assesses these matters as a participant — and indeed as a partisan whose judgment of personalities and motives must be scanned.

By the early part of 1713 clouds were gathering. It became clear that the divisions among the Tories and the bitter rift between Harley and Bolingbroke would have disastrous effects. Swift watched with despair as the ministry went to its destruction. Its fall and the death of Queen Anne in 1714 closed what he considered the most brilliant chapter in his life. For him personally the future was to be "exile" in Ireland, with only two visits to England in the long years ahead. Fortunately, before the Tories fell from power he was given the long-deferred advancement in the Church, though it was after all an appointment that to him and to his friends seemed less than his deserts. He had devoutly hoped to remain in England, not necessarily as a bishop or a dean, as he had some reason to expect in the light of contemporary custom. A canonry at Windsor or Westminster would have satisfied him. But the Queen and the Archbishop of York were set against it; and there were others, the Duchess of Somerset, for example, whose enmity may have influenced the Queen, not to mention the culpability of his friend Harley, whose aggrandizement of his own family led him to bestow bishoprics that might with more justice have gone to Swift. It was particularly disconcerting that he stood by month after month in expectation of preferment, as he had with the Whigs, listening to promises and rumors, while deaneries and bishoprics fell vacant and were filled by the appointment of others. His anger and resentment mounted, and finally in April 1713, he informed Harley that he would no longer endure the embarrassment of remaining in England unless he received an honorable preferment. This brought action, not however without some wrangling, and he was made Dean of St. Patrick's on April 23, 1713.

"My enemies [are] busy," Swift wrote to Stella at this time. They continued to be busy. The news of his appointment to a deanery made them clamorous. Legend has it that the following lines were affixed to the door of the cathedral on the day of his installation:

> Look down, St. Patrick, look, we pray,
>   On thine own Church and steeple;
> Convert thy Dean, on this great day;
>   Or else God help the people.

The violence of the Whig attack on Swift, as a turncoat, an obscene and irreverent clergyman, a party scribbler and hireling, suggests how effective he had been as a political journalist. Even in parliament he was denounced — as "a divine hardly suspected of being a Christian, but in a fair way of being a bishop." Now as a dignitary of the Church he was to continue in the realm of controversy. As he took up his decanal duties in 1714, he was confronted with formidable opposition from politically inclined members of the cathedral and from the influential Archbishop of Dublin, William King, a staunch Whig with whom Swift fought fiercely at times but with whom he also joined on occasions in defense of the Church and of Ireland. No small part of his energies in the two decades following 1714 went into struggles for the welfare of the Anglican Establishment in Ireland. He was one of the few who had the courage to fight the powerful bishops when they endeavored to take advantage of the lower clergy. He was a leader of the clergy in their perpetual economic warfare with laymen who resisted payment of tithes or unscrupulously benefited from church lands; and he kept close watch over the Irish parliament, to prevent legislation unfavorable to the vulnerable clergy. This phase of his career is well exhibited in his church tracts, so little read in modern times because they are concerned with outmoded matters, though they were of vast importance to his age. His greatness as a churchman, universally acknowledged, does not derive from defense of theological doctrine. This was not his métier. He was, all the evidence shows, a man of deep and untroubled faith, who thought it folly to enter into controversies about the infallible doctrines of Christianity. His efforts were directed instead to the support of the privileged position of the Anglican religion and of its temporal prosperity, so necessary in his eyes if a reasonable and moderate Christianity was to survive. The threats as he conceived them were social, economic, religious, and political, and both from within and without the Church. He combatted them where he could, often with notable success. But in this sphere, as elsewhere, he had many moments of despair and pessimism. As he approached his seventieth year he wrote gloomily, "I have long given up all hopes of Church or Christianity."

The debility of the Church was matched by the debility of the Irish economy; and Swift's struggle for the Anglican Establishment was paralleled by his endeavors in behalf of the impoverished, oppressed nation. For the first few years after his return to Ireland in 1714, sunken in spirits and weighed down with other matters, he did not play a vital part in public affairs. The events in England subsequent to the fall of the Harley cabinet were hardly to be borne. Harley was imprisoned; Bolingbroke, accused of Jacobite intrigue, fled to France; other friends were dispersed or out of power, and Swift himself was under suspicion. His mail was intercepted, and he was in danger of being brought to England to testify, perhaps to stand trial. These events, which Swift later wove into the political allegory in *Gulliver's Travels*, resulted from the determination of the Whigs, restored to power by the accession of George I, to punish those who had thrown away the fruits of Marlborough's victories on the Continent by making peace with France. Swift, as journalist for the Harley ministry, had defended the peace, attacked Marlborough, and made himself obnoxious to the Whigs. Fortunately the turbulent feelings calmed down. The disquieting personal threat he faced with courage and dignity, but the situation in England from 1714 to 1717, added to the atmosphere of political hostility in Ireland, tended to immobilize him. By 1718 his spirits had revived and he was beginning to concern himself with (in his own phrase) "the wretched condition of Ireland." For two decades thereafter he produced what we now call the Irish tracts, addressed frequently to England as well as to Ireland. The materials of these are economic, political, broadly social, but many of them are not mere documents of the times. They are transformed by greatness of style, irony, wit, and anguish of spirit. One of them, *A Modest Proposal,* is with justice acclaimed the greatest short satire in the language. Perhaps in this brief work best of all we can see how appropriate was his use of the phrase, the lacerated heart. Here, underneath the irony, one finds anger, indignation, and humanity — qualities that generated and gave force to his pessimism. In the years following 1719, when he was writing *Gulliver's Travels,* he was also producing some of these lesser works quite consonant in spirit with his great masterpiece, similarly bitter and despairing. England's opprobrious treatment of Ireland he brought under scathing attack, for example, in the first of the Irish tracts, *A Proposal for the Universal Use of Irish Manufacture* (1720), a plea to the people of Ireland to attempt a measure of economic self sufficiency. The same motive in part animated *The Drapier's Letters* (1724), where he combatted the notion that Ireland was merely a colony of England, existing for the profit of the mother country. He appraised with a clear vision the cold mercantilism of the times by which Ireland's powerful neighbor restricted the trade and agriculture of the hapless Irish. At the same time he lashed the people of Ireland — the absentees for draining the wealth of the country, the tradesmen for dishonesty, the nobility for indifference, the strolling beggars for sloth, the men and women of fashion for shortsighted indulgences. Not surprisingly, the language of these tracts is sometimes that of despair, hopelessness, and disillusionment, yet it is notable that he persisted to the end of his active life in his efforts to achieve reforms and relieve the people of Ireland. Here was no withdrawal to nurse cynical indifference or misanthropy. The emotional coloring and strong rhetoric of the Irish tracts are appropriate to the purpose in hand, quite proper from a reformer bent on seeing maladjustments corrected and human weakness moderated. Swift's clerical profession, his position as dean and dignitary, not only gave him the opportunity, it imposed upon him the obligation to take cognizance of public and private distress. This duty he never scanted, either as a private citizen willingly using his own money or as a public figure with the prestige of his office. It was thus that he became an embodiment of the voice and conscience of Ireland, and was popularly hailed as the Hibernian Patriot. Yeats would have it that Swift's heart "dragged him down into mankind," by which he means (I suppose) that Swift had a compulsion to express his humanity by sharing man's agonies. This suggests what one cannot miss in reading the Irish tracts, their remarkable kinship to *Gulliver's Travels*. Although these lesser works are lamentations over one hapless country, directed at specific evils in the social and economic order, we are always left with a strong sense that basically the troubles derive from the irrational nature of man — his ill use, in the language of *Gulliver's Travels*, of that "small pittance" of reason which has fallen to him "to aggravate [his] *natural* corruptions, and to acquire new ones which Nature had not given [him]."

The many external facts of Swift's career which help to explain his pessimism are not to be divorced from the intellectual currents of his time, certain philosophical and theological influences, which may have shaped his conception of man and the world. It would seem reasonable, for example, to expect that his thinking as a Christian divine might have a strong influence. Were there elements in the traditional Christian view of the nature of man, or its modifications, from which his pessimism was partially derived, or which reinforced it? We get a clue that this approach may be fruitful from the words of Swift's relative and biographer, Deane Swift, who wrote that the Christian conception of the evil nature of man appears to be "the groundwork of the whole satire contained in the voyage to the Houyhnhnms." This is indeed a far cry from the view that the Fourth Voyage grew out of Swift's malignity, personal bitterness, or madness. "Dr. Swift," Deane Swift added, "was not the first preacher whose writings import this kind of philosophy." Deane Swift could easily have pointed to scores of clergymen in the seventeenth and eighteenth centuries who, like their predecessors, expatiated on the corruption of human nature. If they recognized the existence of a divine spark, they seldom forgot that other aspect of man — and in a rhetoric every bit as harsh as Swift's. That mild Anglican, Jeremy Taylor, could remark, "What is man but a vessel of dung, a stink of corruption, and by birth, a slave to the devil" — a remark that his listeners would accept acquiescently as not in the least misanthropic and nothing more than a conventional homiletic reflection on the depravity of man. Even in the "benevolent" Christianity of the early eighteenth century this language did not disappear; and Jeremy Taylor's gnomic description of man in its theological context is a parallel for Gulliver's equally gnomic description — "a lump of deformity and diseases both in body and mind" — in its ethical context. This is that violent rhetoric of denunciation which in its line of descent can be traced back to the medieval preachers as they described proud, lecherous, gluttonous man, a traditional anathematism; and as such it remained a vital element in Christian homiletic literature.

Swift probably would have thought an optimistic divine a contradiction in terms; and his own pessimism is at least consonant with the pessimism at the heart of Christianity. One of his sermons begins:

> The holy Scripture is full of expressions to set forth the miserable condition of man during the whole progress of his life; his weakness, pride, and vanity; his unmeasurable desires, and perpetual disappointments; the prevalence of his passions, and the corruptions of his reason; his deluding hopes . . .; his natural and artificial wants; his cares and anxieties; the diseases of his body, and the diseases of his mind; the shortness of his life; his dread of a future state, with his carelessness to prepare for it: and the wise men of all ages have made the same reflections.

If Swift had written his own comment on *Gulliver's Travels*, he might well have used the words of this sermon. That great work is obviously concerned to set forth the miserable condition of man, his weakness, pride, and vanity, his unmeasurable desires, the prevalency of his passions, the corruption of his reason, and so on through the catalogue. Some of Swift's surviving sermons, as well as those of his fellow divines, could easily be used to annotate *Gulliver's Travels*. It seems clear that there is an affinity between this work and many of the quite conventional sermons on depraved human nature and the evils of this life. The satirist and the divine tend to merge, or at the very least to come together in striking compatibility as they envisage man. If Swift sounds like those whose emphasis on man's depravity derives from Augustinian and Calvinistic roots, this is a result of the intensity of his attack and his extreme rhetoric and not, it must be firmly stated, the result of his agreement with the doctrines which buttressed the Augustinian view or the Calvinistic restatement of it. He felt too keenly man's moral responsibility, and would have been embarrassed, had he been alive at mid-century, to hear John Wesley approve his conception of man's corruption. Soon after the publication of *Gulliver's Travels*, a Dublin essayist, commenting on the theme of human corruption, complained that it had been preached upon to the point of exhaustion, yet continues to be "a darling theme [among] great numbers of grave and orthodox divines." They hold the doctrine of man's depravity, he added, to be of the utmost importance in religion, and belief in it "absolutely necessary to denominate a man a good Christian."

Swift's sermons indicate that he was one of these "grave and orthodox divines" who reaffirmed the taint in man's nature as a cardinal principle of Christian theology. He reaffirmed it all the more strongly because, it may be, he scented heresy in the air; or, if heresy is too extreme a term, he felt uneasily a threat to Christianity in a host of writers who were showing only "the fair side of human nature in Adam's posterity" and asserting man's natural goodness. A moderated Pelagianism was current, a heresy which St. Augustine had combatted in the 5th century A.D., draining the doctrine of original sin of its full efficacy and, as a consequence, weakening the doctrines of redemption and grace. Article IX of the Anglican Church, on original sin, formally signified the "infection of nature" in man and referred to the vain talk of Pelagians. But there were "mighty softeners" (Deane Swift's phrase) of this doctrine in Swift's day, John Locke, for example, who denied, without raising much serious protest, that the fall of Adam implied the corruption of human nature in Adam's posterity (*The Reasonableness of Christianity*, 1695). Theologians joined with others in panegyrics on human nature, in showing it "in its proper dignity" and affirming man's natural goodness, an aspect of that current of thought which we now label "sentimentalism." In two of his sermons, *On the Testimony of the Conscience* and *Upon the Excellence of Christianity*, Swift considers those who express this theory of human nature. He finds their views both false and dangerous, false in that they minimize the powerful defect in man's will, dangerous in that they reflect an "undue conceit of human sufficiency." To the extent that they endow man, they take away from God. They tend towards a secular ethics, a freeing of man from the restraints of a religious conscience which alone can ensure right behavior since, as he maintains, "there is no other tie [other than religion] thro' which the pride, or lust, or avarice, or ambition of mankind will not certainly break at one time or other." Thus Swift topples over "these mighty softeners" of man's corrupt nature — the sentimental proponents of "benevolent" man, the neo-stoics who hypothesized a proud, magnanimous man sufficient unto himself, the theorists who had created "the man of honor" and the "mere moral man" with a capacity for virtue for virtue's own sake, and the deists with their rational man. By contrast Swift depicts man as he is, a creature of passions, pride, and self-love, a frail and sinful being in need of redemption and anything but self-sufficient or inclined by his nature to virtue.

Even though the view of man as formulated in *Gulliver's Travels* may have received both coloring and substance from the currents of traditional Christian thought, we are obviously not to conceive of the work as a religious tract or as concerned with doctrine. *Gulliver's Travels* is secular, an exploration of man's social and moral nature in non-theological terms, done in the allegorical mode and embedded in fantasy. Nevertheless we may reasonably suppose that Swift's thinking as a divine had a yeasty influence, however difficult it is to define that influence precisely or indicate its full extent. It seems to go beyond the obvious use of the traditional symbols of sin — that is, those figures and images of the flesh which he utilizes in describing the Yahoos. The noisome putridity of these creatures, their envelopment in stench and dungy vileness, is, of course, emblematic of their moral natures. Swift has employed an old device abundant in Christian literature (though not only there) — the metaphorical association of physical corruption with moral corruption. And it is this same device which has disturbed many critics in their reading of his anti-sentimental, anti-Petrarchan poems, those few scatalogical verses out of several hundred he composed, such as *A Beautiful Young Nymph Going to Bed*, *The Lady's Dressing Room*, and *Strephon and Chloe.* Here indeed he has employed an extreme naturalistic language, occasional flashes of which we find also in *Gulliver's Travels*. Our more fastidious age has found these unwholesome, an "obsessive . . . preoccupation" one critic has said, "with the visceral and excrementitious"; and another, after peeping into the depths of Swift's subconscious, has endowed him with "an excremental vision" — an explanation that needs an explanation. The language itself might well have seemed to an eighteenth-century reader not excessively shocking. Taboo words go in and out of fashion. Words concerned with bodily functions, dirt, disease, squalor in general, jarred the sensibilities less in Swift's day, as did the facts they described. But apart from the mere uninhibited language he uses, the privilege of any satirist, Swift reflects traditional views in these scatalogical poems. Their staple is woman as the embodiment of vice, her hypocrisy, her deceptiveness, her filthiness beneath a fair exterior. The tradition is both classical and Christian. The Latin satirist Juvenal (of the Sixth satire) and a medieval church father descanting on womankind as the devil incarnate tend to sound alike on this subject; and Swift sounds like both of them. There are as well other, more purely literary traditions to which Swift strongly reacted, "the high raptures and romantic flights" of pastoral writers and Petrarchan sonneteers, for example. The difficulty of disentangling the traditions is clear enough, but both overtly and implicitly Swift reflects a basic religious idea, the dichotomy of body and soul, and the implications which flow from this idea. The romantic glorification of what, after all, is only flesh and blood, the exaltation of values concerned with the body, exterior beauty — his corrosive attack on this way of thinking has a strong ethical intention such as we find enduringly in homiletic literature. How base it is, said a contemporary preacher, "to serve an Idol of flesh and blood; a paunch of guts, that's full of filth and excrements within, and the skin itself, the cleanest part, is ashamed to be uncovered." Are this clergyman and Swift coprophilous, as the psychoanalyst would have it? Or are they concerned with a vital and perennial notion about the dual nature of man?

The difficulty in separating the strands of influence is further complicated by the prevalence in contemporary thought of a libertine strain in which the denigration of human nature was no less severe than that of the divines in their Augustinian and Calvinistic moods. This vilification of man in "modish French authors" and in "loose and profligate writers" in England was uncomfortably close in language, however different in purpose, to the language of "grave and orthodox divines." When Addison, in *The Tatler*, No. 108, praised the ancient moralists for exhibiting the "natural grandeur" of man, he contrasts them with those recent writers who basely depreciate human nature, such as La Rochefoucauld, the celebrated author of the *Maxims*, who does not distinguish, so Addison complained, between "the species of men and brutes." Swift, on the other hand, pays a tribute to La Rochefoucauld at the opening of the *Verses on the Death of Dr. Swift* (1731):

> As Rochefoucault his maxims drew
> From nature, I believe 'em true:
> They argue no corrupted mind
> In him; the fault is in mankind.

Even more significant, as *Gulliver's Travels* was nearing completion in 1725, Pope's announced intention of writing maxims in opposition to La Rochefoucauld found no favor in Swift's eyes. Rochefoucauld, he wrote to Pope, "is my favorite, because I found my whole character in him." Here then is another current of thought, stressing man's egoistic and subrational nature, reflected most baldly in such widely read writers as La Rochefoucauld, Bayle, Rochester, Hobbes, and Mandeville, which merits consideration as a formative influence on Swift. This *libertin* appraisal of human nature existed in a worldly and secular context quite opposed in spirit and intention to the orthodox Christian conception, which was concerned with man's ultimate salvation. Both served Swift's satiric purposes. That he was disturbed by the contradiction in spirit between the two views or felt the need to reconcile them is not evident. This need not surprise us, as it would not surprise him, who wrote: "How inconsistent is man with himself!"

Finally, it may help us to assess Swift more competently if we rob him of a little of his uniqueness (though not of his literary greatness) in viewing the age. Envision him as one of a collective body of eighteenth-century Jeremiahs whose lamentations were filling the air. The Tory wits, as Professor Louis Bredvold has so persuasively shown in his excellent essay, "The Gloom of the Tory Satirists," reflected, even generated, their fair share of the gloom-thickened atmosphere of the period of Queen Anne and the first Georges. But in this limited respect there was nothing singular, except their talents, about Swift and his friends — Pope, Gay, Prior, Arbuthnot, and

Parnell. "We are doomed to be undone," wrote Bishop George Berkeley in 1721, in his tract significantly titled, *An Essay towards Preventing the Ruin of Great Britain,* one of numerous dark pictures of the character and destiny of the British. Many looked about and saw widely prevailing infection, a culture losing its vigor and its better values, under the impact of bribery, luxury, political faction, deteriorated education, an immoral stage, ostentatious fashions, a dissolute and slothful poor, an irresponsible aristocracy, loss of public spirit, imitation of French and Italian fopperies, the vulgarization of the arts, and a dozen other such evils. But only a person of the rarest gifts, such as Swift, could transmute these into an imperishable imaginative comment on the nature of man and society.

A CHRONOLOGICAL TABLE

Swift born in Dublin of English parents	Nov. 30, 1667
Attended Kilkenny Grammar School	c. 1673–1682
Esther Johnson [Stella] born	Mar. 13, 1681
Swift entered Trinity College, Dublin	April 24, 1682
B. A. degree, *speciali gratia.* Continued at Trinity College, Dublin	Feb. 15, 1686
Left Ireland for England as a result of troubles incident to the fall of James II. Lived with his mother	1688 or early in 1689
Entered household of Sir William Temple. Probably first acquaintance with Stella.	1689
Returned to Ireland	May, 1690
Returned to England (August) and to Temple in Moor Park. Early poems, 1690–93	Dec. (?), 1691
M. A. degree, Hart Hall, University of Oxford	July 5, 1692
Ordained in Ireland: (1) Deacon and	Oct. 28, 1694
(2) Priest	Jan. 13, 1695
Appointed to the prebend of Kilroot, near Belfast, (Jan. 28) and began to reside in Kilroot	March, 1695
Returned to Moor Park. (Temple's death, 1699)	1696
Domestic chaplain to Lord Berkeley (Lord Justice of Ireland) in Dublin	Summer, 1699
Presented to livings of Laracor and two other country parishes	Feb. 1700
Installed prebendary of St. Patrick's Cathedral, Dublin	Oct. 22, 1700
To England with Lord Berkeley. Soon published first political tract, in defence of impeached Whig statesmen, *Contests and Dissensions . . . in Athens and Rome*	April, 1701
Doctor of Divinity degree, Trinity College, Dublin	Feb. 1702
A Tale of a Tub and *The Battle of the Books* published	1704
Emissary of Church of Ireland to seek remission of First Fruits from Queen Anne. Resident in London. Wrote tracts on church and state, including *Argument Against Abolishing Christianity* (pub. 1711). Published *Bickerstaff Papers.* Failed to win support of Whig cabinet for his mission or to win preferment in the Church. Returned to Ireland, June, 1709	Nov., 1707– May, 1709
To England again seeking remission of First Fruits.	Sept. 1710
Journal to Stella. Letters to Esther Johnson in Ireland begin, to continue until June, 1713	Sept. 1710

Swift met Robert Harley, head of Queen Anne's new ministry (Tory). Harley supports his project. Swift joined Tories, became editor of *The Examiner* (Nov. 2, 1710), a Tory journal. — Oct. 4, 1710

Active as political journalist. Wrote poems and tracts in support of the Tory ministry. Attacked Marlborough and other Whigs. Friendship with Addison and Steele cools. Friendship with Gay, Pope, Congreve, Arbuthnot, and Esther Vanhomrigh (Vanessa) developed. — 1710–14

Installed as Dean of St. Patrick's Cathedral, Dublin. Returned to London, Sept. 9, 1713 — June 13, 1713

Returned to Ireland to take up duties as Dean after the fall of the Harley cabinet (July) and death of Anne (Aug. 1, 1714). — Sept. 1714

Ill-founded rumors report his marriage to Stella — 1716

Published *A Proposal for the Universal Use of Irish Manufacture,* first of the significant Irish tracts — 1720

The Drapier's Letters. Swift became the Hibernian Patriot. Reward offered by English authorities for the discovery of the Drapier — 1724

Visited England. Stayed with Pope at Twickenham (summer) — March–Aug., 1726

Discussed Irish problems with Sir Robert Walpole, Lord Treasurer, to no avail — April 27, 1726

Cadenus and Vanessa published. This poem tells of the relationship between Swift and Esther Vanhomrigh, who had died June 2, 1723. — May, 1726

Gulliver's Travels published in London soon after Swift returned to Ireland — Oct. 28, 1726

Last visit to England (April–Sept.) — 1727

Death of Stella — Jan. 28, 1728

Conducts *The Intelligencer,* with Sheridan — 1728

A Modest Proposal published — 1729

Verses on the Death of Dr. Swift composed (pub. 1739) — 1731

Wrote *The Legion Club,* a violent attack on the Irish House of Commons — 1736

Found to be "of unsound mind and memory" — Aug. 17, 1742

Death. Buried in St. Patrick's Cathedral, Oct. 22. Left the greater part of his estate for the founding of a hospital for the insane — Oct. 19, 1745

TRAVELS

INTO SEVERAL

Remote NATIONS

OF THE

WORLD.

In FOUR PARTS.

By *LEMUEL GULLIVER,*
First a SURGEON, and then a CAP-
TAIN of several SHIPS.

VOL. I.

LONDON:

Printed for BENJ. MOTTE, *at the*
Middle Temple-Gate *in* Fleet-street.
MDCCXXVI.

Title-page of the First Edition, 1726

A LETTER FROM CAPT. GULLIVER
TO HIS COUSIN SYMPSON.

I hope you will be ready to own publicly, whenever you shall be called to it, that by your great and frequent urgency you prevailed on me to publish a very loose and uncorrect account of my travels; with direction to hire some young gentlemen of either university to put them in order, and correct the style, as my cousin Dampier did by my advice, in his book called *A Voyage round the World*. But I do not remember I gave you power to consent, that any thing should be omitted, and much less that any thing should be inserted: therefore, as to the latter, I do here renounce every thing of that kind; particularly a paragraph about her Majesty the late Queen Anne, of most pious and glorious memory; although I did reverence and esteem her more than any of human species. But you, or your inter-polator, ought to have considered, that as it was not my inclina-tion, so was it not decent to praise any animal of our composition before my master Houyhnhnm: and besides, the fact was alto-gether false; for to my knowledge, being in England during some part of her Majesty's reign, she did govern by a chief minister; nay, even by two successively; the first whereof was the Lord of Godolphin, and the second the Lord of Oxford; so that you have made me *say the thing that was not*. Likewise, in the account of the Academy of Projectors, and several passages of my dis-course to my master Houyhnhnm, you have either omitted some material circumstances, or minced or changed them in such a man-ner, that I do hardly know mine own work. When I formerly hinted to you something of this in a letter, you were pleased to answer, that you were afraid of giving offence; that people in power were very watchful over the press, and apt not only to interpret, but to punish every thing which looked like an *innuendo* (as I think you called it). But pray, how could that which I spoke so many years ago, and at above five thousand leagues distance, in another reign, be applied to any of the yahoos who now are said to govern the herd; especially at a time when I little thought on or feared the unhappiness of living under them? Have not I the most reason to complain, when I see these very yahoos carried by Houyhnhnms in a vehicle, as if these were brutes, and those the rational creatures? And, indeed, to avoid so monstrous and detestable a sight was one principal motive of my retirement hither.

3

Thus much I thought proper to tell you in relation to your self, and to the trust I reposed in you.

I do in the next place complain of my own great want of judgment, in being prevailed upon by the intreaties and false reasonings of you and some others, very much against mine own opinion, to suffer my travels to be published. Pray bring to your mind how often I desired you to consider, when you insisted on the motive of public good, that the yahoos were a species of animals utterly incapable of amendment by precepts or examples, and so it hath proved; for instead of seeing a full stop put to all abuses and corruptions, at least in this little island, as I had reason to expect: behold, after above six months' warning, I cannot learn that my book hath produced one single effect according to mine intentions: I desired you would let me know by a letter, when party and faction were extinguished; judges learned and upright; pleaders honest and modest, with some tincture of common sense; and Smithfield blazing with pyramids of law-books; the young nobility's education entirely changed; the physicians banished; the female yahoos abounding in virtue, honour, truth and good sense; courts and levees of great ministers thoroughly weeded and swept; wit, merit and learning rewarded; all disgracers of the press in prose and verse condemned to eat nothing but their own cotton, and quench their thirst with their own ink. These, and a thousand other reformations, I firmly counted upon by your encouragement; as indeed they were plainly deducible from the precepts delivered in my book. And, it must be owned, that seven months were a sufficient time to correct every vice and folly to which yahoos are subject, if their natures had been capable of the least disposition to virtue or wisdom; yet so far have you been from answering mine expectation in any of your letters, that on the contrary you are loading our carrier every week with libels, and keys, and reflections, and memoirs, and second parts; wherein I see myself accused of reflecting upon great states-folk; of degrading human nature (for so they have still the confidence to style it), and of abusing the female sex. I find likewise, that the writers of those bundles are not agreed among themselves; for some of them will not allow me to be author of mine own travels; and others make me author of books to which I am wholly a stranger.

I find likewise that your printer hath been so careless as to confound the times, and mistake the dates of my several voyages and returns, neither assigning the true year, or the true month, or day of the month; and I hear the original manuscript is all destroyed since the publication of my book. Neither have I any copy left;

however, I have sent you some corrections, which you may insert if ever there should be a second edition: and yet I cannot stand to them, but shall leave that matter to my judicious and candid readers, to adjust it as they please.

I hear some of our sea-yahoos find fault with my sea-language, as not proper in many parts, nor now in use. I cannot help it. In my first voyages, while I was young, I was instructed by the oldest mariners, and learned to speak as they did. But I have since found that the sea-yahoos are apt, like the land ones, to become new-fangled in their words; which the latter change every year, insomuch as I remember upon each return to mine own country, their old dialect was so altered that I could hardly understand the new. And I observe, when any yahoo comes from London out of curiosity to visit me at mine own house, we neither of us are able to deliver our conceptions in a manner intelligible to the other.

If the censure of yahoos could any way affect me, I should have great reason to complain that some of them are so bold as to think my book of travels a mere fiction out of mine own brain; and have gone so far as to drop hints that the Houyhnhnms and yahoos have no more existence than the inhabitants of Utopia.

Indeed I must confess, that as to the people of Lilliput, Brobdingrag (for so the word should have been spelt, and not erroneously 'Brobdingnag') and Laputa, I have never yet heard of any yahoo so presumptuous as to dispute their being, or the facts I have related concerning them; because the truth immediately strikes every reader with conviction. And is there less probability in my account of the Houyhnhnms or yahoos, when it is manifest as to the latter, there are so many thousands even in this city, who only differ from their brother brutes in Houyhnhnmland, because they use a sort of a jabber, and do not go naked? I wrote for their amendment, and not their approbation. The united praise of the whole race would be of less consequence to me than the neighing of those two degenerate Houyhnhnms I keep in my stable; because from these, degenerate as they are, I still improve in some virtues, without any mixture of vice.

Do these miserable animals presume to think that I am so far degenerated as to defend my veracity? Yahoo as I am, it is well known through all Houyhnhnmland, that by the instructions and example of my illustrious master, I was able in the compass of two years (although I confess with the utmost difficulty) to remove that infernal habit of lying, shuffling, deceiving, and equivocating, so deeply rooted in the very souls of all my species, especially the Europeans.

I have other complaints to make upon this vexatious occasion; but I forbear troubling myself or you any further. I must freely confess, that since my last return some corruptions of my yahoo nature have revived in me by conversing with a few of your species, and particularly those of mine own family, by an unavoidable necessity; else I should never have attempted so absurd a project as that of reforming the yahoo race in this kingdom; but I have now done with all such visionary schemes for ever.

April 2, 1727.

THE PUBLISHER TO THE READER

The author of these *Travels*, Mr. Lemuel Gulliver, is my ancient and intimate friend; there is likewise some relation between us by the mother's side. About three years ago Mr. Gulliver, growing weary of the concourse of curious people coming to him at his house in Redriff, made a small purchase of land, with a convenient house, near Newark in Nottinghamshire, his native country; where he now lives retired, yet in good esteem among his neighbours.

Although Mr. Gulliver was born in Nottinghamshire, where his father dwelt, yet I have heard him say, his family came from Oxfordshire; to confirm which, I have observed in the churchyard at Banbury, in that county, several tombs and monuments of the Gullivers.

Before he quitted Redriff, he left the custody of the following papers in my hands, with the liberty to dispose of them as I should think fit. I have carefully perused them three times: the style is very plain and simple; and the only fault I find is, that the author, after the manner of travellers, is a little too circumstantial. There is an air of truth apparent through the whole; and indeed, the author was so distinguished for his veracity, that it became a sort of proverb among his neighbours at Redriff, when any one affirmed a thing, to say, it was as true as if Mr. Gulliver had spoke it.

By the advice of several worthy persons, to whom, with the author's permission, I communicated these papers, I now venture to send them into the world, hoping they may be at least, for some time, a better entertainment to our young noblemen than the common scribbles of politics and party.

This volume would have been at least twice as large, if I had not made bold to strike out innumerable passages relating to the winds and tides, as well as to the variations and bearings in the several voyages; together with the minute descriptions of the management of the ship in storms, in the style of sailors: likewise the account of the longitudes and latitudes; wherein I have reason to apprehend that Mr. Gulliver may be a little dissatisfied: but I was resolved to fit the work as much as possible to the general capacity of readers. However, if my own ignorance in sea-affairs shall have led me to commit some mistakes, I alone am answerable for them: and if any traveller hath a curiosity to see the whole work at large, as it came from the hand of the author, I will be ready to gratify him.

As for any further particulars relating to the author, the reader will receive satisfaction from the first pages of the book.

RICHARD SYMPSON.

THE
CONTENTS.

PART I.

[A VOYAGE TO LILLIPUT]

PART II.

[A VOYAGE TO BROBDINGNAG]

PART III.

[A VOYAGE TO LAPUTA, BALNIBARBI, GLUBBDUBDRIB, LUGGNAGG, AND JAPAN]

PART IV.

[A VOYAGE TO THE COUNTRY OF THE HOUYHNHNMS]

Plate.1 Part.1 Page.1   Hogs I

P Mint aon

I Good Fortune

I Naſſow

SUNDA

SUMATRA

Sillabar

Straits of Sunda

Blefuſcut

Mendendo   Lilliput

Diſcovered A.D. 1699.

Dimens Land

TRAVELS.

PART I.

A VOYAGE TO LILLIPUT.

CHAPTER I.

The author gives some account of himself and family; his first induce-
ments to travel. He is shipwrecked, and swims for his life, gets
safe on shore in the country of Lilliput, is made a prisoner, and
carried up the country.

MY father had a small estate in Nottinghamshire; I was the
third of five sons. He sent me to Emanuel College in
Cambridge, at fourteen years old, where I resided three
years, and applied my self close to my studies: but the charge of
maintaining me (although I had a very scanty allowance) being
too great for a narrow fortune, I was bound apprentice to Mr.
James Bates, an eminent surgeon in London, with whom I continued four years; and my father now and then sending me small
sums of money, I laid them out in learning navigation, and other
parts of the mathematics, useful to those who intend to travel, as
I always believed it would be some time or other my fortune to
do. When I left Mr. Bates, I went down to my father; where, by
the assistance of him and my uncle John, and some other relations I got forty pounds, and a promise of thirty pounds a year
to maintain me at Leyden: there I studied physic two years and
seven months, knowing it would be useful in long voyages.

Soon after my return from Leyden, I was recommended, by
my good master Mr. Bates, to be surgeon to the *Swallow*, Captain Abraham Pannell commander; with whom I continued three
years and a half, making a voyage or two into the Levant, and
some other parts. When I came back, I resolved to settle in London, to which Mr. Bates, my master, encouraged me, and by him
I was recommended to several patients. I took part of a small
house in the Old Jury; and being advised to alter my condition,
I married Mrs. Mary Burton, second daughter to Mr. Edmond
Burton hosier in Newgate Street, with whom I received four
hundred pounds for a portion.

But, my good master Bates dying in two years after, and I having few friends, my business began to fail; for my conscience would not suffer me to imitate the bad practice of too many among my brethren. Having therefore consulted with my wife, and some of my acquaintance, I determined to go again to sea. I was surgeon successively in two ships, and made several voyages, for six years, to the East and West Indies, by which I got some addition to my fortune. My hours of leisure I spent in reading the best authors ancient and modern, being always provided with a good number of books; and when I was ashore, in observing the manners and dispositions of the people, as well as learning their language, wherein I had a great facility by the strength of my memory.

The last of these voyages not proving very fortunate, I grew weary of the sea, and intended to stay at home with my wife and family. I removed from the Old Jury to Fetter Lane, and from thence to Wapping, hoping to get business among the sailors; but it would not turn to account. After three years' expectation that things would mend, I accepted an advantageous offer from Captain William Prichard, master of the *Antelope*, who was making a voyage to the South Sea. We set sail from Bristol May 4th, 1699, and our voyage at first was very prosperous.

It would not be proper, for some reasons, to trouble the reader with the particulars of our adventures in those seas: let it suffice to inform him, that in our passage from thence to the East Indies we were driven by a violent storm to the northwest of Van Diemen's Land. By an observation, we found ourselves in the latitude of 30 degrees 2 minutes south. Twelve of our crew were dead by immoderate labour, and ill food, the rest were in a very weak condition. On the fifth of November, which was the beginning of summer in those parts, the weather being very hazy, the seamen spied a rock, within half a cable's length of the ship; but the wind was so strong, that we were driven directly upon it, and immediately split. Six of the crew, of whom I was one, having let down the boat into the sea, made a shift to get clear of the ship, and the rock. We rowed by my computation about three leagues, till we were able to work no longer, being already spent with labour while we were in the ship. We therefore trusted ourselves to the mercy of the waves, and in about half an hour the boat was overset by a sudden flurry from the north. What became of my companions in the boat, as well as of those who escaped on the rock, or were left in the vessel, I cannot tell; but conclude they were all lost. For my own part, I swam as fortune directed me, and was pushed forward by wind and tide. I often

let my legs drop, and could feel no bottom: but when I was almost gone and able to struggle no longer, I found myself within
my depth; and by this time the storm was much abated. The declivity was so small, that I walked near a mile before I got to the
shore, which I conjectured was about eight o'clock in the evening. I then advanced forward near half a mile, but could not
discover any sign of houses or inhabitants; at least I was in so
weak a condition, that I did not observe them. I was extremely
tired, and with that, and the heat of the weather, and about half
a pint of brandy that I drank as I left the ship, I found myself
much inclined to sleep. I lay down on the grass, which was very
short and soft, where I slept sounder than ever I remember to
have done in my life, and, as I reckoned, above nine hours; for
when I awaked, it was just daylight. I attempted to rise, but was
not able to stir: for as I happened to lie on my back, I found
my arms and legs were strongly fastened on each side to the
ground; and my hair, which was long and thick, tied down
in the same manner. I likewise felt several slender ligatures
across my body, from my armpits to my thighs. I could only
look upwards, the sun began to grow hot, and the light offended my eyes. I heard a confused noise about me, but, in the
posture I lay, could see nothing except the sky. In a little time
I felt something alive moving on my left leg, which advancing
gently forward over my breast, came almost up to my chin;
when, bending my eyes downwards as much as I could, I perceived it to be a human creature not six inches high, with a bow
and arrow in his hands, and a quiver at his back. In the mean
time, I felt at least forty more of the same kind (as I conjectured)
following the first. I was in the utmost astonishment, and roared
so loud, that they all ran back in a fright; and some of them, as
I was afterwards told, were hurt with the falls they got by leaping from my sides upon the ground. However, they soon returned, and one of them, who ventured so far as to get a full
sight of my face, lifting up his hands and eyes by way of admiration, cried out in a shrill, but distinct voice, *Hekinah degul:* the
others repeated the same words several times, but I then knew
not what they meant. I lay all this while, as the reader may believe, in great uneasiness: at length, struggling to get loose, I had
the fortune to break the strings and wrench out the pegs that
fastened my left arm to the ground; for, by lifting it up to my
face, I discovered the methods they had taken to bind me; and,
at the same time, with a violent pull, which gave me excessive
pain, I a little loosened the strings that tied down my hair on the
left side, so that I was just able to turn my head about two inches.

But the creatures ran off a second time, before I could seize them; whereupon there was a great shout in a very shrill accent, and after it ceased, I heard one of them cry aloud, *Tolgo phonac*; when in an instant I felt above an hundred arrows discharged on my left hand, which pricked me like so many needles; and besides they shot another flight into the air, as we do bombs in Europe, whereof many, I suppose, fell on my body (though I felt them not) and some on my face, which I immediately covered with my left hand. When this shower of arrows was over, I fell a groaning with grief and pain, and then striving again to get loose, they discharged another volley larger than the first, and some of them attempted with spears to stick me in the sides; but, by good luck, I had on me a buff jerkin, which they could not pierce. I thought it the most prudent method to lie still, and my design was to continue so till night, when, my left hand being already loose, I could easily free myself: and as for the inhabitants, I had reason to believe I might be a match for the greatest armies they could bring against me, if they were all of the same size with him that I saw. But fortune disposed otherwise of me. When the people observed I was quiet, they discharged no more arrows: but by the noise increasing, I knew their numbers were greater; and about four yards from me, over-against my right ear, I heard a knocking for above an hour, like people at work; when, turning my head that way, as well as the pegs and strings would permit me, I saw a stage erected about a foot and a half from the ground, capable of holding four of the inhabitants, with two or three ladders to mount it: from whence one of them, who seemed to be a person of quality, made me a long speech, whereof I understood not one syllable. But I should have mentioned, that before the principal person began his oration, he cried out three times, *Langro dehul san*: (these words and the former were afterwards repeated and explained to me). Whereupon immediately about fifty of the inhabitants came, and cut the strings that fastened the left side of my head, which gave me the liberty of turning it to the right, and of observing the person and gesture of him who was to speak. He appeared to be of a middle age, and taller than any of the other three who attended him, whereof one was a page who held up his train, and seemed to be somewhat longer than my middle finger; the other two stood one on each side to support him. He acted every part of an orator, and I could observe many periods of threatenings, and others of promises, pity and kindness. I answered in a few words, but in the most submissive manner, lifting up my left hand and both eyes to the sun, as calling him for a witness; and being almost famished with hunger, having not eaten a morsel for some hours before I left the ship, I found the demands of nature so strong upon me, that I could not forbear showing my impatience (perhaps against the strict rules of decency) by putting my finger frequently on my mouth, to signify that I wanted food. The *Hurgo* (for so they call a great lord, as I afterwards learnt) understood me very well. He descended from the stage, and commanded that several ladders should be applied to my sides, on which above an hundred of the inhabitants mounted, and walked towards my mouth, laden with baskets full of meat, which had been provided and sent thither by the King's orders upon the first intelligence he received of me. I observed there was the flesh of several animals, but could not distinguish them by the taste. There were shoulders, legs and loins shaped like those of mutton, and very well dressed, but smaller than the wings of a lark. I eat them by two or three at a mouthful, and took three loaves at a time, about the bigness of musket bullets. They supplied me as fast as they could, showing a thousand marks of wonder and astonishment at my bulk and appetite. I then made another sign that I wanted drink. They found by my eating that a small quantity would not suffice me, and being a most ingenious people, they slung up with great dexterity one of their largest hogsheads, then rolled it towards my hand, and beat out the top; I drank it off at a draught, which I might well do, for it hardly held half a pint, and tasted like a small wine of Burgundy, but much more delicious. They brought me a second hogshead, which I drank in the same manner, and made signs for more, but they had none to give me. When I had performed these wonders, they shouted for joy, and danced upon my breast, repeating several times as they did at first, *Hekinah degul.* They made me a sign that I should throw down the two hogsheads, but first warned the people below to stand out of the way, crying aloud, *Borach mivola,* and when they saw the vessels in the air, there was an universal shout of *Hekinah degul.* I confess I was often tempted, while they were passing backwards and forwards on my body, to seize forty or fifty of the first that came in my reach, and dash them against the ground. But the remembrance of what I had felt, which probably might not be the worst they could do, and the promise of honour I made them, for so I interpreted my submissive behaviour, soon drove out those imaginations. Besides, I now considered my self as bound by the laws of hospitality to a people who had treated me with so much expense and magnificence. However, in my thoughts I could not sufficiently wonder at the intrepidity of these diminutive mortals, who durst venture to mount and walk on my body, while one of my hands was at liberty, without trembling at the very sight of so prodigious a creature as I must appear to them. After some time, when they observed that I made no more demands for meat, there appeared before me a person of high rank from his Imperial Majesty. His Excellency, having mounted on the small of my right leg, advanced forwards up to my face, with about a dozen of his retinue. And producing his credentials under the Signet Royal, which he applied close to my eyes, spoke about ten minutes, without any signs of anger, but with a kind of determinate resolution; often pointing forwards, which, as I afterwards found, was towards the capital city, about half a mile distant, whither it was agreed by his Majesty in council that I must be conveyed. I answered in few words, but to no purpose, and made a sign with my hand that was loose, putting it to the other (but over his Excellency's head, for fear of hurting him or his train) and then to my own head and body, to signify that I desired my liberty. It appeared that he understood me well enough, for he shook his head by way of disapprobation, and held his hand in a posture to show that I must be carried as a prisoner. However, he made other signs to let me understand that I should have meat and drink enough, and very good treatment. Whereupon I once more thought of attempting to break my bonds, but again, when I felt the smart of their arrows upon my face and hands, which were all in blisters, and many of the darts still sticking in them, and observing likewise that the number of my enemies encreased, I gave tokens to let them know that they might do with me what they pleased. Upon this the *Hurgo* and his train withdrew with much civility and cheerful countenances. Soon after I heard a general shout, with frequent repetitions of the words, *Peplom selan*, and I felt great numbers of the people on my left side relaxing the cords to such a degree, that I was able to turn upon my right, and to ease myself with making water; which I very plentifully did, to the great astonishment of the people, who conjecturing by my motions what I was going to do, immediately opened to the right and left on that side to avoid the torrent which fell with such noise and violence from me. But before this, they had daubed my face and both my hands with a sort of ointment very pleasant to the smell, which in a few minutes removed all the smart of their arrows. These circumstances, added to the refreshment I had received by their victuals and drink, which were very nourishing, disposed me to sleep. I slept about eight hours, as I was afterwards assured; and it was no wonder, for the physicians, by the Emperor's order, had mingled a sleeping potion in the hogsheads of wine.

It seems that upon the first moment I was discovered sleeping on the ground after my landing, the Emperor had early notice of it by an express, and determined in council that I should be tied in the manner I have related (which was done in the night while I slept), that plenty of meat and drink should be sent me, and a machine prepared to carry me to the capital city.

This resolution perhaps may appear very bold and dangerous, and I am confident would not be imitated by any prince in Europe on the like occasion; however, in my opinion, it was extremely prudent as well as generous. For supposing these people had endeavoured to kill me with their spears and arrows while I was asleep, I should certainly have awaked with the first sense of smart, which might so far have roused my rage and strength, as to enable me to break the strings wherewith I was tied; after which, as they were not able to make resistance, so they could expect no mercy.

These people are most excellent mathematicians, and arrived to a great perfection in mechanics by the countenance and encouragement of the Emperor, who is a renowned patron of learning. This prince hath several machines fixed on wheels for the carriage of trees and other great weights. He often builds his largest men of war, whereof some are nine foot long, in the woods where the timber grows, and has them carried on these engines three or four hundred yards to the sea. Five hundred carpenters and engineers were immediately set at work to prepare the greatest engine they had. It was a frame of wood raised three inches from the ground, about seven foot long and four wide, moving upon twenty-two wheels. The shout I heard was upon the arrival of this engine, which it seems set out in four hours after my landing. It was brought parallel to me as I lay. But the principal difficulty was to raise and place me in this vehicle. Eighty poles, each of one foot high, were erected for this purpose, and very strong cords of the bigness of packthread were fastened by hooks to many bandages, which the workmen had girt round my neck, my hands, my body, and my legs. Nine hundred of the strongest men were employed to draw up these cords by many pulleys fastened on the poles, and thus, in less than three hours, I was raised and slung into the engine, and there tied fast. All this I was told, for while the whole operation was performing, I lay in a profound sleep, by the force of that soporiferous medicine infused into my liquor. Fifteen hundred of the Emperor's largest horses, each about four inches and a half high, were employed to draw me towards the metropolis, which, as I said, was half a mile distant.

About four hours after we began our journey, I awaked by a very ridiculous accident; for, the carriage being stopped a while to adjust something that was out of order, two or three of the young natives had the curiosity to see how I looked when I was asleep; they climbed up into the engine, and advancing very softly to my face, one of them, an officer in the guards, put the sharp end of his half-pike a good way up into my left nostril, which tickled my nose like a straw, and made me sneeze violently: whereupon they stole off unperceived, and it was three weeks before I knew the cause of my awaking so suddenly. We made a long march the remaining part of the day, and rested at night with five hundred guards on each side of me, half with torches, and half with bows and arrows, ready to shoot me if I should offer to stir. The next morning at sunrise we continued our march, and arrived within two hundred yards of the city gates about noon. The Emperor and all his court came out to meet us, but his great officers would by no means suffer his Majesty to endanger his person by mounting on my body.

At the place where the carriage stopped, there stood an ancient temple, esteemed to be the largest in the whole kingdom, which having been polluted some years before by an unnatural murder, was, according to the zeal of those people, looked on as profane, and therefore had been applied to common use, and all the ornaments and furniture carried away. In this edifice it was determined I should lodge. The great gate fronting to the north was about four foot high, and almost two foot wide, through which I could easily creep. On each side of the gate was a small window not above six inches from the ground: into that on the left side, the King's smiths conveyed fourscore and eleven chains, like those that hang to a lady's watch in Europe, and almost as large, which were locked to my left leg with six and thirty padlocks. Over against this temple, on the other side of the great highway, at twenty foot distance, there was a turret at least five foot high. Here the Emperor ascended with many principal lords of his court, to have an opportunity of viewing me, as I was told, for I could not see them. It was reckoned that above an hundred thousand inhabitants came out of the town upon the same errand; and in spite of my guards, I believe there could not be fewer than ten thousand, at several times, who mounted upon my body by the help of ladders. But a proclamation was soon issued to forbid it upon pain of death. When the workmen found it was impossible for me to break loose, they cut all the strings

that bound me; whereupon I rose up with as melancholy a disposition as ever I had in my life. But the noise and astonishment
of the people at seeing me rise and walk are not to be expressed.
The chains that held my left leg were about two yards long, and
gave me not only the liberty of walking backwards and forwards
in a semicircle; but, being fixed within four inches of the gate,
allowed me to creep in, and lie at my full length in the temple.

CHAPTER II.

*The Emperor of Lilliput, attended by several of the nobility, comes
to see the author in his confinement. The Emperor's person and
habit described. Learned men appointed to teach the author their
language. He gains favour by his mild disposition. His pockets
are searched, and his sword and pistols taken from him.*

When I found myself on my feet, I looked about me, and
must confess I never beheld a more entertaining prospect. The
country round appeared like a continued garden, and the inclosed fields, which were generally forty foot square, resembled
so many beds of flowers. These fields were intermingled with
woods of half a stang, and the tallest trees, as I could judge, appeared to be seven foot high. I viewed the town on my left hand,
which looked like the painted scene of a city in a theatre.

I had been for some hours extremely pressed by the necessities
of nature; which was no wonder, it being almost two days since
I had last disburthened myself. I was under great difficulties between urgency and shame. The best expedient I could think on,
was to creep into my house, which I accordingly did; and shut-
ting the gate after me, I went as far as the length of my chain
would suffer, and discharged my body of that uneasy load. But
this was the only time I was ever guilty of so uncleanly an action;
for which I cannot but hope the candid reader will give some
allowance, after he hath maturely and impartially considered my
case, and the distress I was in. From this time my constant practice was, as soon as I rose, to perform that business in open air,
at the full extent of my chain, and due care was taken every
morning before company came, that the offensive matter should
be carried off in wheelbarrows by two servants appointed for
that purpose. I would not have dwelt so long upon a circumstance, that perhaps at first sight may appear not very momen-
tous, if I had not thought it necessary to justify my character
in point of cleanliness to the world; which I am told some of my

maligners have been pleased, upon this and other occasions, to call in question.

When this adventure was at an end, I came back out of my house, having occasion for fresh air. The Emperor was already descended from the tower, and advancing on horseback towards me, which had like to have cost him dear; for the beast, although very well trained, yet wholly unused to such a sight, which appeared as if a mountain moved before him, reared up on his hinder feet: but that prince, who is an excellent horseman, kept his seat, until his attendants ran in, and held the bridle, while his Majesty had time to dismount. When he alighted, he surveyed me round with great admiration, but kept beyond the length of my chains. He ordered his cooks and butlers, who were already prepared, to give me victuals and drink, which they pushed forward in a sort of vehicles upon wheels until I could reach them. I took these vehicles, and soon emptied them all; twenty of them were filled with meat, and ten with liquor; each of the former afforded me two or three good mouthfuls, and I emptied the liquor of ten vessels, which was contained in earthen vials, into one vehicle, drinking it off at a draught, and so I did with the rest. The Empress, and young princes of the blood, of both sexes, attended by many ladies, sat at some distance in their chairs; but upon the accident that happened to the Emperor's horse, they alighted, and came near his person, which I am now going to describe. He is taller, by almost the breadth of my nail, than any of his court, which alone is enough to strike an awe into the beholders. His features are strong and masculine, with an Austrian lip and arched nose, his complexion olive, his countenance erect, his body and limbs well proportioned, all his motions graceful, and his deportment majestic. He was then past his prime, being twenty-eight years and three quarters old, of which he had reigned about seven, in great felicity, and generally victorious. For the better convenience of beholding him, I lay on my side, so that my face was parallel to his, and he stood but three yards off: however, I have had him since many times in my hand, and therefore cannot be deceived in the description. His dress was very plain and simple, and the fashion of it between the Asiatic and the European; but he had on his head a light helmet of gold, adorned with jewels, and a plume on the crest. He held his sword drawn in his hand, to defend himself, if I should happen to break loose; it was almost three inches long, the hilt and scabbard were gold enriched with diamonds. His voice was shrill, but very clear and articulate, and I could distinctly hear it when I stood up. The ladies and

courtiers were all most magnificently clad, so that the spot they
stood upon seemed to resemble a petticoat spread on the ground,
embroidered with figures of gold and silver. His Imperial Majesty spoke often to me, and I returned answers, but neither of us
could understand a syllable. There were several of his priests
and lawyers present (as I conjectured by their habits) who were
commanded to address themselves to me, and I spoke to them in
as many languages as I had the least smattering of, which were
High and Low Dutch, Latin, French, Spanish, Italian, and Lingua
Franca; but all to no purpose. After about two hours the court
retired, and I was left with a strong guard, to prevent the impertinence, and probably the malice of the rabble, who were
very impatient to crowd about me as near as they durst, and some
of them had the impudence to shoot their arrows at me as I sat
on the ground by the door of my house, whereof one very narrowly missed my left eye. But the colonel ordered six of the
ringleaders to be seized, and thought no punishment so proper
as to deliver them bound into my hands, which some of his soldiers accordingly did, pushing them forwards with the butt-ends
of their pikes into my reach; I took them all in my right hand,
put five of them into my coat-pocket, and as to the sixth, I made
a countenance as if I would eat him alive. The poor man squalled
terribly, and the colonel and his officers were in much pain, especially when they saw me take out my penknife: but I soon put
them out of fear; for, looking mildly, and immediately cutting
the strings he was bound with, I set him gently on the ground,
and away he ran; I treated the rest in the same manner, taking
them one by one out of my pocket, and I observed both the soldiers and people were highly obliged at this mark of my clemency, which was represented very much to my advantage at
court.

Towards night I got with some difficulty into my house,
where I lay on the ground, and continued to do so about a fortnight; during which time the Emperor gave orders to have a
bed prepared for me. Six hundred beds of the common measure
were brought in carriages, and worked up in my house; an hundred and fifty of their beds sewn together made up the breadth
and length, and these were four double, which however kept me
but very indifferently from the hardness of the floor, that was of
smooth stone. By the same computation they provided me with
sheets, blankets, and coverlets, tolerable enough for one who had
been so long enured to hardships as I.

As the news of my arrival spread through the kingdom, it
brought prodigious numbers of rich, idle, and curious people to

see me; so that the villages were almost emptied, and great neglect of tillage and household affairs must have ensued, if his Imperial Majesty had not provided by several proclamations and
orders of state against this inconveniency. He directed that those
who had already beheld me should return home, and not presume to come within fifty yards of my house without licence
from court: whereby the secretaries of state got considerable
fees.

In the mean time, the Emperor held frequent councils to debate what course should be taken with me; and I was afterwards
assured by a particular friend, a person of great quality, who was
as much in the secret as any, that the court was under many difficulties concerning me. They apprehended my breaking loose,
that my diet would be very expensive, and might cause a famine. Sometimes they determined to starve me, or at least to shoot
me in the face and hands with poisoned arrows, which would
soon dispatch me: but again they considered, that the stench of
so large a carcase might produce a plague in the metropolis, and
probably spread through the whole kingdom. In the midst of
these consultations, several officers of the army went to the door
of the great council-chamber; and two of them being admitted,
gave an account of my behaviour to the six criminals above-mentioned, which made so favourable an impression in the breast of
his Majesty and the whole board in my behalf, that an imperial
commission was issued out, obliging all the villages nine hundred
yards round the city to deliver in every morning six beeves,
forty sheep, and other victuals for my sustenance; together with
a proportionable quantity of bread, and wine, and other liquors:
for the due payment of which his Majesty gave assignments upon
his treasury. For this prince lives chiefly upon his own demesnes,
seldom except upon great occasions raising any subsidies upon
his subjects, who are bound to attend him in his wars at their
own expense. An establishment was also made of six hundred
persons to be my domestics, who had board-wages allowed for
their maintenance, and tents built for them very conveniently
on each side of my door. It was likewise ordered, that three hundred tailors should make me a suit of clothes after the fashion of
the country: that six of his Majesty's greatest scholars should be
employed to instruct me in their language: and, lastly, that the
Emperor's horses, and those of the nobility and troops of guards,
should be exercised in my sight, to accustom themselves to me.
All these orders were duly put in execution, and in about three
weeks I made a great progress in learning their language; during
which time the Emperor frequently honoured me with his visits,

and was pleased to assist my masters in teaching me. We began already to converse together in some sort; and the first words I learnt were to express my desire that he would please to give me my liberty, which I every day repeated on my knees. His answer, as I could apprehend was, that this must be a work of time, not to be thought on without the advice of his council, and that first I must *lumos kelmin pesso desmar lon emposo;* that is, swear a peace with him and his kingdom. However, that I should be used with all kindness, and he advised me to acquire, by my patience, and discreet behaviour, the good opinion of himself and his subjects. He desired I would not take it ill, if he gave orders to certain proper officers to search me; for probably I might carry about me several weapons, which must needs be dangerous things, if they answered the bulk of so prodigious a person. I said, his Majesty should be satisfied, for I was ready to strip myself, and turn up my pockets before him. This I delivered part in words, and part in signs. He replied, that by the laws of the kingdom I must be searched by two of his officers; that he knew this could not be done without my consent and assistance; that he had so good an opinion of my generosity and justice, as to trust their persons in my hands: that whatever they took from me should be returned when I left the country, or paid for at the rate which I would set upon them. I took up the two officers in my hands, put them first into my coat-pockets, and then into every other pocket about me, except my two fobs, and another secret pocket which I had no mind should be searched, wherein I had some little necessaries of no consequence to any but myself. In one of my fobs there was a silver watch, and in the other a small quantity of gold in a purse. These gentlemen, having pen, ink and paper about them, made an exact inventory of every thing they saw; and when they had done, desired I would set them down, that they might deliver it to the Emperor. This inventory I afterwards translated into English, and is word for word as follows.

Imprimis, In the right coat-pocket of the Great Man-Mountain (for so I interpret the words *Quinbus Flestrin*) after the strictest search, we found only one great piece of coarse cloth, large enough to be a foot-cloth for your Majesty's chief room of state. In the left pocket, we saw a huge silver chest, with a cover of the same metal, which we the searchers were not able to lift. We desired it should be opened, and one of us, stepping into it, found himself up to the mid leg in a sort of dust, some part whereof, flying up to our faces, set us both a sneezing for several times together. In his right waistcoat-pocket, we found a prodigious bundle of white thin substances, folded one over another, about the bigness of three men, tied with a strong cable, and marked with black figures; which we humbly conceive to be writings, every letter almost half as large as the palm of our hands. In the left, there was a sort of engine, from the back of which were extended twenty long poles, resembling the palisados before your Majesty's court; wherewith we conjecture the Man-Mountain combs his head, for we did not always trouble him with questions, because we found it a great difficulty to make him understand us. In the large pocket on the right side of his middle cover (so I translate the word *ranfu-lo*, by which they meant my breeches) we saw a hollow pillar of iron, about the length of a man, fastened to a strong piece of timber, larger than the pillar; and upon one side of the pillar were huge pieces of iron sticking out, cut into strange figures, which we know not what to make of. In the left pocket, another engine of the same kind. In the smaller pocket on the right side, were several round flat pieces of white and red metal, of different bulk; some of the white, which seemed to be silver, were so large and heavy, that my comrade and I could hardly lift them. In the left pocket were two black pillars irregularly shaped: we could not, without difficulty, reach the top of them as we stood at the bottom of his pocket. One of them was covered, and seemed all of a piece: but at the upper end of the other, there appeared a white round substance, about twice the bigness of our heads. Within each of these was inclosed a prodigious plate of steel; which, by our orders, we obliged him to show us, because we apprehended they might be dangerous engines. He took them out of their cases, and told us, that in his own country his practice was to shave his beard with one of these, and to cut his meat with the other. There were two pockets which we could not enter: these he called his fobs; they were two large slits cut into the top of his middle cover, but squeezed close by the pressure of his belly. Out of the right fob hung a great silver chain, with a wonderful kind of engine at the bottom. We directed him to draw out whatever was at the end of that chain; which appeared to be a globe, half silver, and half of some transparent metal: for on the transparent side we saw certain strange figures circularly drawn, and thought we could touch them, until we found our fingers stopped with that lucid substance. He put this engine to our ears, which made an incessant noise like that of a watermill. And we conjecture it is either some unknown animal, or the god that he worships: but we are more inclined to the latter opinion, because he assured us (if we understood him right, for he expressed himself very imperfectly), that he seldom did any thing without consulting it. He called it his oracle, and said it pointed out the time for every action of his life. From the left fob he took out a net almost large enough for a fisherman, but contrived to open and shut like a purse, and served him for the same use: we found therein several massy pieces of yellow metal, which, if they be of real gold, must be of immense value.

Having thus, in obedience to your Majesty's commands, diligently searched all his pockets, we observed a girdle about his waist made of the hide of some prodigious animal; from which, on the left side, hung a sword of the length of five men, and on the right, a bag or pouch divided into two cells, each cell capable of holding three of your Majesty's subjects. In one of these cells were several globes or balls of a most ponderous metal, about the bigness of our heads, and required a strong hand to lift them: the other cell contained a heap of certain black grains, but of no great bulk or weight, for we could hold above fifty of them in the palms of our hands.

This is an exact inventory of what we found about the body of the Man-Mountain, who used us with great civility, and due respect to your Majesty's commission. Signed and sealed on the fourth day of the eighty-ninth moon of your Majesty's auspicious reign.

CLEFREN FRELOCK, MARSI FRELOCK.

When this inventory was read over to the Emperor, he directed me to deliver up the several particulars. He first called for my scimitar, which I took out, scabbard and all. In the mean time he ordered three thousand of his choicest troops (who then attended him) to surround me at a distance, with their bows and arrows just ready to discharge: but I did not observe it, for my eyes were wholly fixed upon his Majesty. He then desired me to draw my scimitar, which, although it had got some rust by the sea-water, was in most parts exceeding bright. I did so, and immediately all the troops gave a shout between terror and surprise; for the sun shone clear, and the reflection dazzled their eyes as I waved the scimitar to and fro in my hand. His Majesty, who is a most magnanimous prince, was less daunted than I could expect; he ordered me to return it into the scabbard, and cast it on the ground as gently as I could, about six foot from the end of my chain. The next thing he demanded was one of the hollow iron pillars, by which he meant my pocket-pistols. I drew it out, and at his desire, as well as I could, expressed to him the use of it; and charging it only with powder, which by the closeness of my pouch happened to escape wetting in the sea (an inconvenience that all prudent mariners take special care to provide against), I first cautioned the Emperor not to be afraid, and then I let it off in the air. The astonishment here was much greater than at the sight of my scimitar. Hundreds fell down as if they had been struck dead; and even the Emperor, although he stood his ground, could not recover himself in some time. I delivered up both my pistols in the same manner as I had done my scimitar, and then my pouch of powder and bullets; begging him that the former might be kept from the fire, for it would kindle with the smallest spark, and blow up his imperial palace into the air. I likewise delivered up my watch, which the Emperor was very curious to see, and commanded two of his tallest yeomen of the guards to bear it on a pole upon their shoulders, as draymen in England do a barrel of ale. He was amazed at the continual noise it made, and the motion of the minute-hand, which he could easily discern; for their sight is much more acute than ours: he asked the opinions of his learned men about him, which were various and remote, as the reader may well imagine without my repeating; although indeed I could not very perfectly understand them. I then gave up my silver and copper money, my purse with nine large pieces of gold, and some smaller ones; my knife and razor, my comb and silver snuff-box, my handkerchief and journal book. My scimitar, pistols, and pouch, were conveyed in carriages to his Majesty's stores; but the rest of my goods were returned me.

I had, as I before observed, one private pocket which escaped their search, wherein there was a pair of spectacles (which I sometimes use for the weakness of my eyes), a pocket perspective, and several other little conveniences; which, being of no consequence to the Emperor, I did not think my self bound in honour to discover, and I apprehended they might be lost or spoiled if I ventured them out of my possession.

CHAPTER III.

The author diverts the Emperor and his nobility of both sexes in a very uncommon manner. The diversions of the court of Lilliput described. The author hath his liberty granted him upon certain conditions.

My gentleness and good behaviour had gained so far on the Emperor and his court, and indeed upon the army and people in general, that I began to conceive hopes of getting my liberty in a short time. I took all possible methods to cultivate this favourable disposition. The natives came by degrees to be less apprehensive of any danger from me. I would sometimes lie down, and let five or six of them dance on my hand. And at last the boys and girls would venture to come and play at hide and seek in my hair. I had now made a good progress in understanding and speaking their language. The Emperor had a mind one day to entertain me with several of the country shows, wherein they exceed all nations I have known, both for dexterity and magnificence. I was diverted with none so much as that of the rope-dancers, performed upon a slender white thread, extended about two foot, and twelve inches from the ground. Upon which I shall desire liberty, with the reader's patience, to enlarge a little.

This diversion is only practised by those persons who are candidates for great employments, and high favour, at court. They are trained in this art from their youth, and are not always of noble birth, or liberal education. When a great office is vacant either by death or disgrace (which often happens) five or six of those candidates petition the Emperor to entertain his Majesty and the court with a dance on the rope, and whoever jumps the highest without falling, succeeds in the office. Very often the chief ministers themselves are commanded to show their skill, and to convince the Emperor that they have not lost their faculty. Flimnap, the Treasurer, is allowed to cut a caper on the strait rope, at least an inch higher than any other lord in the whole empire. I have seen him do the summerset several times together upon a trencher fixed on the rope, which is no thicker than a common packthread in England. My friend Reldresal, Principal Secretary for Private Affairs, is, in my opinion, if I am not partial, the second after the Treasurer; the rest of the great officers are much upon a par.

These diversions are often attended with fatal accidents, whereof great numbers are on record. I my self have seen two or three candidates break a limb. But the danger is much greater when the ministers themselves are commanded to show their dexterity; for by contending to excel themselves and their fellows, they strain so far, that there is hardly one of them who hath not received a fall, and some of them two or three. I was assured that a year or two before my arrival, Flimnap would have infallibly broke his neck, if one of the King's cushions, that accidentally lay on the ground, had not weakened the force of his fall.

There is likewise another diversion, which is only shown before the Emperor and Empress, and first minister, upon particular occasions. The Emperor lays on a table three fine silken threads of six inches long. One is blue, the other red, and the third green. These threads are proposed as prizes for those persons whom the Emperor hath a mind to distinguish by a peculiar mark of his favour. The ceremony is performed in his Majesty's great chamber of state, where the candidates are to undergo a trial of dexterity very different from the former, and such as I have not observed the least resemblance of in any other country of the old or the new world. The Emperor holds a stick in his hands, both ends parallel to the horizon, while the candidates, advancing one by one, sometimes leap over the stick, sometimes creep under it backwards and forwards several times, according as the stick is advanced or depressed. Sometimes the Emperor holds one end of the stick, and his first minister the other; sometimes the minister has it entirely to himself. Whoever performs his part with most agility, and holds out the longest in leaping and creeping, is rewarded with the blue-coloured silk; the red is given to the next, and the green to the third, which they all wear girt twice round about the middle; and you see few great persons about this court who are not adorned with one of these girdles.

The horses of the army, and those of the royal stables, having been daily led before me, were no longer shy, but would come up to my very feet without starting. The riders would leap them over my hand as I held it on the ground, and one of the Emperor's huntsmen, upon a large courser, took my foot, shoe and all; which was indeed a prodigious leap. I had the good fortune to divert the Emperor one day after a very extraordinary manner. I desired he would order several sticks of two foot high, and the thickness of an ordinary cane, to be brought me; whereupon his Majesty commanded the master of his woods to give directions accordingly, and the next morning six woodmen arrived with as many carriages, drawn by eight horses to each. I took nine of these sticks, and fixing them firmly in the ground in a quadrangular figure, two foot and a half square, I took four other sticks, and tied them parallel at each corner, about two foot from the ground; then I fastened my handkerchief to the nine sticks that stood erect, and extended it on all sides till it was as tight as the top of a drum; and the four parallel sticks, rising about five inches higher than the handkerchief, served as ledges on each side. When I had finished my work, I desired the Emperor to let a troop of his best horse, twenty-four in number, come and exercise upon this plain. His Majesty approved of the proposal, and I took them up one by one in my hands, ready mounted and armed, with the proper officers to exercise them. As soon as they got into order, they divided into two parties, performed mock skirmishes, discharged blunt arrows, drew their swords, fled and pursued, attacked and retired, and in short discovered the best military discipline I ever beheld. The parallel sticks secured them and their horses from falling over the stage; and the Emperor was so much delighted, that he ordered this entertainment to be repeated several days, and once was pleased to be lifted up, and give the word of command; and, with great difficulty, persuaded even the Empress her self to let me hold her in her close chair within two yards of the stage, from whence she was able to take a full view of the whole performance. It was my good fortune that no ill accident happened in these entertainments, only once a fiery horse that belonged to one of the captains pawing with his hoof struck a hole in my handkerchief, and his foot slipping, he overthrew his rider and himself; but I immediately relieved them both, for covering the hole with one hand, I set down the troop with the other, in the same manner as I took them up. The horse that fell was strained in the left shoulder, but the rider got no hurt, and I repaired my handkerchief as well as I could; however, I would not trust to the strength of it any more in such dangerous enterprises.

About two or three days before I was set at liberty, as I was entertaining the court with these kinds of feats, there arrived an express to inform his Majesty that some of his subjects, riding near the place where I was first taken up, had seen a great black substance lying on the ground, very oddly shaped, extending its edges round as wide as his Majesty's bedchamber, and rising up in the middle as high as a man; that it was no living creature, as they at first apprehended, for it lay on the grass without motion, and some of them had walked round it several times; that by mounting upon each others' shoulders, they had got to the top, which was flat and even, and stamping upon it they found it was hollow within; that they humbly conceived it might be something belonging to the Man-Mountain, and if his Majesty pleased, they would undertake to bring it with only five horses. I presently knew what they meant, and was glad at heart to receive this intelligence. It seems upon my first reaching the shore after our shipwreck, I was in such confusion, that before I came to the place where I went to sleep, my hat, which I had fastened with a string to my head while I was rowing, and had stuck on all the time I was swimming, fell off after I came to land; the string, as I conjecture, breaking by some accident which I never observed, but thought my hat had been lost at sea. I intreated his Imperial Majesty to give orders it might be brought to me as soon

as possible, describing to him the use and the nature of it:
and the next day the waggoners arrived with it, but not in a
very good condition; they had bored two holes in the brim, within
an inch and half of the edge, and fastened two hooks in the
holes; these hooks were tied by a long cord to the harness, and
thus my hat was dragged along for above half an English mile:
but the ground in that country being extremely smooth and level,
it received less damage than I expected.

Two days after this adventure, the Emperor having ordered
that part of his army which quarters in and about his metropolis
to be in a readiness, took a fancy of diverting himself in a very
singular manner. He desired I would stand like a colossus, with
my legs as far asunder as I conveniently could. He then commanded his general (who was an old experienced leader, and a
great patron of mine) to draw up the troops in close order, and
march them under me, the foot by twenty-four in a breast,
and the horse by sixteen, with drums beating, colours flying, and
pikes advanced. This body consisted of three thousand foot,
and a thousand horse. His Majesty gave orders, upon pain of
death, that every soldier in his march should observe the strictest
decency with regard to my person; which, however, could not
prevent some of the younger officers from turning up their eyes
as they passed under me. And, to confess the truth, my breeches
were at that time in so ill a condition, that they afforded some
opportunities for laughter and admiration.

I had sent so many memorials and petitions for my liberty, that
his Majesty at length mentioned the matter, first in the cabinet,
and then in a full council; where it was opposed by none, except
Skyresh Bolgolam, who was pleased, without any provocation, to
be my mortal enemy. But it was carried against him by the whole
board, and confirmed by the Emperor. That minister was *Galbet*,
or Admiral of the Realm, very much in his master's confidence,
and a person well versed in affairs, but of a morose and sour
complexion. However, he was at length persuaded to comply;
but prevailed that the articles and conditions upon which I should
be set free, and to which I must swear, should be drawn up by
himself. These articles were brought to me by Skyresh Bolgolam
in person, attended by two under-secretaries, and several persons
of distinction. After they were read, I was demanded to swear to
the performance of them; first in the manner of my own country,
and afterwards in the method prescribed by their laws; which
was to hold my right foot in my left hand, to place the middle
finger of my right hand on the crown of my head, and my thumb
on the tip of my right ear. But because the reader may perhaps

be curious to have some idea of the style and manner of expression peculiar to that people, as well as to know the articles upon which I recovered my liberty, I have made a translation of the whole instrument word for word, as near as I was able, which I here offer to the public.

GOLBASTO MOMAREN EVLAME GURDILO SHEFIN MULLY ULLY GUE, most mighty Emperor of Lilliput, delight and terror of the universe, whose dominions extend five thousand blustrugs (about twelve miles in circumference) to the extremities of the globe; monarch of all monarchs, taller than the sons of men; whose feet press down to the center, and whose head strikes against the sun: at whose nod the princes of the earth shake their knees; pleasant as the spring, comfortable as the summer, fruitful as autumn, dreadful as winter. His most sublime Majesty proposeth to the Man-Mountain, lately arrived at our celestial dominions, the following articles, which by a solemn oath he shall be obliged to perform.

First, The Man-Mountain shall not depart from our dominions, without our licence under our great seal.

Secondly, He shall not presume to come into our metropolis, without our express order; at which time the inhabitants shall have two hours warning to keep within their doors.

Thirdly, The said Man-Mountain shall confine his walks to our principal high roads, and not offer to walk or lie down in a meadow or field of corn.

Fourthly, As he walks the said roads, he shall take the utmost care not to trample upon the bodies of any of our loving subjects, their horses, or carriages, nor take any of our said subjects into his hands, without their own consent.

Fifthly, If an express require extraordinary dispatch, the Man-Mountain shall be obliged to carry in his pocket the messenger and horse a six days' journey once in every moon, and return the said messenger back (if so required) safe to our Imperial Presence.

Sixthly, He shall be our ally against our enemies in the island of Blefuscu, and do his utmost to destroy their fleet, which is now preparing to invade us.

Seventhly, That the said Man-Mountain shall, at his times of leisure, be aiding and assisting to our workmen, in helping to raise certain great stones, towards covering the wall of the principal park, and other our royal buildings.

Eighthly, That the said Man-Mountain shall, in two moons' time, deliver in an exact survey of the circumference of our dominions by a computation of his own paces round the coast.

Lastly, That upon his solemn oath to observe all the above articles, the said Man-Mountain shall have a daily allowance of meat and drink sufficient for the support of 1728 of our subjects, with free access to our Royal Person, and other marks of our favour. Given at our palace at Belfaborac the twelfth day of the ninety-first moon of our reign.

I swore and subscribed to these articles with great cheerfulness and content, although some of them were not so honourable as I could have wished; which proceeded wholly from the malice of Skyresh Bolgolam the High Admiral: whereupon my chains were immediately unlocked, and I was at full liberty; the Emperor himself in person did me the honour to be by at the whole ceremony. I made my acknowledgements by prostrating myself at his Majesty's feet: but he commanded me to rise; and after many gracious expressions, which, to avoid the censure of vanity, I shall not repeat, he added, that he hoped I should prove a useful servant, and well deserve all the favours he had already conferred upon me, or might do for the future.

The reader may please to observe, that in the last article for the recovery of my liberty, the Emperor stipulates to allow me a quantity of meat and drink sufficient for the support of 1728 Lilliputians. Some time after, asking a friend at court how they came to fix on that determinate number, he told me, that his Majesty's mathematicians, having taken the height of my body by the help of a quadrant, and finding it to exceed theirs in the proportion of twelve to one, they concluded from the similarity of their bodies, that mine must contain at least 1728 of theirs, and consequently would require as much food as was necessary to support that number of Lilliputians. By which the reader may conceive an idea of the ingenuity of that people, as well as the prudent and exact œconomy of so great a prince.

CHAPTER IV.

Mildendo, the metropolis of Lilliput, described, together with the Emperor's palace. A conversation between the author and a principal secretary, concerning the affairs of that empire; the author's offers to serve the Emperor in his wars.

The first request I made after I had obtained my liberty, was, that I might have licence to see Mildendo, the metropolis; which the Emperor easily granted me, but with a special charge to do no hurt, either to the inhabitants, or their houses. The people had notice by proclamation of my design to visit the town. The wall which encompassed it is two foot and an half high, and at least eleven inches broad, so that a coach and horses may be driven very safely round it; and it is flanked with strong towers at ten foot distance. I stepped over the great western gate, and passed very gently, and sideling through the two principal streets, only in my short waistcoat, for fear of damaging the roofs and eaves of the houses with the skirts of my coat. I walked with the utmost circumspection, to avoid treading on any stragglers, who might remain in the streets, although the orders were very strict, that all people should keep in their houses, at their own peril. The garret windows and tops of houses were so crowded with spectators, that I thought in all my travels I had not seen a more populous place. The city is an exact square, each side of the wall being five hundred foot long. The two great streets, which run cross and divide it into four quarters, are five foot wide. The lanes and alleys, which I could not enter, but only viewed them as I passed, are from twelve to eighteen inches. The town is capable of holding five hundred thousand souls. The houses are from three to five stories. The shops and markets well provided.

The Emperor's palace is in the center of the city, where the two great streets meet. It is inclosed by a wall of two foot high, and twenty foot distant from the buildings. I had his Majesty's permission to step over this wall; and the space being so wide between that and the palace, I could easily view it on every side. The outward court is a square of forty foot, and includes two other courts: in the inmost are the royal apartments, which I was very desirous to see, but found it extremely difficult; for the great gates, from one square into another, were but eighteen inches high, and seven inches wide. Now the buildings of the outer court were at least five foot high, and it was impossible for me to stride over them, without infinite damage to the pile, although the walls were strongly built of hewn stone, and four inches thick. At the same time the Emperor had a great desire that I should see the magnificence of his palace; but this I was not able to do till three days after, which I spent in cutting down with my knife some of the largest trees in the royal park, about an hundred yards distant from the city. Of these trees I made two stools, each about three foot high, and strong enough to bear my weight. The people having received notice a second time, I went again through the city to the palace, with my two stools in my hands. When I came to the side of the outer court, I stood upon one stool, and took the other in my hand: this I lifted over the roof, and gently set it down on the space between the first and second court, which was eight foot wide. I then stepped over the buildings very conveniently from one stool to the other, and drew up the first after me with a hooked stick. By this contrivance I got into the inmost court; and lying down upon my side, I applied my face to the windows of the middle stories, which were left open on purpose, and discovered the most splendid apartments that can be imagined. There I saw the Empress, and the young princes in their several lodgings, with their chief attendants about them. Her Imperial Majesty was pleased to smile very graciously upon me, and gave me out of the window her hand to kiss.

But I shall not anticipate the reader with farther descriptions of this kind, because I reserve them for a greater work, which is now almost ready for the press, containing a general description of this empire, from its first erection, through a long series of princes, with a particular account of their wars and politics, laws, learning, and religion; their plants and animals, their peculiar manners and customs, with other matters very curious and useful; my chief design at present being only to relate such events and transactions as happened to the public, or to myself, during a residence of about nine months in that empire.

One morning, about a fortnight after I had obtained my liberty, Reldresal, Principal Secretary (as they style him) of Private Affairs, came to my house, attended only by one servant. He ordered his coach to wait at a distance, and desired I would give him an hour's audience; which I readily consented to, on account of his quality, and personal merits, as well as of the many good offices he had done me during my solicitations at court. I offered to lie down, that he might the more conveniently reach my ear; but he chose rather to let me hold him in my hand during our conversation. He began with compliments on my liberty, said he might pretend to some merit in it; but, however, added, that if it had not been for the present situation of things at court, perhaps I might not have obtained it so soon. For, said he, as flourishing a condition as we appear to be in to foreigners, we labour under two mighty evils; a violent faction at home, and the danger of an invasion by a most potent enemy from abroad. As to the first, you are to understand, that for above seventy moons past, there have been two struggling parties in the empire, under the names of *Tramecksan* and *Slamecksan*, from the high and low heels on their shoes, by which they distinguish themselves. It is alleged indeed, that the high heels are most agreeable to our ancient constitution: but however this be, his Majesty hath determined to make use of only low heels in the administration of the govern-

ment and all offices in the gift of the crown, as you cannot but
observe; and particularly, that his Majesty's imperial heels are
lower at least by a *drurr* than any of his court; (*drurr* is a measure about the fourteenth part of an inch). The animosities between these two parties run so high, that they will neither eat nor
drink, nor talk with each other. We compute the *Tramecksan*, or
High-Heels, to exceed us in number; but the power is wholly on
our side. We apprehend his Imperial Highness, the heir to the
crown, to have some tendency towards the High-Heels; at least
we can plainly discover one of his heels higher than the other,
which gives him a hobble in his gait. Now, in the midst of these
intestine disquiets, we are threatened with an invasion from the
island of Blefuscu, which is the other great empire of the universe, almost as large and powerful as this of his Majesty. For as
to what we have heard you affirm, that there are other kingdoms
and states in the world, inhabited by human creatures as large as
yourself, our philosophers are in much doubt, and would rather
conjecture that you dropped from the moon, or one of the stars;
because it is certain, that an hundred mortals of your bulk would,
in a short time, destroy all the fruits and cattle of his Majesty's
dominions. Besides, our histories of six thousand moons make no
mention of any other regions, than the two great empires of Lilliput and Blefuscu. Which two mighty powers have, as I was going
to tell you, been engaged in a most obstinate war for six and thirty
moons past. It began upon the following occasion. It is allowed on all hands, that the primitive way of breaking eggs before we eat them, was upon the larger end: but his present Majesty's grandfather, while he was a boy, going to eat an egg, and
breaking it according to the ancient practice, happened to cut one
of his fingers. Whereupon the Emperor his father published an
edict, commanding all his subjects, upon great penalties, to break
the smaller end of their eggs. The people so highly resented this
law, that our histories tell us there have been six rebellions raised
on that account; wherein one emperor lost his life, and another
his crown. These civil commotions were constantly fomented by
the monarchs of Blefuscu; and when they were quelled, the exiles always fled for refuge to that empire. It is computed, that
eleven thousand persons have, at several times, suffered death,
rather than submit to break their eggs at the smaller end. Many
hundred large volumes have been published upon this controversy: but the books of the Big-Endians have been long forbidden,
and the whole party rendered incapable by law of holding employments. During the course of these troubles, the emperors of
Blefuscu did frequently expostulate by their ambassadors, accus-

ing us of making a schism in religion, by offending against a fundamental doctrine of our great prophet Lustrog, in the fifty-fourth chapter of the *Brundecral* (which is their Alcoran). This, however, is thought to be a mere strain upon the text: for the words are these; That all true believers shall break their eggs at the convenient end: and which is the convenient end, seems, in my humble opinion, to be left to every man's conscience, or at least in the power of the chief magistrate to determine. Now the Big-Endian exiles have found so much credit in the Emperor of Blefuscu's court, and so much private assistance and encouragement from their party here at home, that a bloody war hath been carried on between the two empires for six and thirty moons with various success; during which time we have lost forty capital ships, and a much greater number of smaller vessels, together with thirty thousand of our best seamen and soldiers; and the damage received by the enemy is reckoned to be somewhat greater than ours. However, they have now equipped a numerous fleet, and are just preparing to make a descent upon us; and his Imperial Majesty, placing great confidence in your valour and strength, hath commanded me to lay this account of his affairs before you.

I desired the Secretary to present my humble duty to the Emperor, and to let him know, that I thought it would not become me, who was a foreigner, to interfere with parties; but I was ready, with the hazard of my life, to defend his person and state against all invaders.

Chapter V.

The author by an extraordinary stratagem prevents an invasion. A high title of honour is conferred upon him. Ambassadors arrive from the Emperor of Blefuscu, and sue for peace. The Empress's apartment on fire by an accident; the author instrumental in saving the rest of the palace.

The empire of Blesfuscu is an island situated to the north-northeast side of Lilliput, from whence it is parted only by a channel of eight hundred yards wide. I had not yet seen it, and upon this notice of an intended invasion, I avoided appearing on that side of the coast, for fear of being discovered by some of the enemy's ships, who had received no intelligence of me, all intercourse between the two empires having been strictly forbidden during the war, upon pain of death, and an embargo laid by our

Emperor upon all vessels whatsoever. I communicated to his Majesty a project I had formed of seizing the enemy's whole fleet; which, as our scouts assured us, lay at anchor in the harbour ready to sail with the first fair wind. I consulted the most experienced seamen upon the depth of the channel, which they had often plumbed, who told me, that in the middle at high water it was seventy *glumgluffs* deep, which is about six foot of European measure; and the rest of it fifty *glumgluffs* at most. I walked to the northeast coast over against Blefuscu; where, lying down behind a hillock, I took out my small pocket perspective-glass, and viewed the enemy's fleet at anchor, consisting of about fifty men of war, and a great number of transports: I then came back to my house, and gave order (for which I had a warrant) for a great quantity of the strongest cable and bars of iron. The cable was about as thick as packthread, and the bars of the length and size of a knitting-needle. I trebled the cable to make it stronger, and for the same reason I twisted three of the iron bars together, bending the extremities into a hook. Having thus fixed fifty hooks to as many cables, I went back to the northeast coast, and putting off my coat, shoes, and stockings, walked into the sea in my leathern jerkin, about half an hour before high water. I waded with what haste I could, and swam in the middle about thirty yards until I felt ground; I arrived at the fleet in less than half an hour. The enemy was so frighted when they saw me, that they leaped out of their ships, and swam to shore, where there could not be fewer than thirty thousand souls. I then took my tackling, and fastening a hook to the hole at the prow of each, I tied all the cords together at the end. While I was thus employed, the enemy discharged several thousand arrows, many of which stuck in my hands and face; and besides the excessive smart, gave me much disturbance in my work. My greatest apprehension was for my eyes, which I should have infallibly lost, if I had not suddenly thought of an expedient. I kept among other little necessaries a pair of spectacles in a private pocket, which, as I observed before, had escaped the Emperor's searchers. These I took out and fastened as strongly as I could upon my nose, and thus armed went on boldly with my work in spite of the enemy's arrows, many of which struck against the glasses of my spectacles, but without any other effect, further than a little to discompose them. I had now fastened all the hooks, and taking the knot in my hand, began to pull; but not a ship would stir, for they were all too fast held by their anchors, so that the boldest part of my enterprise remained. I therefore let go the cord, and leaving the hooks fixed to the ships, I resolutely cut with my knife the cables that fastened the anchors, receiving above two hundred shots in my face and hands; then I took up the knotted end of the cables to which my hooks were tied, and with great ease drew fifty of the enemy's largest men-of-war after me.

The Blefuscudians, who had not the least imagination of what I intended, were at first confounded with astonishment. They had seen me cut the cables, and thought my design was only to let the ships run adrift, or fall foul on each other: but when they perceived the whole fleet, moving in order, and saw me pulling at the end, they set up such a scream of grief and despair, that it is almost impossible to describe or conceive. When I had got out of danger, I stopped a while to pick out the arrows that stuck in my hands and face, and rubbed on some of the same ointment that was given me at my first arrival, as I have formerly mentioned. I then took off my spectacles, and waiting about an hour until the tide was a little fallen, I waded through the middle with my cargo, and arrived safe at the royal port of Lilliput.

The Emperor and his whole court stood on the shore expecting the issue of this great adventure. They saw the ships move forward in a large half-moon, but could not discern me, who was up to my breast in water. When I advanced to the middle of the channel, they were yet more in pain, because I was under water to my neck. The Emperor concluded me to be drowned, and that the enemy's fleet was approaching in a hostile manner: but he was soon eased of his fears, for, the channel growing shallower every step I made, I came in a short time within hearing, and holding up the end of the cable by which the fleet was fastened, I cried in a loud voice, Long live the most puissant Emperor of Lilliput! This great prince received me at my landing with all possible encomiums, and created me a *Nardac* upon the spot, which is the highest title of honour among them.

His Majesty desired I would take some other opportunity of bringing all the rest of his enemy's ships into his ports. And so unmeasureable is the ambition of princes, that he seemed to think of nothing less than reducing the whole empire of Blefuscu into a province, and governing it by a viceroy; of destroying the Big-Endian exiles, and compelling that people to break the smaller end of their eggs, by which he would remain sole monarch of the whole world. But I endeavoured to divert him from this design, by many arguments drawn from the topics of policy as well as justice: and I plainly protested, that I would never be an instrument of bringing a free and brave people into slavery. And when the matter was debated in council, the wisest part of the ministry were of my opinion.

This open bold declaration of mine was so opposite to the schemes and politics of his Imperial Majesty, that he could never forgive me; he mentioned it in a very artful manner at council, where I was told that some of the wisest appeared, at least, by their silence, to be of my opinion; but others, who were my secret enemies, could not forbear some expressions, which by a side-wind reflected on me. And from this time began an intrigue between his Majesty and a junta of ministers maliciously bent against me, which broke out in less than two months, and had like to have ended in my utter destruction. Of so little weight are the greatest services to princes, when put into the balance with a refusal to gratify their passions.

About three weeks after this exploit, there arrived a solemn embassy from Blefuscu, with humble offers of a peace; which was soon concluded upon conditions very advantageous to our Emperor, wherewith I shall not trouble the reader. There were six ambassadors, with a train of about five hundred persons, and their entry was very magnificent, suitable to the grandeur of their master, and the importance of their business. When their treaty was finished, wherein I did them several good offices by the credit I now had, or at least appeared to have at court, their Excellencies, who were privately told how much I had been their friend, made me a visit in form. They began with many compliments upon my valour and generosity, invited me to that kingdom in the Emperor their master's name, and desired me to show them some proofs of my prodigious strength, of which they had heard so many wonders; wherein I readily obliged them, but shall not interrupt the reader with the particulars.

When I had for some time entertained their Excellencies to their infinite satisfaction and surprise, I desired they would do me the honour to present my most humble respects to the Emperor their master, the renown of whose virtues had so justly filled the whole world with admiration, and whose royal person I resolved to attend before I returned to my own country: accordingly, the next time I had the honour to see our Emperor, I desired his general licence to wait on the Blefuscudian monarch, which he was pleased to grant me, as I could plainly perceive, in a very cold manner; but could not guess the reason, till I had a whisper from a certain person, that Flimnap and Bolgolam had represented my intercourse with those ambassadors as a mark of disaffection, from which I am sure my heart was wholly free. And this was the first time I began to conceive some imperfect idea of courts and ministers.

It is to be observed, that these ambassadors spoke to me by an interpreter, the languages of both empires differing as much from each other as any two in Europe, and each nation priding itself upon the antiquity, beauty, and energy of their own tongues, with an avowed contempt for that of their neighbour; yet our Emperor, standing upon the advantage he had got by the seizure of their fleet, obliged them to deliver their credentials, and make their speech, in the Lilliputian tongue. And it must be confessed, that from the great intercourse of trade and commerce between both realms, from the continual reception of exiles, which is mutual among them, and from the custom in each empire to send their young nobility and richer gentry to the other, in order to polish themselves, by seeing the world, and understanding men and manners, there are few persons of distinction, or merchants, or seamen, who dwell in the maritime parts, but what can hold conversation in both tongues; as I found some weeks after, when I went to pay my respects to the Emperor of Blefuscu, which in the midst of great misfortunes, through the malice of my ene-mies, proved a very happy adventure to me, as I shall relate in its proper place.

The reader may remember, that when I signed those articles upon which I recovered my liberty, there were some which I disliked upon account of their being too servile, neither could any thing but an extreme necessity have forced me to submit. But being now a *Nardac*, of the highest rank in that empire, such offices were looked upon as below my dignity, and the Emperor (to do him justice) never once mentioned them to me. However, it was not long before I had an opportunity of doing his Majesty, at least as I then thought, a most signal service. I was alarmed at midnight with the cries of many hundred people at my door; by which being suddenly awaked, I was in some kind of terror. I heard the word *burglum* repeated incessantly: several of the Em-peror's court, making their way through the crowd, intreated me to come immediately to the palace, where her Imperial Majesty's apartment was on fire, by the carelessness of a maid of honour, who fell asleep while she was reading a romance. I got up in an instant; and orders being given to clear the way before me, and it being likewise a moonshine night, I made a shift to get to the palace without trampling on any of the people. I found they had already applied ladders to the walls of the apartment, and were well provided with buckets, but the water was at some distance. These buckets were about the size of a large thimble, and the poor people supplied me with them as fast as they could; but the flame was so violent that they did little good. I might easily have stifled it with my coat, which I unfortunately left behind me for haste, and came away only in my leathern jerkin. The case seemed wholly desperate and deplorable, and this magnificent palace would have infallibly been burnt down to the ground, if, by a presence of mind, unusual to me, I had not suddenly thought of an expedient. I had the evening before drank plentifully of a most delicious wine, called *glimigrim* (the Blefuscudians call it *flunec*, but ours is esteemed the better sort), which is very diuretic. By the luckiest chance in the world, I had not discharged myself of any part of it. The heat I had contracted by coming very near the flames, and by my labouring to quench them, made the wine begin to operate by urine; which I voided in such a quantity, and applied so well to the proper places, that in three minutes the fire was wholly extinguished, and the rest of that noble pile, which had cost so many ages in erecting, preserved from destruction.

It was now daylight, and I returned to my house, without waiting to congratulate with the Emperor; because, although I had done a very eminent piece of service, yet I could not tell how his Majesty might resent the manner by which I had performed it: for, by the fundamental laws of the realm, it is capital in any person, of what quality soever, to make water within the precints of the palace. But I was a little comforted by a message from his Majesty, that he would give orders to the Grand Justiciary for passing my pardon in form; which, however, I could not obtain. And I was privately assured, that the Empress, conceiving the greatest abhorrence of what I had done, removed to the most distant side of the court, firmly resolved that those buildings should never be repaired for her use; and, in the presence of her chief confidents, could not forbear vowing revenge.

Chapter VI.

Of the inhabitants of Lilliput; their learning, laws, and customs, the manner of educating their children. The author's way of living in that country. His vindication of a great lady.

Although I intend to leave the description of this empire to a particular treatise, yet in the mean time I am content to gratify the curious reader with some general ideas. As the common size of the natives is somewhat under six inches, so there is an exact proportion in all other animals, as well as plants and trees: for instance, the tallest horses and oxen are between four and five inches in height, the sheep an inch and a half, more or less; their

geese about the bigness of a sparrow, and so the several gradations downwards, till you come to the smallest, which, to my
sight, were almost invisible; but nature hath adapted the eyes of
the Lilliputians to all objects proper for their view: they see with
great exactness, but at no great distance. And to show the sharpness of their sight towards objects that are near, I have been
much pleased with observing a cook pulling a lark, which was
not so large as a common fly; and a young girl threading an
invisible needle with invisible silk. Their tallest trees are about
seven foot high; I mean some of those in the great royal park, the
tops whereof I could but just reach with my fist clenched. The
other vegetables are in the same proportion; but this I leave to the
reader's imagination.

I shall say but little at present of their learning, which for
many ages hath flourished in all its branches among them: but
their manner of writing is very peculiar, being neither from the
left to the right, like the Europeans; nor from the right to the
left, like the Arabians; nor from up to down, like the Chinese;
nor from down to up, like the Cascagians, but aslant from one
corner of the paper to the other, like ladies in England.

They bury their dead with their heads directly downwards,
because they hold an opinion that in eleven thousand moons they
are all to rise again, in which period the earth (which they conceive to be flat) will turn upside down, and by this means they
shall, at their resurrection, be found ready standing on their feet.
The learned among them confess the absurdity of this doctrine,
but the practice still continues, in compliance to the vulgar.

There are some laws and customs in this empire very peculiar,
and if they were not so directly contrary to those of my own
dear country, I should be tempted to say a little in their justifi-
cation. It is only to be wished, that they were as well executed.
The first I shall mention relates to informers. All crimes against
the state are punished here with the utmost severity; but if the
person accused make his innocence plainly to appear upon his
trial, the accuser is immediately put to an ignominious death; and
out of his goods or lands, the innocent person is quadruply
recompensed for the loss of his time, for the danger he underwent, for the hardship of his imprisonment, and for all the
charges he hath been at in making his defence. Or, if that fund
be deficient, it is largely supplied by the crown. The Emperor
doth also confer on him some public mark of his favour, and
proclamation is made of his innocence through the whole city.

They look upon fraud as a greater crime than theft, and therefore seldom fail to punish it with death; for they allege, that

care and vigilance, with a very common understanding, may preserve a man's goods from thieves, but honesty hath no fence against superior cunning: and since it is necessary that there should be a perpetual intercourse of buying and selling, and dealing upon credit, where fraud is permitted and connived at, or hath no law to punish it, the honest dealer is always undone, and the knave gets the advantage. I remember when I was once interceding with the King for a criminal who had wronged his master of a great sum of money, which he had received by order, and ran away with; and happening to tell his Majesty, by way of extenuation, that it was only a breach of trust; the Emperor thought it monstrous in me to offer, as a defence, the greatest aggravation of the crime: and truly I had little to say in return, farther than the common answer, that different nations had different customs; for, I confess, I was heartily ashamed.

Although we usually call reward and punishment the two hinges upon which all government turns, yet I could never observe this maxim to be put in practice by any nation except that of Lilliput. Whoever can there bring sufficient proof that he hath strictly observed the laws of his country for seventy-three moons, hath a claim to certain privileges, according to his quality and condition of life, with a proportionable sum of money out of a fund appropriated for that use: he likewise acquires the title of *Snilpall*, or *Legal*, which is added to his name, but doth not descend to his posterity. And these people thought it a prodigious defect of policy among us, when I told them that our laws were enforced only by penalties without any mention of reward. It is upon this account that the image of Justice, in their courts of judicature, is formed with six eyes, two before, as many behind, and on each side one, to signify circumspection; with a bag of gold open in her right hand, and a sword sheathed in her left, to show she is more disposed to reward than to punish.

In choosing persons for all employments, they have more regard to good morals than to great abilities; for, since government is necessary to mankind, they believe that the common size of human understandings is fitted to some station or other, and that Providence never intended to make the management of public affairs a mystery, to be comprehended only by a few persons of sublime genius, of which there seldom are three born in an age: but they suppose truth, justice, temperance, and the like, to be in every man's power; the practice of which virtues, assisted by experience and a good intention, would qualify any man for the service of his country, except where a course of study is required. But they thought the want of moral virtues was so far from being supplied by superior endowments of the minds, that employments could never be put into such dangerous hands as those of persons so qualified; and at least, that the mistakes committed by ignorance in a virtuous disposition would never be of such fatal consequence to the public weal, as the practices of a man whose inclinations led him to be corrupt, and had great abilities to manage, to multiply, and defend his corruptions.

In like manner, the disbelief of a divine Providence renders a man uncapable of holding any public station; for since kings avow themselves to be the deputies of Providence, the Lilliputians think nothing can be more absurd than for a prince to employ such men as disown the authority under which he acts.

In relating these and the following laws, I would only be understood to mean the original institutions, and not the most scandalous corruptions into which these people are fallen by the degenerate nature of man. For as to that infamous practice of acquiring great employments by dancing on the ropes, or badges of favour and distinction by leaping over sticks, and creeping under them, the reader is to observe, that they were first introduced by the grandfather of the Emperor now reigning, and grew to the present height by the gradual increase of party and faction.

Ingratitude is among them a capital crime, as we read it to have been in some other countries; for they reason thus, that whoever makes ill returns to his benefactor, must needs be a common enemy to the rest of mankind, from whom he hath received no obligation, and therefore such a man is not fit to live.

Their notions relating to the duties of parents and children differ extremely from ours. For, since the conjunction of male and female is founded upon the great law of nature, in order to propagate and continue the species, the Lilliputians will needs have it, that men and women are joined together like other animals, by the motives of concupiscence; and that their tenderness towards their young proceeds from the like natural principle: for which reason they will never allow, that a child is under any obligation to his father for begetting him, or to his mother for bringing him into the world; which, considering the miseries of human life, was neither a benefit in itself, nor intended so by his parents, whose thoughts in their love-encounters were otherwise employed. Upon these, and the like reasonings, their opinion is, that parents are the last of all others to be trusted with the education of their own children: and therefore they have in every town public nurseries, where all parents, except cottagers and labourers, are obliged to send their infants of both sexes to be reared and educated when they come to the age of twenty moons, at which time they are supposed to have some rudiments of docility. These schools are of several kinds, suited to different qualities, and to both sexes. They have certain professors well skilled in preparing children for such a condition of life as befits the rank of their parents, and their own capacities as well as inclinations. I shall first say something of the male nurseries, and then of the female.

The nurseries for males of noble or eminent birth are provided with grave and learned professors, and their several deputies. The clothes and food of the children are plain and simple. They are bred up in the principles of honour, justice, courage, modesty, clemency, religion, and love of their country; they are always employed in some business, except in the times of eating and sleeping, which are very short, and two hours for diversions, consisting of bodily exercises. They are dressed by men until four years of age, and then are obliged to dress themselves, although their quality be ever so great; and the women attendants, who are aged proportionably to ours at fifty, perform only the most menial offices. They are never suffered to converse with servants, but go together in small or greater numbers to take their diversions, and always in the presence of a professor, or one of his deputies; whereby they avoid those early bad impressions of folly and vice to which our children are subject. Their parents are suffered to see them only twice a year; the visit is not to last above an hour. They are allowed to kiss the child at meeting and parting; but a professor, who always stands by on those occasions, will not suffer them to whisper, or use any fondling expressions, or bring any presents of toys, sweetmeats, and the like.

The pension from each family for the education and entertainment of a child, upon failure of due payment, is levied by the Emperor's officers.

The nurseries for children of ordinary gentlemen, merchants, traders, and handicrafts, are managed proportionably after the same manner; only those designed for trades are put out apprentices at seven years old, whereas those of persons of quality continue in their nurseries till fifteen, which answers to one and twenty with us: but the confinement is gradually lessened for the last three years.

In the female nurseries, the young girls of quality are educated much like the males, only they are dressed by orderly servants of their own sex, but always in the presence of a professor or deputy, until they come to dress themselves, which is at five years old. And if it be found that these nurses ever presume to entertain the girls with frightful or foolish stories, or the common follies practiced by chambermaids among us, they are publicly whipped thrice about the city, imprisoned for a year, and banished for life to the most desolate parts of the country. Thus the young ladies there are as much ashamed of being cowards and fools as the men, and despise all personal ornaments beyond decency and cleanliness: neither did I perceive any difference in their education, made by their difference of sex, only that the exercises of the females were not altogether so robust, and that some rules were given them relating to domestic life, and a smaller compass of learning was enjoined them: for their maxim is, that among people of quality, a wife should be always a reasonable and agreeable companion, because she cannot always be young. When the girls are twelve years old, which among them is the marriageable age, their parents or guardians take them home, with great expressions of gratitude to the professors, and seldom without tears of the young lady and her companions.

In the nurseries of females of the meaner sort, the children are instructed in all kinds of works proper for their sex, and their several degrees: those intended for apprentices are dismissed at seven years old, the rest are kept to eleven.

The meaner families who have children at these nurseries are obliged, besides their annual pension, which is as low as possible, to return to the steward of the nursery a small monthly share of their gettings, to be a portion for the child; and therefore all parents are limited in their expenses by the law. For the Lilliputians think nothing can be more unjust, than that people, in subservience to their own appetites, should bring children into the world, and leave the burthen of supporting them on the public. As to persons of quality, they give security to appropriate a certain sum for each child, suitable to their condition; and these funds are always managed with good husbandry, and the most exact justice.

The cottagers and labourers keep their children at home, their business being only to till and cultivate the earth, and therefore their education is of little consequence to the public; but the old and diseased among them are supported by hospitals: for begging is a trade unknown in this empire.

And here it may perhaps divert the curious reader, to give some account of my domestic, and my manner of living in this country, during a residence of nine months and thirteen days. Having a head mechanically turned, and being likewise forced by necessity, I had made for myself a table and chair convenient enough, out of the largest trees in the royal park. Two hundred sempstresses were employed to make me shirts, and linen for my bed and table, all of the strongest and coarsest kind they could get; which, however, they were forced to quilt together in several folds, for the thickest was some degrees finer than lawn. Their linen is usually three inches wide, and three foot make a piece. The sempstresses took my measure as I lay on the ground, one standing at my neck, and another at my midleg, with a strong cord extended, that each held by the end, while the third measured the length of the cord with a rule of an inch long. Then they measured my right thumb, and desired no more; for by a mathematical computation, that twice round the thumb is once round the wrist, and so on to the neck and the waist, and by the help of my old shirt, which I displayed on the ground before them for a pattern, they fitted me exactly. Three hundred tailors were employed in the same manner to make me clothes; but they had another contrivance for taking my measure. I kneeled down, and they raised a ladder from the ground to my neck; upon this ladder one of them mounted, and let fall a plumb-line from my collar to the floor, which just answered the length of my coat; but my waist and arms I measured myself. When my clothes were finished, which was done in my house (for the largest of theirs would not have been able to hold them) they looked like the patchwork made by the ladies in England, only that mine were all of a colour.

I had three hundred cooks to dress my victuals, in little convenient huts built about my house, where they and their families lived, and prepared me two dishes apiece. I took up twenty waiters in my hand, and placed them on the table; an hundred more attended below on the ground, some with dishes of meat, and some with barrels of wine, and other liquors, slung on their shoulders; all which the waiters above drew up as I wanted, in a very ingenious manner, by certain cords, as we draw the bucket up a well in Europe. A dish of their meat was a good mouthful, and a barrel of their liquor a reasonable draught. Their mutton yields to ours, but their beef is excellent. I have had a sirloin so large, that I have been forced to make three bits of it; but this is rare. My servants were astonished to see me eat it bones and all, as in our country we do the leg of a lark. Their geese and turkeys I usually eat at a mouthful, and I must confess they far exceed ours. Of their smaller fowl I could take up twenty or thirty at the end of my knife.

One day his Imperial Majesty, being informed of my way of living, desired that himself and his royal consort, with the young princes of the blood of both sexes, might have the happiness (as he was pleased to call it) of dining with me. They came accordingly, and I placed them upon chairs of state on my table, just over-against me, with their guards about them. Flimnap the Lord High Treasurer attended there likewise, with his white staff; and I observed he often looked on me with a sour countenance, which I would not seem to regard, but eat more than usual, in honour to my dear country, as well as to fill the court with admiration. I have some private reasons to believe, that this visit from his Majesty gave Flimnap an opportunity of doing me ill offices to his master. That minister had always been my secret enemy, although he outwardly caressed me more than was usual to the moroseness of his nature. He represented to the Emperor the low condition of his treasury; that he was forced to take up money at great discount; that exchequer bills would not circulate under nine per cent below par; that I had cost his Majesty above a million and a half of *sprugs* (their greatest gold coin, about the bigness of a spangle); and upon the whole, that it would be advisable in the Emperor to take the first fair occasion of dismissing me.

I am here obliged to vindicate the reputation of an excellent lady, who was an innocent sufferer upon my account. The Treasurer took a fancy to be jealous of his wife, from the malice of some evil tongues, who informed him that her Grace had taken a violent affection for my person, and the court-scandal ran for some time, that she once came privately to my lodging. This I solemnly declare to be a most infamous falsehood, without any grounds, farther than that her Grace was pleased to treat me with all innocent marks of freedom and friendship. I own she came often to my house, but always publicly, nor ever without three more in the coach, who were usually her sister and young daughter, and some particular acquaintance; but this was common to many other ladies of the court. And I still appeal to my servants round, whether they at any time saw a coach at my door without knowing what persons were in it. On those occasions, when a servant had given me notice, my custom was to go immediately to the door; and, after paying my respects, to take up the coach and two horses very carefully in my hands (for if there were six horses, the postillion always unharnessed four) and place them on a table, where I had fixed a moveable rim quite round, of five inches high, to prevent accidents. And I have often had four coaches and horses at once on my table full of company, while I sat in my chair leaning my face towards them; and when I was engaged with one set, the coachmen would gently drive the others round my table. I have passed many an afternoon very agreeably in these conversations. But I defy the Treasurer, or his two informers (I will name them, and let them make their best of it) Clustril and Drunlo, to prove that any person ever came to me *incognito*, except the Secretary Reldresal, who was sent by express command of his Imperial Majesty, as I have before related. I should not have dwelt so long upon this particular, if it had not been a point wherein the reputation of a great lady is so nearly concerned, to say nothing of my own; although I had the honour to be a *Nardac*, which the Treasurer himself is not; for all the world knows he is only a *Clumglum*, a title inferior by one degree, as that of a marquis is to a duke in England, yet I allow he preceded me in right of his post. These false informations, which I afterwards came to the knowledge of, by an accident not proper to mention, made the Treasurer show his lady for some time an ill countenance, and me a worse; for although he was at last undeceived and reconciled to her, yet I lost all credit with him, and found my interest decline very fast with the Emperor himself, who was indeed too much governed by that favourite.

CHAPTER VII.

The author, being informed of a design to accuse him of high treason, makes his escape to Blefuscu. His reception there.

Before I proceed to give an account of my leaving this kingdom, it may be proper to inform the reader of a private intrigue which had been for two months forming against me.

I had been hitherto all my life a stranger to courts, for which I was unqualified by the meanness of my condition. I had indeed heard and read enough of the dispositions of great princes and ministers; but never expected to have found such terrible effects of them in so remote a country, governed, as I thought, by very different maxims from those in Europe.

When I was just preparing to pay my attendance on the Emperor of Blefuscu, a considerable person at court (to whom I had been very serviceable at a time when he lay under the highest displeasure of his Imperial Majesty) came to my house very privately at night in a close chair, and without sending his name, desired admittance: the chairmen were dismissed; I put the chair, with his Lordship in it, into my coat-pocket; and giving orders to a trusty servant to say I was indisposed and gone to sleep, I fastened the door of my house, placed the chair on the table, according to my usual custom, and sat down by it. After the common salutations were over, observing his Lordship's countenance full of concern, and enquiring into the reason, he desired I would hear him with patience in a matter that highly concerned my honour and my life. His speech was to the following effect, for I took notes of it as soon as he left me.

You are to know, said he, that several committees of council have been lately called in the most private manner on your account: and it is but two days since his Majesty came to a full resolution.

You are very sensible that Skyresh Bolgolam (*Galbet*, or High Admiral) hath been your mortal enemy almost ever since your arrival. His original reasons I know not, but his hatred is much encreased since your great success against Blefuscu, by which his glory, as Admiral, is obscured. This lord, in conjunction with Flimnap the High Treasurer, whose enmity against you is notorious on account of his lady, Limtoc the General, Lalcon the Chamberlain, and Balmuff the Grand Justiciary, have prepared articles of impeachment against you, for treason, and other capital crimes.

This preface made me so impatient, being conscious of my own merits and innocence, that I was going to interrupt; when he entreated me to be silent, and thus proceeded.

Out of gratitude for the favours you have done me, I procured information of the whole proceedings, and a copy of the articles, wherein I venture my head for your service.

Articles of Impeachment against Quinbus Flestrin (*the* Man-Moutain).

ARTICLE I.

Whereas, by a statute made in the reign of his Imperial Majesty Calin Deffar Plune, it is enacted, that whoever shall make water within the precincts of the royal palace shall be liable to the pains and penalties of high treason: notwithstanding, the said Quinbus Flestrin, in open breach of the said law, under colour of extinguishing the fire kindled in the apartment of his Majesty's most dear imperial consort, did maliciously, traitorously, and devilishly, by discharge of his urine, put out the said fire kindled in the said apartment, lying and being within the precincts of the said royal palace, against the statute in that case provided, etc., against the duty, etc.

ARTICLE II.

That the said Quinbus Flestrin, having brought the imperial fleet of Blefuscu into the royal port, and being afterwards commanded by his Imperial Majesty to seize all the other ships of the said empire of Blefuscu, and reduce that empire to a province, to be governed by a viceroy from hence, and to destroy and put to death not only all the Big-Endian exiles, but likewise all the people of that empire who would not immediately forsake the Big-Endian heresy: he, the said Flestrin, like a false traitor against his most Auspicious, Serene, Imperial Majesty, did petition to be excused from the said service, upon pretence of unwillingness to force the consciences, or destroy the liberties and lives of an innocent people.

ARTICLE III.

That, whereas certain ambassadors arrived from the court of Blefuscu to sue for peace in his Majesty's court: he the said Flestrin did, like a false traitor, aid, abet, comfort, and divert the said ambassadors, although he knew them to be servants to a prince who was lately an open enemy to his Imperial Majesty, and in open war against his said Majesty.

ARTICLE IV.

That the said Quinbus Flestrin, contrary to the duty of a faithful subject, is now preparing to make a voyage to the court and empire of Blefuscu, for which he hath received only verbal licence from his Imperial Majesty; and under colour of the said licence, doth falsely and traitorously intend to take the said voyage, and thereby to aid, comfort, and abet the Emperor of Blefuscu, so late an enemy, and in open war with his Imperial Majesty aforesaid.

There are some other articles, but these are the most important, of which I have read you an abstract.

In the several debates upon this impeachment, it must be confessed that his Majesty gave many marks of his great lenity, often urging the services you had done him, and endeavouring to extenuate your crimes. The Treasurer and Admiral insisted that you should be put to the most painful and ignominious death, by setting fire on your house at night, and the General was to attend with twenty thousand men armed with poisoned arrows to shoot you on the face and hands. Some of your servants were to have private orders to strew a poisonous juice on your shirts and sheets, which would soon make you tear your own flesh, and die in the utmost torture. The General came into the same opinion, so that for a long time there was a majority against you. But his Majesty resolving, if possible, to spare your life, at last brought off the Chamberlain.

Upon this incident, Reldresal, Principal Secretary for Private Affairs, who always approved himself your true friend, was commanded by the Emperor to deliver his opinion, which he accordingly did; and therein justified the good thoughts you have of him. He allowed your crimes to be great, but that still there was room for mercy, the most commendable virtue in a prince, and for which his Majesty was so justly celebrated. He said the friendship between you and him was so well known to the world, that perhaps the most honourable board might think him partial: however, in obedience to the command he had received, he would freely offer his sentiments. That if his Majesty, in consideration of your services, and pursuant to his own merciful disposition, would please to spare your life, and only give order to put out both your eyes, he humbly conceived, that by this expedient justice might in some measure be satisfied, and all the world would applaud the lenity of the Emperor, as well as the fair and generous proceedings of those who have the honour to be his counsellors. That the loss of your eyes would be no impediment to your bodily strength, by which you might still be useful to his Majesty. That blindness is an addition to courage, by concealing dangers from us; that the fear you had for your eyes was the greatest difficulty in bringing over the enemy's fleet, and it would be sufficient for you to see by the eyes of the ministers, since the greatest princes do no more.

This proposal was received with the utmost disapprobation by the whole board. Bolgolam, the Admiral, could not preserve his temper; but rising up in fury, said, he wondered how the Secretary durst presume to give his opinion for preserving the life of a traitor: that the services you had performed were, by all true reasons of state, the great aggravation of your crimes; that you, who were able to extinguish the fire by discharge of urine in her Majesty's apartment (which he mentioned with horror), might, at another time, raise an inundation by the same means, to drown the whole palace; and the same strength which enabled you to bring over the enemy's fleet might serve, upon the first discontent, to carry it back: that he had good reasons to think you were a Big-Endian in your heart; and as treason begins in the heart before it appears in overt acts, so he accused you as a traitor on that account, and therefore insisted you should be put to death.

The Treasurer was of the same opinion; he showed to what straits his Majesty's revenue was reduced by the charge of maintaining you, which would soon grow insupportable: that the Secretary's expedient of putting out your eyes was so far from being a remedy against this evil, that it would probably increase it, as it is manifest from the common practice of blinding some kind of fowl, after which they fed the faster, and grew sooner fat: that his sacred Majesty, and the council, who are your judges, were in their own consciences fully convinced of your guilt, which was a sufficient argument to condemn you to death, without the formal proofs required by the strict letter of the law.

But his Imperial Majesty, fully determined against capital punishment, was graciously pleased to say, that since the council thought the loss of your eyes too easy a censure, some other may be inflicted hereafter. And your friend the Secretary humbly desiring to be heard again, in answer to what the Treasurer had objected concerning the great charge his Majesty was at in maintaining you, said, that his Excellency, who had the sole disposal of the Emperor's revenue, might easily provide against this evil, by gradually lessening your establishment; by which, for want of sufficient food, you would grow weak and faint, and lose your appetite, and consequently decay and consume in a few months; neither would the stench of your carcass be then so dangerous, when it should become more than half diminished; and immediately upon your death, five or six thousand of his Majesty's subjects might, in two or three days, cut your flesh from your bones, take it away by cart-loads, and bury it in distant parts to prevent infection, leaving the skeleton as a monument of admiration to posterity.

Thus by the great friendship of the Secretary, the whole affair was compromised. It was strictly enjoined, that the project of starving you by degrees should be kept a secret, but the sentence of putting out your eyes was entered on the books; none dissenting except Bolgolam the Admiral, who being a creature of the Empress, was perpetually instigated by her Majesty to insist upon your death, she having borne perpetual malice against you, on account of that infamous and illegal method you took to extinguish the fire in her apartment.

In three days your friend the Secretary will be directed to come to your house, and read before you the articles of impeachment; and then to signify the great lenity and favour of his Maj-

esty and council, whereby you are only condemned to the loss
of your eyes, which his Majesty doth not question you will
gratefully and humbly submit to; and twenty of his Majesty's
surgeons will attend, in order to see the operation well performed, by discharging very sharp-pointed arrows into the balls
of your eyes, as you lie on the ground.

I leave to your prudence what measures you will take; and to
avoid suspicion, I must immediately return in as private a manner
as I came.

His Lordship did so, and I remained alone, under many doubts
and perplexities of mind.

It was a custom introduced by this prince and his ministry
(very different, as I have been assured, from the practices of
former times) that after the court had decreed any cruel execution, either to gratify the monarch's resentment, or the malice of
a favourite, the Emperor always made a speech to his whole
council, expressing his great lenity and tenderness, as qualities
known and confessed by all the world. This speech was immediately published through the kingdom; nor did any thing
terrify the people so much as those encomiums on his Majesty's
mercy; because it was observed, that the more these praises were
enlarged and insisted on, the more inhuman was the punishment,
and the sufferer more innocent. Yet as to myself, I must confess,
having never been designed for a courtier either by my birth or
education, I was so ill a judge of things, that I could not discover
the lenity and favour of this sentence, but conceived it (perhaps
erroneously) rather to be rigorous than gentle. I sometimes
thought of standing my trial, for although I could not deny the
facts alleged in the several articles, yet I hoped they would admit
of some extenuations. But having in my life perused many state
trials, which I ever observed to terminate as the judges thought
fit to direct, I durst not rely on so dangerous a decision, in so
critical a juncture, and against such powerful enemies. Once I
was strongly bent upon resistance, for while I had liberty, the
whole strength of that empire could hardly subdue me, and I
might easily with stones pelt the metropolis to pieces; but I
soon rejected that project with horror, by remembering the oath
I had made to the Emperor, the favours I received from him, and
the high title of *Nardac* he conferred upon me. Neither had I so
soon learned the gratitude of courtiers, to persuade myself that
his Majesty's present severities acquitted me of all past obligations.

At last I fixed upon a resolution, for which it is probable I
may incur some censure, and not unjustly; for I confess I owe

the preserving my eyes, and consequently my liberty, to my own great rashness and want of experience: because if I had then known the nature of princes and ministers, which I have since observed in many other courts, and their methods of treating criminals less obnoxious than myself, I should with great alacrity and readiness have submitted to so easy a punishment. But hurried on by the precipitancy of youth, and having his Imperial Majesty's licence to pay my attendance upon the Emperor of Blefuscu, I took this opportunity, before the three days were elapsed, to send a letter to my friend the Secretary, signifying my resolution of setting out that morning for Blefuscu pursuant to the leave I had got; and without waiting for an answer, I went to that side of the island where our fleet lay. I seized a large man of war, tied a cable to the prow, and, lifting up the anchors, I stripped myself, put my clothes (together with my coverlet, which I carried under my arm) into the vessel, and drawing it after me between wading and swimming, arrived at the royal port of Blefuscu, where the people had long expected me; they lent me two guides to direct me to the capital city, which is of the same name. I held them in my hands until I came within two hundred yards of the gate, and desired them to signify my arrival to one of the secretaries, and let him know, I there waited his Majesty's commands. I had an answer in about an hour, that his Majesty, attended by the royal family, and great officers of the court, was coming out to receive me. I advanced a hundred yards. The Emperor, and his train, alighted from their horses, the Empress and ladies from their coaches, and I did not perceive they were in any fright or concern. I lay on the ground to kiss his Majesty's and the Empress's hand. I told his Majesty that I was come according to my promise, and with the licence of the Emperor my master, to have the honour of seeing so mighty a monarch, and to offer him any service in my power, consistent with my duty to my own prince; not mentioning a word of my disgrace, because I had hitherto no regular information of it, and might suppose myself wholly ignorant of any such design; neither could I reasonably conceive that the Emperor would discover the secret while I was out of his power: wherein, however, it soon appeared I was deceived.

I shall not trouble the reader with the particular account of my reception at this court, which was suitable to the generosity of so great a prince; nor of the difficulties I was in for want of a house and bed, being forced to lie on the ground, wrapped up in my coverlet.

CHAPTER VIII.

The author, by a lucky accident, finds means to leave Blefuscu; and, after some difficulties, returns safe to his native country.

Three days after my arrival, walking out of curiosity to the northeast coast of the island, I observed, about half a league off, in the sea, somewhat that looked like a boat overturned. I pulled off my shoes and stockings, and wading two or three hundred yards, I found the object to approach nearer by force of the tide, and then plainly saw it to be a real boat, which I supposed might, by some tempest, have been driven from a ship; whereupon I returned immediately towards the city, and desired his Imperial Majesty to lend me twenty of the tallest vessels he had left after the loss of his fleet, and three thousand seamen under the command of his Vice-Admiral. This fleet sailed round, while I went back the shortest way to the coast where I first discovered the boat; I found the tide had driven it still nearer. The seamen were all provided with cordage, which I had beforehand twisted to a sufficient strength. When the ships came up, I stripped myself, and waded till I came within an hundred yards of the boat, after which I was forced to swim till I got up to it. The seamen threw me the end of the cord, which I fastened to a hole in the fore-part of the boat, and the other end to a man of war: but I found all my labour to little purpose; for being out of my depth, I was not able to work. In this necessity, I was forced to swim behind, and push the boat forwards as often as I could, with one of my hands; and the tide favouring me, I advanced so far, that I could just hold up my chin and feel the ground. I rested two or three minutes, and then gave the boat another shove, and so on till the sea was no higher than my armpits; and now the most laborious part being over, I took out my other cables, which were stowed in one of the ships, and fastening them first to the boat, and then to nine of the vessels which attended me; the wind being favourable the seamen towed, and I shoved till we arrived within forty yards of the shore, and waiting till the tide was out, I got dry to the boat, and by the assistance of two thousand men, with ropes and engines, I made a shift to turn it on its bottom, and found it was but little damaged.

I shall not trouble the reader with the difficulties I was under by the help of certain paddles, which cost me ten days making, to get my boat to the royal port of Blefuscu, where a mighty concourse of people appeared upon my arrival, full of wonder at the sight of so prodigious a vessel. I told the Emperor that my good fortune had thrown this boat in my way, to carry me to some place from whence I might return into my native country, and begged his Majesty's orders for getting materials to fit it up, together with his licence to depart; which, after some kind expostulations, he was pleased to grant.

I did very much wonder, in all this time, not to have heard of any express relating to me from our Emperor to the court of Blefuscu. But I was afterwards given privately to understand, that his Imperial Majesty, never imagining I had the least notice of his designs, believed I was only gone to Blefuscu in performance of my promise, according to the licence he had given me, which was well known at our court, and would return in a few days when that ceremony was ended. But he was at last in pain at my long absence; and after consulting with the Treasurer, and the rest of that cabal, a person of quality was dispatched with the copy of the articles against me. This envoy had instructions to represent to the monarch of Blefuscu the great lenity of his master, who was content to punish me no further than with the loss of my eyes; that I had fled from justice, and if I did not return in two hours, I should be deprived of my title of *Nardac*, and declared a traitor. The envoy further added, that in order to maintain the peace and amity between both empires, his master expected, that his brother of Blefuscu would give orders to have me sent back to Lilliput, bound hand and foot, to be punished as a traitor.

The Emperor of Blefuscu, having taken three days to consult, returned an answer consisting of many civilities and excuses. He said, that as for sending me bound, his brother knew it was impossible; that although I had deprived him of his fleet, yet he owed great obligations to me for many good offices I had done him in making the peace. That however both their Majesties would soon be made easy; for I had found a prodigious vessel on the shore, able to carry me on the sea, which he had given order to fit up with my own assistance and direction, and he hoped in a few weeks both empires would be freed from so insupportable an incumbrance.

With this answer the envoy returned to Lilliput, and the monarch of Blefuscu related to me all that had passed, offering me at the same time (but under the strictest confidence) his gracious protection if I would continue in his service; wherein although I believed him sincere, yet I resolved never more to put any confidence in princes or ministers, where I could possibly avoid it; and therefore, with all due acknowledgements for his favourable intentions, I humbly begged to be excused. I told him, that since fortune, whether good or evil, had thrown a vessel in my way, I was resolved to venture myself in the ocean, rather than be an occasion of difference between two such mighty monarchs. Neither did I find the Emperor at all displeased; and I discovered by a certain accident, that he was very glad of my resolution, and so were most of his ministers.

These considerations moved me to hasten my departure somewhat sooner than I intended; to which the court, impatient to have me gone, very readily contributed. Five hundred workmen were employed to make two sails to my boat, according to my directions, by quilting thirteen fold of their strongest linen together. I was at the pains of making ropes and cables, by twisting ten, twenty or thirty of the thickest and strongest of theirs. A great stone that I happened to find, after a long search by the seashore, served me for an anchor. I had the tallow of three hundred cows for greasing my boat, and other uses. I was at incredible pains in cutting down some of the largest timber trees for oars and masts, wherein I was, however, much assisted by his Majesty's ship-carpenters, who helped me in smoothing them, after I had done the rough work.

In about a month, when all was prepared, I sent to receive his Majesty's commands, and to take my leave. The Emperor and royal family came out of the palace; I lay down on my face to kiss his hand, which he very graciously gave me: so did the Empress, and young princes of the blood. His Majesty presented me with fifty purses of two hundred *sprugs* apiece, together with his picture at full length, which I put immediately into one of my gloves, to keep it from being hurt. The ceremonies at my departure were too many to trouble the reader with at this time.

I stored the boat with the carcasses of an hundred oxen, and three hundred sheep, with bread and drink proportionable, and as much meat ready dressed as four hundred cooks could provide. I took with me six cows and two bulls alive, with as many ewes and rams, intending to carry them into my own country, and propagate the breed. And to feed them on board, I had a good bundle of hay, and a bag of corn. I would gladly have taken a dozen of the natives, but this was a thing the Emperor would by no means permit; and besides a diligent search into my pockets, his Majesty engaged my honour not to carry away any of his subjects, although with their own consent and desire.

Having thus prepared all things as well as I was able, I set sail on the twenty-fourth day of September, 1701, at six in the morning; and when I had gone about four leagues to the northward, the wind being at southeast, at six in the evening, I descried a

small island about half a league to the northwest. I advanced forward, and cast anchor on the lee-side of the island, which seemed
to be uninhabited. I then took some refreshment, and went to
my rest. I slept well, and as I conjecture at least six hours, for I
found the day broke in two hours after I awaked. It was a clear
night. I eat my breakfast before the sun was up; and heaving
anchor, the wind being favourable, I steered the same course that
I had done the day before, wherein I was directed by my pocket-
compass. My intention was to reach, if possible, one of those
islands which I had reason to believe lay to the northeast of Van
Diemen's Land. I discovered nothing all that day; but upon the
next, about three in the afternoon, when I had by my computation made twenty-four leagues from Blefuscu, I descried a sail
steering to the southeast; my course was due east. I hailed her,
but could get no answer; yet I found I gained upon her, for the
wind slackened. I made all the sail I could, and in half an hour
she spied me, then hung out her ancient, and discharged a gun.
It is not easy to express the joy I was in upon the unexpected
hope of once more seeing my beloved country, and the dear
pledges I had left in it. The ship slackened her sails, and I came
up with her between five and six in the evening, September 26;
but my heart leapt within me to see her English colours. I put
my cows and sheep into my coat-pockets, and got on board with
all my little cargo of provisions. The vessel was an English
merchantman, returning from Japan by the North and South
Seas; the captain, Mr. John Biddel of Deptford, a very civil man,
and an excellent sailor. We were now in the latitude of 30
degrees south; there were about fifty men in the ship; and here I
met an old comrade of mine, one Peter Williams, who gave me a
good character to the captain. This gentleman treated me with
kindness, and desired I would let him know what place I came
from last, and whither I was bound; which I did in few words,
but he thought I was raving, and that the dangers I underwent
had disturbed my head; whereupon I took my black cattle and
sheep out of my pocket, which, after great astonishment, clearly
convinced him of my veracity. I then showed him the gold
given me by the Emperor of Blefuscu, together with his Majesty's picture at full length, and some other rarities of that country. I gave him two purses of two hundred *sprugs* each, and
promised, when we arrived in England, to make him a present of
a cow and a sheep big with young.

I shall not trouble the reader with a particular account of this
voyage, which was very prosperous for the most part. We arrived in the Downs on the 13th of April, 1702. I had only one

misfortune, that the rats on board carried away one of my sheep; I found her bones in a hole, picked clean from the flesh. The rest of my cattle I got safe on shore, and set them a grazing in a bowling-green at Greenwich, where the fineness of the grass made them feed very heartily, though I had always feared the contrary; neither could I possibly have preserved them in so long a voyage, if the captain had not allowed me some of his best biscuit, which, rubbed to powder, and mingled with water, was their constant food. The short time I continued in England, I made a considerable profit by showing my cattle to many persons of quality, and others: and before I began my second voyage, I sold them for six hundred pounds. Since my last return, I find the breed is considerably increased, especially the sheep; which I hope will prove much to the advantage of the woollen manufacture, by the fineness of the fleeces.

I stayed but two months with my wife and family; for my insatiable desire of seeing foreign countries would suffer me to continue no longer. I left fifteen hundred pounds with my wife, and fixed her in a good house at Redriff. My remaining stock I carried with me, part in money, and part in goods, in hopes to improve my fortunes. My eldest uncle John had left me an estate in land, near Epping, of about thirty pounds a year; and I had a long lease of the Black Bull in Fetter Lane, which yielded me as much more: so that I was not in any danger of leaving my family upon the parish. My son Johnny, named so after his uncle, was at the grammar school, and a towardly child. My daughter Betty (who is now well married, and has children) was then at her needlework. I took leave of my wife, and boy and girl with tears on both sides, and went on board the *Adventure*, a merchant-ship of three hundred tons, bound for Surat, Captain John Nicholas of Liverpool, commander. But my account of this voyage must be referred to the second part of my *Travels*.

THE END OF THE FIRST PART.

Plate 2.nd Part 2.nd Page 93.

BROBDINGNAG

Flanflasnic

Lorbrulgrud

Discovered A D 1703

NORTH AMERICA

Streights of Annian

C Blanco

St Sebastian

NEW ALBION

C Mendocino

Mount St Martin

Po. St Francis Drake

P Monterey

TRAVELS.

A VOYAGE TO BROBDINGNAG.

CHAPTER I.

A great storm described. The longboat sent to fetch water, the author goes with it to discover the country. He is left on shore, is seized by one of the natives, and carried to a farmer's house. His reception there, with several accidents that happened there. A description of the inhabitants.

HAVING been condemned by nature and fortune to an active and restless life, in two months after my return I again left my native country, and took shipping in the Downs on the 20th day of June, 1702, in the *Adventure*, Capt. John Nicholas, a Cornish man, commander, bound for Surat. We had a very prosperous gale till we arrived at the Cape of Good Hope, where we landed for fresh water, but discovering a leak we unshipped our goods, and wintered there; for the captain falling sick of an ague, we could not leave the Cape till the end of March. We then set sail, and had a good voyage till we passed the Straits of Madagascar; but having got northward of that island, and to about five degrees south latitude, the winds, which in those seas are observed to blow a constant equal gale between the north and west from the beginning of December to the beginning of May, on the 19th of April began to blow with much greater violence, and more westerly than usual, continuing so for twenty days together, during which time we were driven a little to the east of the Molucca Islands, and about three degrees northward of the Line, as our captain found by an observation he took the 2nd of May, at which time the wind ceased, and it was a perfect calm, whereat I was not a little rejoiced. But he, being a man well experienced in the navigation of those seas, bid us all prepare against a storm, which accordingly happened the day following: for a southern wind, called the southern monsoon, began to set in.

Finding it was like to overblow, we took in our spritsail, and stood by to hand the foresail; but making foul weather, we looked the guns were all fast, and handed the missen. The ship lay very broad off, so we thought it better spooning before the sea, than trying or hulling. We reefed the foresail and set him, we hauled aft the fore-sheet; the helm was hard a weather. The ship wore bravely. We belayed the fore-downhaul; but the sail was split, and we hauled down the yard, and got the sail into the ship, and unbound all the things clear of it. It was a very fierce storm; the sea broke strange and dangerous. We hauled off upon the lanyard of the whipstaff, and helped the man at helm. We would not get down our topmast, but let all stand, because she scudded before the sea very well, and we knew that the topmast being aloft, the ship was the wholesomer, and made better way through the sea, seeing we had searoom. When the storm was over, we set foresail and mainsail, and brought the ship to. Then we set the missen, main-topsail and the fore-topsail. Our course was east-northeast, the wind was at southwest. We got the starboard tacks aboard, we cast off our weatherbraces and lifts; we set in the lee braces, and hauled forward by the weather bowlings, and hauled them tight, and belayed them, and hauled over the missen tack to windward, and kept her full and by as near as she would lie.

During this storm, which was followed by a strong wind west-southwest, we were carried by my computation about five hundred leagues to the east, so that the oldest sailor on board could not tell in what part of the world we were. Our provisions held out well, our ship was staunch, and our crew all in good health; but we lay in the utmost distress for water. We thought it best to hold on the same course rather than turn more northerly, which might have brought us to the northwest parts of Great Tartary, and into the frozen sea.

On the 16th day of June, 1703, a boy on the topmast discovered land. On the 17th we came in full view of a great island or continent (for we knew not whether) on the south side whereof was a small neck of land jutting out into the sea, and a creek too shallow to hold a ship of above one hundred tons. We cast anchor within a league of this creek, and our captain sent a dozen of his men well armed in the longboat, with vessels for water if any could be found. I desired his leave to go with them, that I might see the country, and make what discoveries I could. When we came to land we saw no river or spring, nor any sign of inhabitants. Our men therefore wandered on the shore to find out some fresh water near the sea, and I walked alone about a mile on the other side, where I observed the country all barren and rocky. I now began to be weary, and seeing nothing to entertain my curiosity, I returned gently down towards the creek; and the sea being full in my view, I saw our men already got into the boat, and rowing for life to the ship. I was going to hollow after them, although it had been to little purpose, when I observed a huge creature walking after them in the sea, as fast as he could: he waded not much deeper than his knees, and took prodigious strides: but our men had the start of him half a league, and the sea thereabouts being full of sharp pointed rocks, the monster was not able to overtake the boat. This I was afterwards told, for I durst not stay to see the issue of that adventure; but ran as fast as I could the way I first went; and then climbed up a steep hill which gave me some prospect of the country. I found it fully cultivated; but that which first surprised me was the length of the grass, which in those grounds that seemed to be kept for hay was above twenty foot high.

I fell into a high road, for so I took it to be, although it served to the inhabitants only as a footpath through a field of barley. Here I walked on for some time, but could see little on either side, it being now near harvest, and the corn rising at least forty foot. I was an hour walking to the end of this field, which was fenced in with a hedge of at least one hundred and twenty foot high, and the trees so lofty that I could make no computation of their altitude. There was a stile to pass from this field into the next. It had four steps, and a stone to cross over when you came to the uppermost. It was impossible for me to climb this stile, because every step was six foot high, and the upper stone above twenty. I was endeavouring to find some gap in the hedge, when I discovered one of the inhabitants in the next field advancing towards the stile, of the same size with him whom I saw in the sea pursuing our boat. He appeared as tall as an ordinary spire-steeple, and took about ten yards at every stride, as near as I could guess. I was struck with the utmost fear and astonishment, and ran to hide my self in the corn, from whence I saw him at the top of the stile, looking back into the next field on the right hand, and heard him call in a voice many degrees louder than a speaking-trumpet; but the noise was so high in the air, that at first I certainly thought it was thunder. Whereupon seven monsters like himself came towards him with reaping-hooks in their hands, each hook about the largeness of six scythes. These people were not so well clad as the first, whose servants or labourers they seemed to be. For, upon some words he spoke, they went to reap the corn in the field where I lay. I kept from them at as great a distance as I could, but was forced to move with extreme difficulty, for the stalks of the corn were sometimes not above a

foot distant, so that I could hardly squeeze my body betwixt
them. However, I made a shift to go forward till I came to a part
of the field where the corn had been laid by the rain and wind.
Here it was impossible for me to advance a step: for the stalks
were so interwoven that I could not creep through, and the
beards of the fallen ears so strong and pointed that they pierced
through my clothes into my flesh. At the same time I heard the
reapers not above an hundred yards behind me. Being quite dispirited with toil, and wholly overcome by grief and despair, I
lay down between two ridges, and heartily wished I might there
end my days. I bemoaned my desolate widow, and fatherless
children. I lamented my own folly and wilfulness in attempting
a second voyage against the advice of all my friends and relations.
In this terrible agitation of mind I could not forbear thinking of
Lilliput, whose inhabitants looked upon me as the greatest
prodigy that ever appeared in the world: where I was able to
draw an imperial fleet in my hand, and perform those other
actions which will be recorded for ever in the chronicles of that
empire, while posterity shall hardly believe them, although at-
tested by millions. I reflected what a mortification it must prove
to me to appear as inconsiderable in this nation as one single Lilliputian would be among us. But this I conceived was to be the
least of my misfortunes: for, as human creatures are observed to
be more savage and cruel in proportion to their bulk, what could
I expect but to be a morsel in the mouth of the first among these
enormous barbarians who should happen to seize me? Undoubt-
edly philosophers are in the right when they tell us, that nothing
is great or little otherwise than by comparison. It might have
pleased fortune to let the Lilliputians find some nation, where the
people were as diminutive with respect to them, as they were to
me. And who knows but that even this prodigious race of mortals might be equally overmatched in some distant part of the
world, whereof we have yet no discovery?

Scared and confounded as I was, I could not forbear going on
with these reflections, when one of the reapers, approaching
within ten yards of the ridge where I lay, made me apprehend
that with the next step I should be squashed to death under his
foot, or cut in two with his reaping hook. And therefore, when
he was again about to move, I screamed as loud as fear could
make me. Whereupon the huge creature trod short, and looking
round about under him for some time, at last espied me as I lay on
the ground. He considered a while with the caution of one who
endeavours to lay hold on a small dangerous animal in such a
manner that it shall not be able either to scratch or to bite him,

as I my self have sometimes done with a weasel in England. At length he ventured to take me up behind by the middle between his forefinger and thumb, and brought me within three yards of his eyes, that he might behold my shape more perfectly. I guessed his meaning, and my good fortune gave me so much presence of mind, that I resolved not to struggle in the least as he held me in the air above sixty foot from the ground, although he grievously pinched my sides, for fear I should slip through his fingers. All I ventured was to raise my eyes towards the sun, and place my hands together in a supplicating posture, and to speak some words in an humble melancholy tone, suitable to the condition I then was in. For I apprehended every moment that he would dash me against the ground, as we usually do any little hateful animal which we have a mind to destroy. But my good star would have it, that he appeared pleased with my voice and gestures, and began to look upon me as a curiosity, much wondering to hear me pronounce articulate words, although he could not understand them. In the mean time I was not able to forbear groaning and shedding tears, and turning my head towards my sides; letting him know, as well as I could, how cruelly I was hurt by the pressure of his thumb and finger. He seemed to apprehend my meaning; for, lifting up the lappet of his coat, he put me gently into it, and immediately ran along with me to his master, who was a substantial farmer, and the same person I had first seen in the field.

The farmer, having (as I supposed by their talk) received such an account of me as his servant could give him, took a piece of a small straw, about the size of a walking staff, and therewith lifted up the lappets of my coat; which it seems he thought to be some kind of covering that nature had given me. He blew my hairs aside to take a better view of my face. He called his hinds about him, and asked them (as I afterwards learned) whether they had ever seen in the fields any little creature that resembled me. He then placed me softly on the ground upon all four, but I got immediately up, and walked slowly backwards and forwards, to let those people see I had no intent to run away. They all sat down in a circle about me, the better to observe my motions. I pulled off my hat, and made a low bow towards the farmer. I fell on my knees, and lifted up my hands and eyes, and spoke several words as loud as I could: I took a purse of gold out of my pocket, and humbly presented it to him. He received it on the palm of his hand, then applied it close to his eye, to see what it was, and afterwards turned it several times with the point of a pin (which he took out of his sleeve), but could make nothing of it. Whereupon I made a sign that he should place his hand on the ground. I then took the purse, and opening it, poured all the gold into his palm. There were six Spanish pieces of four pistoles each, beside twenty or thirty smaller coins. I saw him wet the tip of his little finger upon his tongue, and take up one of my largest pieces, and then another, but he seemed to be wholly ignorant what they were. He made me a sign to put them again into my purse, and the purse again into my pocket, which after offering to him several times, I thought it best to do.

The farmer by this time was convinced I must be a rational creature. He spoke often to me, but the sound of his voice pierced my ears like that of a watermill, yet his words were articulate enough. I answered as loud as I could, in several languages, and he often laid his ear within two yards of me, but all in vain, for we were wholly unintelligible to each other. He then sent his servants to their work, and taking his handkerchief out of his pocket, he doubled and spread it on his left hand, which he placed flat on the ground, with the palm upwards, making me a sign to step into it, as I could easily do, for it was not above a foot in thickness. I thought it my part to obey, and for fear of falling, laid my self at full length upon the handkerchief, with the remainder of which he lapped me up to the head for further security, and in this manner carried me home to his house. There he called his wife, and showed me to her; but she screamed and ran back as women in England do at the sight of a toad or a spider. However, when she had a while seen my behaviour, and how well I observed the signs her husband made, she was soon reconciled, and by degrees grew extremely tender of me.

It was about twelve at noon, and a servant brought in dinner. It was only one substantial dish of meat (fit for the plain condition of an husbandman) in a dish of about four and twenty foot diameter. The company were the farmer and his wife, three children, and an old grandmother: when they were sat down, the farmer placed me at some distance from him on the table, which was thirty foot high from the floor. I was in a terrible fright, and kept as far as I could from the edge for fear of falling. The wife minced a bit of meat, then crumbled some bread on a trencher, and placed it before me. I made her a low bow, took out my knife and fork, and fell to eat, which gave them exceeding delight. The mistress sent her maid for a small dram cup, which held about two gallons, and filled it with drink; I took up the vessel with much difficulty in both hands, and in a most respectful manner drank to her ladyship's health, expressing the words as loud as I could in English, which made the company laugh so heartily, that I was almost deafened with the noise. This liquor tasted like a small cider, and was not unpleasant. Then the master made me a sign to come to his trencher side; but as I walked on the table, being in great surprise all the time, as the indulgent reader will easily conceive and excuse, I happened to stumble against a crust, and fell flat on my face, but received no hurt. I got up immediately, and observing the good people to be in much concern, I took my hat (which I held under my arm out of good manners) and waving it over my head, made three huzzas to show I had got no mischief by the fall. But advancing forwards toward my master (as I shall henceforth call him) his youngest son who sat next him, an arch boy of about ten years old, took me up by the legs, and held me so high in the air, that I trembled every limb; but his father snatched me from him, and at the same time gave him such a box on the left ear, as would have felled an European troop of horse to the earth, ordering him to be taken from the table. But being afraid the boy might owe me a spite, and well remembering how mischievous all children among us naturally are to sparrows, rabbits, young kittens, and puppy dogs, I fell on my knees, and pointing to the boy, made my master understand, as well as I could, that I desired his son might be pardoned. The father complied, and the lad took his seat again; whereupon I went to him and kissed his hand, which my master took, and made him stroke me gently with it.

In the midst of dinner, my mistress's favourite cat leapt into her lap. I heard a noise behind me like that of a dozen stocking-weavers at work; and turning my head I found it proceeded from the purring of this animal, who seemed to be three times larger than an ox, as I computed by the view of her head, and one of her paws, while her mistress was feeding and stroking her. The fierceness of this creature's countenance altogether discomposed me; although I stood at the further end of the table, above fifty foot off, and although my mistress held her fast for fear she might give a spring, and seize me in her talons. But it happened there was no danger; for the cat took not the least notice of me when my master placed me within three yards of her. And as I have been always told, and found true by experience in my travels, that flying, or discovering fear before a fierce animal, is a certain way to make it pursue or attack you, so I resolved in this dangerous juncture to show no manner of concern. I walked with intrepidity five or six times before the very head of the cat, and came within half a yard of her; whereupon she drew her self back, as if she were more afraid of me: I had less apprehension concerning the dogs, whereof three or four came into the room, as it is usual in farmers' houses; one of which was a mastiff equal in bulk to four elephants, and a greyhound somewhat taller than the mastiff, but not so large.

When dinner was almost done, the nurse came in with a child of a year old in her arms, who immediately spied me, and began a squall that you might have heard from London Bridge to Chelsea, after the usual oratory of infants, to get me for a plaything. The mother out of pure indulgence took me up, and put me towards the child, who presently seized me by the middle, and got my head in his mouth, where I roared so loud that the urchin was frighted, and let me drop, and I should infallibly have broke my neck if the mother had not held her apron under me. The nurse to quiet her babe made use of a rattle, which was a kind of hollow vessel filled with great stones, and fastened by a cable to the child's waist: but all in vain, so that she was forced to apply the last remedy by giving it suck. I must confess no object ever disgusted me so much as the sight of her monstrous breast, which I cannot tell what to compare with, so as to give the curious reader an idea of its bulk, shape and colour. It stood prominent six foot, and could not be less than sixteen in circumference. The nipple was about half the bigness of my head, and the hue both of that and the dug so varified with spots, pimples and freckles, that nothing could appear more nauseous: for I had a near sight of her, she sitting down the more conveniently to give suck, and I standing on the table. This made me reflect upon the fair skins of our English ladies, who appear so beautiful to us, only because they are of our own size, and their defects not to be seen but through a magnifying glass, where we find by experiment that the smoothest and whitest skins look rough and coarse, and ill coloured.

I remember when I was at Lilliput, the complexions of those diminutive people appeared to me the fairest in the world; and talking upon this subject with a person of learning there, who was an intimate friend of mine, he said that my face appeared much fairer and smoother when he looked on me from the ground, than it did upon a nearer view when I took him up in my hand, and brought him close, which he confessed was at first a very shocking sight. He said he could discover great holes in my skin, that the stumps of my beard were ten times stronger than the bristles of a boar, and my complexion made up of several colours altogether disagreeable: although I must beg leave to say for my self, that I am as fair as most of my sex and country, and very little sunburnt by all my travels. On the other side, discoursing of the ladies in that emperor's court, he used to tell me, one had freckles, another too wide a mouth, a third too large a nose, nothing of which I was able to distinguish. I confess this reflection was obvious enough; which however I could not forbear, lest the reader might think those vast creatures were actually deformed: for I must do them justice to say they are a comely race of people; and particularly the features of my master's countenance, although he were but a farmer, when I beheld him from the height of sixty foot, appeared very well proportioned.

When dinner was done, my master went out to his labourers, and, as I could discover by his voice and gesture, gave his wife a strict charge to take care of me. I was very much tired and disposed to sleep, which my mistress perceiving, she put me on her own bed, and covered me with a clean white handkerchief, but larger and coarser than the mainsail of a man of war.

I slept about two hours, and dreamed I was at home with my wife and children, which aggravated my sorrows when I awaked and found my self alone in a vast room, between two and three hundred foot wide, and above two hundred high, lying in a bed twenty yards wide. My mistress was gone about her household affairs, and had locked me in. The bed was eight yards from the floor. Some natural necessities required me to get down; I durst not presume to call, and if I had, it would have been in vain with such a voice as mine at so great a distance from the room where I lay to the kitchen where the family kept. While I was under these circumstances two rats crept up the curtains, and ran smelling backwards and forwards on the bed. One of them came up almost to my face, whereupon I rose in a fright, and drew out my hanger to defend my self. These horrible animals had the boldness to attack me on both sides, and one of them held his fore-feet at my collar; but I had the good fortune to rip up his belly before he could do me any mischief. He fell down at my feet, and the other, seeing the fate of his comrade, made his escape, but not without one good wound on the back, which I gave him as he fled, and made the blood run trickling from him. After this exploit, I walked gently to and fro on the bed, to recover my breath and loss of spirits. These creatures were of the size of a large mastiff, but infinitely more nimble and fierce, so that if I had taken off my belt before I went to sleep, I must have infallibly been torn to pieces and devoured. I measured the tail of the dead rat, and found it to be two yards long wanting an inch; but it went against my stomach to drag the carcass off the bed, where it lay still bleeding; I observed it had yet some life, but with a strong slash cross the neck I thoroughly dispatched it.

Soon after my mistress came into the room, who seeing me all bloody, ran and took me up in her hand. I pointed to the dead rat, smiling and making other signs to show I was not hurt, whereat she was extremely rejoiced, calling the maid to take up the dead rat with a pair of tongs, and throw it out of the window. Then she set me on a table, where I showed her my hanger all bloody, and wiping it on the lappet of my coat, returned it to the scabbard. I was pressed to do more than one thing which another could not do for me, and therefore endeavoured to make my mistress understand that I desired to be set down on the floor; which after she had done, my bashfulness would not suffer me to express my self farther than by pointing to the door, and bowing several times. The good woman with much difficulty at last perceived what I would be at, and taking me up again in her hand, walked into the garden, where she set me down. I went on one side about two hundred yards, and beckoning to her not to look or to follow me, I hid myself between two leaves of sorrel, and there discharged the necessities of nature.

I hope the gentle reader will excuse me for dwelling on these and the like particulars, which, however insignificant they may appear to grovelling vulgar minds, yet will certainly help a philosopher to enlarge his thoughts and imagination, and apply them to the benefit of public as well as private life, which was my sole design in presenting this and other accounts of my travels to the world; wherein I have been chiefly studious of truth, without affecting any ornaments of learning or of style. But the whole scene of this voyage made so strong an impression on my mind, and is so deeply fixed in my memory, that in committing it to paper I did not omit one material circumstance: however, upon a strict review, I blotted out several passages of less moment which were in my first copy, for fear of being censured as tedious and trifling, whereof travellers are often, perhaps not without justice, accused.

CHAPTER II.

A description of the farmer's daughter. The author carried to a market-town, and then to the metropolis. The particulars of his journey.

My mistress had a daughter of nine years old, a child of forward parts for her age, very dextrous at her needle, and skilful in dressing her baby. Her mother and she contrived to fit up the baby's cradle for me against night: the cradle was put into a small drawer of a cabinet, and the drawer placed upon a hanging shelf for fear of the rats. This was my bed all the time I stayed with those people, although made more convenient by degrees, as I began to learn their language, and make my wants known. This young girl was so handy, that after I had once or twice pulled off my clothes before her, she was able to dress and undress me, although I never gave her that trouble when she would let me do either my self. She made me seven shirts, and some other linen, of as fine cloth as could be got, which indeed was coarser than sackcloth; and these she constantly washed for me with her own hands. She was likewise my school-mistress to teach me the language: when I pointed to any thing, she told me the name of it in her own tongue, so that in a few days I was able to call for whatever I had a mind to. She was very good natured, and not above forty foot high, being little for her age. She gave me the name of *Grildrig*, which the family took up, and afterwards the whole kingdom. The word imports what the Latins call *nanunculus*, the Italians *homunceletino*, and the English *mannikin*. To her I chiefly owe my preservation in that country: we never parted while I was there; I called her my *glumdalclitch*, or 'little nurse': and I should be guilty of great ingratitude if I omitted this honourable mention of her care and affection towards me, which I heartily wish it lay in my power to requite as she deserves, instead of being the innocent but unhappy instrument of her disgrace, as I have too much reason to fear.

It now began to be known and talked of in the neighbourhood, that my master had found a strange animal in the field, about the bigness of a *splacknuck*, but exactly shaped in every part like a human creature; which it likewise imitated in all its actions; seemed to speak in a little language of its own, had already learned several words of theirs, went erect upon two legs, was tame and gentle, would come when it was called, do whatever it was bid, had the finest limbs in the world, and a complexion fairer than a nobleman's daughter of three years old. Another farmer who lived hard by, and was a particular friend of my master, came on a visit on purpose to enquire into the truth of this story. I was immediately produced, and placed upon a table, where I walked as I was commanded, drew my hanger, put it up again, made my reverence to my master's guest, asked him in his own language how he did, and told him he was welcome, just as my little nurse had instructed me. This man, who was old and dim-sighted, put on his spectacles to behold me better, at which

I could not forbear laughing very heartily, for his eyes appeared like the full moon shining into a chamber at two windows. Our people, who discovered the cause of my mirth, bore me company in laughing, at which the old fellow was fool enough to be angry and out of countenance. He had the character of a great miser, and to my misfortune he well deserved it, by the cursed advice he gave my master to show me as a sight upon a market-day in the next town, which was half an hour's riding, about two and twenty miles from our house. I guessed there was some mischief contriving, when I observed my master and his friend whispering long together, sometimes pointing at me; and my fears made me fancy that I overheard and understood some of their words. But the next morning Glumdalclitch my little nurse told me the whole matter, which she had cunningly picked out from her mother. The poor girl laid me on her bosom, and fell a weeping with shame and grief. She apprehended some mischief would happen to me from rude vulgar folks, who might squeeze me to death, or break one of my limbs by taking me in their hands. She had also observed how modest I was in my nature, how nicely I regarded my honour, and what an indignity I should conceive it to be exposed for money as a public spectacle to the meanest of the people. She said, her papa and mamma had promised that Grildrig should be hers, but now she found they meant to serve her as they did last year, when they pretended to give her a lamb, and yet, as soon as it was fat, sold it to a butcher. For my own part, I may truly affirm that I was less concerned than my nurse. I had a strong hope, which never left me, that I should one day recover my liberty; and as to the ignominy of being carried about for a monster, I considered my self to be a perfect stranger in the country, and that such a misfortune could never be charged upon me as a reproach if ever I should return to England; since the King of Great Britain himself, in my condition, must have undergone the same distress.

My master, pursuant to the advice of my friend, carried me in a box the next market-day to the neighbouring town, and took along with him his little daughter my nurse upon a pillion behind him. The box was close on every side, with a little door for me to go in and out, and a few gimlet-holes to let in air. The girl had been so careful to put the quilt of her baby's bed into it, for me to lie down on. However, I was terribly shaken and discomposed in this journey, although it were but of half an hour. For the horse went about forty foot at every step, and trotted so high, that the agitation was equal to the rising and falling of a ship in a great storm, but much more frequent: our journey was somewhat further than from London to St. Albans. My master alighted at an inn which he used to frequent; and after consulting a while with the inn-keeper, and making some necessary preparations, he hired the *Grultrud,* or crier, to give notice through the town of a strange creature to be seen at the Sign of the Green Eagle, not so big as a *splacknuck* (an animal in that country very finely shaped, about six foot long) and in every part of the body resembling an human creature, could speak several words, and perform an hundred diverting tricks.

I was placed upon a table in the largest room of the inn, which might be near three hundred foot square. My little nurse stood on a low stool close to the table, to take care of me, and direct what I should do. My master, to avoid a crowd, would suffer only thirty people at a time to see me. I walked about on the table as the girl commanded; she asked me questions as far as she knew my understanding of the language reached, and I answered them as loud as I could. I turned about several times to the company, paid my humble respects, said they were welcome, and used some other speeches I had been taught. I took up a thimble filled with liquor, which Glumdalclitch had given me for a cup, and drank their health. I drew out my hanger, and flourished with it after the manner of fencers in England. My nurse gave me part of a straw, which I exercised as a pike, having learned the art in my youth. I was that day shown to twelve sets of company, and as often forced to go over again with the same fopperies, till I was half dead with weariness and vexation. For those who had seen me made such wonderful reports, that the people were ready to break down the doors to come in. My master for his own interest would not suffer any one to touch me except my nurse; and, to prevent danger, benches were set round the table at such a distance as put me out of every body's reach. However, an unlucky school-boy aimed a hazel nut directly at my head, which very narrowly missed me; otherwise, it came with so much violence that it would have infallibly knocked out my brains, for it was almost as large as a small pumpion: but I had the satisfaction to see the young rogue well beaten, and turned out of the room.

My master gave public notice, that he would show me again the next market-day, and in the mean time he prepared a more convenient vehicle for me, which he had reason enough to do; for I was so tired with my first journey, and with entertaining company for eight hours together, that I could hardly stand upon my legs, or speak a word. It was at least three days before I recovered my strength; and that I might have no rest at home, all the neighbouring gentlemen from an hundred miles round, hearing of my fame, came to see me at my master's own house. There could not be fewer than thirty persons with their wives and children (for the country is very populous); and my master demanded the rate of a full room whenever he showed me at home, although it were only to a single family. So that for some time I had but little ease every day of the week (except Wednesday, which is their Sabbath) although I were not carried to the town.

My master, finding how profitable I was like to be, resolved to carry me to the most considerable cities of the kingdom. Having therefore provided himself with all things necessary for a long journey, and settled his affairs at home, he took leave of his wife, and upon the 17th of August, 1703, about two months after my arrival, we set out for the metropolis, situated near the middle of that empire, and about three thousand miles distance from our house: my master made his daughter Glumdalclitch ride behind him. She carried me on her lap in a box tied about her waist. The girl had lined it on all sides with the softest cloth she could get, well quilted underneath, furnished it with her baby's bed, provided me with linen and other necessaries, and made every thing as convenient as she could. We had no other company but a boy of the house, who rode after us with the luggage.

My master's design was to show me in all the towns by the way, and to step out of the road for fifty or an hundred miles, to any village or person of quality's house where he might expect custom. We made easy journeys of not above seven or eight-score miles a day: for Glumdalclitch, on purpose to spare me, complained she was tired with the trotting of the horse. She often took me out of my box at my own desire, to give me air, and show me the country, but always held me fast by leading-strings. We passed over five or six rivers many degrees broader and deeper than the Nile or the Ganges; and there was hardly a rivulet so small as the Thames at London Bridge. We were ten weeks in our journeys, and I was shown in eighteen large towns, besides many villages and private families.

On the 26th day of October, we arrived at the metropolis, called in their language Lorbrulgrud, or Pride of the Universe. My master took a lodging in the principal street of the city, not far from the royal palace, and put out bills in the usual form, containing an exact description of my person and parts. He hired a large room between three and four hundred foot wide. He provided a table sixty foot in diameter, upon which I was to act my part, and palisadoed it round three feet from the edge, and as many high, to prevent my falling over. I was shown ten times a day to the wonder and satisfaction of all people. I could now speak the language tolerably well, and perfectly understood every word that was spoken to me. Besides, I had learnt their alphabet, and could make a shift to explain a sentence here and there; for Glumdalclitch had been my instructor while we were at home, and at leisure hours during our journey. She carried a little book in her pocket, not much larger than a Sanson's *Atlas;* it was a common treatise for the use of young girls, giving a short account of their religion; out of this she taught me my letters, and interpreted the words.

CHAPTER III.

The author sent for to court. The Queen buys him of his master the farmer, and presents him to the King. He disputes with his Majesty's great scholars. An apartment at court provided for the author. He is in high favour with the Queen. He stands up for the honour of his own country. His quarrels with the Queen's dwarf.

The frequent labours I underwent every day made in a few weeks a very considerable change in my health: the more my master got by me, the more unsatiable he grew. I had quite lost my stomach, and was almost reduced to a skeleton. The farmer observed it, and concluding I soon must die, resolved to make as good a hand of me as he could. While he was thus reasoning and resolving with himself, a *slardral*, or gentleman usher, came from court, commanding my master to bring me immediately thither for the diversion of the Queen and her ladies. Some of the latter had already been to see me, and reported strange things of my beauty, behaviour, and good sense. Her Majesty and those who attended her were beyond measure delighted with my demeanor. I fell on my knees, and begged the honour of kissing her imperial foot; but this gracious princess held out her little finger towards me (after I was set on a table) which I embraced in both my arms, and put the tip of it, with the utmost respect, to my lip. She made me some general questions about my country and my travels, which I answered as distinctly and in as few words as I could. She asked whether I would be content to live at court. I bowed down to the board of the table, and humbly answered that I was my master's slave, but if I were at my own disposal, I should be proud to devote my life to her Majesty's service. She then asked my master whether he were willing to sell me at a good price. He, who apprehended I could not live a month, was

ready enough to part with me, and demanded a thousand pieces
of gold, which were ordered him on the spot, each piece being
about the bigness of eight hundred moidores; but, allowing for
the proportion of all things between that country and Europe,
and the high price of gold among them, was hardly so great a
sum as a thousand guineas would be in England. I then said to
the Queen, since I was now her Majesty's most humble creature
and vassal, I must beg the favour, that Glumdalclitch, who had
always tended me with so much care and kindness, and understood to do it so well, might be admitted into her service, and
continue to be my nurse and instructor. Her Majesty agreed to
my petition, and easily got the farmer's consent, who was glad
enough to have his daughter preferred at court: and the poor girl
herself was not able to hide her joy: my late master withdrew,
bidding me farewell, and saying he had left me in a good service;
to which I replied not a word, only making him a slight bow.

The Queen observed my coldness, and when the farmer was
gone out of the apartment, asked me the reason. I made bold to
tell her Majesty that I owed no other obligation to my late
master, than his not dashing out the brains of a poor harmless
creature found by chance in his field; which obligation was
amply recompensed by the gain he had made in showing me
through half the kingdom, and the price he had now sold me for.
That the life I had since led was laborious enough to kill an animal of ten times my strength. That my health was much
impaired by the continual drudgery of entertaining the rabble
every hour of the day, and that if my master had not thought
my life in danger, her Majesty perhaps would not have got so
cheap a bargain. But as I was out of all fear of being ill treated
under the protection of so great and good an empress, the Ornament of Nature, the Darling of the World, the Delight of her
Subjects, the Phoenix of the Creation; so, I hoped, my late
master's apprehensions would appear to be groundless, for I
already found my spirits to revive by the influence of her most
august presence.

This was the sum of my speech, delivered with great im-
proprieties and hesitation; the latter part was altogether framed
in the style peculiar to that people, whereof I learned some
phrases from Glumdalclitch, while she was carrying me to court.

The Queen, giving great allowance for my defectiveness in
speaking, was however surprised at so much wit and good sense
in so diminutive an animal. She took me in her own hand, and
carried me to the King, who was then retired to his cabinet. His
Majesty, a prince of much gravity, and austere countenance, not

well observing my shape at first view, asked the Queen after a cold manner, how long it was since she grew fond of a *splack-nuck;* for such it seems he took me to be, as I lay upon my breast in her Majesty's right hand. But this princess, who hath an infinite deal of wit and humour, set me gently on my feet upon the scrutore, and commanded me to give his Majesty an account of my self, which I did in a very few words; and Glumdalclitch, who attended at the cabinet door, and could not endure I should be out of her sight, being admitted, confirmed all that had passed from my arrival at her father's house.

The King, although he be as learned a person as any in his dominions, had been educated in the study of philosophy, and particularly mathematics; yet when he observed my shape exactly, and saw me walk erect, before I began to speak, conceived I might be a piece of clock-work (which is in that country arrived to a very great perfection), contrived by some ingenious artist. But, when he heard my voice, and found what I delivered to be regular and rational, he could not conceal his astonishment. He was by no means satisfied with the relation I gave him of the manner I came into his kingdom, but thought it a story concerted between Glumdalclitch and her father, who had taught me a set of words to make me sell at a higher price. Upon this imagination he put several other questions to me, and still received rational answers, no otherwise defective than by a foreign accent, and an imperfect knowledge in the language, with some rustic phrases which I had learned at the farmer's house, and did not suit the polite style of a court.

His Majesty sent for three great scholars who were then in their weekly waiting (according to the custom in that country). These gentlemen, after they had a while examined my shape with much nicety, were of different opinions concerning me. They all agreed that I could not be produced according to the regular laws of nature, because I was not framed with a capacity of preserving my life, either by swiftness, or climbing of trees, or digging holes in the earth. They observed by my teeth, which they viewed with great exactness, that I was a carnivorous animal; yet most quadrupeds being an overmatch for me, and field mice, with some others, too nimble, they could not imagine how I should be able to support my self, unless I fed upon snails and other insects, which they offered by many learned arguments to evince that I could not possibly do. One of them seemed to think that I might be an embryo, or abortive birth. But this opinion was rejected by the other two, who observed my limbs to be perfect and finished, and that I had lived several years, as it was mani-

fested from my beard, the stumps whereof they plainly discovered through a magnifying-glass. They would not allow me
to be a dwarf, because my littleness was beyond all degrees of
comparison; for the Queen's favourite dwarf, the smallest ever
known in that kingdom, was near thirty foot high. After much
debate, they concluded unanimously that I was only *relplum
scalcath*, which is interpreted literally, *lusus naturæ;* a determination exactly agreeable to the modern philosophy of Europe,
whose professors, disdaining the old evasion of occult causes,
whereby the followers of Aristotle endeavour in vain to disguise
their ignorance, have invented this wonderful solution of all
difficulties to the unspeakable advancement of human knowledge.

After this decisive conclusion, I entreated to be heard a word
or two. I applied myself to the King, and assured his Majesty
that I came from a country which abounded with several millions
of both sexes, and of my own stature; where the animals, trees,
and houses were all in proportion, and where by consequence I
might be as able to defend my self, and to find sustenance, as any
of his Majesty's subjects could do here; which I took for a full
answer to those gentlemen's arguments. To this they only
replied with a smile of contempt, saying, that the farmer had
instructed me very well in my lesson. The King, who had a
much better understanding, dismissing his learned men, sent for
the farmer, who by good fortune was not yet gone out of town;
having therefore first examined him privately, and then confronted him with me and the young girl, his Majesty began to
think that what we told him might possibly be true. He desired
the Queen to order that a particular care should be taken of me,
and was of opinion, that Glumdalclitch should still continue in
her office of tending me, because he observed we had a great
affection for each other. A convenient apartment was provided
for her at court; she had a sort of governess appointed to take
care of her education, a maid to dress her, and two other
servants for menial offices; but the care of me was wholly appropriated to her self. The Queen commanded her own cabinet-
maker to contrive a box that might serve me for a bed-chamber,
after the model that Glumdalclitch and I should agree upon.
This man was a most ingenious artist, and according to my directions, in three weeks finished for me a wooden chamber of
sixteen foot square, and twelve high, with sash-windows, a door,
and two closets, like a London bed-chamber. The board that
made the ceiling was to be lifted up and down by two hinges, to
put in a bed ready furnished by her Majesty's upholsterer, which
Glumdalclitch took out every day to air, made it with her own

hands, and letting it down at night, locked up the roof over me. A nice workman, who was famous for little curiosities, undertook to make me two chairs, with backs and frames, of a substance not unlike ivory, and two tables, with a cabinet to put my things in. The room was quilted on all sides, as well as the floor and the ceiling, to prevent any accident from the carelessness of those who carried me, and to break the force of a jolt when I went in a coach. I desired a lock for my door to prevent rats and mice from coming in: the smith after several attempts made the smallest that was ever seen among them, for I have known a larger at the gate of a gentleman's house in England. I made a shift to keep the key in a pocket of my own, fearing Glumdalclitch might lose it. The Queen likewise ordered the thinnest silks that could be gotten, to make me clothes, not much thicker than an English blanket, very cumbersome till I was accustomed to them. They were after the fashion of the kingdom, partly resembling the Persian, and partly the Chinese, and are a very grave decent habit.

The Queen became so fond of my company, that she could not dine without me. I had a table placed upon the same at which her Majesty eat, just at her left elbow, and a chair to sit on. Glumdalclitch stood upon a stool on the floor, near my table, to assist and take care of me. I had an entire set of silver dishes and plates, and other necessaries, which, in proportion to those of the Queen, were not much bigger than what I have seen in a London toy-shop, for the furniture of a baby-house: these my little nurse kept in her pocket, in a silver box, and gave me at meals as I wanted them, always cleaning them her self. No person dined with the Queen but the two princesses royal, the elder sixteen years old, and the younger at that time thirteen and a month. Her Majesty used to put a bit of meat upon one of my dishes, out of which I carved for my self; and her diversion was to see me eat in miniature. For the Queen (who had indeed but a weak stomach) took up at one mouthful as much as a dozen English farmers could eat at a meal, which to me was for some time a very nauseous sight. She would craunch the wing of a lark, bones and all, between her teeth, although it were nine times as large as that of a full-grown turkey; and put a bit of bread in her mouth, as big as two twelve-penny loaves. She drank out of a golden cup, above a hogshead at a draught. Her knives were twice as long as a scythe set straight upon the handle. The spoons, forks, and other instruments were all in the same proportion. I remember when Glumdalclitch carried me out of curiosity to see some of the tables at court, where ten or a dozen of these enormous knives and forks were lifted up together, I thought I had never till then beheld so terrible a sight.

It is the custom that every Wednesday (which, as I have before observed, was their Sabbath) the King and Queen, with the royal issue of both sexes, dine together in the apartment of his Majesty, to whom I was now become a favourite; and at these times my little chair and table were placed at his left hand before one of the salt-cellars. This prince took a pleasure in conversing with me, enquiring into the manners, religion, laws, government, and learning of Europe, wherein I gave him the best account I was able. His apprehension was so clear, and his judgment so exact, that he made very wise reflections and observations upon all I said. But I confess, that after I had been a little too copious in talking of my own beloved country, of our trade, and wars by sea and land, of our schisms in religion, and parties in the state, the prejudices of his education prevailed so far, that he could not forbear taking me up in his right hand, and stroking me gently with the other, after an hearty fit of laughing, asked me whether I were a Whig or a Tory. Then turning to his first minister, who waited behind him with a white staff, near as tall as the main-mast of the *Royal Sovereign*, he observed how contemptible a thing was human grandeur, which could be mimicked by such diminutive insects as I: And yet, said he, I dare engage, those creatures have their titles and distinctions of honour, they contrive little nests and burrows, that they call houses and cities; they make a figure in dress and equipage; they love, they fight, they dispute, they cheat, they betray. And thus he continued on, while my colour came and went several times, with indignation to hear our noble country, the mistress of arts and arms, the scourge of France, the arbitress of Europe, the seat of virtue, piety, honour and truth, the pride and envy of the world, so contemptuously treated.

But, as I was not in a condition to resent injuries, so, upon mature thoughts, I began to doubt whether I were injured or no. For, after having been accustomed several months to the sight and converse of this people, and observed every object upon which I cast my eyes to be of proportionable magnitude, the horror I had first conceived from their bulk and aspect was so far worn off, that if I had then beheld a company of English lords and ladies in their finery and birthday clothes, acting their several parts in the most courtly manner of strutting, and bowing, and prating, to say the truth, I should have been strongly tempted to laugh as much at them as this king and his grandees did at me. Neither indeed could I forbear smiling at my self, when the

Queen used to place me upon her hand towards a looking-glass, by which both our persons appeared before me in full view together; and there could nothing be more ridiculous than the comparison: so that I really began to imagine my self dwindled many degrees below my usual size.

Nothing angered and mortified me so much as the Queen's dwarf, who being of the lowest stature that was ever in that country (for I verily think he was not full thirty foot high) became so insolent at seeing a creature so much beneath him, that he would always affect to swagger and look big as he passed by me in the Queen's antechamber, while I was standing on some table talking with the lords or ladies of the court, and he seldom failed of a smart word or two upon my littleness; against which I could only revenge my self by calling him brother, challenging him to wrestle, and such repartees as are usual in the mouths of court pages. One day at dinner this malicious little cub was so nettled with something I had said to him, that raising himself upon the frame of her Majesty's chair, he took me up by the middle, as I was sitting down, not thinking any harm, and let me drop into a large silver bowl of cream, and then ran away as fast as he could. I fell over head and ears, and if I had not been a good swimmer, it might have gone very hard with me; for Glumdalclitch in that instant happened to be at the other end of the room, and the Queen was in such a fright that she wanted presence of mind to assist me. But my little nurse ran to my relief, and took me out, after I had swallowed above a quart of cream. I was put to bed; however I received no other damage than the loss of a suit of clothes, which was utterly spoiled. The dwarf was soundly whipped, and as a further punishment, forced to drink up the bowl of cream into which he had thrown me; neither was he ever restored to favour: for, soon after, the Queen bestowed him to a lady of high quality, so that I saw him no more, to my very great satisfaction; for I could not tell to what extremities such a malicious urchin might have carried his resentment.

He had before served me a scurvy trick, which set the Queen a laughing, although at the same time she were heartily vexed, and would have immediately cashiered him, if I had not been so generous as to intercede. Her Majesty had taken a marrow-bone upon her plate, and after knocking out the marrow, placed the bone again in the dish erect as it stood before; the dwarf watching his opportunity, while Glumdalclitch was gone to the sideboard, mounted the stool she stood on to take care of me at meals, took me up in both hands, and squeezing my legs together,

wedged them into the marrow-bone above my waist, where I
stuck for some time, and made a very ridiculous figure. I believe
it was near a minute before any one knew what was become of
me, for I thought it below me to cry out. But, as princes seldom
get their meat hot, my legs were not scalded, only my stockings
and breeches in a sad condition. The dwarf at my entreaty had
no other punishment than a sound whipping.

I was frequently rallied by the Queen upon account of my
fearfulness, and she used to ask me whether the people of my
country were as great cowards as my self. The occasion was
this. The kingdom is much pestered with flies in summer, and
these odious insects, each of them as big as a Dunstable lark,
hardly gave me any rest while I sat at dinner, with their continual
humming and buzzing about my ears. They would sometimes
alight upon my victuals, and leave their loathsome excrement or
spawn behind, which to me was very visible, although not to the
natives of that country, whose large optics were not so acute as
mine in viewing smaller objects. Sometimes they would fix upon
my nose or forehead, where they stung me to the quick, smelling
very offensively, and I could easily trace that viscous matter,
which our naturalists tell us enables those creatures to walk with
their feet upwards upon a ceiling. I had much ado to defend my
self against these detestable animals, and could not forbear starting when they came on my face. It was the common practice of
the dwarf to catch a number of these insects in his hand as
schoolboys do among us, and let them out suddenly under my
nose on purpose to frighten me, and divert the Queen. My
remedy was to cut them in pieces with my knife as they flew in
the air, wherein my dexterity was much admired.

I remember one morning when Glumdalclitch had set me in
my box upon a window, as she usually did in fair days to give me
air (for I durst not venture to let the box be hung on a nail out of
the window, as we do with cages in England) after I had lifted up
one of my sashes, and sat down at my table to eat a piece of
sweet cake for my breakfast, above twenty wasps, allured by
the smell, came flying into the room, humming louder than the
drones of as many bagpipes. Some of them seized my cake, and
carried it piecemeal away, others flew about my head and face,
confounding me with the noise, and putting me in the utmost
terror of their stings. However I had the courage to rise and
draw my hanger, and attack them in the air. I dispatched four of
them, but the rest got away, and I presently shut my window.
These insects were as large as partridges: I took out their stings,
found them an inch and a half long, and as sharp as needles. I

carefully preserved them all, and having since shown them with some other curiosities in several parts of Europe, upon my return to England I gave three of them to Gresham College, and kept the fourth for my self.

CHAPTER IV.

The country described. A proposal for correcting modern maps. The King's palace, and some account of the metropolis. The author's way of travelling. The chief temple described.

I now intend to give the reader a short description of this country, as far as I travelled in it, which was not above two thousand miles round Lorbrulgrud the metropolis. For the Queen, whom I always attended, never went further when she accompanied the King in his progresses, and there stayed till his Majesty returned from viewing his frontiers. The whole extent of this prince's dominions reacheth about six thousand miles in length, and from three to five in breadth. From whence I cannot but conclude that our geographers of Europe are in a great error, by supposing nothing but sea between Japan and California; for it was ever my opinion, that there must be a balance of earth to counterpoise the great continent of Tartary; and therefore they ought to correct their maps and charts, by joining this vast tract of land to the northwest parts of America, wherein I shall be ready to lend them my assistance.

The kingdom is a peninsula, terminated to the northeast by a ridge of mountains thirty miles high, which are altogether impassable by reason of the volcanoes upon the tops. Neither do the most learned know what sort of mortals inhabit beyond these mountains, or whether they be inhabited at all. On the three other sides it is bounded by the ocean. There is not one seaport in the whole kingdom, and those parts of the coasts into which the rivers issue are so full of pointed rocks, and the sea generally so rough, that there is no venturing with the smallest of their boats, so that these people are wholly excluded from any commerce with the rest of the world. But the large rivers are full of vessels, and abound with excellent fish, for they seldom get any from the sea, because the sea-fish are of the same size with those in Europe, and consequently not worth catching; whereby it is manifest, that nature in the production of plants and animals of so extraordinary a bulk is wholly confined to this continent, of which I leave the reasons to be determined by philosophers.

However, now and then they take a whale that happens to be
dashed against the rocks, which the common people feed on
heartily. These whales I have known so large that a man could
hardly carry one upon his shoulders; and sometimes for curiosity
they are brought in hampers to Lorbrulgrud: I saw one of them
in a dish at the King's table, which passed for a rarity, but I did
not observe he was fond of it; for I think indeed the bigness
disgusted him, although I have seen one somewhat larger in
Greenland.

The country is well inhabited, for it contains fifty-one cities,
near an hundred walled towns, and a great number of villages.
To satisfy my curious reader, it may be sufficient to describe
Lorbrulgrud. This city stands upon almost two equal parts on
each side the river that passes through. It contains above eighty
thousand houses, and about six hundred thousand inhabitants. It
is in length three *glonglungs* (which make about fifty-four English miles) and two and a half in breadth, as I measured it my
self in the royal map made by the King's order, which was laid
on the ground on purpose for me, and extended an hundred feet;
I paced the diameter and circumference several times barefoot,
and computing by the scale, measured it pretty exactly.

The King's palace is no regular edifice, but an heap of buildings
about seven miles round: the chief rooms are generally two
hundred and forty foot high, and broad and long in proportion.
A coach was allowed to Glumdalclitch and me, wherein her
governess frequently took her out to see the town, or go among
the shops; and I was always of the party, carried in my box;
although the girl at my own desire would often take me out, and
hold me in her hand, that I might more conveniently view the
houses and the people as we passed along the streets. I reckoned
our coach to be about a square of Westminster Hall, but not
altogether so high; however, I cannot be very exact. One day
the governess ordered our coachman to stop at several shops,
where the beggars, watching their opportunity, crowded to the
sides of the coach, and gave me the most horrible spectacles that
ever an European eye beheld. There was a woman with a cancer
in her breast, swelled to a monstrous size, full of holes, in two or
three of which I could have easily crept, and covered my whole
body. There was a fellow with a wen in his neck, larger than
five woolpacks, and another with a couple of wooden legs, each
about twenty foot high. But the most hateful sight of all was
the lice crawling on their clothes. I could see distinctly the
limbs of these vermin with my naked eye, much better than
those of an European louse through a microscope, and their

snouts with which they rooted like swine. They were the first I had ever beheld, and I should have been curious enough to dissect one of them, if I had proper instruments (which I unluckily left behind me in the ship) although indeed the sight was so nauseous, that it perfectly turned my stomach.

Beside the large box in which I was usually carried, the Queen ordered a smaller one to be made for me, of about twelve foot square, and ten high, for the convenience of travelling, because the other was somewhat too large for Glumdalclitch's lap, and cumbersome in the coach; it was made by the same artist, whom I directed in the whole contrivance. This travelling closet was an exact square with a window in the middle of three of the squares, and each window was latticed with iron wire on the outside, to prevent accidents in long journeys. On the fourth side, which had no window, two strong staples were fixed, through which the person that carried me, when I had a mind to be on horseback, put in a leathern belt, and buckled it about his waist. This was always the office of some grave trusty servant in whom I could confide, whether I attended the King and Queen in their progresses, or were disposed to see the gardens, or pay a visit to some great lady or minister of state in the court, when Glumdalclitch happened to be out of order: for I soon began to be known and esteemed among the greatest officers, I suppose more upon account of their Majesties' favour than any merit of my own. In journeys, when I was weary of the coach, a servant on horseback would buckle my box, and place it on a cushion before him; and there I had a full prospect of the country on three sides from my three windows. I had in this closet a field-bed and a hammock hung from the ceiling, two chairs and a table, neatly screwed to the floor, to prevent being tossed about by the agitation of the horse or the coach. And having been long used to sea-voyages, those motions, although sometimes very violent, did not much discompose me.

Whenever I had a mind to see the town, it was always in my travelling-closet, which Glumdalclitch held in her lap in a kind of open sedan, after the fashion of the country, borne by four men, and attended by two others in the Queen's livery. The people, who had often heard of me, were very curious to crowd about the sedan, and the girl was complaisant enough to make the bearers stop, and to take me in her hand that I might be more conveniently seen.

I was very desirous to see the chief temple, and particularly the tower belonging to it, which is reckoned the highest in the kingdom. Accordingly one day my nurse carried me thither, but

I may truly say I came back disappointed; for the height is not above three thousand foot, reckoning from the ground to the highest pinnacle top; which, allowing for the difference between the size of those people and us in Europe, is no great matter for admiration, nor at all equal in proportion (if I rightly remember) to Salisbury steeple. But, not to detract from a nation to which during my life I shall acknowledge my self extremely obliged, it must be allowed that whatever this famous tower wants in height is amply made up in beauty and strength. For the walls are near an hundred foot thick, built of hewn stone, whereof each is about forty foot square, and adorned on all sides with statues of gods and emperors cut in marble larger than the life, placed in their several niches. I measured a little finger which had fallen down from one of these statues, and lay unperceived among some rubbish, and found it exactly four foot and an inch in length. Glumdalclitch wrapped it up in a handkerchief, and carried it home in her pocket to keep among other trinkets, of which the girl was very fond, as children at her age usually are.

The King's kitchen is indeed a noble building, vaulted at top, and about six hundred foot high. The great oven is not so wide by ten paces as the cupola at St. Paul's: for I measured the latter on purpose after my return. But if I should describe the kitchen-grate, the prodigious pots and kettles, the joints of meat turning on the spits, with many other particulars, perhaps I should be hardly believed; at least a severe critic would be apt to think I enlarged a little, as travellers are often suspected to do. To avoid which censure, I fear I have run too much into the other extreme; and that if this treatise should happen to be translated into the language of Brobdingnag (which is the general name of that kingdom) and transmitted thither, the King and his people would have reason to complain that I had done them an injury by a false and diminutive representation.

His Majesty seldom keeps above six hundred horses in his stables: they are generally from fifty-four to sixty foot high. But, when he goes abroad on solemn days, he is attended for state by a militia guard of five hundred horse, which indeed I thought was the most splendid sight that could be ever beheld, till I saw part of his army in battalia, whereof I shall find another occasion to speak.

Chapter V.

Several adventures that happened to the author. The execution of a criminal. The author shows his skill in navigation.

I should have lived happy enough in that country, if my littleness had not exposed me to several ridiculous and troublesome accidents, some of which I shall venture to relate. Glumdalclitch often carried me into the gardens of the court in my smaller box, and would sometimes take me out of it and hold me in her hand, or set me down to walk. I remember, before the dwarf left the Queen, he followed us one day into those gardens, and my nurse having set me down, he and I being close together, near some dwarf apple-trees, I must needs show my wit by a silly allusion between him and the trees, which happens to hold in their language as it doth in ours. Whereupon the malicious rogue, watching his opportunity, when I was walking under one of them, shook it directly over my head, by which a dozen apples, each of them near as large as a Bristol barrel, came tumbling about my ears; one of them hit me on the back as I chanced to stoop, and knocked me down flat on my face, but I received no other hurt, and the dwarf was pardoned at my desire, because I had given the provocation.

Another day Glumdalclitch left me on a smooth grass-plot to divert my self while she walked at some distance with her governess. In the mean time there suddenly fell such a violent shower of hail, that I was immediately by the force of it struck to the ground: and when I was down, the hailstones gave me such cruel bangs all over the body, as if I had been pelted with tennis-balls; however I made a shift to creep on all four, and shelter my self by lying flat on my face on the lee-side of a border of lemon thyme, but so bruised from head to foot that I could not go abroad in ten days. Neither is this at all to be wondered at, because nature in that country observing the same proportion through all her operations, a hailstone is near eighteen hundred times as large as one in Europe, which I can assert upon experience, having been so curious to weigh and measure them.

But a more dangerous accident happened to me in the same garden, when my little nurse, believing she had put me in a secure place, which I often entreated her to do, that I might enjoy my own thoughts, and having left my box at home to avoid the trouble of carrying it, went to another part of the gardens with her governess and some ladies of her acquaintance. While she was absent and out of hearing, a small white spaniel

belonging to one of the chief gardeners, having got by accident
into the garden, happened to range near the place where I lay.
The dog, following the scent, came directly up, and taking me
in his mouth ran straight to his master, wagging his tail, and set
me gently on the ground. By good fortune he had been so well
taught, that I was carried between his teeth without the least
hurt, or even tearing my clothes. But the poor gardener, who
knew me well, and had a great kindness for me, was in a terrible
fright. He gently took me up in both his hands, and asked me
how I did; but I was so amazed and out of breath, that I could
not speak a word. In a few minutes I came to my self, and he
carried me safe to my little nurse, who by this time had returned
to the place where she left me, and was in cruel agonies when
I did not appear, nor answer when she called: she severely reprimanded the gardener on account of his dog. But the thing
was hushed up, and never known at court; for the girl was afraid
of the Queen's anger, and truly as to my self, I thought it would
not be for my reputation that such a story should go about.

This accident absolutely determined Glumdalclitch never to
trust me abroad for the future out of her sight. I had been long
afraid of this resolution, and therefore concealed from her some
little unlucky adventures that happened in those times when I was
left by my self. Once a kite hovering over the garden made a
stoop at me, and if I had not resolutely drawn my hanger, and
run under a thick espalier, he would have certainly carried me
away in his talons. Another time walking to the top of a fresh
mole-hill, I fell to my neck in the hole through which that animal
had cast up the earth, and coined some lie not worth remembering,
to excuse my self for spoiling my clothes. I likewise broke my
right shin against the shell of a snail, which I happened to stumble
over, as I was walking alone, and thinking on poor England.

I cannot tell whether I were more pleased or mortified to observe in those solitary walks, that the smaller birds did not appear
to be at all afraid of me, but would hop about within a yard
distance, looking for worms and other food with as much indifference and security as if no creature at all were near them. I
remember a thrush had the confidence to snatch out of my hand
with his bill a piece of cake that Glumdalclitch had just given me
for my breakfast. When I attempted to catch any of these birds,
they would boldly turn against me, endeavouring to pick my
fingers, which I durst not venture within their reach; and then
they would hop back unconcerned to hunt for worms or snails,
as they did before. But one day I took a thick cudgel, and threw
it with all my strength so luckily at a linnet, that I knocked him

down, and seizing him by the neck with both my hands, ran with him in triumph to my nurse. However, the bird, who had only been stunned, recovering himself, gave me so many boxes with his wings on both sides of my head and body, although I held him at arm's length, and was out of the reach of his claws, that I was twenty times thinking to let him go. But I was soon relieved by one of our servants, who wrung off the bird's neck, and I had him next day for dinner by the Queen's command. This linnet, as near as I can remember, seemed to be somewhat larger than an English swan.

The maids of honour often invited Glumdalclitch to their apartments, and desired she would bring me along with her, on purpose to have the pleasure of seeing and touching me. They would often strip me naked from top to toe, and lay me at full length in their bosoms; wherewith I was much disgusted; because, to say the truth, a very offensive smell came from their skins; which I do not mention or intend to the disadvantage of those excellent ladies, for whom I have all manner of respect; but I conceive that my sense was more acute in proportion to my littleness, and that those illustrious persons were no more disagreeable to their lovers, or to each other, than people of the same quality are with us in England. And, after all, I found their natural smell was much more supportable than when they used perfumes, under which I immediately swooned away. I cannot forget that an intimate friend of mine in Lilliput took the freedom, in a warm day, when I had used a good deal of exercise, to complain of a strong smell about me, although I am as little faulty that way as most of my sex: but I suppose his faculty of smelling was as nice with regard to me, as mine was to that of this people. Upon this point, I cannot forbear doing justice to the Queen my mistress, and Glumdalclitch my nurse, whose persons were as sweet as those of any lady in England.

That which gave me most uneasiness among these maids of honour, when my nurse carried me to visit them, was to see them use me without any manner of ceremony, like a creature who had no sort of consequence. For they would strip themselves to the skin, and put on their smocks in my presence, while I was placed on their toilet directly before their naked bodies, which, I am sure, to me was very far from being a tempting sight, or from giving me any other emotions than those of horror and disgust. Their skins appeared so coarse and uneven, so variously coloured, when I saw them near, with a mole here and there as broad as a trencher, and hairs hanging from it thicker than pack-threads; to say nothing further concerning the rest of their

persons. Neither did they at all scruple while I was by to discharge what they had drunk, to the quantity of at least two
hogsheads, in a vessel that held above three tuns. The hand-
somest among these maids of honour, a pleasant frolicsome girl of
sixteen, would sometimes set me astride upon one of her nipples,
with many other tricks, wherein the reader will excuse me for not
being over particular. But I was so much displeased, that I
entreated Glumdalclitch to contrive some excuse for not seeing
that young lady any more.

One day a young gentleman, who was nephew to my nurse's
governess, came and pressed them both to see an execution. It
was of a man who had murdered one of that gentleman's
intimate acquaintance. Glumdalclitch was prevailed on to be of
the company, very much against her inclination, for she was
naturally tender-hearted: and as for my self, although I abhorred
such kind of spectacles, yet my curiosity tempted me to see
something that I thought must be extraordinary. The malefactor
was fixed in a chair upon a scaffold erected for the purpose, and
his head cut off at one blow with a sword of about forty foot
long. The veins and arteries spouted up such a prodigious
quantity of blood, and so high in the air, that the great *jet d'eau*
at Versailles was not equal for the time it lasted; and the head,
when it fell on the scaffold floor, gave such a bounce as made
me start, although I was at least an English mile distant.

The Queen, who often used to hear me talk of my sea-
voyages, and took all occasions to divert me when I was
melancholy, asked me whether I understood how to handle a
sail or an oar, and whether a little exercise of rowing might not
be convenient for my health. I answered that I understood both
very well. For although my proper employment had been to be
surgeon or doctor to the ship, yet often, upon a pinch, I was
forced to work like a common mariner. But I could not see how
this could be done in their country, where the smallest wherry
was equal to a first rate man of war among us, and such a boat as
I could manage would never live in any of their rivers: her
Majesty said, if I would contrive a boat, her own joiner should
make it, and she would provide a place for me to sail in. The
fellow was an ingenious workman, and by my instructions in
ten days finished a pleasure-boat with all its tackling, able conveniently to hold eight Europeans. When it was finished, the
Queen was so delighted, that she ran with it in her lap to the
King, who ordered it to be put in a cistern full of water, with me
in it, by way of trial, where I could not manage my two sculls
or little oars for want of room. But the Queen had before con-

trived another project. She ordered the joiner to make a wooden trough of three hundred foot long, fifty broad, and eight deep; which being well pitched to prevent leaking, was placed on the floor along the wall, in an outer room of the palace. It had a cock near the bottom to let out the water when it began to grow stale, and two servants could easily fill it in half an hour. Here I often used to row for my diversion, as well as that of the Queen and her ladies, who thought themselves agreeably entertained with my skill and agility. Sometimes I would put up my sail, and then my business was only to steer, while the ladies gave me a gale with their fans; and when they were weary, some of the pages would blow my sail forward with their breath, while I showed my art by steering starboard or larboard as I pleased. When I had done, Glumdalclitch always carried back my boat into her closet, and hung it on a nail to dry.

In this exercise I once met an accident which had like to have cost me my life. For, one of the pages having put my boat into the trough, the governess who attended Glumdalclitch very officiously lifted me up to place me in the boat, but I happened to slip through her fingers, and should have infallibly fallen down forty foot upon the floor if, by the luckiest chance in the world, I had not been stopped by a corking-pin that stuck in the good gentlewoman's stomacher; the head of the pin passed between my shirt and the waistband of my breeches, and thus I was held by the middle in the air till Glumdalclitch ran to my relief.

Another time, one of the servants, whose office it was to fill my trough every third day with fresh water, was so careless to let a huge frog (not perceiving it) slip out of his pail. The frog lay concealed till I was put into my boat, but then seeing a resting place, climbed up, and made it lean so much on one side, that I was forced to balance it with all my weight on the other, to prevent overturning. When the frog was got in, it hopped at once half the length of the boat, and then over my head, backwards and forwards, daubing my face and clothes with its odious slime. The largeness of its features made it appear the most deformed animal that can be conceived. However, I desired Glumdalclitch to let me deal with it alone. I banged it a good while with one of my sculls, and at last forced it to leap out of the boat.

But the greatest danger I ever underwent in that kingdom was from a monkey, who belonged to one of the clerks of the kitchen. Glumdalclitch had locked me up in her closet, while she went somewhere upon business or a visit. The weather being very warm, the closet window was left open, as well as the windows and the door of my bigger box, in which I usually lived, because of its largeness and conveniency. As I sat quietly meditating at my table, I heard something bounce in at the closet window, and skip about from one side to the other; whereat, although I were much alarmed, yet I ventured to look out, but not stirring from my seat; and then I saw this frolicsome animal, frisking and leaping up and down till at last he came to my box, which he seemed to view with great pleasure and curiosity, peeping in at the door and every window. I retreated to the farther corner of my room, or box, but the monkey, looking in at every side, put me into such a fright, that I wanted presence of mind to conceal my self under the bed, as I might easily have done. After some time spent in peeping, grinning, and chattering, he at last espied me, and reaching one of his paws in at the door, as a cat does when she plays with a mouse, although I often shifted place to avoid him, he at length seized the lappet of my coat (which being made of that country silk, was very thick and strong) and dragged me out. He took me up in his right forefoot, and held me as a nurse does a child she is going to suckle, just as I have seen the same sort of creature do with a kitten in Europe: and when I offered to struggle, he squeezed me so hard, that I thought it more prudent to submit. I have good reason to believe that he took me for a young one of his own species, by his often stroking my face very gently with his other paw. In these diversions he was interrupted by a noise at the closet door, as if some body were opening it; whereupon he suddenly leaped up to the window at which he had come in, and thence upon the leads and gutters, walking upon three legs, and holding me in the fourth, till he clambered up to a roof that was next to ours. I heard Glumdalclitch give a shriek at the moment he was carrying me out. The poor girl was almost distracted: that quarter of the palace was all in an uproar; the servants ran for ladders; the monkey was seen by hundreds in the court sitting upon the ridge of a building, holding me like a baby in one of his fore-paws, and feeding me with the other, by cramming into my mouth some victuals he had squeezed out of the bag on one side of his chaps, and patting me when I would not eat; whereat many of the rabble below could not forbear laughing; neither do I think they justly ought to be blamed, for without question the sight was ridiculous enough to every body but my self. Some of the people threw up stones, hoping to drive the monkey down; but this was strictly forbidden, or else very probably my brains had been dashed out.

The ladders were now applied, and mounted by several men,

which the monkey observing, and finding himself almost encompassed, not being able to make speed enough with his three legs, let me drop on a ridge tile, and made his escape. Here I sat for some time five hundred yards from the ground, expecting every moment to be blown down by the wind, or to fall by my own giddiness, and come tumbling over and over from the ridge to the eaves. But an honest lad, one of my nurse's footmen, climbed up, and putting me into his breeches pocket, brought me down safe.

I was almost choked with the filthy stuff the monkey had crammed down my throat; but my dear little nurse picked it out of my mouth with a small needle, and then I fell a vomiting, which gave me great relief. Yet I was so weak and bruised in the sides with the squeezes given me by this odious animal, that I was forced to keep my bed a fortnight. The King, Queen and all the court sent every day to enquire after my health, and her Majesty made me several visits during my sickness. The monkey was killed, and an order made that no such animal should be kept about the palace.

When I attended the King after my recovery, to return him thanks for his favours, he was pleased to rally me a good deal upon this adventure. He asked me what my thoughts and speculations were while I lay in the monkey's paw, how I liked the victuals he gave me, his manner of feeding, and whether the fresh air on the roof had sharpened my stomach. He desired to know what I would have done upon such an occasion in my own country. I told his Majesty, that in Europe we had no monkeys, except such as were brought for curiosities from other places, and so small, that I could deal with a dozen of them together, if they presumed to attack me. And as for that monstrous animal with whom I was so lately engaged (it was indeed as large as an elephant), if my fears had suffered me to think so far as to make use of my hanger (looking fiercely and clapping my hand upon the hilt as I spoke) when he poked his paw into my chamber, perhaps I should have given him such a wound as would have made him glad to withdraw it with more haste than he put it in. This I delivered in a firm tone, like a person who was jealous lest his courage should be called in question. However, my speech produced nothing else besides a loud laughter, which all the respect due to his Majesty from those about him could not make them contain. This made me reflect how vain an attempt it is for a man to endeavour doing himself honour among those who are out of all degree of equality or comparison with him. And yet I have seen the moral of my own behaviour very frequent in England since my return, where a little contemptible varlet, without the least title to birth, person, wit, or common sense, shall presume to look with importance, and put himself upon a foot with the greatest persons of the kingdom.

I was every day furnishing the court with some ridiculous story; and Glumdalclitch, although she loved me to excess, yet was arch enough to inform the Queen whenever I committed any folly that she thought would be diverting to her Majesty. The girl, who had been out of order, was carried by her governess to take the air about an hour's distance, or thirty miles from town. They alighted out of the coach near a small footpath in a field, and Glumdalclitch setting down my travelling box, I went out of it to walk. There was a cow-dung in the path, and I must needs try my activity by attempting to leap over it. I took a run, but unfortunately jumped short, and found my self just in the middle up to my knees. I waded through with some difficulty, and one of the footmen wiped me as clean as he could with his handkerchief; for I was filthily bemired, and my nurse confined me to my box till we returned home; where the Queen was soon informed of what had passed, and the footmen spread it about the court, so that all the mirth, for some days, was at my expense.

CHAPTER VI.

Several contrivances of the author to please the King and Queen. He shows his skill in music. The King enquires into the state of Europe, which the author relates to him. The King's observations thereon.

I used to attend the King's levee once or twice a week, and had often seen him under the barber's hand, which indeed was at first very terrible to behold. For the razor was almost twice as long as an ordinary scythe. His Majesty according to the custom of the country was only shaved twice a week. I once prevailed on the barber to give me some of the suds or lather, out of which I picked forty or fifty of the strongest stumps of hair. I then took a piece of fine wood, and cut it like the back of a comb, making several holes in it at equal distance with as small a needle as I could get from Glumdalclitch. I fixed in the stumps so artificially, scraping and sloping them with my knife towards the points, that I made a very tolerable comb; which was a seasonable supply, my own being so much broken in the teeth, that it was almost useless: neither did I know any artist in that country so nice and exact, as would undertake to make me another.

And this puts me in mind of an amusement wherein I spent many of my leisure hours. I desired the Queen's woman to save for me the combings of her Majesty's hair, whereof in time I got a good quantity, and consulting with my friend the cabinet-maker, who had received general orders to do little jobs for me, I directed him to make two chair-frames, no larger than those I had in my box, and then to bore little holes with a fine awl round those parts where I designed the backs and seats; through these holes I wove the strongest hairs I could pick out, just after the manner of cane-chairs in England. When they were finished, I made a present of them to her Majesty, who kept them in her cabinet, and used to show them for curiosities, as indeed they were the wonder of every one who beheld them. The Queen would have had me sit upon one of these chairs, but I absolutely refused to obey her, protesting I would rather die a thousand deaths than place a dishonourable part of my body on those precious hairs that once adorned her Majesty's head. Of these hairs (as I had always a mechanical genius) I likewise made a neat little purse about five foot long, with her Majesty's name deciphered in gold letters, which I gave to Glumdalclitch, by the Queen's consent. To say the truth, it was more for show than use, being not of strength to bear the weight of the larger coins, and therefore she kept nothing in it, but some little toys that girls are fond of.

The King, who delighted in music, had frequent concerts at court, to which I was sometimes carried, and set in my box on a table to hear them: but the noise was so great, that I could hardly distinguish the tunes. I am confident that all the drums and trumpets of a royal army, beating and sounding together just at your ears, could not equal it. My practice was to have my box removed from the places where the performers sat, as far as I could, then to shut the doors and windows of it, and draw the window curtains; after which I found their music not disagreeable.

I had learned in my youth to play a little upon the spinet. Glumdalclitch kept one in her chamber, and a master attended twice a week to teach her: I call it a spinet, because it somewhat resembled that instrument, and was played upon in the same manner. A fancy came into my head that I would entertain the King and Queen with an English tune upon this instrument. But this appeared extremely difficult: for the spinet was near sixty foot long, each key being almost a foot wide, so that, with my arms extended, I could not reach to above five keys, and to press them down required a good smart stroke with my fist, which would be too great a labour, and to no purpose. The method I contrived was this. I prepared two round sticks about the bigness of common cudgels; they were thicker at one end than the other, and I covered the thicker ends with a piece of a mouse's skin, that by rapping on them I might neither damage the tops of the keys, nor interrupt the sound. Before the spinet a bench was placed about four foot below the keys, and I was put upon the bench. I ran sideling upon it that way and this, as fast as I could, banging the proper keys with my two sticks, and made a shift to play a jig to the great satisfaction of both their Majesties: but it was the most violent exercise I ever underwent, and yet I could not strike above sixteen keys, nor, consequently, play the bass and treble together, as other artists do; which was a great disadvantage to my performance.

The King, who, as I before observed, was a prince of excellent understanding, would frequently order that I should be brought in my box, and set upon the table in his closet. He would then command me to bring one of my chairs out of the box, and sit down within three yards distance upon the top of the cabinet, which brought me almost to a level with his face. In this manner I had several conversations with him. I one day took the freedom to tell his Majesty, that the contempt he discovered towards Europe, and the rest of the world, did not seem answerable to those excellent qualities of mind he was master of. That reason did not extend it self with the bulk of the body: on the contrary, we observed in our country that the tallest persons were usually least provided with it. That among other animals, bees and ants had the reputation of more industry, art and sagacity than many of the larger kinds. And that, as inconsiderable as he took me to be, I hoped I might live to do his Majesty some signal service. The King heard me with attention, and began to conceive a much better opinion of me than he had ever before. He desired I would give him as exact an account of the government of England as I possibly could; because, as fond as princes commonly are of their own customs (for so he conjectured of other monarchs by my former discourses), he should be glad to hear of any thing that might deserve imitation.

Imagine with thy self, courteous reader, how often I then wished for the tongue of Demosthenes or Cicero, that might have enabled me to celebrate the praise of my own dear native country in a style equal to its merits and felicity.

I began my discourse by informing his Majesty that our dominions consisted of two islands, which composed three mighty kingdoms under one sovereign, besides our plantations in America. I dwelt long upon the fertility of our soil, and the temperature of our climate. I then spoke at large upon the constitution of an English parliament, partly made up of an illustrious body called the House of Peers, persons of the noblest blood, and of the most ancient and ample patrimonies. I described that extraordinary care always taken of their education in arts and arms, to qualify them for being counsellors born to the king and kingdom, to have a share in the legislature, to be members of the highest court of judicature from whence there could be no appeal; and to be champions always ready for the defence of their prince and country by their valour, conduct and fidelity. That these were the ornament and bulwark of the kingdom, worthy followers of their most renowned ancestors, whose honour had been the reward of their virtue, from which their posterity were never once known to degenerate. To these were joined several holy persons, as part of that assembly, under the title of bishops, whose peculiar business it is to take care of religion, and of those who instruct the people therein. These were searched and sought out through the whole nation, by the prince and wisest counsellors, among such of the priesthood as were most deservedly distinguished by the sanctity of their lives, and the depth of their erudition; who were indeed the spiritual fathers of the clergy and the people.

That the other part of the parliament consisted of an assembly called the House of Commons, who were all principal gentlemen, freely picked and culled out by the people themselves, for their great abilities, and love of their country, to represent the wisdom of the whole nation. And these two bodies make up the most august assembly in Europe, to whom, in conjunction with the prince, the whole legislature is committed.

I then descended to the courts of justice, over which the judges, those venerable sages and interpreters of the law, presided, for determining the disputed rights and properties of men, as well as for the punishment of vice, and protection of innocence. I mentioned the prudent management of our treasury, the valour and achievements of our forces by sea and land. I computed the number of our people, by reckoning how many millions there might be of each religious sect, or political party among us. I did not omit even our sports and pastimes, or any other particular which I thought might redound to the honour of my country. And I finished all with a brief historical account of affairs and events in England for about an hundred years past. This conversation was not ended under five audiences, each of several hours, and the King heard the whole with great attention, frequently taking notes of what I spoke, as well as memorandums of what questions he intended to ask me.

When I had put an end to these long discourses, his Majesty in a sixth audience, consulting his notes, proposed many doubts, queries, and objections, upon every article. He asked, what methods were used to cultivate the minds and bodies of our young nobility, and in what kind of business they commonly spent the first and teachable part of their lives. What course was taken to supply that assembly when any noble family became extinct. What qualifications were necessary in those who are to be created new lords: whether the humour of the prince, a sum of money to a court-lady, or a prime minister, or a design of strengthening a party opposite to the public interest, ever happened to be motives in those advancements. What share of knowledge these lords had in the laws of their country, and how they came by it, so as to enable them to decide the properties of their fellow-subjects in the last resort. Whether they were always so free from avarice, partialities, or want, that a bribe, or some other sinister view, could have no place among them. Whether those holy lords I spoke of were constantly promoted to that rank upon account of their knowledge in religious matters, and the sanctity of their lives; had never been compliers with the times while they were common priests, or slavish prostitute chaplains to some nobleman, whose opinions they continued servilely to follow after they were admitted into that assembly.

He then desired to know what arts were practised in electing those whom I called commoners. Whether a stranger with a strong purse might not influence the vulgar voters to choose him before their own landlords, or the most considerable gentleman in the neighbourhood. How it came to pass, that people were so violently bent upon getting into this assembly, which I allowed to be a great trouble and expense, often to the ruin of their families, without any salary or pension: because this appeared such an exalted strain of virtue and public spirit, that his Majesty seemed to doubt it might possibly not be always sincere: and he desired to know whether such zealous gentlemen could have any views of refunding themselves for the charges and trouble they were at, by sacrificing the public good to the designs of a weak and vicious prince in conjunction with a corrupted ministry. He multiplied his questions, and sifted me thoroughly upon every part of this head, proposing numberless enquiries and objections, which I think it not prudent or convenient to repeat.

Upon what I said in relation to our courts of justice, his Majesty desired to be satisfied in several points: and this I was the better able to do, having been formerly almost ruined by a long suit in chancery, which was decreed for me with costs. He asked, what time was usually spent in determining between right and wrong, and what degree of expense. Whether advocates and orators had liberty to plead in causes manifestly known to be unjust, vexatious, or oppressive. Whether party in religion or politics were observed to be of any weight in the scale of justice. Whether those pleading orators were persons educated in the general knowledge of equity, or only in provincial, national, and other local customs. Whether they or their judges had any part in penning those laws which they assumed the liberty of interpreting and glossing upon at their pleasure. Whether they had ever at different times pleaded for and against the same cause, and cited precedents to prove contrary opinions. Whether they were a rich or a poor corporation. Whether they received any pecuniary reward for pleading or delivering their opinions. And particularly whether they were ever admitted as members in the lower senate.

He fell next upon the management of our treasury; and said, he thought my memory had failed me, because I computed our taxes at about five or six millions a year, and when I came to mention the issues, he found they sometimes amounted to more than double; for the notes he had taken were very particular in this point, because he hoped, as he told me, that the knowledge of our conduct might be useful to him, and he could not be deceived in his calculations. But, if what I told him were true, he was still at a loss how a kingdom could run out of its estate like a private person. He asked me, who were our creditors; and where we found money to pay them. He wondered to hear me talk of such chargeable and extensive wars; that certainly we must be a quarrelsome people, or live among very bad neighbours, and that our generals must needs be richer than our kings. He asked what business we had out of our own islands, unless upon the score of trade or treaty, or to defend the coasts with our fleet. Above all, he was amazed to hear me talk of a mercenary standing army in the midst of peace, and among a free people. He said if we were governed by our own consent in the persons of our representatives, he could not imagine of whom we were afraid, or against whom we were to fight, and would hear my opinion, whether a private man's house might not better be defended by himself, his children, and family, than by a half a dozen rascals picked up at a venture in the streets, for small wages, who might get an hundred times more by cutting their throats.

He laughed at my odd kind of arithmetic (as he was pleased to call it) in reckoning the numbers of our people by a computation drawn from the several sects among us in religion and politics. He said, he knew no reason, why those who entertain opinions prejudicial to the public should be obliged to change, or should not be obliged to conceal them. And as it was tyranny in any government to require the first, so it was weakness not to enforce the second: for a man may be allowed to keep poisons in his closets, but not to vend them about as cordials.

He observed, that among the diversions of our nobility and gentry I had mentioned gaming. He desired to know at what age this entertainment was usually taken up, and when it was laid down. How much of their time it employed; whether it ever went so high as to affect their fortunes. Whether mean vicious people by their dexterity in that art might not arrive at great riches, and sometimes keep our very nobles in dependence, as well as habituate them to vile companions, wholly take them from the improvement of their minds, and force them, by the losses they received, to learn and practice that infamous dexterity upon others.

He was perfectly astonished with the historical account I gave him of our affairs during the last century, protesting it was only an heap of conspiracies, rebellions, murders, massacres, revolutions, banishments, the very worst effects that avarice, faction, hypocrisy, perfidiousness, cruelty, rage, madness, hatred, envy, lust, malice, and ambition could produce.

His Majesty in another audience was at the pains to recapitulate the sum of all I had spoken, compared the questions he made with the answers I had given; then taking me into his hands, and stroking me gently, delivered himself in these words, which I shall never forget, nor the manner he spoke them in: My little friend Grildrig, you have made a most admirable panegyric upon your country. You have clearly proved that ignorance, idleness and vice are the proper ingredients for qualifying a legislator. That laws are best explained, interpreted, and applied by those whose interest and abilities lie in perverting, confounding, and eluding them. I observe among you some lines of an institution, which in its original might have been tolerable, but these half erased, and the rest wholly blurred and blotted by corruptions. It doth not appear from all you have said, how any one perfection is required towards the procurement of any one station among

you, much less that men are ennobled on account of their virtue,
that priests are advanced for their piety or learning, soldiers for
their conduct or valour, judges for their integrity, senators for
the love of their country, or counsellors for their wisdom. As
for yourself, continued the King, who have spent the greatest
part of your life in travelling, I am well disposed to hope you
may hitherto have escaped many vices of your country. But, by
what I have gathered from your own relation, and the answers I
have with much pains wringed and extorted from you, I cannot
but conclude the bulk of your natives to be the most pernicious
race of little odious vermin that nature ever suffered to crawl
upon the surface of the earth.

CHAPTER VII.

*The author's love of his country. He makes a proposal of much ad-
vantage to the King, which is rejected. The King's great ignorance
in politics. The learning of that country very imperfect and confined. Their laws, and military affairs, and parties in the state.*

Nothing but an extreme love of truth could have hindered me
from concealing this part of my story. It was in vain to discover
my resentments, which were always turned into ridicule; and I
was forced to rest with patience while my noble and most
beloved country was so injuriously treated. I am heartily sorry
as any of my readers can possibly be, that such an occasion was
given: but this prince happened to be so curious and inquisitive
upon every particular, that it could not consist either with gratitude or good manners to refuse giving him what satisfaction I
was able. Yet thus much I may be allowed to say in my own
vindication, that I artfully eluded many of his questions, and
gave to every point a more favourable turn by many degrees
than the strictness of truth would allow. For I have always
borne that laudable partiality to my own country, which Dionysius Halicarnassensis with so much justice recommends to an
historian. I would hide the frailties and deformities of my political mother, and place her virtues and beauties in the most advantageous light. This was my sincere endeavour in those many
discourses I had with that mighty monarch, although it unfortunately failed of success.

But great allowances should be given to a king who lives
wholly secluded from the rest of the world, and must therefore
be altogether unacquainted with the manners and customs that

most prevail in other nations: the want of which knowledge will ever produce many prejudices, and a certain narrowness of thinking, from which we and the politer countries of Europe are wholly exempted. And it would be hard indeed, if so remote a prince's notions of virtue and vice were to be offered as a standard for all mankind.

To confirm what I have now said, and further to show the miserable effects of a confined education, I shall here insert a passage which will hardly obtain belief. In hopes to ingratiate my self farther into his Majesty's favour, I told him of an invention discovered between three and four hundred years ago, to make a certain powder, into an heap of which the smallest spark of fire falling, would kindle the whole in a moment, although it were as big as a mountain, and make it all fly up in the air together, with a noise and agitation greater than thunder. That a proper quantity of this powder rammed into an hollow tube of brass or iron, according to its bigness, would drive a ball of iron or lead with such violence and speed as nothing was able to sustain its force. That the largest balls, thus discharged, would not only destroy whole ranks of an army at once, but batter the strongest walls to the ground, sink down ships, with a thousand men in each, to the bottom of the sea; and when linked together by a chain, would cut through masts and rigging, divide hundreds of bodies in the middle, and lay all waste before them. That we often put this powder into large hollow balls of iron, and discharged them by an engine into some city we were besieging, which would rip up the pavement, tear the houses to pieces, burst and throw splinters on every side, dashing out the brains of all who came near. That I knew the ingredients very well, which were cheap, and common; I understood the manner of compounding them, and could direct his workmen how to make those tubes of a size proportionable to all other things in his Majesty's kingdom, and the largest need not be above two hundred foot long; twenty or thirty of which tubes, charged with the proper quantity of powder and balls, would batter down the walls of the strongest town in his dominions in a few hours, or destroy the whole metropolis, if ever it should pretend to dispute his absolute commands. This I humbly offered to his Majesty as a small tribute of acknowledgment in return of so many marks that I had received of his royal favour and protection.

The King was struck with horror at the description I had given of those terrible engines, and the proposal I had made. He was amazed how so impotent and groveling an insect as I (these were his expressions) could entertain such inhuman ideas, and in so familiar a manner as to appear wholly unmoved at all the scenes of blood and desolation, which I had painted as the common effects of those destructive machines, whereof he said, some evil genius, enemy to mankind, must have been the first contriver. As for himself, he protested, that although few things delighted him so much as new discoveries in art or in nature, yet he would rather lose half his kingdom than be privy to such a secret, which he commanded me, as I valued my life, never to mention any more.

A strange effect of narrow principles and short views! that a prince possessed of every quality which procures veneration, love, and esteem; of strong parts, great wisdom and profound learning, endued with admirable talents for government, and almost adored by his subjects, should from a nice unnecessary scruple, whereof in Europe we can have no conception, let slip an opportunity put into his hands, that would have made him absolute master of the lives, the liberties, and the fortunes of his people. Neither do I say this with the least intention to detract from the many virtues of that excellent king, whose character I am sensible will on this account be very much lessened in the opinion of an English reader: but I take this defect among them to have risen from their ignorance, by not having hitherto reduced politics into a science, as the more acute wits of Europe have done. For I remember very well, in a discourse one day with the King, when I happened to say there were several thousand books among us written upon the art of government, it gave him (directly contrary to my intention) a very mean opinion of our understandings. He professed both to abominate and despise all mystery, refinement, and intrigue, either in a prince or a minister. He could not tell what I meant by secrets of state, where an enemy or some rival nation were not in the case. He confined the knowledge of governing within very narrow bounds; to common sense and reason, to justice and lenity, to the speedy determination of civil and criminal causes; with some other obvious topics which are not worth considering. And he gave it for his opinion, that whoever could make two ears of corn, or two blades of grass to grow upon a spot of ground where only one grew before, would deserve better of mankind, and do more essential service to his country, than the whole race of politicians put together.

The learning of this people is very defective, consisting only in morality, history, poetry, and mathematics, wherein they must be allowed to excel. But the last of these is wholly applied to what may be useful in life, to the improvement of agriculture and all mechanical arts; so that among us it would be little esteemed. And as to ideas, entities, abstractions and transcendentals, I could never drive the least conception into their heads.

No law of that country must exceed in words the number of letters in their alphabet, which consists only of two and twenty. But indeed, few of them extend even to that length. They are expressed in the most plain and simple terms, wherein those people are not mercurial enough to discover above one interpretation. And to write a comment upon any law is a capital crime. As to the decision of civil causes, or proceedings against criminals, their precedents are so few, that they have little reason to boast of any extraordinary skill in either.

They have had the art of printing, as well as the Chinese, time out of mind. But their libraries are not very large; for that of the King's, which is reckoned the largest, doth not amount to above a thousand volumes, placed in a gallery of twelve hundred foot long, from whence I had liberty to borrow what books I pleased. The Queen's joiner had contrived in one of Glumdalclitch's rooms a kind of wooden machine five and twenty foot high, formed like a standing ladder; the steps were each fifty foot long. It was indeed a moveable pair of stairs, the lowest end placed at ten foot distance from the wall of the chamber. The book I had a mind to read was put up leaning against the wall. I first mounted to the upper step of the ladder, and turning my face towards the book, began at the top of the page, and so walking to the right and left about eight or ten paces, according to the length of the lines, till I had gotten a little below the level of my eyes, and then descending gradually till I came to the bottom: after which I mounted again, and began the other page in the same manner, and so turned over the leaf, which I could easily do with both my hands, for it was as thick and stiff as a pasteboard, and in the largest folios not above eighteen or twenty foot long.

Their style is clear, masculine, and smooth, but not florid, for they avoid nothing more than multiplying unnecessary words, or using various expressions. I have perused many of their books, especially those in history and morality. Among the latter I was much diverted with a little old treatise, which always lay in Glumdalclitch's bedchamber, and belonged to her governess, a grave elderly gentlewoman, who dealt in writings of morality and devotion. The book treats of the weakness of human kind, and is in little esteem except among women and the vulgar. However, I was curious to see what an author of that country could say upon such a subject. This writer went through all the usual topics of European moralists, showing how diminutive, contemptible, and helpless an animal was man in his own nature; how unable to defend himself from the inclemencies of the air, or the fury of wild beasts. How much he was excelled by one creature in strength, by another in speed, by a third in foresight, by a fourth in industry. He added, that nature was degenerated in these latter declining ages of the world, and could now produce only small abortive births in comparison of those in ancient times. He said it was very reasonable to think, not only that the species of men were originally much larger, but also that there must have been giants in former ages, which, as it is asserted by history and tradition, so it hath been confirmed by huge bones and skulls casually dug up in several parts of the kingdom, far exceeding the common dwindled race of man in our days. He argued, that the very laws of nature absolutely required we should have been made, in the beginning, of a size more large and robust, not so liable to destruction from every little accident of a tile falling from an house, or a stone cast from the hand of a boy, or of being drowned in a little brook. From this way of reasoning the author drew several moral applications useful in the conduct of life, but needless here to repeat. For my own part, I could not avoid reflecting how universally this talent was spread of drawing lectures in morality, or indeed rather matter of discontent and repining, from the quarrels we raise with nature. And, I believe, upon a strict enquiry those quarrels might be shown as ill-grounded among us as they are among that people.

As to their military affairs, they boast that the King's army consists of an hundred and seventy-six thousand foot, and thirty-two thousand horse, if that may be called an army which is made up of tradesmen in the several cities, and farmers in the country, whose commanders are only the nobility and gentry without pay or reward. They are indeed perfect enough in their exercises, and under very good discipline, wherein I saw no great merit; for how should it be otherwise, where every farmer is under the command of his own landlord, and every citizen under that of the principal men in his own city, chosen after the manner of Venice by ballot?

I have often seen the militia of Lorbrulgrud drawn out to exercise in a great field near the city, of twenty miles square. They were in all not above twenty-five thousand foot, and six thousand horse; but it was impossible for me to compute their number, considering the space of ground they took up. A cavalier mounted on a large steed might be about ninety foot high. I have seen this whole body of horse upon the word of command draw their swords at once, and brandish them in the air. Imagination can figure nothing so grand, so surprising and so astonishing. It looked as if ten thousand flashes of lightning were darting at the same time from every quarter of the sky.

I was curious to know how this prince, to whose dominions there is no access from any other country, came to think of armies, or to teach his people the practice of military discipline. But I was soon informed, both by conversation, and reading their histories. For in the course of many ages they have been troubled with the same disease to which the whole race of mankind is subject; the nobility often contending for power, the people for liberty, and the King for absolute dominion. All which, however happily tempered by the laws of that kingdom, have been sometimes violated by each of the three parties, and have more than once occasioned civil wars, the last whereof was happily put an end to by this prince's grandfather in a general composition; and the militia then settled with common consent hath been ever since kept in the strictest duty.

CHAPTER VIII.

The King and Queen make a progress to the frontiers. The author attends them. The manner in which he leaves the country very particularly related. He returns to England.

I had always a strong impulse that I should sometime recover my liberty, although it was impossible to conjecture by what means, or to form any project with the least hope of succeeding. The ship in which I sailed was the first ever known to be driven within sight of that coast, and the King had given strict orders, that if at any time another appeared, it should be taken ashore, and with all its crew and passengers brought in a tumbril to Lorbrulgrud. He was strongly bent to get me a woman of my own size, by whom I might propagate the breed: but I think I should rather have died than undergone the disgrace of leaving a posterity to be kept in cages like tame canary birds, and perhaps in time sold about the kingdom to persons of quality for curiosities. I was indeed treated with much kindness; I was the favourite of a great king and queen, and the delight of the whole court, but it was upon such a foot as ill became the dignity of human kind. I could never forget those domestic pledges I had left behind me. I wanted to be among people with whom I could converse upon even terms, and walk about the streets and fields without fear of being trod to death like a frog or young puppy. But my deliverance came sooner than I expected, and in a manner not very common: the whole story and circumstances of which I shall faithfully relate.

I had now been two years in this country; and about the beginning of the third, Glumdalclitch and I attended the King and Queen in progress to the south coast of the kingdom. I was carried as usual in my travelling-box, which, as I have already described, was a very convenient closet of twelve foot wide. I had ordered a hammock to be fixed by silken ropes from the four corners at the top, to break the jolts, when a servant carried me before him on horseback, as I sometimes desired, and would often sleep in my hammock while we were upon the road. On the roof of my closet, just over the middle of the hammock, I ordered the joiner to cut out a hole of a foot square to give me air in hot weather as I slept, which hole I shut at pleasure with a board that drew backwards and forwards through a groove.

When we came to our journey's end, the King thought proper to pass a few days at a palace he hath near Flanflasnic, a city within eighteen English miles of the seaside. Glumdalclitch and I were much fatigued; I had gotten a small cold, but the poor girl was so ill as to be confined to her chamber. I longed to see the ocean, which must be the only scene of my escape, if ever it should happen. I pretended to be worse than I really was, and desired leave to take the fresh air of the sea, with a page whom I was very fond of, and who had sometimes been trusted with me. I shall never forget with what unwillingness Glumdalclitch consented, nor the strict charge she gave the page to be careful of me, bursting at the same time into a flood of tears, as if she had some foreboding of what was to happen. The boy took me out in my box about half an hour's walk from the palace towards the rocks on the seashore. I ordered him to set me down, and lifting up one of my sashes, cast many a wistful melancholy look towards the sea. I found my self not very well, and told the page that I had a mind to take a nap in my hammock, which I hoped would do me good. I got in, and the boy shut the window close down to keep out the cold. I soon fell asleep, and all I can conjecture is, that while I slept, the page, thinking no danger could happen, went among the rocks to look for birds' eggs, having before observed him from my window searching about, and picking up one or two in the clefts. Be that as it will, I found my self suddenly awaked with a violent pull upon the ring which was fastened at the top of my box for the conven-

iency of carriage. I felt the box raised very high in the air, and
then borne forward with prodigious speed. The first jolt had like
to have shaken me out of my hammock, but afterwards the
motion was easy enough. I called out several times as loud as I
could raise my voice, but all to no purpose. I looked towards my
windows, and could see nothing but the clouds and sky. I heard
a noise just over my head like the clapping of wings, and then
began to perceive the woful condition I was in; that some eagle
had got the ring of my box in his beak, with an intent to let it fall
on a rock like a tortoise in a shell, and then pick out my body
and devour it. For the sagacity and smell of this bird enable him
to discover his quarry at a great distance, although better concealed than I could be within a two-inch board.

In a little time I observed the noise and flutter of wings to
encrease very fast, and my box was tossed up and down like a
signpost in a windy day. I heard several bangs or buffets, as I
thought, given to the eagle (for such I am certain it must have
been that held the ring of my box in his beak) and then all on a
sudden felt my self falling perpendicularly down for above a
minute, but with such incredible swiftness that I almost lost my
breath. My fall was stopped by a terrible squash, that sounded
louder to my ears than the cataract of Niagara; after which I was
quite in the dark for another minute, and then my box began to
rise so high that I could see light from the tops of my windows.
I now perceived that I was fallen into the sea. My box, by the
weight of my body, the goods that were in, and the broad plates
of iron fixed for strength at the four corners of the top and bottom, floated about five foot deep in water. I did then, and do
now suppose that the eagle which flew away with my box was
pursued by two or three others, and forced to let me drop while
he was defending himself against the rest, who hoped to share
in the prey. The plates of iron fastened at the bottom of the box
(for those were the strongest) preserved the balance while it fell,
and hindered it from being broken on the surface of the water.
Every joint of it was well grooved, and the door did not move
on hinges, but up and down like a sash, which kept my closet so
tight that very little water came in. I got with much difficulty
out of my hammock, having first ventured to draw back the
slip-board on the roof already mentioned, contrived on purpose
to let in air, for want of which I found my self almost stifled.

How often did I then wish my self with my dear Glumdalclitch, from whom one single hour had so far divided me! And
I may say with truth, that in the midst of my own misfortune I
could not forbear lamenting my poor nurse, the grief she would

suffer for my loss, the displeasure of the Queen, and the ruin of her fortune. Perhaps many travellers have not been under greater difficulties and distress than I was at this juncture, expecting every moment to see my box dashed in pieces, or at least overset by the first violent blast, or a rising wave. A breach in one single pane of glass would have been immediate death: nor could any thing have preserved the windows but the strong lattice wires placed on the outside against accidents in travelling. I saw the water ooze in at several crannies, although the leaks were not considerable, and I endeavoured to stop them as well as I could. I was not able to lift up the roof of my closet, which otherwise I certainly should have done, and sat on the top of it, where I might at least preserve my self from being shut up, as I may call it, in the hold. Or, if I escaped these dangers for a day or two, what could I expect but a miserable death of cold and hunger! I was four hours under these circumstances, expecting and indeed wishing every moment to be my last.

I have already told the reader, that there were two strong staples fixed upon the side of my box which had no window, and into which the servant who used to carry me on horseback would put a leathern belt, and buckle it about his waist. Being in this disconsolate state, I heard or at least thought I heard some kind of grating noise on that side of my box where the staples were fixed, and soon after I began to fancy that the box was pulled or towed along in the sea; for I now and then felt a sort of tugging which made the waves rise near the tops of my windows, leaving me almost in the dark. This gave me some faint hopes of relief, although I was not able to imagine how it could be brought about. I ventured to unscrew one of my chairs, which were always fastened to the floor; and having made a hard shift to screw it down again directly under the slipping-board that I had lately opened, I mounted on the chair, and putting my mouth as near as I could to the hole, I called for help in a loud voice, and in all the languages I understood. I then fastened my handkerchief to a stick I usually carried, and thrusting it up the hole, waved it several times in the air, that if any boat or ship were near, the seamen might conjecture some unhappy mortal to be shut up in the box.

I found no effect from all I could do, but plainly perceived my closet to be moved along; and in the space of an hour, or better, that side of the box where the staples were, and had no window, struck against something that was hard. I apprehended it to be a rock, and found my self tossed more than ever. I plainly heard a noise upon the cover of my closet, like that of a cable, and the grating of it as it passed through the ring. I then found my self hoisted up by degrees at least three foot higher than I was before. Whereupon I again thrust up my stick and handkerchief, calling for help till I was almost hoarse. In return to which, I heard a great shout repeated three times, giving me such transports of joy as are not to be conceived but by those who feel them. I now heard a trampling over my head, and somebody calling through the hole with a loud voice in the English tongue, If there be any body below let them speak. I answered, I was an Englishman, drawn by ill fortune into the greatest calamity that ever any creature underwent, and begged, by all that was moving, to be delivered out of the dungeon I was in. The voice replied, I was safe, for my box was fastened to their ship; and the carpenter should immediately come, and saw an hole in the cover, large enough to pull me out. I answered, that was needless, and would take up too much time, for there was no more to be done, but let one of the crew put his finger into the ring, and take the box out of the sea into the ship, and so into the captain's cabin. Some of them upon hearing me talk so wildly thought I was mad; others laughed; for indeed it never came into my head that I was now got among people of my own stature and strength. The carpenter came, and in a few minutes sawed a passage about four foot square, then let down a small ladder, upon which I mounted, and from thence was taken into the ship in a very weak condition.

The sailors were all in amazement, and asked me a thousand questions, which I had no inclination to answer. I was equally confounded at the sight of so many pigmies, for such I took them to be, after having so long accustomed my eyes to the monstrous objects I had left. But the captain, Mr. Thomas Wilcocks, an honest worthy Shropshire man, observing I was ready to faint, took me into his cabin, gave me a cordial to comfort me, and made me turn in upon his own bed, advising me to take a little rest, of which I had great need. Before I went to sleep I gave him to understand that I had some valuable furniture in my box, too good to be lost; a fine hammock, an handsome field-bed, two chairs, a table and a cabinet: that my closet was hung on all sides, or rather quilted, with silk and cotton: that if he would let one of the crew bring my closet into his cabin, I would open it there before him, and show him my goods. The captain, hearing me utter these absurdities, concluded I was raving: however (I suppose to pacify me), he promised to give order as I desired, and going upon deck sent some of his men down into my closet, from whence (as I afterwards found) they drew up all my goods, and stripped off the quilting; but the chairs, cabinet and bedstead, being screwed to the floor, were much damaged by the ignorance of the seamen, who tore them up by force. Then they knocked off some of the boards for the use of the ship, and when they had got all they had a mind for, let the hulk drop into the sea, which, by reason of many breaches made in the bottom and sides, sunk to rights. And indeed I was glad not to have been a spectator of the havoc they made; because I am confident it would have sensibly touched me, by bringing former passages into my mind, which I had rather forget.

I slept some hours, but perpetually disturbed with dreams of the place I had left, and the dangers I had escaped. However, upon waking I found my self much recovered. It was now about eight o'clock at night, and the captain ordered supper immediately, thinking I had already fasted too long. He entertained me with great kindness, observing me not to look wildly, or talk inconsistently; and when we were left alone, desired I would give him a relation of my travels, and by what accident I came to be set adrift in that monstrous wooden chest. He said, that about twelve o'clock at noon, as he was looking through his glass, he spied it at a distance, and thought it was a sail, which he had a mind to make, being not much out of his course, in hopes of buying some biscuit, his own beginning to fall short. That upon coming nearer, and finding his error, he sent out his longboat to discover what I was; that his men came back in a fright, swearing they had seen a swimming house. That he laughed at their folly, and went himself in the boat, ordering his men to take a strong cable along with them. That the weather being calm, he rowed round me several times, observed my windows, and the wire lattices that defended them. That he discovered two staples upon one side, which was all of boards, without any passage for light. He then commanded his men to row up to that side, and fastening a cable to one of the staples, ordered his men to tow my chest (as he called it) towards the ship. When it was there, he gave directions to fasten another cable to the ring fixed in the cover, and to raise up my chest with pulleys, which all the sailors were not able to do above two or three foot. He said, they saw my stick and handkerchief thrust out of the hole, and concluded that some unhappy man must be shut up in the cavity. I asked whether he or the crew had seen any prodigious birds in the air about the time he first discovered me. To which he answered, that discoursing this matter with the sailors while I was asleep, one of them said he had observed three eagles flying towards the north, but remarked nothing of their being larger than the

usual size, which I suppose must be imputed to the great height
they were at: and he could not guess the reason of my question.
I then asked the captain how far he reckoned we might be from
land; he said, by the best computation he could make, we were
at least an hundred leagues. I assured him, that he must be mistaken by almost half, for I had not left the country from whence
I came above two hours before I dropped into the sea. Whereupon he began again to think that my brain was disturbed, of
which he gave me a hint, and advised me to go to bed in a cabin
he had provided. I assured him I was well refreshed with his
good entertainment and company, and as much in my senses as
ever I was in my life. He then grew serious, and desired to ask
me freely whether I were not troubled in mind by the consciousness of some enormous crime, for which I was punished at the
command of some prince, by exposing me in that chest, as great
criminals in other countries have been forced to sea in a leaky
vessel without provisions: for although he should be sorry to
have taken so ill a man into his ship, yet he would engage his
word to set me safe on shore in the first port where we arrived.
He added, that his suspicions were much increased by some very
absurd speeches I had delivered at first to the sailors, and afterwards to himself, in relation to my closet or chest, as well as by
my odd looks and behaviour while I was at supper.

I begged his patience to hear me tell my story, which I faithfully did from the last time I left England to the moment he first
discovered me. And, as truth always forceth its way into rational minds, so this honest worthy gentleman, who had some
tincture of learning, and very good sense, was immediately
convinced of my candor and veracity. But further to confirm
all I had said, I entreated him to give order that my cabinet should
be brought, of which I kept the key in my pocket (for he had
already informed me how the seamen disposed of my closet);
I opened it in his presence, and showed him the small collection
of rarities I made in the country from whence I had been so
strangely delivered. There was the comb I had contrived out of
the stumps of the King's beard, and another of the same materials, but fixed into a paring of her Majesty's thumb-nail, which
served for the back. There was a collection of needles and pins
from a foot to half a yard long. Four wasp-stings, like joiners'
tacks: some combings of the Queen's hair: a gold ring which one
day she made me a present of in a most obliging manner, taking
it from her little finger, and throwing it over my head like a
collar. I desired the captain would please to accept this ring in
return of his civilities, which he absolutely refused. I showed

him a corn that I had cut off with my own hand from a maid of honour's toe; it was about the bigness of a Kentish pippin, and grown so hard, that when I returned to England, I got it hollowed into a cup and set in silver. Lastly, I desired him to see the breeches I had then on, which were made of a mouse's skin.

I could force nothing on him but a footman's tooth, which I observed him to examine with great curiosity, and found he had a fancy for it. He received it with abundance of thanks, more than such a trifle could deserve. It was drawn by an unskilful surgeon in a mistake from one of Glumdalclitch's men, who was afflicted with the toothache, but it was as sound as any in his head. I got it cleaned, and put it into my cabinet. It was about a foot long, and four inches in diameter.

The captain was very well satisfied with this plain relation I had given him; and said, he hoped, when we returned to England I would oblige the world by putting it in paper, and making it public. My answer was, that I thought we were already over-stocked with books of travels: that nothing could now pass which was not extraordinary, wherein I doubted some authors less consulted truth than their own vanity or interest, or the diversion of ignorant readers. That my story could contain little besides common events, without those ornamental descriptions of strange plants, trees, birds, and other animals, or of the barbarous customs and idolatry of savage people, with which most writers abound. However, I thanked him for his good opinion, and promised to take the matter into my thoughts.

He said he wondered at one thing very much, which was to hear me speak so loud, asking me whether the King or Queen of that country were thick of hearing. I told him it was what I had been used to for above two years past, and that I admired as much at the voices of him and his men, who seemed to me only to whisper, and yet I could hear them well enough. But when I spoke in that country, it was like a man talking in the street to another looking out from the top of a steeple, unless when I was placed on a table, or held in any person's hand. I told him I had likewise observed another thing, that when I first got into the ship, and the sailors stood all about me, I thought they were the most little contemptible creatures I had ever be-held. For, indeed, while I was in that prince's country, I could never endure to look in a glass after my eyes had been accustomed to such prodigious objects, because the comparison gave me so despicable a conceit of my self. The captain said, that while we were at supper, he observed me to look at every thing with a sort of wonder, and that I often seemed hardly able to contain my laughter, which he knew not well how to take, but imputed it to some disorder in my brain. I answered, it was very true, and I wondered how I could forbear, when I saw his dishes of the size of a silver threepence, a leg of pork hardly a mouthful, a cup not so big as a nutshell: and so I went on, describing the rest of his household-stuff and provisions after the same manner. For although the Queen had ordered a little equipage of all things necessary for me while I was in her service, yet my ideas were wholly taken up with what I saw on every side of me, and I winked at my own littleness as people do at their own faults. The captain understood my raillery very well, and merrily replied with the old English proverb, that he doubted my eyes were bigger than my belly, for he did not observe my stomach so good, although I had fasted all day; and continuing in his mirth, protested he would have gladly given an hundred pounds to have seen my closet in the eagle's bill, and afterwards in its fall from so great an height into the sea; which would certainly have been a most astonishing object, worthy to have the description of it transmitted to future ages: and the comparison of Phaeton was so obvious, that he could not forbear applying it, although I did not much admire the conceit.

The captain, having been at Tonquin, was in his return to England driven northeastward to the latitude of 44 degrees, and of longitude 143. But meeting a trade wind two days after I came on board him, we sailed southward a long time, and coasting New Holland kept our course west-southwest, and then south-southwest till we doubled the Cape of Good Hope. Our voyage was very prosperous, but I shall not trouble the reader with a journal of it. Tht captain called in at one or two ports and sent in his longboat for provisions and fresh water, but I never went out of the ship till we came into the Downs, which was on the 3d day of June, 1706, about nine months after my escape. I offered to leave my goods in security for payment of my freight; but the captain protested he would not receive one farthing. We took kind leave of each other, and I made him promise he would come to see me at my house in Redriff. I hired a horse and guide for five shillings, which I borrowed of the captain.

As I was on the road, observing the littleness of the houses, the trees, the cattle and the people, I began to think my self in Lilliput. I was afraid of trampling on every traveller I met, and often called aloud to have them stand out of the way, so that I had like to have gotten one or two broken heads for my impertinence.

When I came to my own house, for which I was forced to

enquire, one of the servants opening the door, I bent down to go in (like a goose under a gate) for fear of striking my head. My wife ran out to embrace me, but I stooped lower than her knees, thinking she could otherwise never be able to reach my mouth. My daughter kneeled to ask me blessing, but I could not see her till she arose, having been so long used to stand with my head and eyes erect to above sixty foot; and then I went to take her up with one hand, by the waist. I looked down upon the servants and one or two friends who were in the house, as if they had been pigmies, and I a giant. I told my wife she had been too thrifty, for I found she had starved herself and her daughter to nothing. In short, I behaved my self so unaccountably, that they were all of the captain's opinion when he first saw me, and concluded I had lost my wits. This I mention as an instance of the great power of habit and prejudice.

In a little time I and my family and friends came to a right understanding: but my wife protested I should never go to sea any more; although my evil destiny so ordered that she had not power to hinder me, as the reader may know hereafter. In the mean time I here conclude the second part of my unfortunate voyages.

THE END of the SECOND PART.

Plate III. *Part* III.   *Page* 190.

Parts Unknown

LAND OF
St James Bay
Robbin I
IESSO
Salmon B
C Canal

C Patience
Straits of the Vries

Companys
Land
Stats I

Laputa

BALNIBARBI
Lagado

Dicovered. A.D 1701

Sea of Corea
Sando I
Teroul
Meaco
Jedo
Inwale
JAPON
Osaca
Ouanoo
Tonsa
Bungo I
Dimoris Straits
I Tanaxuma

Tou Pt
Red Pt
Bosho Pt
Barnevelts
Ongeluckig I
South I
Sialo
Glangurn
Maldoneda

LUGN-AGG
Waldrigdul

Clamrynig

I Deserta

Urat
Tunal

Glubdnubdnb

TRAVELS.

PART III.

A VOYAGE TO LAPUTA, BALNIBARBI, GLUBBDUBDRIB, LUGGNAGG, AND JAPAN.

CHAPTER I.

The author sets out on his third voyage. Is taken by pirates. The malice of a Dutchman. His arrival at an island. He is received into Laputa.

I had not been at home above ten days, when Captain William Robinson, a Cornish man, commander of the *Hope-well*, a stout ship of three hundred tons, came to my house. I had formerly been surgeon of another ship where he was master, and a fourth part owner, in a voyage to the Levant; he had always treated me more like a brother than an inferior officer, and hearing of my arrival made me a visit, as I apprehended, only out of friendship, for nothing passed more than what is usual after long absence. But repeating his visits often, expressing his joy to find me in good health, asking whether I were now settled for life, adding that he intended a voyage to the East Indies, in two months, at last plainly invited me, although with some apologies, to be surgeon of the ship; that I should have another surgeon under me besides our two mates; that my salary should be double to the usual pay; and that having experienced my knowledge in sea-affairs to be at least equal to his, he would enter into any engagement to follow my advice, as much as if I had share in the command.

He said so many other obliging things, and I knew him to be so honest a man, that I could not reject his proposal; the thirst I had of seeing the world, notwithstanding my past misfortunes, continuing as violent as ever. The only difficulty that remained was to persuade my wife, whose consent however I at last obtained, by the prospect of advantage she proposed to her children.

We set out the 5th day of August, 1706, and arrived at Fort St. George the 11th of April, 1707. We stayed there three weeks to refresh our crew, many of whom were sick. From thence we went to Tonquin, where the captain resolved to continue some time, because many of the goods he intended to buy were not ready, nor could he expect to be dispatched in several months. Therefore in hopes to defray some of the charges he must be at, he bought a sloop, loaded it with several sorts of goods, wherewith the Tonquinese usually trade to the neighbouring islands, and putting fourteen men on board, whereof three were of the country, he appointed me master of the sloop, and gave me power to traffic while he transacted his affairs at Tonquin.

We had not sailed above three days, when, a great storm arising, we were driven five days to the north-northeast, and then to the east, after which we had fair weather, but still with a pretty strong gale from the west. Upon the tenth day we were chased by two pirates, who soon overtook us; for my sloop was so deep loaden, that she sailed very slow, neither were we in a condition to defend our selves.

We were boarded about the same time by both the pirates, who entered furiously at the head of their men, but finding us all prostrate upon our faces (for so I gave order), they pinioned us with strong ropes, and setting a guard upon us, went to search the sloop.

I observed among them a Dutchman, who seemed to be of some authority, although he was not commander of either ship. He knew us by our countenances to be Englishmen, and jabbering to us in his own language, swore we should be tied back to back, and thrown into the sea. I spoke Dutch tolerably well; I told him who we were, and begged him in consideration of our being Christians and Protestants, of neighbouring countries, in strict alliance, that he would move the captains to take some pity on us. This inflamed his rage, he repeated his threatenings, and turning to his companions, spoke with great vehemence, in the Japanese language, as I suppose, often using the word *Christianos*.

The largest of the two pirate ships was commanded by a Japanese captain, who spoke a little Dutch, but very imperfectly. He came up to me, and after several questions, which I answered in great humility, he said we should not die. I made the captain a very low bow, and then turning to the Dutchman, said, I was sorry to find more mercy in a heathen, than in a brother Christian. But I had soon reason to repent those foolish words; for that malicious reprobate, having often endeavoured in vain to persuade both the captains that I might be thrown into the sea (which they would not yield to after the promise made me, that

I should not die), however prevailed so far as to have a punishment inflicted on me, worse in all human appearance than death it self. My men were sent by an equal division into both the pirate ships, and my sloop new manned. As to my self, it was determined that I should be set adrift in a small canoe, with paddles and a sail, and four days' provisions, which last the Japanese captain was so kind to double out of his own stores, and would permit no man to search me. I got down into the canoe, while the Dutchman, standing upon the deck, loaded me with all the curses and injurious terms his language could afford.

About an hour before we saw the pirates, I had taken an observation, and found we were in the latitude of 46 N. and of longitude 183. When I was at some distance from the pirates, I discovered by my pocket-glass several islands to the southeast. I set up my sail, the wind being fair, with a design to reach the nearest of those islands, which I made a shift to do in about three hours. It was all rocky; however I got many birds' eggs, and striking fire I kindled some heath and dry seaweed, by which I roasted my eggs. I eat no other supper, being resolved to spare my provisions as much as I could. I passed the night under the shelter of a rock, strowing some heath under me, and slept pretty well.

The next day I sailed to another island, and thence to a third and fourth, sometimes using my sail, and sometimes my paddles. But not to trouble the reader with a particular account of my distresses, let it suffice that on the 5th day I arrived at the last island in my sight, which lay south-southeast to the former.

This island was at a greater distance than I expected, and I did not reach it in less than five hours. I encompassed it almost round before I could find a convenient place to land in, which was a small creek, about three times the wideness of my canoe. I found the island to be all rocky, only a little intermingled with tufts of grass, and sweet-smelling herbs. I took out my small provisions, and after having refreshed myself, I secured the remainder in a cave, whereof there were great numbers. I gathered plenty of eggs upon the rocks, and got a quantity of dry seaweed, and parched grass, which I designed to kindle the next day, and roast my eggs as well as I could. (For I had about me my flint, steel, match, and burning-glass.) I lay all night in the cave where I had lodged my provisions. My bed was the same dry grass and seaweed which I intended for fuel. I slept very little, for the disquiets of my mind prevailed over my weariness, and kept me awake. I considered how impossible it was to preserve my life in so desolate a place, and how miserable my end must be. Yet I found my self so listless and desponding, that I had not the heart to rise, and before I could get spirits enough to creep out of my cave, the day was far advanced. I walked a while among the rocks; the sky was perfectly clear, and the sun so hot, that I was forced to turn my face from it: when all on a sudden it became obscured, as I thought, in a manner very different from what happens by the interposition of a cloud. I turned back, and perceived a vast opaque body between me and the sun, moving forwards towards the island: it seemed to be about two miles high, and hid the sun six or seven minutes, but I did not observe the air to be much colder, or the sky more darkened, than if I had stood under the shade of a mountain. As it approached nearer over the place where I was, it appeared to be a firm substance, the bottom flat, smooth, and shining very bright from the reflection of the sea below. I stood upon a height about two hundred yards from the shore, and saw this vast body descending almost to a parallel with me, at less than an English mile distance. I took out my pocket-perspective, and could plainly discover numbers of people moving up and down the sides of it, which appeared to be sloping, but what those people were doing I was not able to distinguish.

The natural love of life gave me some inward motions of joy, and I was ready to entertain a hope, that this adventure might some way or other help to deliver me from the desolate place and condition I was in. But at the same time the reader can hardly conceive my astonishment, to behold an island in the air, inhabited by men, who were able (as it should seem) to raise, or sink, or put it into a progressive motion, as they pleased. But not being at that time in a disposition to philosophize upon this phenomenon, I rather chose to observe what course the island would take, because it seemed for a while to stand still. Yet soon after it advanced nearer, and I could see the sides of it, encompassed with several gradations of galleries, and stairs, at certain intervals, to descend from one to the other. In the lowest gallery, I beheld some people fishing with long angling rods, and others looking on. I waved my cap (for my hat was long since worn out) and my handkerchief towards the island; and upon its nearer approach, I called and shouted with the utmost strength of my voice; and then looking circumspectly, I beheld a crowd gathered to that side which was most in my view. I found by their pointing towards me and to each other, that they plainly discovered me, although they made no return to my shouting. But I could see four or five men running in great haste up the stairs to the top of the island, who then disappeared. I happened rightly to conjecture, that these were sent for orders to some person in authority upon this occasion.

The number of people increased, and in less than half an hour the island was moved and raised in such a manner, that the lowest gallery appeared in a parallel of less than an hundred yards' distance from the height where I stood. I then put my self into the most supplicating postures, and spoke in the humblest accent, but received no answer. Those who stood nearest over-against me seemed to be persons of distinction, as I supposed by their habit. They conferred earnestly with each other, looking often upon me. At length one of them called out in a clear, polite, smooth dialect, not unlike in sound to the Italian; and therefore I returned an answer in that language, hoping at least that the cadence might be more agreeable to his ears. Although neither of us understood the other, yet my meaning was easily known, for the people saw the distress I was in.

They made signs for me to come down from the rock, and go towards the shore, which I accordingly did; and the flying island being raised to a convenient height, the verge directly over me, a chain was let down from the lowest gallery, with a seat fastened to the bottom, to which I fixed my self, and was drawn up by pulleys.

CHAPTER II.

The humours and dispositions of the Laputans described. An account of their learning. Of the King and his court. The author's reception there. The inhabitants subject to fears and disquietudes. An account of the women.

At my alighting I was surrounded by a crowd of people, but those who stood nearest seemed to be of better quality. They beheld me with all the marks and circumstances of wonder, neither indeed was I much in their debt, having never till then seen a race of mortals so singular in their shapes, habits, and countenances. Their heads were all reclined either to the right, or the left; one of their eyes turned inward, and the other directly up to the zenith. Their outward garments were adorned with the figures of suns, moons, and stars, interwoven with those of fiddles, flutes, harps, trumpets, guitars, harpsichords, and many more instruments of music, unknown to us in Europe. I observed here and there many in the habits of servants, with a blown bladder fastened like a flail to the end of a short stick,

which they carried in their hands. In each bladder was a small
quantity of dried pease or little pebbles (as I was afterwards
informed). With these bladders they now and then flapped the
mouths and ears of those who stood near them, of which practice I could not then conceive the meaning; it seems, the minds
of these people are so taken up with intense speculations, that
they neither can speak, nor attend to the discourses of others, without being roused by some external taction upon the organs of
speech and hearing; for which reason those persons who are able
to afford it always keep a flapper (the original is *climenole*) in
their family, as one of their domestics, nor ever walk abroad or
make visits without him. And the business of this officer is,
when two or more persons are in company, gently to strike with
his bladder the mouth of him who is to speak, and the right ear
of him or them to whom the speaker addresseth himself. This
flapper is likewise employed diligently to attend his master in
his walks, and upon occasion to give him a soft flap on his eyes,
because he is always so wrapped up in cogitation, that he is in
manifest danger of falling down every precipice, and bouncing
his head against every post, and in the streets, of jostling others
or being jostled himself into the kennel.

It was necessary to give the reader this information, without
which he would be at the same loss with me, to understand the
proceedings of these people, as they conducted me up the stairs,
to the top of the island, and from thence to the royal palace.
While we were ascending, they forgot several times what they
were about, and left me to my self, till their memories were again
roused by their flappers; for they appeared altogether unmoved
by the sight of my foreign habit and countenance, and by the
shouts of the vulgar, whose thoughts and minds were more
disengaged.

At last we entered the palace, and proceeded into the chamber
of presence, where I saw the King seated on his throne, attended
on each side by persons of prime quality. Before the throne was
a large table filled with globes and spheres, and mathematical
instruments of all kinds. His Majesty took not the least notice of
us, although our entrance was not without sufficient noise, by the
concourse of all persons belonging to the court. But he was then
deep in a problem, and we attended at least an hour before he
could solve it. There stood by him, on each side, a young page,
with flaps in their hands, and when they saw he was at leisure,
one of them gently struck his mouth, and the other his right ear,
at which he started like one awaked on the sudden, and looking
towards me, and the company I was in, recollected the occasion

of our coming, whereof he had been informed before. He spoke some words, whereupon immediately a young man with a flap came up to my side, and flapped me gently on the right ear; but I made signs as well as I could, that I had no occasion for such an instrument; which as I afterwards found gave his Majesty and the whole court a very mean opinion of my understanding. The King, as far as I could conjecture, asked me several questions, and I addressed my self to him in all the languages I had. When it was found that I could neither understand nor be understood, I was conducted by his order to an apartment in his palace (this prince being distinguished above all his predecessors for his hospitality to strangers), where two servants were appointed to attend me. My dinner was brought, and four persons of quality, whom I remembered to have seen very near the King's person, did me the honour to dine with me. We had two courses, of three dishes each. In the first course there was a shoulder of mutton, cut into an equilateral triangle, a piece of beef into a rhomboides, and a pudding into a cycloid. The second course was two ducks, trussed up into the form of fiddles; sausages and puddings resembling flutes and hautboys, and a breast of veal in the shape of a harp. The servants cut our bread into cones, cylinders, parallelograms, and several other mathematical figures.

While we were at dinner, I made bold to ask the names of several things in their language, and those noble persons, by the assistance of their flappers, delighted to give me answers, hoping to raise my admiration of their great abilities, if I could be brought to converse with them. I was soon able to call for bread and drink, or whatever else I wanted.

After dinner my company withdrew, and a person was sent to me by the King's order, attended by a flapper. He brought with him pen, ink, and paper, and three or four books, giving me to understand by signs, that he was sent to teach me the language. We sat together four hours, in which time I wrote down a great number of words in columns, with the translations over against them. I likewise made a shift to learn several short sentences. For my tutor would order one of my servants to fetch something, to turn about, to make a bow, to sit, or stand, or walk and the like. Then I took down the sentence in writing. He showed me also in one of his books the figures of the sun, moon, and stars, the zodiac, the tropics, and polar circles, together with the denominations of many figures of planes and solids. He gave me the names and descriptions of all the musical instruments, and the general terms of art in playing on each of them. After he had left me, I placed all my words with their interpretations in alphabetical order. And thus in a few days, by the help of a very faithful memory, I got some insight into their language.

The word which I interpret the *Flying* or *Floating Island* is in the original *Laputa*, whereof I could never learn the true etymology. *Lap* in the old obsolete language signifieth *high*, and *untuh* a *governor*, from which they say by corruption was derived *Laputa*, from *Lapuntuh*. But I do not approve of this derivation, which seems to be a little strained. I ventured to offer to the learned among them a conjecture of my own, that *Laputa* was *quasi Lap outed; Lap* signifying properly the dancing of the sunbeams in the sea, and *outed* a wing, which however I shall not obtrude, but submit to the judicious reader.

Those to whom the King had entrusted me, observing how ill I was clad, ordered a tailor to come next morning, and take my measure for a suit of clothes. This operator did his office after a different manner from those of his trade in Europe. He first took my altitude by a quadrant, and then, with rule and compasses, described the dimensions and outlines of my whole body, all which he entered upon paper, and in six days brought my clothes very ill made, and quite out of shape, by happening to mistake a figure in the calculation. But my comfort was, that I observed such accidents very frequent and little regarded.

During my confinement for want of clothes, and by an indisposition that held me some days longer, I much enlarged my dictionary; and when I went next to court, was able to understand many things the King spoke, and to return him some kind of answers. His Majesty had given orders that the island should move northeast and by east, to the vertical point over Lagado, the metropolis of the whole kingdom below upon the firm earth. It was about ninety leagues distant, and our voyage lasted four days and an half. I was not in the least sensible of the progressive motion made in the air by the island. On the second morning about eleven o'clock, the King himself in person, attended by his nobility, courtiers, and officers, having prepared all their musical instruments, played on them for three hours without intermission, so that I was quite stunned with the noise; neither could I possibly guess the meaning till my tutor informed me. He said that the people of their island had their ears adapted to hear the music of the spheres, which always played at certain periods, and the court was now prepared to bear their part in what ever instrument they most excelled.

In our journey towards Lagado, the capital city, his Majesty ordered that the island should stop over certain towns and villages, from whence he might receive the petitions of his subjects.

And to this purpose several packthreads were let down with small weights at the bottom. On these packthreads the people strung their petitions, which mounted up directly like the scraps of paper fastened by schoolboys at the end of the string that holds their kite. Sometimes we received wine and victuals from below, which were drawn up by pulleys.

The knowledge I had in mathematics gave me great assistance in acquiring their phraseology, which depended much upon that science and music; and in the latter I was not unskilled. Their ideas are perpetually conversant in lines and figures. If they would, for example, praise the beauty of a woman or any other animal, they describe it by rhombs, circles, parallelograms, ellipses, and other geometrical terms, or else by words of art drawn from music, needless here to repeat. I observed in the King's kitchen all sorts of mathematical and musical instruments, after the figures of which they cut up the joints that were served to his Majesty's table.

Their houses are very ill built, the walls bevil, without one right angle in any apartment, and this defect ariseth from the contempt they bear for practical geometry, which they despise as vulgar and mechanic, those instructions they give being too refined for the intellectuals of their workmen, which occasions perpetual mistakes. And although they are dextrous enough upon a piece of paper in the management of the rule, the pencil, and the divider, yet in the common actions and behaviour of life I have not seen a more clumsy, awkward, and unhandy people, nor so slow and perplexed in their conceptions upon all other subjects, except those of mathematics and music. They are very bad reasoners, and vehemently given to opposition, unless when they happen to be of the right opinion, which is seldom their case. Imagination, fancy, and invention, they are wholly strangers to, nor have any words in their language by which those ideas can be expressed; the whole compass of their thoughts and mind being shut up within the two forementioned sciences.

Most of them, and especially those who deal in the astronomical part, have great faith in judicial astrology, although they are ashamed to own it publicly. But what I chiefly admired, and thought altogether unaccountable, was the strong disposition I observed in them towards news and politics, perpetually enquiring into public affairs, giving their judgments in matters of state, and passionately disputing every inch of a party opinion. I have indeed observed the same disposition among most of the mathematicians I have known in Europe, although I could never discover the least analogy between the two sciences; unless those people suppose, that because the smallest circle hath as many degrees as the largest, therefore the regulation and management of the world require no more abilities than the handling and turning of a globe. But I rather take this quality to spring from a very common infirmity of human nature, inclining us to be more curious and conceited in matters where we have least concern, and for which we are least adapted either by study or nature.

These people are under continual disquietudes, never enjoying a minute's peace of mind; and their disturbances proceed from causes which very little affect the rest of mortals. Their apprehensions arise from several changes they dread in the celestial bodies. For instance; that the earth, by the continual approaches of the sun towards it, must in course of time be absorbed or swallowed up. That the face of the sun will by degrees be encrusted with its own effluvia, and give no more light to the world. That the earth very narrowly escaped a brush from the tail of the last comet, which would have infallibly reduced it to ashes; and that the next, which they have calculated for one and thirty years hence, will probably destroy us. For, if in its perihelion it should approach within a certain degree of the sun (as by their calculations they have reason to dread), it will conceive a degree of heat ten thousand times more intense than that of red-hot glowing iron; and in its absence from the sun, carry a blazing tail ten hundred thousand and fourteen miles long; through which if the earth should pass at the distance of one hundred thousand miles from the nucleus or main body of the comet, it must in its passage be set on fire, and reduced to ashes. That the sun daily spending its rays without any nutriment to supply them, will at last be wholly consumed and annihilated; which must be attended with the destruction of this earth, and of all the planets that receive their light from it.

They are so perpetually alarmed with the apprehensions of these and the like impending dangers, that they can neither sleep quietly in their beds, nor have any relish for the common pleasures or amusements of life. When they meet an acquaintance in the morning, the first question is about the sun's health, how he looked at his setting and rising, and what hopes they have to avoid the stroke of the approaching comet. This conversation they are apt to run into with the same temper that boys discover in delighting to hear terrible stories of sprites and hobgoblins, which they greedily listen to, and dare not go to bed for fear.

The women of the island have abundance of vivacity; they contemn their husbands, and are exceedingly fond of strangers, whereof there is always a considerable number from the continent below, attending at court, either upon affairs of the several towns and corporations, or their own particular occasions, but are much despised, because they want the same endowments. Among these the ladies choose their gallants: but the vexation is, that they act with too much ease and security, for the husband is always so rapt in speculation, that the mistress and lover may proceed to the greatest familiarities before his face, if he be but provided with paper and implements, and without his flapper at his side.

The wives and daughters lament their confinement to the island, although I think it the most delicious spot of ground in the world; and although they live here in the greatest plenty and magnificence, and are allowed to do whatever they please, they long to see the world, and take the diversions of the metropolis, which they are not allowed to do without a particular licence from the King; and this is not easy to be obtained because the people of quality have found by frequent experience how hard it is to persuade their women to return from below. I was told that a great court lady, who had several children, is married to the prime minister, the richest subject in the kingdom, a very graceful person, extremely fond of her, and lives in the finest palace of the island, went down to Lagado, on the pretence of health, there hid her self for several months, till the King sent a warrant to search for her, and she was found in an obscure eating house all in rags, having pawned her clothes to maintain an old deformed footman, who beat her every day, and in whose company she was taken much against her will. And although her husband received her with all possible kindness, and without the least reproach, she soon after contrived to steal down again with all her jewels, to the same gallant, and hath not been heard of since.

This may perhaps pass with the reader rather for an European or English story, than for one of a country so remote. But he may please to consider, that the caprices of womankind are not limited by any climate or nation, and that they are much more uniform than can be easily imagined.

In about a month's time I had made a tolerable proficiency in their language, and was able to answer most of the King's questions, when I had the honour to attend him. His Majesty discovered not the least curiosity to enquire into the laws, government, history, religion, or manners of the countries where I had been, but confined his questions to the state of mathematics, and received the account I gave him with great contempt and indifference, though often roused by his flapper on each side.

CHAPTER III

*A phenomenon solved by modern philosophy and astronomy. The
Laputians' great improvements in the latter. The King's method
of suppressing insurrections.*

I desired leave of this prince to see the curiosities of the island,
which he was graciously pleased to grant, and ordered my tutor
to attend me. I chiefly wanted to know to what cause in art or in
nature it owed its several motions, whereof I will now give a
philosophical account to the reader.

The Flying or Floating Island is exactly circular, its diameter
7,837 yards, or about four miles and an half, and consequently
contains ten thousand acres. It is three hundred yards thick.
The bottom or under surface, which appears to those who view it
from below, is one even regular plate of adamant, shooting up to
the height of about two hundred yards. Above it lie the several
minerals in their usual order, and over all is a coat of rich mould
ten or twelve foot deep. The declivity of the upper surface,
from the circumference to the center, is the natural cause why
all the dews and rains which fall upon the island are conveyed in
small rivulets towards the middle, where they are emptied into
four large basons, each of about half a mile in circuit, and two
hundred yards distant from the center. From these basons the
water is continually exhaled by the sun in the day time, which
effectually prevents their overflowing. Besides, as it is in the
power of the monarch to raise the island above the region of
clouds and vapours, he can prevent the falling of dews and rains
when ever he pleases. For the highest clouds cannot rise above
two miles, as naturalists agree, at least they were never known to
do so in that country.

At the center of the island there is a chasm about fifty yards in
diameter, from whence the astronomers descend into a large
dome, which is therefore called *Flandona Gagnole*, or the *Astronomer's Cave*, situated at the depth of an hundred yards beneath
the upper surface of the adamant. In this cave are twenty lamps
continually burning, which from the reflection of the adamant
cast a strong light into every part. The place is stored with great
variety of sextants, quadrants, telescopes, astrolabes, and other
astronomical instruments. But the greatest curiosity, upon which
the fate of the island depends, is a loadstone of a prodigious size,
in shape resembling a weaver's shuttle. It is in length six yards,
and in the thickest part at least three yards over. This magnet
is sustained by a very strong axle of adamant passing through its
middle, upon which it plays, and is poised so exactly that the

weakest hand can turn it. It is hooped round with an hollow cylinder of adamant, four foot deep, as many thick, and twelve yards in diameter, placed horizontally, and supported by eight adamantine feet, each six yards high. In the middle of the concave side there is a groove twelve inches deep, in which the extremities of the axle are lodged, and turned round as there is occasion.

The stone cannot be moved from its place by any force, because the hoop and its feet are one continued piece with that body of adamant which constitutes the bottom of the island.

By means of this loadstone, the island is made to rise and fall, and move from one place to another. For, with respect to that part of the earth over which the monarch presides, the stone is endued at one of its sides with an attractive power, and at the other with a repulsive. Upon placing the magnet erect with its attracting end towards the earth, the island descends; but when the repelling extremity points downwards, the island mounts directly upwards. When the position of the stone is oblique, the motion of the island is so too. For in this magnet the forces always act in lines parallel to its direction.

By this oblique motion the island is conveyed to different parts of the monarch's dominions. To explain the manner of its progress, let *A B* represent a line drawn cross the dominions of Balnibarbi, let the line *c d* represent the loadstone, of which let *d* be the repelling end, and *c* the attracting end, the island being over *C;* let the stone be placed in the position *c d* with its repelling end downwards; then the island will be driven upwards obliquely towards *D*. When it is arrived at *D*, let the stone be turned upon its axle till its attracting end points towards *E*, and then the island will be carried obliquely towards *E;* where if the stone be again turned upon its axle till it stands in the position *E F*, with its repelling point downwards, the island will rise obliquely towards *F*, where by directing the attracting end towards *G*, the island may be carried to *G*, and from *G* to *H*, by turning the stone, so as to make its repelling extremity point directly downwards. And thus by changing the situation of the stone as often as there is occasion, the island is made to rise and fall by turns in an oblique direction, and by those alternate risings and fallings (the obliquity being not considerable) is conveyed from one part of the dominions to the other.

But it must be observed, that this island cannot move beyond the extent of the dominions below, nor can it rise above the height of four miles. For which the astronomers (who have

Plate 4. Part 3.   Page 218.

Laputa

D   F   H

E   G

C

B   A

BALNIBARBI

Lagado

Malonada

written large systems concerning the stone) assign the following reason: that the magnetic virtue does not extend beyond the distance of four miles, and that the mineral which acts upon the stone in the bowels of the earth, and in the sea about six leagues distant from the shore, is not diffused through the whole globe, but terminated with the limits of the King's dominions; and it was easy, from the great advantage of such a superior situation, for a prince to bring under his obedience whatever country lay within the attraction of that magnet.

When the stone is put parallel to the plane of the horizon, the island standeth still; for in that case, the extremities of it, being at equal distance from the earth, act with equal force, the one in drawing downwards, the other in pushing upwards, and consequently no motion can ensue.

This loadstone is under the care of certain astronomers, who from time to time give it such positions as the monarch directs. They spend the greatest part of their lives in observing the celestial bodies, which they do by the assistance of glasses far excelling ours in goodness. For although their largest telescopes do not exceed three feet, they magnify much more than those of a hundred with us, and at the same time show the stars with greater clearness. For this advantage hath enabled them to extend their discoveries much farther than our astronomers in Europe. They have made a catalogue of ten thousand fixed stars, whereas the largest of ours do not contain above one third part of that number. They have likewise discovered two lesser stars, or 'satellites', which revolve about Mars, whereof the innermost is distant from the center of the primary planet exactly three of his diameters, and the outermost five; the former revolves in the space of ten hours, and the latter in twenty-one and an half; so that the squares of their periodical times are very near in the same proportion with the cubes of their distance from the center of Mars, which evidently shows them to be governed by the same law of gravitation, that influences the other heavenly bodies.

They have observed ninety-three different comets, and settled their periods with great exactness. If this be true (and they affirm it with great confidence) it is much to be wished that their observations were made public, whereby the theory of comets, which at present is very lame and defective, might be brought to the same perfection with other parts of astronomy.

The King would be the most absolute prince in the universe, if he could but prevail on a ministry to join with him; but these having their estates below on the continent, and considering that the office of a favourite hath a very uncertain tenure, would never consent to the enslaving their country.

If any town should engage in rebellion or mutiny, fall into violent factions, or refuse to pay the usual tribute, the King hath two methods of reducing them to obedience. The first and the mildest course is by keeping the island hovering over such a town, and the lands about it, whereby he can deprive them of the benefit of the sun and the rain, and consequently afflict the inhabitants with dearth and diseases. And if the crime deserve it they are at the same time pelted from above with great stones, against which they have no defence but by creeping into cellars or caves, while the roofs of their houses are beaten to pieces. But if they still continue obstinate, or offer to raise insurrections, he proceeds to the last remedy, by letting the island drop directly upon their heads, which makes a universal destruction both of houses and men. However, this is an extremity to which the prince is seldom driven, neither indeed is he willing to put it in execution, nor dare his ministers advise him to an action which, as it would render them odious to the people, so it would be a great damage to their own estates, that lie all below, for the island is the King's demesne.

But there is still indeed a more weighty reason, why the kings of this country have been always averse from executing so terrible an action, unless upon the utmost necessity. For if the town intended to be destroyed should have in it any tall rocks, as it generally falls out in the larger cities, a situation probably chosen at first with a view to prevent such a catastrophe; or if it abound in high spires or pillars of stone, a sudden fall might endanger the bottom or under surface of the island, which although it consist, as I have said, of one entire adamant two hundred yards thick, might happen to crack by too great a shock, or burst by approaching too near the fires from the houses below, as the backs both of iron and stone will often do in our chimneys. Of all this the people are well apprised, and understand how far to carry their obstinacy, where their liberty or property is concerned. And the King, when he is highest provoked, and most determined to press a city to rubbish, orders the island to descend with great gentleness, out of a pretence of tenderness to his people, but indeed for fear of breaking the adamantine bottom; in which case it is the opinion of all their philosophers, that the loadstone could no longer hold it up, and the whole mass would fall to the ground.

About three years before my arrival among them, while the King was in his progress over his dominions, there happened an extraordinary accident which had like to have put a period to the fate of that monarchy, at least as it is now instituted. Lindalino, the second city in the kingdom, was the first his Majesty visited in his progress. Three days after his departure, the inhabitants, who had often complained of great oppressions, shut the town gates, seized on the governor, and with incredible speed and labour erected four large towers, one at every corner of the city (which is an exact square), equal in height to a strong pointed rock that stands directly in the center of the city. Upon the top of each tower, as well as upon the rock, they fixed a great loadstone, and in case their design should fail, they had provided a vast quantity of the most combustible fuel, hoping to burst therewith the adamantine bottom of the island, if the loadstone project should miscarry.

It was eight months before the King had perfect notice that the Lindalinians were in rebellion. He then commanded that the island should be wafted over the city. The people were unanimous, and had laid in store of provisions, and a great river runs through the middle of the town. The King hovered over them several days to deprive them of the sun and the rain. He ordered many packthreads to be let down, yet not a person offered to send up a petition, but instead thereof, very bold demands, the redress of all their grievances, great immunities, the choice of their own governor, and other the like exorbitances. Upon which his Majesty commanded all the inhabitants of the island to cast great stones from the lower gallery into the town; but the citizens had provided against this mischief by conveying their persons and effects into the four towers, and other strong buildings, and vaults underground.

The King being now determined to reduce this proud people, ordered that the island should descend gently within forty yards of the top of the towers and rock. This was accordingly done; but the officers employed in that work found the descent much speedier than usual, and by turning the loadstone could not without great difficulty keep it in a firm position, but found the island inclining to fall. They sent the King immediate intelligence of this astonishing event and begged his Majesty's permission to raise the island higher; the King consented, a general council was called, and the officers of the loadstone ordered to attend. One of the oldest and expertest among them obtained leave to try an experiment. He took a strong line of an hundred yards, and the island being raised over the town above the attracting power they had felt, he fastened a piece of adamant to the end of his line which had in it a mixture of iron mineral, of the same nature with that whereof the bottom or lower surface of the island is composed, and from the lower gallery let it down slowly towards the top of the towers. The adamant was not descended four yards, before the officer felt it drawn so strongly downwards, that he could hardly pull it back. He then threw down several small pieces of adamant, and observed that they were all violently attracted by the top of the tower. The same experiment was made on the other three towers, and on the rock with the same effect.

This incident broke entirely the King's measures and (to dwell no longer on other circumstances) he was forced to give the town their own conditions.

I was assured by a great minister, that if the island had descended so near the town as not to be able to raise it self, the citizens were determined to fix it for ever, to kill the King and all his servants, and entirely change the government.

By a fundamental law of this realm, neither the King nor either of his two elder sons are permitted to leave the island, nor the Queen, till she is past child-bearing.

CHAPTER IV.

The author leaves Laputa, is conveyed to Balnibarbi, arrives at the metropolis. A description of the metropolis and the country adjoining. The author hospitably received by a great lord. His conversation with that lord.

Although I cannot say that I was ill treated in this island, yet I must confess I thought my self too much neglected, not without some degree of contempt. For neither prince nor people appeared to be curious in any part of knowledge, except mathematics and music, wherein I was far their inferior, and upon that account very little regarded.

On the other side, after having seen all the curiosities of the island, I was very desirous to leave it, being heartily weary of those people. They were indeed excellent in two sciences for which I have great esteem, and wherein I am not unversed, but at the same time so abstracted and involved in speculation that I never met with such disagreeable companions. I conversed only with women, tradesmen, flappers, and court-pages, during two months of my abode there, by which at last I rendered my self extremely contemptible, yet these were the only people from whom I could ever receive a reasonable answer.

I had obtained by hard study a good degree of knowledge in their language; I was weary of being confined to an island where I received so little countenance, and resolved to leave it with the first opportunity.

There was a great lord at court, nearly related to the King, and for that reason alone used with respect. He was universally reckoned the most ignorant and stupid person among them. He had performed many eminent services for the crown, had great natural and acquired parts, adorned with integrity and honour, but so ill an ear for music, that his detractors reported he had been often known to beat time in the wrong place; neither could his tutors without extreme difficulty teach him to demonstrate the most easy proposition in the mathematics. He was pleased to show me many marks of favour, often did me the honour of a visit, desired to be informed in the affairs of Europe, the laws and customs, the manners and learning of the several countries where I had travelled. He listened to me with great attention, and made very wise observations on all I spoke. He had two flappers attending him for state, but never made use of them except at court, and in visits of ceremony, and would always command them to withdraw when we were alone together.

I intreated this illustrious person to intercede in my behalf with his Majesty for leave to depart, which he accordingly did, as he was pleased to tell me, with regret: for indeed he had made me several offers very advantageous, which however I refused with expressions of the highest acknowledgement.

On the 16th day of February, I took leave of his Majesty and the court. The King made me a present to the value of about two hundred pounds English, and my protector his kinsman as much more, together with a letter of recommendation to a friend of his in Lagado, the metropolis; the island being then hovering over a mountain about two miles from it, I was let down from the lowest gallery, in the same manner as I had been taken up.

The continent, as far as it is subject to the monarch of the Flying Island, passes under the general name of Balnibarbi, and the metropolis, as I said before, is called Lagado. I felt some little satisfaction in finding my self on firm ground. I walked to the city without any concern, being clad like one of the natives, and sufficiently instructed to converse with them. I soon found out the person's house to whom I was recommended, presented my letter from his friend the grandee in the island, and was received with much kindness. This great lord, whose name was Munodi, ordered me an apartment in his own house, where I continued during my stay, and was entertained in a most hospitable manner.

The next morning after my arrival he took me in his chariot to see the town, which is about half the bigness of London, but the houses very strangely built, and most of them out of repair. The people in the streets walked fast, looked wild, their eyes fixed, and were generally in rags. We passed through one of the town gates, and went about three miles into the country, where I saw many labourers working with several sorts of tools in the ground, but was not able to conjecture what they were about, neither did I observe any expectation either of corn or grass, although the soil appeared to be excellent. I could not forbear admiring at these odd appearances both in town and country, and I made bold to desire my conductor, that he would be pleased to explain to me what could be meant by so many busy heads, hands, and faces, both in the streets and the fields, because I did not discover any good effects they produced; but on the contrary, I never knew a soil so unhappily cultivated, houses so ill contrived and so ruinous, or a people whose countenances and habit expressed so much misery and want.

This Lord Munodi was a person of the first rank, and had been some years Governor of Lagado, but by a cabal of ministers was discharged for insufficiency. However, the King treated him with tenderness, as a well-meaning man, but of a low contemptible understanding.

When I gave that free censure of the country and its inhabitants, he made no further answer than by telling me that I had not been long enough among them to form a judgment, and that the different nations of the world had different customs, with other common topics to the same purpose. But when we returned to his palace, he asked me how I liked the building, what absurdities I observed, and what quarrel I had with the dress and looks of his domestics. This he might safely do, because every thing about him was magnificent, regular, and polite. I answered that his Excellency's prudence, quality, and fortune had exempted him from those defects which folly and beggary had produced in others. He said if I would go with him to his country house, about twenty miles distant, where his estate lay, there would be more leisure for this kind of conversation. I told his Excellency that I was entirely at his disposal, and accordingly we set out next morning.

During our journey, he made me observe the several methods used by farmers in managing their lands, which to me were wholly unaccountable, for, except in some very few places, I could not discover one ear of corn or blade of grass. But in three hours travelling the scene was wholly altered; we came into a most beautiful country; farmers' houses at small distances, neatly built, the fields enclosed, containing vineyards, corn-grounds and meadows. Neither do I remember to have seen a more delightful prospect. His Excellency observed my countenance to clear up; he told me with a sigh, that there his estate began, and would continue the same till we should come to his house. That his countrymen ridiculed and despised him for managing his affairs no better, and for setting so ill an example to the kingdom, which however was followed by very few, such as were old and wilful, and weak like himself.

We came at length to the house, which was indeed a noble structure, built according to the best rules of ancient architecture. The fountains, gardens, walks, avenues, and groves were all disposed with exact judgment and taste. I gave due praises to every thing I saw, whereof his Excellency took not the least notice till after supper, when, there being no third companion, he told me with a very melancholy air, that he doubted he must throw down his houses in town and country, to rebuild them after the present mode, destroy all his plantations, and cast others into such a form as modern usage required, and give the same directions to all his tenants, unless he would submit to incur the censure of pride, singularity, affectation, ignorance, caprice, and perhaps encrease his Majesty's displeasure.

That the admiration I appeared to be under would cease or diminish when he had informed me of some particulars, which probably I never heard of at court, the people there being too much taken up in their own speculations to have regard to what passed here below.

The sum of his discourse was to this effect. That about forty years ago, certain persons went up to Laputa either upon business or diversion, and after five months continuance came back with a very little smattering in mathematics, but full of volatile spirits acquired in that airy region. That these persons upon their return began to dislike the management of every thing below, and fell into schemes of putting all arts, sciences, languages, and mechanics upon a new foot. To this end they procured a royal patent for erecting an academy of PROJECTORS in Lagado; and the humour prevailed so strongly among the people, that there is not a town of any consequence in the kingdom without such an academy. In these colleges the professors contrive new rules and methods of agriculture and building, and new instruments and tools for all trades and manufactures, whereby, as they undertake, one man shall do the work of ten; a palace may be built in a week, of materials so durable as to last for ever without repairing. All the fruits of the earth shall come to maturity at whatever season we think fit to choose, and increase an hundred fold more than they do at present, with innumerable other happy proposals. The only inconvenience is, that none of these projects are yet brought to perfection, and in the mean time the whole country lies miserably waste, the houses in ruins, and the people without food or clothes. By all which, instead of being discouraged, they are fifty times more violently bent upon prosecuting their schemes, driven equally on by hope and despair; that as for himself, being not of an enterprising spirit, he was content to go on in the old forms, to live in the houses his ancestors had built, and act as they did in every part of life without innovation. That some few other persons of quality and gentry had done the same, but were looked on with an eye of contempt and ill will, as enemies to art, ignorant, and ill commonwealth's-men, preferring their own ease and sloth before the general improvement of their country.

His Lordship added, that he would not by any further particulars prevent the pleasure I should certainly take in viewing the Grand Academy, whither he was resolved I should go. He only desired me to observe a ruined building upon the side of a mountain about three miles distant, of which he gave me this account. That he had a very convenient mill within half a mile of his house, turned by a current from a large river, and sufficient for his own family as well as a great number of his tenants. That about seven years ago a club of those projectors came to him with proposals to destroy this mill, and build another on the side of that mountain, on the long ridge whereof a long canal must be cut for a repository of water, to be conveyed up by pipes and engines to supply the mill: because the wind and air upon a height agitated the water, and thereby made it fitter for motion: and because the water descending down a declivity would turn the mill with half the current of a river whose course is more upon a level. He said, that being then not very well with the court, and pressed by many of his friends, he complied with the proposal; and after employing an hundred men for two years, the work miscarried, the projectors went off, laying the blame entirely upon him, railing at him ever since, and putting others upon the same experiment, with equal assurance of success, as well as equal disappointment.

In a few days we came back to town, and his Excellency, considering the bad character he had in the Academy, would not go with me himself, but recommended me to a friend of his to bear me company thither. My Lord was pleased to represent me as a great admirer of projects, and a person of much curiosity and easy belief, which indeed was not without truth, for I had my self been a sort of projector in my younger days.

Chapter V.

The author permitted to see the Grand Academy of Lagado. The Academy largely described. The arts wherein the professors employ themselves.

This academy is not an entire single building, but a continuation of several houses on both sides of a street, which growing waste was purchased and applied to that use.

I was received very kindly by the Warden, and went for many days to the Academy. Every room hath in it one or more projectors, and I believe I could not be in fewer than five hundred rooms.

The first man I saw was of a meagre aspect, with sooty hands and face, his hair and beard long, ragged and singed in several places. His clothes, shirt, and skin were all of the same colour. He had been eight years upon a project for extracting sunbeams out of cucumbers, which were to be put into vials hermetically sealed, and let out to warm the air in raw inclement summers. He told me, he did not doubt in eight years more that he should be able to supply the Governor's gardens with sunshine at a reasonable rate; but he complained that his stock was low, and entreated me to give him something as an encouragement to ingenuity, especially since this had been a very dear season for cucumbers. I made him a small present, for my Lord had furnished me with money on purpose, because he knew their practice of begging from all who go to see them.

I went into another chamber, but was ready to hasten back, being almost overcome with a horrible stink. My conductor pressed me forward, conjuring me in a whisper to give no offence, which would be highly resented, and therefore I durst not so much as stop my nose. The projector of this cell was the most ancient student of the Academy. His face and beard were of a pale yellow; his hands and clothes daubed over with filth. When I was presented to him, he gave me a very close embrace (a compliment I could well have excused). His employment from his first coming into the Academy was an operation to reduce human excrement to its original food, by separating the several parts, removing the tincture which it receives from the gall, making the odour exhale, and scumming off the saliva. He had a weekly allowance from the society of a vessel filled with human ordure, about the bigness of a Bristol barrel.

I saw another at work to calcine ice into gunpowder, who likewise showed me a treatise he had written concerning the malleability of fire, which he intended to publish.

There was a most ingenious architect who had contrived a new method for building houses, by beginning at the roof and working downwards to the foundation, which he justified to me by the like practice of those two prudent insects, the bee and the spider.

There was a man born blind, who had several apprentices in his own condition: their employment was to mix colours for painters, which their master taught them to distinguish by feeling and smelling. It was indeed my misfortune to find them at that time not very perfect in their lessons, and the professor himself happened to be generally mistaken; this artist is much encouraged and esteemed by the whole fraternity.

In another apartment I was highly pleased with a projector, who had found a device of plowing the ground with hogs, to save the charges of plows, cattle, and labour. The method is this: in an acre of ground you bury, at six inches distance, and eight deep, a quantity of acorns, dates, chestnuts, and other mast or vegetables whereof these animals are fondest: then you drive six hundred or more of them into the field, where in a few days they will root up the whole ground in search of their food, and make it fit for sowing, at the same time manuring it with their dung; it is true upon experiment they found the charge and trouble very great, and they had little or no crop. However, it is not doubted that this invention may be capable of great improvement.

I went into another room, where the walls and ceiling were all hung round with cobwebs, except a narrow passage for the artist to go in and out. At my entrance he called aloud to me not to disturb his webs. He lamented the fatal mistake the world had been so long in of using silkworms, while we had such plenty of domestic insects, who infinitely excelled the former, because they understood how to weave as well as spin. And he proposed farther, that by employing spiders the charge of dyeing silks would be wholly saved, whereof I was fully convinced when he showed me a vast number of flies most beautifully coloured, wherewith he fed his spiders, assuring us that the webs would take a tincture from them; and as he had them of all hues, he hoped to fit every body's fancy, as soon as he could find proper food for the flies, of certain gums, oils, and other glutinous matter, to give a strength and consistence to the threads.

There was an astronomer who had undertaken to place a sundial upon the great weathercock on the town-house, by adjusting the annual and diurnal motions of the earth and sun, so as to answer and coincide with all accidental turnings by the wind.

I was complaining of a small fit of the colic, upon which my conductor led me into a room, where a great physician resided, who was famous for curing that disease by contrary operations from the same instrument. He had a large pair of bellows with a long slender muzzle of ivory. This he conveyed eight inches up the anus, and drawing in the wind, he affirmed he could make the guts as lank as a dried bladder. But when the disease was more stubborn and violent, he let in the muzzle while the bellows were full of wind, which he discharged into the body of the patient, then withdrew the instrument to replenish it, clapping his thumb strongly against the orifice of the fundament; and this being repeated three or four times, the adventitious wind would rush out, bringing the noxious along with it (like water put into a pump) and the patient recovers. I saw him try both experiments upon a dog, but could not discern any effect from the former. After the latter, the animal was ready to burst, and made so violent a discharge, as was very offensive to me and my companions. The dog died on the spot, and we left the doctor endeavouring to recover him by the same operation.

I visited many other apartments, but shall not trouble my reader with all the curiosities I observed, being studious of brevity.

I had hitherto seen only one side of the Academy, the other being appropriated to the advancers of speculative learning, of whom I shall say something when I have mentioned one illustrious person more, who is called among them 'the universal artist'. He told us he had been thirty years employing his thoughts for the improvement of human life. He had two large rooms full of wonderful curiosities, and fifty men at work. Some were condensing air into a dry tangible substance, by extracting the nitre, and letting the aqueous or fluid particles percolate; others softening marble for pillows and pincushions; others petrifying the hoofs of a living horse to preserve them from foundering. The artist himself was at that time busy upon two great designs; the first, to sow land with chaff, wherein he affirmed the true seminal virtue to be contained, as he demonstrated by several experiments which I was not skilful enough to comprehend. The other was, by a certain composition of gums, minerals, and vegetables outwardly applied to prevent the growth of wool upon two young lambs; and he hoped in a reasonable time to propagate the breed of naked sheep all over the kingdom.

We crossed a walk to the other part of the Academy, where, as I have already said, the projectors in speculative learning resided.

The first professor I saw was in a very large room, with forty pupils about him. After salutation, observing me to look earnestly upon a frame, which took up the greatest part of both the length and breadth of the room, he said perhaps I might wonder to see him employed in a project for improving speculative knowledge by practical and mechanical operations. But the world would soon be sensible of its usefulness, and he flattered himself that a more noble, exalted thought never sprang in any other man's head. Every one knows how laborious the usual method is of attaining to arts and sciences; whereas by his contrivance the most ignorant person at a reasonable charge, and with a little bodily labour, may write books in philosophy, poetry, politics, law, mathematics and theology, without the least assistance from genius or study. He then led me to the frame, about the sides whereof all his pupils stood in ranks. It was twenty foot square, placed in the middle of the room. The superficies was composed of several bits of wood, about the bigness of a die, but some larger than others. They were all linked together by slender wires. These bits of wood were covered on every square with papers pasted on them, and on these papers were written all the words of their language in their several moods, tenses, and declensions, but without any order. The professor then desired me to observe, for he was going to set his engine at work. The pupils at his command took each of them hold of an iron handle, whereof there were forty fixed round the edges of the frame, and giving them a sudden turn, the whole disposition of the words was entirely changed. He then commanded six and thirty of the lads to read the several lines softly as they appeared upon the frame; and where they found three or four words together that might make part of a sentence, they dictated to the four remaining boys who were scribes. This work was repeated three or four times, and at every turn the engine was so contrived, that the words shifted into new places, as the square bits of wood moved upside down.

Plate 5 Part 3.

Six hours a day the young students were employed in this labour, and the professor showed me several volumes in large folio already collected, of broken sentences, which he intended to piece together, and out of those rich materials to give the world a complete body of all arts and sciences; which however might be still improved, and much expedited, if the public would raise a fund for making and employing five hundred such frames in Lagado, and oblige the managers to contribute in common their several collections.

He assured me, that this invention had employed all his thoughts from his youth, that he had emptied the whole vocabulary into his frame, and made the strictest computation of the general proportion there is in books between the numbers of particles, nouns, and verbs, and other parts of speech.

I made my humblest acknowledgements to this illustrious person for his great communicativeness, and promised if ever I had the good fortune to return to my native country, that I would do him justice, as the sole inventor of this wonderful machine; the form and contrivance of which I desired leave to delineate upon paper as in the figure here annexed. I told him, although it were the custom of our learned in Europe to steal inventions from each other, who had thereby at least this advantage, that it became a controversy which was the right owner, yet I would take such caution, that he should have the honour entire without a rival.

We next went to the school of languages, where three professors sat in consultation upon improving that of their own country.

The first project was to shorten discourse by cutting polysyllables into one, and leaving out verbs and participles, because in reality all things imaginable are but nouns.

The other was a scheme for entirely abolishing all words whatsoever; and this was urged as a great advantage in point of health as well as brevity. For it is plain, that every word we speak is in some degree a diminution of our lungs by corrosion, and consequently contributes to the shortening of our lives. An expedient was therefore offered, that since words are only names for *things*, it would be more convenient for all men to carry about them such *things* as were necessary to express the particular business they are to discourse on. And this invention would certainly have taken place, to the great ease as well as health of the subject, if the women in conjunction with the vulgar and illiterate had not threatened to raise a rebellion, unless they might be allowed the liberty to speak with their tongues, after the manner of their forefathers; such constant ir-reconcilable enemies to science are the common people. How-ever, many of the most learned and wise adhere to the new scheme of expressing themselves by *things*, which hath only this inconvenience attending it, that if a man's business be very great, and of various kinds, he must be obliged in proportion to carry a greater bundle of *things* upon his back, unless he can afford one or two strong servants to attend him. I have often beheld two of those sages almost sinking under the weight of their packs, like pedlars among us; who when they met in the streets would lay down their loads, open their sacks and hold conversation for an hour together; then put up their imple-ments, help each other to resume their burthens, and take their leave.

But for short conversations a man may carry implements in his pockets and under his arms, enough to supply him, and in his house he cannot be at a loss; therefore the room where com-pany meet who practise this art is full of all *things* ready at hand, requisite to furnish matter for this kind of artificial converse.

Another great advantage proposed by this invention was that it would serve as an universal language to be understood in all civilised nations, whose goods and utensils are generally of the same kind, or nearly resembling, so that their uses might easily be comprehended. And thus ambassadors would be qualified to treat with foreign princes or ministers of state to whose tongues they were utter strangers.

I was at the mathematical school, where the master taught his pupils after a method scarce imaginable to us in Europe. The proposition and demonstration were fairly written on a thin wafer, with ink composed of a cephalic tincture. This the stu-dent was to swallow upon a fasting stomach, and for three days following eat nothing but bread and water. As the wafer digested, the tincture mounted to his brain, bearing the proposi-tion along with it. But the success hath not hitherto been answerable, partly by some error in the *quantum* or composition, and partly by the perverseness of lads, to whom this bolus is so nauseous that they generally steal aside, and discharge it upwards before it can operate; neither have they been yet persuaded to use so long an abstinence as the prescription requires.

Chapter VI.

A further account of the Academy. The author proposes some improvements which are honourably received.

In the school of political projectors I was but ill entertained, the professors appearing in my judgment wholly out of their senses, which is a scene that never fails to make me melancholy. These unhappy people were proposing schemes for persuading monarchs to choose favourites upon the score of their wisdom, capacity and virtue; of teaching ministers to consult the public good; of rewarding merit, great abilities and eminent services; of instructing princes to know their true interest by placing it on the same foundation with that of their people: of choosing for employments persons qualified to exercise them; with many other wild impossible chimæras, that never entered before into the heart of man to conceive, and confirmed in me the old observation, that there is nothing so extravagant and irrational which some philosophers have not maintained for truth.

But, however, I shall so far do justice to this part of the Academy, as to acknowledge that all of them were not so visionary. There was a most ingenious doctor who seemed to be perfectly versed in the whole nature and system of government. This illustrious person had very usefully employed his studies in finding out effectual remedies for all diseases and corruptions to which the several kinds of public administration are subject by the vices or infirmities of those who govern, as well as by the licentiousness of those who are to obey. For instance: whereas all writers and reasoners have agreed, that there is a strict universal resemblance between the natural and the political body; can there be any thing more evident, than that the health of both must be preserved, and the diseases cured, by the same prescriptions? It is allowed that senates and great councils are often troubled with redundant, ebullient, and other peccant humours, with many diseases of the head, and more of the heart; with strong convulsions, with grievous contractions of the nerves and sinews in both hands, but especially the right; with spleen, flatus, vertigos and deliriums; with scrofulous tumours full of fœtid purulent matter; with sour frothy ructations, with canine appetites and crudeness of digestion, besides many others needless to mention. This doctor therefore proposed, that upon the meeting of a senate, certain physicians should attend at the three first days of their sitting, and, at the close of each day's debate, feel the pulses of every senator; after which, having maturely considered, and consulted upon the nature of the several maladies, and the methods of cure, they should on the fourth day return to the senate house, attended by their apothecaries stored with proper medicines, and before the members sat, administer to each of them lenitives, aperitives, abstersives, corrosives, restringents, palliatives, laxatives, cephalalgics, icterics, apophlegmatics, acoustics, as their several cases required; and according as these medicines should operate, repeat, alter, or omit them at the next meeting.

This project could not be of any great expense to the public, and might, in my poor opinion, be of much use for the dispatch of business in those countries where senates have any share in the legislative power, beget unanimity, shorten debates, open a few mouths which are now closed, and close many more which are now open; curb the petulancy of the young, and correct the positiveness of the old; rouse the stupid, and damp the pert.

Again, because it is a general complaint that the favourites of princes are troubled with short and weak memories, the same doctor proposed, that whoever attended a first minister, after having told his business with the utmost brevity, and in the plainest words, should at his departure give the said minister a tweak by the nose, or a kick in the belly, or tread on his corns, or lug him thrice by both ears, or run a pin into his breech, or pinch his arm black and blue, to prevent forgetfulness: and at every levee day repeat the same operation, till the business were done or absolutely refused.

He likewise directed, that every senator in the great council of a nation, after he had delivered his opinion, and argued in the defence of it, should be obliged to give his vote directly contrary; because if that were done, the result would infallibly terminate in the good of the public.

When parties in a state are violent, he offered a wonderful contrivance to reconcile them. The method is this. You take an hundred leaders of each party, you dispose them into couples of such whose heads are nearest of a size; then let two nice operators saw off the occiput of each couple at the same time, in such a manner that the brain may be equally divided. Let the occiputs thus cut off be interchanged, applying each to the head of his opposite party-man. It seems indeed to be a work that requireth some exactness, but the professor assured us, that if it were dextrously performed the cure would be infallible. For he argued thus; that the two half brains being left to debate the matter between themselves within the space of one skull, would soon come to a good understanding, and produce that moderation, as well as regularity of thinking, so much to be

wished for in the heads of those who imagine they came into the
world only to watch and govern its motion: and as to the difference of brains in quantity or quality, among those who are
directors in faction, the doctor assured us from his own knowledge, that it was a perfect trifle.

I heard a very warm debate between two professors, about
the most commodious and effectual ways and means of raising
money without grieving the subject. The first affirmed the
justest method would be to lay a certain tax upon vices and
folly, and the sum fixed upon every man to be rated after the
fairest manner by a jury of his neighbours. The second was of
an opinion directly contrary, to tax those qualities of body and
mind for which men chiefly value themselves, the rate to be
more or less according to the degrees of excelling, the decision
whereof should be left entirely to their own breast. The highest
tax was upon men who are the greatest favourites of the other
sex, and the assessments according to the number and natures of
the favours they have received; for which they are allowed to be
their own vouchers. Wit, valour, and politeness were likewise
proposed to be largely taxed, and collected in the same manner,
by every person's giving his own word for the quantum of what
he possessed. But as to honour, justice, wisdom and learning,
they should not be taxed at all, because they are qualifications
of so singular a kind, that no man will either allow them in his
neighbour, or value them in himself.

The women were proposed to be taxed according to their
beauty and skill in dressing, wherein they had the same privilege
with the men, to be determined by their own judgment. But
constancy, chastity, good sense, and good nature were not rated,
because they would not bear the charge of collecting.

To keep senators in the interest of the crown, it was proposed
that the members should raffle for employments, every man
first taking an oath, and giving security that he would vote for
the court, whether he won or no, after which the losers had
in their turn the liberty of raffling upon the next vacancy. Thus
hope and expectation would be kept alive, none would complain
of broken promises, but impute their disappointments wholly to
Fortune, whose shoulders are broader and stronger than those
of a ministry.

Another professor showed me a large paper of instructions
for discovering plots and conspiracies against the government.
He advised great statesmen to examine into the diet of all
suspected persons; their times of eating; upon which side they
lay in bed; with which hand they wiped their posteriors; to take

a strict view of their excrements, and from the colour, the odour, the taste, the consistence, the crudeness or maturity of digestion, form a judgment of their thoughts and designs. Because men are never so serious, thoughtful, and intent, as when they are at stool, which he found by frequent experiment: for in such conjunctures, when he used merely as a trial to consider which was the best way of murdering the King, his ordure would have a tincture of green, but quite different when he thought only of raising an insurrection or burning the metropolis.

The whole discourse was written with great acuteness, containing many observations both curious and useful for politicians, but as I conceived not altogether complete. This I ventured to tell the author, and offered if he pleased to supply him with some additions. He received my proposition with more compliance than is usual among writers, especially those of the projecting species, professing he would be glad to receive farther information.

I told him, that in the kingdom of Tribnia, by the natives called Langden, where I had long sojourned, the bulk of the people consisted wholly of discoverers, witnesses, informers, accusers, prosecutors, evidences, swearers, together with their several subservient and subaltern instruments, all under the colours, the conduct, and pay of ministers and their deputies. The plots in that kingdom are usually the workmanship of those persons who desire to raise their own characters of profound politicians, to restore new vigour to a crazy administration, to stifle or divert general discontents, to fill their coffers with forfeitures, and raise or sink the opinion of public credit, as either shall best answer their private advantage. It is first agreed and settled among them what suspected persons shall be accused of a plot: then effectual care is taken to secure all their letters and other papers, and put the owners in chains. These papers are delivered to a set of artists, very dextrous in finding out the mysterious meanings of words, syllables, and letters. For instance, they can decipher a close-stool to signify a privy-council, a flock of geese a senate, a lame dog an invader, a codshead a ————, the plague a standing army, a buzzard a prime minister, the gout a high priest, a gibbet a secretary of state, a chamber-pot a committee of grandees, a sieve a court lady, a broom a revolution, a mousetrap an employment, a bottomless pit the treasury, a sink a court, a cap and bells a favourite, a broken reed a court of justice, an empty tun a general, a running sore the administration.

When this method fails, they have two others more ef-

fectual, which the learned among them call acrostics and anagrams. First they can decipher all initial letters into political
meanings. Thus N shall signify a plot, B a regiment of horse, L
a fleet at sea. Or secondly by transposing the letters of the
alphabet in any suspected paper, they can lay open the deepest
designs of a discontented party. So, for example, if I should say
in a letter to a friend, Our brother Tom has just got the piles, a
man of skill in this art would discover how the same letters
which compose that sentence may be analysed into the following
words: Resist — a plot is brought home — the tour. And this is
the anagrammatic method.

The professor made me great acknowledgments for communi-
cating these observations, and promised to make honourable
mention of me in his treatise.

I saw nothing in this country that could invite me to a longer
continuance, and began to think of returning home to England.

CHAPTER VII.

*The author leaves Lagado, arrives at Maldonada. No ship ready. He
takes a short voyage to Glubbdubdrib. His reception by the
Governor.*

The continent of which this kingdom is a part extends itself,
as I have reason to believe, eastward to that unknown tract of
America, westward of California and north to the Pacific Ocean,
which is not above an hundred and fifty miles from Lagado,
where there is a good port and much commerce with the great
island of Luggnagg, situated to the northwest about 29 degrees
north latitude, and 140 longitude. This island of Luggnagg
stands southeastwards of Japan, about an hundred leagues distant. There is a strict alliance between the Japanese Emperor
and the King of Luggnagg, which affords frequent opportunities
of sailing from one island to the other. I determined therefore to
direct my course this way in order to my return to Europe. I
hired two mules with a guide to show me the way, and carry
my small baggage. I took leave of my noble protector, who had
shown me so much favour, and made me a generous present at
my departure.

My journey was without any accident or adventure worth relating. When I arrived at the port of Maldonada (for so it is called)
there was no ship in the harbour bound for Luggnagg, nor like to
be in some time. The town is about as large as Portsmouth. I

soon fell into some acquaintance, and was very hospitably received. A gentleman of distinction said to me, that since the ships bound for Luggnagg could not be ready in less than a month, it might be no disagreeable amusement for me to take a trip to the little island of Glubbdubdrib, about five leagues off to the southwest. He offered himself and a friend to accompany me, and that I should be provided with a small convenient barque for the voyage.

Glubbdubdrib, as nearly as I can interpret the word, signifies The Island of *Sorcerers* or *Magicians*. It is about one third as large as the Isle of Wight, and extremely fruitful: it is governed by the head of a certain tribe, who are all magicians. This tribe marries only among each other, and the eldest in succession is prince or governor. He hath a noble palace and a park of about three thousand acres, surrounded by a wall of hewn stone twenty foot high. In this park are several smaller inclosures for cattle, corn, and gardening.

The Governor and his family are served and attended by domestics of a kind somewhat unusual. By his skill in necromancy, he hath power of calling whom he pleaseth from the dead, and commanding their service for twenty-four hours, but no longer; nor can he call the same persons up again in less than three months, except upon very extraordinary occasions.

When we arrived at the island, which was about eleven in the morning, one of the gentlemen who accompanied me went to the Governor, and desired admittance for a stranger, who came on purpose to have the honour of attending on his Highness. This was immediately granted, and we all three entered the gate of the palace between two rows of guards, armed and dressed after a very antic manner, and something in their countenances that made my flesh creep with a horror I cannot express. We passed through several apartments between servants of the same sort, ranked on each side as before, till we came to the chamber of presence, where, after three profound obeisances, and a few general questions, we were permitted to sit on three stools near the lowest step of his Highness's throne. He understood the language of Balnibarbi, although it were different from that of his island. He desired me to give him some account of my travels; and to let me see that I should be treated without ceremony, he dismissed all his attendants with a turn of his finger, at which to my great astonishment they vanished in an instant, like visions in a dream, when we awake on a sudden. I could not recover my self in some time, till the Governor assured me that I should receive no hurt; and observing my two companions to be under no concern, who had been often entertained in the same manner, I began to take courage, and relate to his Highness a short history of my several adventures, yet not without some hesitation, and frequently looking behind me to the place where I had seen those domestic spectres. I had the honour to dine with the Governor, where a new set of ghosts served up the meat, and waited at table. I now observed my self to be less terrified than I had been in the morning. I stayed till sunset, but humbly desired his Highness to excuse me for not accepting his invitation of lodging in the palace. My two friends and I lay at a private house in the town adjoining, which is the captial of this little island; and the next morning we returned to pay our duty to the Governor, as he was pleased to command us.

After this manner we continued in the island for ten days, most part of every day with the Governor, and at night in our lodging. I soon grew so familiarized to the sight of spirits, that after the third or fourth time they gave me no emotion at all; or if I had any apprehensions left, my curiosity prevailed over them. For his Highness the Governor ordered me to call up whatever persons I would choose to name, and in whatever numbers among all the dead from the beginning of the world to the present time, and command them to answer any questions I should think fit to ask; with this condition, that my questions must be confined within the compass of the times they lived in. And one thing I might depend upon, that they would certainly tell me truth, for lying was a talent of no use in the lower world.

I made my humble acknowledgements to his Highness for so great a favour. We were in a chamber, from whence there was a fair prospect into the park. And because my first inclination was to be entertained with scenes of pomp and magnificence, I desired to see Alexander the Great, at the head of his army just after the battle of Arbela, which upon a motion of the Governor's finger immediately appeared in a large field under the window, where we stood. Alexander was called up into the room: it was with great difficulty that I understood his Greek, and had but little of my own. He assured me upon his honour that he was not poisoned, but died of a fever by excessive drinking.

Next I saw Hannibal passing the Alps, who told me he had not a drop of vinegar in his camp.

I saw Cæsar and Pompey at the head of their troops, just ready to engage. I saw the former in his last great triumph. I desired that the Senate of Rome might appear before me in one large chamber, and a modern representative in counterview in another.

The first seemed to be an assembly of heroes and demigods; the other a knot of pedlars, pickpockets, highwaymen and bullies.

The Governor at my request gave the sign for Cæsar and Brutus to advance towards us. I was struck with a profound veneration at the sight of Brutus, and could easily discover the most consummate virtue, the greatest intrepidity and firmness of mind, the truest love of his country and general benevolence for mankind in every lineament of his countenance. I observed with much pleasure that these two persons were in good intelligence with each other, and Cæsar freely confessed to me, that the greatest actions of his own life were not equal by many degrees to the glory of taking it away. I had the honour to have much conversation with Brutus; and was told, that his ancestor Junius, Socrates, Epaminondas, Cato the younger, Sir Thomas More and himself were perpetually together: a *sextumvirate* to which all the ages of the world cannot add a seventh.

It would be tedious to trouble the reader with relating what vast numbers of illustrious persons were called up, to gratify that insatiable desire I had to see the world in every period of antiquity placed before me. I chiefly fed my eyes with beholding the destroyers of tyrants and usurpers, and the restorers of liberty to oppressed and injured nations. But it is impossible to express the satisfaction I received in my own mind, after such a manner as to make it a suitable entertainment to the reader.

CHAPTER VIII.

A further account of Glubbdubdrib. Ancient and modern history corrected.

Having a desire to see those ancients who were most renowned for wit and learning, I set apart one day on purpose. I proposed that Homer and Aristotle might appear at the head of all their commentators; but these were so numerous that some hundreds were forced to attend in the court and outward rooms of the palace. I knew and could distinguish those two heroes at first sight, not only from the crowd, but from each other. Homer was the taller and comelier person of the two, walked very erect for one of his age, and his eyes were the most quick and piercing I ever beheld. Aristotle stooped much, and made use of a staff. His visage was meager, his hair lank and thin, and his voice hollow. I soon discovered that both of them were perfect strangers to the rest of the company, and had never seen or heard of them before. And I had a whisper from a ghost, who shall be nameless, that these commentators always kept in the most distant quarters from their principals in the lower world, through a consciousness of shame and guilt, because they had so horribly misrepresented the meaning of those authors to posterity. I introduced Didymus and Eustathius to Homer, and prevailed on him to treat them better than perhaps they deserved, for he soon found they wanted a genius to enter into the spirit of a poet. But Aristotle was out of all patience with the account I gave him of Scotus and Ramus, as I presented them to him, and he asked them whether the rest of the tribe were as great dunces as themselves.

I then desired the Governor to call up Descartes and Gassendi, with whom I prevailed to explain their systems to Aristotle. This great philosopher freely acknowledged his own mistakes in natural philosophy, because he proceeded in many things upon conjecture, as all men must do; and he found that Gassendi, who had made the doctrine of Epicurus as palatable as he could, and the *vortices* of Descartes, were equally exploded. He predicted the same fate to *attraction*, whereof the present learned are such zealous asserters. He said, that new systems of nature were but new fashions, which would vary in every age; and even those who pretend to demonstrate them from mathematical principles would flourish but a short period of time, and be out of vogue when that was determined.

I spent five days in conversing with many others of the ancient learned. I saw most of the first Roman emperors. I prevailed on the Governor to call up Eliogabalus's cooks to dress us a dinner, but they could not show us much of their skill, for want of materials. A helot of Agesilaus made us a dish of Spartan broth, but I was not able to get down a second spoonful.

The two gentlemen who conducted me to the island were pressed by their private affairs to return in three days, which I employed in seeing some of the modern dead who had made the greatest figure for two or three hundred years past in our own and other countries of Europe; and having been always a great admirer of old illustrious families, I desired the Governor would call up a dozen or two of kings with their ancestors in order for eight or nine generations. But my disappointment was grievous and unexpected. For instead of a long train with royal diadems, I saw in one family, two fiddlers, three spruce courtiers, and an Italian prelate. In another, a barber, an abbot, and two cardinals. I have too great a veneration for crowned heads to dwell any longer on so nice a subject. But as to counts, marquesses, dukes, earls, and the like, I was not so scrupulous. And I confess it was not without some pleasure that I found my self able to trace the particular features, by which certain families are distinguished, up to their originals. I could plainly discover from whence one family derives a long chin, why a second hath abounded with knaves for two generations, and fools for two more; why a third happened to be crack-brained, and a fourth to be sharpers. Whence it came what Polydore Virgil says of a certain great house, *Nec vir fortis, nec fœmina casta.* How cruelty, false-hood, and cowardice grew to be characteristics by which certain families are distinguished as much as by their coat of arms. Who first brought the pox into a noble house, which hath lineally descended in scrofulous tumours to their posterity. Neither could I wonder at all this, when I saw such an interruption of lineages by pages, lackeys, valets, coachmen, gamesters, fiddlers, players, captains, and pickpockets.

I was chiefly disgusted with modern history. For having strictly examined all the persons of greatest name in the courts of princes for an hundred years past, I found how the world had been misled by prostitute writers, to ascribe the greatest exploits in war to cowards, the wisest counsel to fools, sincerity to flatterers, Roman virtue to betrayers of their country, piety to atheists, chastity to sodomites, truth to informers. How many innocent and excellent persons had been condemned to death or banishment, by the practising of great ministers upon the corruption of judges, and the malice of factions. How many villains had been exalted to the highest places of trust, power, dignity, and profit: how great a share in the motions and events of courts, councils, and senates might be challenged by bawds, whores, pimps, parasites, and buffoons: how low an opinion I had of human wisdom and integrity, when I was truly informed of the springs and motives of great enterprises and revolutions in the world, and of the contemptible accidents to which they owed their success.

Here I discovered the roguery and ignorance of those who pretend to write *anecdotes*, or secret history, who send so many kings to their graves with a cup of poison; will repeat the discourse between a prince and chief minister, where no witness was by; unlock the thoughts and cabinets of ambassadors and secretaries of state, and have the perpetual misfortune to be mistaken. Here I discovered the true causes of many great events that have surprised the world, how a whore can govern the back-stairs, the back-stairs a council, and the council a senate. A general confessed in my presence, that he got a victory purely by the force of cowardice and ill conduct: and an admiral that for want of proper intelligence, he beat the enemy to whom he intended to betray the fleet. Three kings protested to me, that in their whole reigns they did never once prefer any person of merit, unless by mistake or treachery of some minister in whom they confided: neither would they do it if they were to live again; and they showed with great strength of reason, that the royal throne could not be supported without corruption, because that positive, confident, restive temper, which virtue infused into man, was a perpetual clog to public business.

I had the curiosity to enquire in a particular manner, by what method great numbers had procured to themselves high titles of honour, and prodigious estates; and I confined my enquiry to a very modern period: however, without grating upon present times, because I would be sure to give no offence even to foreigners (for I hope the reader need not be told that I do not in the least intend my own country in what I say upon this occasion) a great number of persons concerned were called up, and upon a very slight examination, discovered such a scene of infamy, that I cannot reflect upon it without some seriousness. Perjury, oppression, subornation, fraud, pandarism, and the like infirmities, were amongst the most excusable arts they had to mention, and for these I gave, as it was reasonable, due allowance. But when some confessed they owed their greatness and wealth to sodomy or incest, others to the prostituting of their own wives and daughters; others to the betraying their country or their prince; some to poisoning, more to the perverting of justice in order to destroy the innocent: I hope I may be pardoned if these discoveries inclined me a little to abate of that profound veneration which I am naturally apt to pay to persons of high rank, who ought to be treated with the utmost respect due to their sublime dignity, by us their inferiors.

I had often read of some great services done to princes and states, and desired to see the persons by whom those services were performed. Upon enquiry I was told that their names were to be found on no record, except a few of them whom history hath represented as the vilest rogues and traitors. As to the rest, I had never once heard of them. They all appeared with dejected looks, and in the meanest habit, most of them telling me they died in poverty and disgrace, and the rest on a scaffold or a gibbet.

Among others there was one person whose case appeared a little singular. He had a youth about eighteen years old standing by his side. He told me he had for many years been commander of a ship, and in the sea fight at Actium had the good fortune to break through the enemy's great line of battle, sink three of their capital ships, and take a fourth, which was the sole cause of Antony's flight, and of the victory that ensued; that the youth standing by him, his only son, was killed in the action. He added, that upon the confidence of some merit, the war being at an end, he went to Rome, and solicited at the court of Augustus to be preferred to a greater ship, whose commander had been killed; but without any regard to his pretensions, it was given to a boy who had never seen the sea, the son of a Libertina, who waited on one of the Emperor's mistresses. Returning back to his own vessel, he was charged with neglect of duty, and the ship given to a favourite page of Publicola the Vice-Admiral; whereupon he retired to a poor farm, at a great distance from Rome, and there ended his life. I was so curious to know the truth of this story, that I desired Agrippa might be called, who was admiral in that fight. He appeared and confirmed the whole account, but with much more advantage to the captain, whose modesty had extenuated or concealed a great part of his merit.

I was surprised to find corruption grown so high and so quick in that empire, by the force of luxury so lately introduced, which made me less wonder at many parallel cases in other countries, where vices of all kinds have reigned so much longer, and where the whole praise as well as pillage hath been engrossed by the chief commander, who perhaps had the least title to either.

As every person called up made exactly the same appearance he had done in the world, it gave me melancholy reflections to observe how much the race of human kind was degenerate among us, within these hundred years past. How the pox under all its consequences and denominations had altered every lineament of an English countenance, shortened the size of bodies, unbraced the nerves, relaxed the sinews and muscles, introduced a sallow complexion, and rendered the flesh loose and rancid.

I descended so low as to desire that some English yeomen of the old stamp might be summoned to appear, once so famous for the simplicity of their manners, diet and dress, for justice in their dealings, for their true spirit of liberty, for their valour and love of their country. Neither could I be wholly unmoved after comparing the living with the dead, when I considered how all these pure native virtues were prostituted for a piece of money by their grandchildren, who in selling their votes, and managing at elections, have acquired every vice and corruption that can possibly be learned in a court.

CHAPTER IX.

The author's return to Maldonada. Sails to the kingdom of Luggnagg.
The author confined. He is sent for to court. The manner of
his admittance. The King's great lenity to his subjects.

The day of our departure being come, I took leave of his
Highness the Governor of Glubbdubdrib, and returned with
my two companions to Maldonada, where after a fortnight's
waiting, a ship was ready to sail for Luggnagg. The two
gentlemen and some others were so generous and kind as to
furnish me with provisions, and see me on board. I was a month
in this voyage. We had one violent storm, and were under a
necessity of steering westward to get into the trade wind, which
holds for above sixty leagues. On the 21st of April, 1709, we
sailed in the river of Clumegnig, which is a seaport town, at
the southeast point of Luggnagg. We cast anchor within a league
of the town, and made a signal for a pilot. Two of them came
on board in less than half an hour, by whom we were guided
between certain shoals and rocks, which are very dangerous in
the passage, to a large basin, where a fleet may ride in safety
within a cable's length of the town wall.

Some of our sailors, whether out of treachery or inadvertence,
had informed the pilots that I was a stranger and a great
traveller, whereof these gave notice to a custom-house officer,
by whom I was examined very strictly upon my landing. This
officer spoke to me in the language of Balnibarbi, which by the
force of much commerce is generally understood in that town,
especially by seamen, and those employed in the customs. I
gave him a short account of some particulars, and made my
story as plausible and consistent as I could; but I thought it
necessary to disguise my country, and call my self a Hollander,
because my intentions were for Japan, and I knew the Dutch
were the only Europeans permitted to enter into that kingdom.
I therefore told the officer, that having been shipwrecked on
the coast of Balnibarbi, and cast on a rock, I was received up
into Laputa, or the Flying Island (of which he had often heard)
and was now endeavouring to get to Japan, from whence I
might find a convenience of returning to my own country. The
officer said I must be confined till he could receive orders from
court, for which he would write immediately, and hoped to
receive an answer in a fortnight. I was carried to a convenient
lodging, with a sentry placed at the door; however I had the
liberty of a large garden, and was treated with humanity enough,
being maintained all the time at the King's charge. I was visited

by several persons, chiefly out of curiosity, because it was reported I came from countries very remote of which they had never heard.

I hired a young man who came in the same ship to be an interpreter; he was a native of Luggnagg, but had lived some years at Maldonada, and was a perfect master of both languages. By his assistance I was able to hold a conversation with those that came to visit me; but this consisted only of their questions, and my answers.

The dispatch came from court about the time we expected. It contained a warrant for conducting me and my retinue to Traldragdubh or Trildrogdrib, for it is pronounced both ways as near as I can remember, by a party of ten horse. All my retinue was that poor lad for an interpreter, whom I persuaded into my service. At my humble request, we had each of us a mule to ride on. A messenger was dispatched half a day's journey before us, to give the King notice of my approach, and to desire that his Majesty would please to appoint a day and hour, when it would be his gracious pleasure that I might have the honour to 'lick the dust before his footstool.' This is the court style, and I found it to be more than matter of form. For upon my admittance two days after my arrival, I was commanded to crawl up on my belly, and lick the floor as I advanced; but on account of my being a stranger, care was taken to have it so clean that the dust was not offensive. However, this was a peculiar grace, not allowed to any but persons of the highest rank, when they desire an admittance. Nay, sometimes the floor is strewed with dust on purpose, when the person to be admitted happens to have powerful enemies at court. And I have seen a great lord with his mouth so crammed, that when he had crept to the proper distance from the throne, he was not able to speak a word. Neither is there any remedy, because it is capital for those who receive an audience to spit or wipe their mouths in his Majesty's presence. There is indeed another custom, which I cannot altogether approve of. When the King hath a mind to put any of his nobles to death in a gentle indulgent manner, he commands to have the floor strowed with a certain brown powder, of a deadly composition, which being licked up infallibly kills him in twenty-four hours. But in justice to this prince's great clemency, and the care he hath of his subjects' lives (wherein it were much to be wished that the monarchs of Europe would imitate him) it must be mentioned for his honour, that strict orders are given to have the infected parts of the floor well washed after every such execution, which if his domestics neglect, they are in danger of incurring his royal displeasure. I my self heard him give directions, that one of his pages should be whipped, whose turn it was to give notice about washing the floor after an execution, but maliciously had omitted it, by which neglect a young lord of great hopes coming to an audience, was unfortunately poisoned, although the King at that time had no design against his life. But this good prince was so gracious as to forgive the page his whipping, upon promise that he would do so no more, without special orders.

To return from this digression; when I had crept within four yards of the throne, I raised my self gently upon my knees, and then striking my forehead seven times against the ground, I pronounced the following words, as they had been taught me the night before, *Ickpling gloffthrobb squutserumm blhiop mlashnalt, zwin tnodbalkguffh slhiophad gurdlubh asht.* This is the compliment established by the laws of the land for all persons admitted to the King's presence. It may be rendered into English thus: May your Cœlestial Majesty outlive the sun, eleven moons and an half. To this the King returned some answer, which although I could not understand, yet I replied as I had been directed: *Fluft drin yalerick dwuldum prastrad mirplush*, which properly signifies, My tongue is in the mouth of my friend, and by this expression was meant that I desired leave to bring my interpreter; whereupon the young man already mentioned was accordingly introduced, by whose intervention I answered as many questions as his Majesty could put in above an hour. I spoke in the Balnibarbian tongue, and my interpreter delivered my meaning in that of Luggnagg.

The King was much delighted with my company, and ordered his *Bliffmarklub* or high chamberlain to appoint a lodging in the court for me and my interpreter, with a daily allowance for my table, and a large purse of gold for my common expenses.

I stayed three months in this country out of perfect obedience to his Majesty, who was pleased highly to favour me, and made me very honourable offers. But I thought it more consistent with prudence and justice to pass the remainder of my days with my wife and family.

CHAPTER X.

The Luggnaggians commended. A particular description of the struld-
bruggs, with many conversations between the author and some
eminent persons upon that subject.

The Luggnaggians are a polite and generous people, and
although they are not without some share of that pride which is
peculiar to all eastern countries, yet they show themselves
courteous to strangers, especially such who are countenanced by
the court. I had many acquaintance among persons of the best
fashion, and being always attended by my interpreter, the conversation we had was not disagreeable.

One day in much good company I was asked by a person of
quality, whether I had seen any of their *struldbruggs* or
immortals. I said I had not, and desired he would explain to me
what he meant by such an appellation applied to a mortal
creature. He told me, that sometimes, although very rarely, a
child happened to be born in a family with a red circular spot
in the forehead, directly over the left eyebrow, which was an infallible mark that it should never die. The spot, as he described
it, was about the compass of a silver three pence, but in the course
of time grew larger, and changed its colour; for at twelve years
old it became green, so continued till five and twenty, then
turned to a deep blue; at five and forty it grew coal black, and as
large as an English shilling, but never admitted any farther alter-
ation. He said these births were so rare, that he did not believe
there could be above eleven hundred *struldbruggs* of both sexes
in the whole kingdom, of which he computed about fifty in the
metropolis, and among the rest a young girl born about three
years ago. That these productions were not peculiar to any
family, but a mere effect of chance, and the children of the
struldbruggs themselves were equally mortal with the rest of the
people.

I freely own my self to have been struck with inexpressible
delight upon hearing this account: and the person who gave it me
happening to understand the Balnibarbian language, which I
spoke very well, I could not forbear breaking out into expressions perhaps a little too extravagant. I cried out as in a rapture:
Happy nation where every child hath at least a chance for being
immortal! Happy people who enjoy so many living examples of
ancient virtue, and have masters ready to instruct them in the
wisdom of all former ages! But happiest beyond all comparison
are those excellent *struldbruggs*, who being born exempt from
that universal calamity of human nature, have their minds free

and disengaged, without the weight and depression of spirits caused by the continual apprehension of death. I discovered my admiration that I had not observed any of these illustrious persons at court, the black spot on the forehead being so remarkable a distinction, that I could not have easily overlooked it and it was impossible that his Majesty, a most judicious prince, should not provide himself with a good number of such wise and able counsellors. Yet perhaps the virtue of those reverend sages was too strict for the corrupt and libertine manners of a court. And we often find by experience that young men are too opinionative and volatile to be guided by the sober dictates of their seniors. However, since the King was pleased to allow me access to his royal person, I was resolved upon the very first occasion to deliver my opinion to him on this matter freely, and at large by the help of my interpreter; and whether he would please to take my advice or no, yet in one thing I was determined, that his Majesty having frequently offered me an establishment in this country, I would with great thankfulness accept the favour, and pass my life here in the conversation of those superior beings the *struldbruggs*, if they would please to admit me.

The gentleman to whom I addressed my discourse, because (as I have already observed) he spoke the language of Balnibarbi, said to me with a sort of a smile, which usually ariseth from pity to the ignorant, that he was glad of any occasion to keep me among them, and desired my permission to explain to the company what I had spoke. He did so, and they talked together for some time in their own language, whereof I understood not a syllable, neither could I observe by their countenances what impression my discourse had made on them. After a short silence the same person told me, that his friends and mine (so he thought fit to express himself) were very much pleased with the judicious remarks I had made on the great happiness and advantages of immortal life, and they were desirous to know in a particular manner, what scheme of living I should have formed to my self, if it had fallen to my lot to have been born a *struldbrugg*.

I answered, it was easy to be eloquent on so copious and delightful a subject, especially to me who have been often apt to amuse my self with visions of what I should do if I were a king, a general, or a great lord; and upon this very case I had frequently run over the whole system how I should employ my self and pass the time if I were sure to live for ever.

That if it had been my good fortune to come into the world a *struldbrugg*, as soon as I could discover my own happiness by understanding the difference between life and death, I would first resolve by all arts and methods whatsoever to procure my self riches. In the pursuit of which by thrift and management, I might reasonably expect in about two hundred years to be the wealthiest man in the kingdom. In the second place, I would from my earliest youth apply myself to the study of arts and sciences, by which I should arrive in time to excel all others in learning. Lastly, I would carefully record every action and event of consequence that happened in the public, impartially draw the characters of the several successions of princes, and great ministers of state, with my own observations on every point. I would exactly set down the several changes in customs, languages, fashions of dress, diet and diversions. By all which acquirements, I should be a living treasury of knowledge and wisdom, and certainly become the oracle of the nation.

I would never marry after threescore, but live in an hospitable manner, yet still on the saving side. I would entertain myself in forming and directing the minds of hopeful young men, by convincing them from my own remembrance, experience and observation, fortified by numerous examples, of the usefulness of virtue in public and private life. But my choice and constant companions should be a set of my own immortal brotherhood, among whom I would elect a dozen from the most ancient down to my own contemporaries. Where any of these wanted fortunes, I would provide them with convenient lodges round my own estate, and have some of them always at my table, only mingling a few of the most valuable among you mortals, whom length of time would harden me to lose with little or no reluctance, and treat your posterity after the same manner, just as a man diverts himself with the annual succession of pinks and tulips in his garden, without regretting the loss of those which withered the preceding year.

These *struldbruggs* and I would mutually communicate our observations and memorials through the course of time, remark the several gradations by which corruption steals into the world, and oppose it in every step, by giving perpetual warning and instruction to mankind; which, added to the strong influence of our own example, would probably prevent that continual degeneracy of human nature so justly complained of in all ages.

Add to all this, the pleasure of seeing the various revolutions of states and empires, the changes in the lower and upper world, ancient cities in ruins, and obscure villages become the seats of kings. Famous rivers lessening into shallow brooks, the ocean leaving one coast dry, and overwhelming another; the discovery of many countries yet unknown. Barbarity overrunning the

politest nations, and the most barbarous becoming civilized. I
should then see the discovery of the longitude, the perpetual
motion, the universal medicine, and many other great inventions
brought to the utmost perfection.

What wonderful discoveries should we make in astronomy,
by outliving and confirming our own predictions, by observing
the progress and returns of comets, with the changes of motion
in the sun, moon and stars.

I enlarged upon many other topics which the natural desire of
endless life and sublunary happiness could easily furnish me with.
When I had ended, and the sum of my discourse had been interpreted as before to the rest of the company, there was a good
deal of talk among them in the language of the country, not without some laughter at my expense. At last the same gentleman
who had been my interpreter said, he was desired by the rest
to set me right in a few mistakes, which I had fallen into through
the common imbecility of human nature, and upon that allowance
was less answerable for them. That this breed of *struldbruggs* was
peculiar to their country, for there were no such people either
in Balnibarbi or Japan, where he had the honour to be ambassador
from his Majesty, and found the natives in both those kingdoms
very hard to believe that the fact was possible, and it appeared
from my astonishment when he first mentioned the matter to me,
that I received it as a thing wholly new, and scarcely to be credited. That in the two kingdoms above mentioned, where during
his residence he had conversed very much, he observed long life to
be the universal desire and wish of mankind. That whoever had
one foot in the grave was sure to hold back the other as strongly
as he could. That the oldest had still hopes of living one day
longer, and looked on death as the greatest evil, from which
nature always prompted him to retreat; only in this island of
Luggnagg the appetite for living was not so eager, from the continual example of the *struldbruggs* before their eyes.

That the system of living contrived by me was unreasonable
and unjust, because it supposed a perpetuity of youth, health, and
vigour, which no man could be so foolish to hope, however
extravagant he might be in his wishes. That the question therefore was not whether a man would choose to be always in the
prime of youth, attended with prosperity and health, but how
he would pass a perpetual life under all the usual disadvantages
which old age brings along with it. For although few men will
avow their desires of being immortal upon such hard conditions,
yet in the two kingdoms before-mentioned of Balnibarbi and
Japan, he observed that every man desired to put off death for

some time longer, let it approach ever so late, and he rarely heard of any man who died willingly, except he were incited by the extremity of grief or torture. And he appealed to me whether in those countries I had travelled, as well as my own, I had not observed the same general disposition.

After this preface he gave me a particular account of the *struldbruggs* among them. He said they commonly acted like mortals, till about thirty years old, after which by degrees they grew melancholy and dejected, increasing in both till they came to fourscore. This he learned from their own confession; for otherwise there not being above two or three of that species born in an age, they were too few to form a general observation by. When they came to fourscore years, which is reckoned the extremity of living in this country, they had not only all the follies and infirmities of other old men, but many more which arose from the dreadful prospect of never dying. They were not only opinionative, peevish, covetous, morose, vain, talkative, but uncapable of friendship, and dead to all natural affection, which never descended below their grandchildren. Envy and impotent desires are their prevailing passions. But those objects against which their envy seems principally directed, are the vices of the younger sort, and the deaths of the old. By reflecting on the former, they find themselves cut off from all possibility of pleasure; and whenever they see a funeral, they lament and repine that others are gone to an harbour of rest, to which they themselves never can hope to arrive. They have no remembrance of any thing but what they learned and observed in their youth and middle age, and even that is very imperfect. And for the truth or particulars of any fact, it is safer to depend on common traditions than upon their best recollections. The least miserable among them appear to be those who turn to dotage and entirely lose their memories; these meet with more pity and assistance, because they want many bad qualities which abound in others.

If a *struldbrugg* happen to marry one of his own kind, the marriage is dissolved of course by the courtesy of the kingdom, as soon as the younger of the two comes to be fourscore. For the law thinks it a reasonable indulgence, that those who are condemned without any fault of their own to a perpetual continuance in the world, should not have their misery doubled by the load of a wife.

As soon as they have completed the term of eighty years, they are looked on as dead in law; their heirs immediately succeed to their estates, only a small pittance is reserved for their support, and the poor ones are maintained at the public charge. After that period they are held incapable of any employment of trust or profit; they cannot purchase lands or take leases, neither are they allowed to be witnesses in any cause, either civil or criminal, not even for the decision of meers and bounds.

At ninety they lose their teeth and hair, they have at that age no distinction of taste, but eat and drink whatever they can get, without relish or appetite. The diseases they were subject to still continue without encreasing or diminishing. In talking they forget the common appellation of things, and the names of persons, even of those who are their nearest friends and relations. For the same reason they never can amuse themselves with reading, because their memory will not serve to carry them from the beginning of a sentence to the end; and by this defect they are deprived of the only entertainment whereof they might otherwise be capable.

The language of this country being always upon the flux, the *struldbruggs* of one age do not understand those of another, neither are they able after two hundred years to hold any conversation (farther than by a few general words) with their neighbours the mortals, and thus they lie under the disadvantage of living like foreigners in their own country.

This was the account given me of the *struldbruggs*, as near as I can remember. I afterwards saw five or six of different ages, the youngest not above two hundred years old, who were brought to me at several times by some of my friends; but although they were told that I was a great traveller, and had seen all the world, they had not the least curiosity to ask me a question; only desired I would give them *slumskudask,* or a token of remembrance, which is a modest way of begging, to avoid the law that strictly forbids it, because they are provided for by the public, although indeed with a very scanty allowance.

They are despised and hated by all sorts of people; when one of them is born, it is reckoned ominous, and their birth is recorded very particularly; so that you may know their age by consulting the registry, which however hath not been kept above a thousand years past, or at least hath been destroyed by time or public disturbances. But the usual way of computing how old they are, is by asking them what kings or great persons they can remember, and then consulting history, for infallibly the last prince in their mind did not begin his reign after they were fourscore years old.

They were the most mortifying sight I ever beheld, and the women more horrible than the men. Besides the usual deformities in extreme old age, they acquired an additional ghastliness in proportion to their number of years, which is not to be described, and among half a dozen I soon distinguished which was the eldest, although there was not above a century or two between them.

The reader will easily believe, that from what I had heard and seen, my keen appetite for perpetuity of life was much abated. I grew heartily ashamed of the pleasing visions I had formed, and thought no tyrant could invent a death into which I would not run with pleasure from such a life. The King heard of all that had passed between me and my friends upon this occasion, and rallied me very pleasantly, wishing I would send a couple of *struldbruggs* to my own country, to arm our people against the fear of death; but this it seems is forbidden by the fundamental laws of the kingdom, or else I should have been well content with the trouble and expense of transporting them.

I could not but agree that the laws of this kingdom, relating to the *struldbruggs*, were founded upon the strongest reasons, and such as any other country would be under the necessity of enacting in the like circumstances. Otherwise, as avarice is the necessary consequent of old age, those immortals would in time become proprietors of the whole nation, and engross the civil power, which, for want of abilities to manage, must end in the ruin of the public.

CHAPTER XI.

The author leaves Luggnagg and sails to Japan. From thence he returns in a Dutch ship to Amsterdam, and from Amsterdam to England.

I thought this account of the *struldbruggs* might be some entertainment to the reader, because it seems to be a little out of the common way, at least, I do not remember to have met the like in any book of travels that hath come to my hands: and if I am deceived, my excuse must be, that it is necessary for travellers who describe the same country very often to agree in dwelling on the same particulars, without deserving the censure of having borrowed or transcribed from those who wrote before them.

There is indeed a perpetual commerce between this kingdom and the great empire of Japan, and it is very probable that the Japanese authors may have given some account of the *struldbruggs;* but my stay in Japan was so short, and I was so entirely a stranger to the language, that I was not qualified to make any enquiries. But I hope the Dutch upon this notice will be curious and able enough to supply my defects.

His Majesty having often pressed me to accept some employment in his court, and finding me absolutely determined to return to my native country, was pleased to give me his licence to depart, and honoured me with a letter of recommendation under his own hand to the Emperor of Japan. He likewise presented me with four hundred forty-four large pieces of gold (this nation delighting in even numbers) and a red diamond which I sold in England for eleven hundred pounds.

On the 6th day of May, 1709, I took a solemn leave of his Majesty, and all my friends. This prince was so gracious as to order a guard to conduct me to Glanguenstald, which is a royal port to the southwest part of the island. In six days I found a vessel ready to carry me to Japan, and spent fifteen days in the voyage. We landed at a small port-town called Xamoschi, situated on the southeast part of Japan; the town lies on the western part where there is a narrow strait, leading northward into a long arm of the sea, upon the northwest part of which Yedo, the metropolis stands. At landing I showed the custom-house officers my letter from the King of Luggnagg to his Imperial Majesty. They knew the seal perfectly well; it was as broad as the palm of my hand. The impression was, *a king lifting up a lame beggar from the earth*. The magistrates of the town, hearing of my letter, received me as a public minister; they provided me with carriages and servants, and bore my charges to Yedo, where I was admitted to an audience, and delivered my letter, which was opened with great ceremony, and explained to the Emperor by an interpreter, who gave me notice of his Majesty's order, that I should signify my request, and whatever it were, it should be granted for the sake of his royal brother of Luggnagg. This interpreter was a person employed to transact affairs with the Hollanders; he soon conjectured by my countenance that I was an European, and therefore repeated his Majesty's commands in Low Dutch, which he spoke perfectly well. I answered (as I had before determined) that I was a Dutch merchant, shipwrecked in a very remote country, from whence I travelled by sea and land to Luggnagg, and then took shipping for Japan, where I knew my countrymen often traded, and with some of these I hoped to get an opportunity of returning into Europe: I therefore most humbly entreated his royal favour to give order, that I should be conducted in safety to Nangasac: to this I added another petition, that for the sake of my patron the King of

Luggnagg, his Majesty would condescend to excuse my performing the ceremony imposed on my countrymen of *trampling upon the crucifix*, because I had been thrown into his kingdom by my misfortunes, without any intention of trading. When this latter petition was interpreted to the Emperor, he seemed a little surprised, and said he believed I was the first of my countrymen who ever made any scruple in this point, and that he began to doubt whether I was a real Hollander or no; but rather suspected I must be a Christian. However, for the reasons I had offered, but chiefly to gratify the King of Luggnagg, by an uncommon mark of his favour, he would comply with the singularity of my humour; but the affair must be managed with dexterity, and his officers should be commanded to let me pass as it were by forgetfulness. For he assured me, that if the secret should be discovered by my countrymen, the Dutch, they would cut my throat in the voyage. I returned my thanks by the interpreter for so unusual a favour, and some troops being at that time on their march to Nangasac, the commanding officer had orders to convey me safe thither, with particular instructions about the business of the crucifix.

On the 9th day of June, 1709, I arrived at Nangasac, after a very long and troublesome journey. I soon fell into company of some Dutch sailors belonging to the *Amboyna* of Amsterdam, a stout ship of 450 tons. I had lived long in Holland, pursuing my studies at Leyden, and I spoke Dutch well. The seamen soon knew from whence I came last; they were curious to enquire into my voyages and course of life. I made up a story as short and probable as I could, but concealed the greatest part. I knew many persons in Holland, I was able to invent names for my parents, whom I pretended to be obscure people in the province of Gelderland. I would have given the captain (one Theodorus Vangrult) what he pleased to ask for my voyage to Holland; but understanding I was a surgeon, he was contented to take half the usual rate, on condition that I would serve him in the way of my calling. Before we took shipping, I was often asked by some of the crew, whether I had performed the ceremony above-mentioned. I evaded the question by general answers, that I had satisfied the Emperor and court in all particulars. However, a malicious rogue of a skipper went to an officer, and pointing to me, told him, I had not yet *trampled on the crucifix* but the other, who had received instructions to let me pass, gave the rascal twenty strokes on the shoulders with a bamboo, after which I was no more troubled with such questions.

Nothing happened worth mentioning in this voyage. We sailed

with a fair wind to the Cape of Good Hope, where we stayed only to take in fresh water. On the 6th of April we arrived safely at Amsterdam, having lost only three men by sickness in the voyage, and a fourth who fell from the foremast into the sea, not far from the coast of Guinea. From Amsterdam I soon after set sail for England in a small vessel belonging to that city.

On the 10th of April, 1710, we put in at the Downs. I landed the next morning, and saw once more my native country after an absence of five years and six months complete. I went straight to Redriff, where I arrived the same day at two in the afternoon, and found my wife and family in good health.

THE END OF THE THIRD PART.

Nuyts Land

Edels Land
Lewins Land   *I St. Francot*   *I St Pieter*

HOUYHNHNMS LAND

Sweers I
I Maelsuyker
De Wits I

Discovered A D 1711.

TRAVELS.

PART IV.

A VOYAGE TO THE COUNTRY OF THE HOUYHNHNMS.

CHAPTER I.

The author sets out as captain of a ship. His men conspire against him, confine him a long time to his cabin, set him on shore in an unknown land. He travels up in the country. The yahoos, a strange sort of animal, described. The author meets two Houyhnhnms.

I continued at home with my wife and children about five months in a very happy condition, if I could have learned the lesson of knowing when I was well. I left my poor wife big with child, and accepted an advantageous offer made me to be captain of the *Adventure,* a stout merchantman of 350 tons: for I understood navigation well, and being grown weary of a surgeon's employment at sea, which however I could exercise upon occasion, I took a skilful young man of that calling, one Robert Purefoy, into my ship. We set sail from Portsmouth upon the 7th day of September, 1710; on the 14th, we met with Captain Pocock of Bristol, at Tenariff, who was going to the bay of Campechy, to cut logwood. On the 16th, he was parted from us by a storm; I heard since my return that his ship foundered, and none escaped, but one cabin-boy. He was an honest man, and a good sailor, but a little too positive in his own opinions, which was the cause of his destruction, as it hath been of several others. For if he had followed my advice, he might at this time have been safe at home with his family as well as myself.

I had several men died in my ship of calentures, so that I was forced to get recruits out of Barbadoes, and the Leeward Islands, where I touched by the direction of the merchants who employed me, which I had soon too much cause to repent; for I found afterwards that most of them had been buccaneers. I had fifty hands on board, and my orders were, that I should trade

with the Indians in the South Sea, and make what discoveries I
could. These rogues whom I had picked up debauched my other
men, and they all formed a conspiracy to seize the ship and secure
me; which they did one morning, rushing into my cabin, and
binding me hand and foot, threatening to throw me overboard,
if I offered to stir. I told them, I was their prisoner, and would
submit. This they made me swear to do, and then unbound me,
only fastening one of my legs with a chain near my bed, and
placed a sentry at my door with his piece charged, who was
commanded to shoot me dead if I attempted my liberty. They
sent me down victuals and drink, and took the government of the
ship to themselves. Their design was to turn pirates, and plunder
the Spaniards, which they could not do till they got more men.
But first they resolved to sell the goods in the ship, and then go
to Madagascar for recruits, several among them having died since
my confinement. They sailed many weeks, and traded with the
Indians, but I knew not what course they took, being kept close
prisoner in my cabin, and expecting nothing less than to be
murdered, as they often threatened me.

Upon the 9th day of May, 1711, one James Welch came
down to my cabin; and said he had orders from the captain to set
me ashore. I expostulated with him, but in vain; neither would
he so much as tell me who their new captain was. They forced
me into the long-boat, letting me put on my best suit of clothes,
which were as good as new, and a small bundle of linen, but no
arms except my hanger; and they were so civil as not to search
my pockets, into which I conveyed what money I had, with some
other little necessaries. They rowed about a league, and then set
me down on a strand. I desired them to tell me what country it
was. They all swore, they knew no more than myself, but said,
that the captain (as they called him) was resolved, after they had
sold the lading, to get rid of me in the first place where they discovered land. They pushed off immediately, advising me to
make haste, for fear of being overtaken by the tide, and bade me
farewell.

In this desolate condition I advanced forward, and soon got
upon firm ground, where I sat down on a bank to rest myself, and
consider what I had best to do. When I was a little refreshed I
went up into the country, resolving to deliver myself to the first
savages I should meet, and purchase my life from them by some
bracelets, glass rings, and other toys, which sailors usually provide themselves with in those voyages, and whereof I had some
about me: the land was divided by long rows of trees, not
regularly planted, but naturally growing; there was great plenty

of grass, and several fields of oats. I walked very circumspectly
for fear of being surprised, or suddenly shot with an arrow from
behind or on either side. I fell into a beaten road, where I saw
many tracks of human feet, and some of cows, but most of
horses. At last I beheld several animals in a field, and one or two
of the same kind sitting in trees. Their shape was very singular,
and deformed, which a little discomposed me, so that I lay down
behind a thicket to observe them better. Some of them coming
forward near the place where I lay, gave me an opportunity of
distinctly marking their form. Their heads and breasts were
covered with a thick hair, some frizzled and others lank; they
had beards like goats, and a long ridge of hair down their backs,
and the foreparts of their legs and feet, but the rest of their
bodies were bare, so that I might see their skins, which were of a
brown buff colour. They had no tails, nor any hair at all on their
buttocks, except about the anus; which, I presume, nature had
placed there to defend them as they sat on the ground; for this
posture they used, as well as lying down, and often stood on their
hind feet. They climbed high trees, as nimbly as a squirrel, for
they had strong extended claws before and behind, terminating
in sharp points, and hooked. They would often spring, and
bound, and leap with prodigious agility. The females were not
so large as the males; they had long lank hair on their heads, and
only a sort of down on the rest of their bodies, except about the
anus, and pudenda. Their dugs hung between their fore-feet,
and often reached almost to the ground as they walked. The hair
of both sexes was of several colours, brown, red, black, and yellow. Upon the whole, I never beheld in all my travels so
disagreeable an animal, or one against which I naturally conceived so strong antipathy. So that thinking I had seen enough,
full of contempt and aversion, I got up and pursued the beaten
road, hoping it might direct me to the cabin of some Indian. I
had not gone far when I met one of these creatures full in my
way, and coming up directly to me. The ugly monster, when
he saw me, distorted several ways every feature of his visage, and
stared as at an object he had never seen before; then approaching
nearer, lifted up his forepaw, whether out of curiosity or mischief, I could not tell. But I drew my hanger, and gave him a
good blow with the flat side of it, for I durst not strike him with
the edge, fearing the inhabitants might be provoked against me,
if they should come to know that I had killed or maimed any of
their cattle. When the beast felt the smart, he drew back, and
roared so loud, that a herd of at least forty came flocking about
me from the next field, howling and making odious faces; but I

ran to the body of a tree, and leaning my back against it, kept
them off, by waving my hanger. Several of this cursed brood
getting hold of the branches behind leaped up into the tree, from
whence they began to discharge their excrements on my head:
however, I escaped pretty well, by sticking close to the stem of
a tree, but was almost stifled with the filth, which fell about me
on every side.

In the midst of this distress, I observed them all to run away
on a sudden as fast as they could, at which I ventured to leave
the tree, and pursue the road, wondering what it was that could
put them into this fright. But looking on my left hand, I saw a
horse walking softly in the field, which my persecutors having
sooner discovered, was the cause of their flight. The horse
started a little when he came near me, but soon recovering
himself, looked full in my face with manifest tokens of wonder:
he viewed my hands and feet, walking round me several times.
I would have pursued my journey, but he placed himself directly
in the way, yet looking with a very mild aspect, never offering
the least violence. We stood gazing at each other for some time;
at last I took the boldness to reach my hand towards his neck,
with a design to stroke it, using the common style and whistle of
jockeys when they are going to handle a strange horse. But this
animal, seeming to receive my civilities with disdain, shook his
head, and bent his brows, softly raising up his left forefoot to
remove my hand. Then he neighed three or four times, but in
so different a cadence, that I almost began to think he was speaking to himself in some language of his own.

While he and I were thus employed, another horse came up;
who applying himself to the first in a very formal manner, they
gently struck each other's right hoof before, neighing several
times by turns, and varying the sound, which seemed to be
almost articulate. They went some paces off, as if it were to
confer together, walking side by side, backward and forward,
like persons deliberating upon some affair of weight, but often
turning their eyes towards me, as it were to watch that I might
not escape. I was amazed to see such actions and behaviour in
brute beasts, and concluded with myself, that if the inhabitants
of this country were endued with a proportionable degree of
reason, they must needs be the wisest people upon earth. This
thought gave me so much comfort, that I resolved to go forward
until I could discover some house or village, or meet with any of
the natives, leaving the two horses to discourse together as they
pleased. But the first, who was a dapple grey, observing me to
steal off, neighed after me in so expressive a tone, that I fancied

myself to understand what he meant; whereupon I turned back, and came near him, to expect his farther commands. But concealing my fear as much as I could, for I began to be in some pain, how this adventure might terminate; and the reader will easily believe I did not much like my present situation.

The two horses came up close to me, looking with great earnestness upon my face and hands. The grey steed rubbed my hat all round with his right fore-hoof, and discomposed it so much, that I was forced to adjust it better, by taking it off, and settling it again; whereat both he and his companion (who was a brown bay) appeared to be much surprised; the latter felt the lappet of my coat, and finding it to hang loose about me, they both looked with new signs of wonder. He stroked my right hand, seeming to admire the softness, and colour; but he squeezed it so hard between his hoof and his pastern, that I was forced to roar; after which they both touched me with all possible tenderness. They were under great perplexity about my shoes and stockings, which they felt very often, neighing to each other, and using various gestures, not unlike those of a philosopher, when he would attempt to solve some new and difficult phænomenon.

Upon the whole, the behaviour of these animals was so orderly and rational, so acute and judicious, that I at last concluded, they must needs be magicians, who had thus metamorphosed themselves upon some design, and seeing a stranger in the way, were resolved to divert themselves with him; or perhaps were really amazed at the sight of a man so very different in habit, feature, and complexion from those who might probably live in so remote a climate. Upon the strength of this reasoning, I ventured to address them in the following manner: Gentlemen, if you be conjurers, as I have good cause to believe, you can understand any language; therefore I make bold to let your Worships know, that I am a poor distressed English man, driven by his misfortunes upon your coast, and I entreat one of you, to let me ride upon his back, as if he were a real horse, to some house or village, where I can be relieved. In return of which favour, I will make you a present of this knife and bracelet (taking them out of my pocket). The two creatures stood silent while I spoke, seeming to listen with great attention; and when I had ended, they neighed frequently towards each other, as if they were engaged in serious conversation. I plainly observed, that their language expressed the passions very well, and the words might with little pains be resolved into an alphabet more easily than the Chinese.

I could frequently distinguish the word *yahoo*, which was repeated by each of them several times; and although it was impossible for me to conjecture what it meant, yet while the two horses were busy in conversation, I endeavoured to practice this word upon my tongue; and as soon as they were silent, I boldly pronounced *yahoo* in a loud voice, imitating, at the same time, as near as I could, the neighing of a horse; at which they were both visibly surprised, and the grey repeated the same word twice, as if he meant to teach me the right accent, wherein I spoke after him as well as I could, and found myself perceivably to improve every time, although very far from any degree of perfection. Then the bay tried me with a second word, much harder to be pronounced; but reducing it to the English orthography, may be spelt thus, *Houyhnhnm*. I did not succeed in this so well as the former, but after two or three farther trials, I had better fortune; and they both appeared amazed at my capacity.

After some farther discourse, which I then conjectured might relate to me, the two friends took their leaves, with the same compliment of striking each other's hoof; and the grey made me signs that I should walk before him, wherein I thought it prudent to comply, till I could find a better director. When I offered to slacken my pace, he would cry *hhuun, hhuun*; I guessed his meaning, and gave him to understand, as well as I could, that I was weary, and not able to walk faster; upon which he would stand a while to let me rest.

CHAPTER II.

The author conducted by a Houyhnhnm to his house. The house described. The author's reception. The food of the Houyhnhnms. The author in distress for want of meat, is at last relieved. His manner of feeding in that country.

Having travelled about three miles, we came to a long kind of building, made of timber stuck in the ground, and wattled across; the roof was low, and covered with straw. I now began to be a little comforted, and took out some toys, which travellers usually carry for presents to the savage Indians of America and other parts, in hopes the people of the house would be thereby encouraged to receive me kindly. The horse made me a sign to go in first; it was a large room with a smooth clay floor, and a rack and manger extending the whole length on one side. There were three nags, and two mares, not eating, but some of them sitting down upon their hams, which I very much wondered at; but wondered more to see the rest employed in domestic business. They seemed but ordinary cattle; however, this confirmed my first opinion, that a people who could so far civilize brute animals must needs excel in wisdom all the nations of the world. The grey came in just after, and thereby prevented any ill treatment which the others might have given me. He neighed to them several times in a style of authority, and received answers.

Beyond this room there were three others, reaching the length of the house, to which you passed through three doors, opposite to each other, in the manner of a vista; we went through the second room towards the third; here the grey walked in first, beckoning me to attend: I waited in the second room, and got ready my presents for the master and mistress of the house: they were two knives, three bracelets of false pearl, a small looking-glass and a bead necklace. The horse neighed three or four times, and I waited to hear some answers in a human voice, but I heard no other returns than in the same dialect, only one or two a little shriller than his. I began to think that this house must belong to some person of great note among them, because there appeared so much ceremony before I could gain admittance. But that a man of quality should be served all by horses was beyond my comprehension. I feared my brain was disturbed by my sufferings and misfortunes: I roused myself, and looked about me in the room where I was left alone; this was furnished as the first, only after a more elegant manner. I rubbed my eyes often, but the same objects still occurred. I pinched my arms and sides, to awake myself, hoping I might be in a dream. I then absolutely concluded, that all these appearances could be nothing else but necromancy and magic. But I had no time to pursue these reflections; for the grey horse came to the door, and made me a sign to follow him into the third room, where I saw a very comely mare, together with a colt and foal, sitting on their haunches, upon mats of straw, not unartfully made, and perfectly neat and clean.

The mare, soon after my entrance, rose from her mat, and coming up close, after having nicely observed my hands and face, gave me a most contemptuous look; then turning to the horse, I heard the word *yahoo* often repeated betwixt them; the meaning of which word I could not then comprehend, although it were the first I had learned to pronounce; but I was soon better informed, to my everlasting mortification: for the horse beckoning to me with his head, and repeating the word *hhuun, hhuun*, as he did upon the road, which I understood was to attend him, led me out into a kind of court, where was another building at some distance from the house. Here we entered, and I saw three of those detestable creatures, which I first met after my landing, feeding upon roots, and the flesh of some animals, which I afterwards found to be that of asses and dogs, and now and then a cow dead by accident or disease. They were all tied by the neck with strong withes, fastened to a beam; they held their food between the claws of their forefeet, and tore it with their teeth.

The master horse ordered a sorrel nag, one of his servants, to untie the largest of these animals, and take him into the yard. The beast and I were brought close together, and our countenances diligently compared, both by master and servant, who thereupon repeated several times the word *yahoo*. My horror and astonishment are not to be described, when I observed, in this abominable animal, a perfect human figure; the face of it indeed was flat and broad, the nose depressed, the lips large, and the mouth wide. But these differences are common to all savage nations, where the lineaments of the countenance are distorted by the natives suffering their infants to lie grovelling on the earth, or by carrying them on their backs, nuzzling with their face against the mother's shoulders. The forefeet of the yahoo differed from my hands in nothing else but the length of the nails, the coarseness and brownness of the palms, and the hairiness on the backs. There was the same resemblance between our feet, with the same differences, which I knew very well, although the horses did not, because of my shoes and stockings; the same in every part of our bodies, except as to hairiness and colour, which I have already described.

The great difficulty that seemed to stick with the two horses, was to see the rest of my body so very different from that of a yahoo, for which I was obliged to my clothes, whereof they had no conception: the sorrel nag offered me a root, which he held (after their manner, as we shall describe in its proper place) between his hoof and pastern; I took it in my hand, and having smelt it, returned it to him as civilly as I could. He brought out of the yahoo's kennel a piece of ass's flesh, but it smelt so offensively that I turned from it with loathing: he then threw it to the yahoo, by whom it was greedily devoured. He afterwards showed me a wisp of hay, and a fetlock full of oats; but I shook my head, to signify, that neither of these were food for me. And indeed, I now apprehended, that I must absolutely starve, if I did not get to some of my own species: for as to those filthy yahoos, although there were few greater lovers of mankind, at that time, than myself, yet I confess I never saw any sensitive

being so detestable on all accounts; and the more I came near
them, the more hateful they grew, while I stayed in that country.
This the master horse observed by my behaviour, and therefore
sent the yahoo back to his kennel. He then put his fore-hoof to
his mouth, at which I was much surprised, although he did it
with ease, and with a motion that appeared perfectly natural,
and made other signs to know what I would eat; but I could not
return him such an answer as he was able to apprehend; and if
he had understood me, I did not see how it was possible to contrive any way for finding myself nourishment. While we were
thus engaged, I observed a cow passing by, whereupon I pointed
to her, and expressed a desire to let me go and milk her. This
had its effect; for he led me back into the house, and ordered a
mare-servant to open a room, where a good store of milk lay in
earthen and wooden vessels, after a very orderly and cleanly
manner. She gave me a large bowl full, of which I drank very
heartily, and found myself well refreshed.

About noon I saw coming towards the house a kind of vehicle
drawn like a sledge by four yahoos. There was in it an old steed,
who seemed to be of quality; he alighted with his hind feet forward, having by accident got a hurt in his left forefoot. He came
to dine with our horse, who received him with great civility.
They dined in the best room, and had oats boiled in milk for the
second course, which the old horse eat warm, but the rest cold.
Their mangers were placed circular in the middle of the room,
and divided into several partitions, round which they sat on their
haunches upon bosses of straw. In the middle was a large rack
with angles answering to every partition of the manger. So that
each horse and mare eat their own hay, and their own mash of
oats and milk, with much decency and regularity. The behaviour
of the young colt and foal appeared very modest, and that of the
master and mistress extremely cheerful and complaisant to their
guest. The grey ordered me to stand by him, and much discourse passed between him and his friend concerning me, as I
found by the stranger's often looking on me, and the frequent
repetition of the word *yahoo*.

I happened to wear my gloves, which the master grey observing, seemed perplexed, discovering signs of wonder what I had
done to my forefeet; he put his hoof three or four times to them,
as if he would signify, that I should reduce them to their former
shape, which I presently did, pulling off both my gloves, and putting them into my pocket. This occasioned farther talk, and I
saw the company was pleased with my behaviour, whereof I soon
found the good effects. I was ordered to speak the few words I

understood, and while they were at dinner, the master taught me the names for oats, milk, fire, water, and some others: which I could readily pronounce after him, having from my youth a great facility in learning languages.

When dinner was done, the master horse took me aside, and by signs and words made me understand the concern he was in, that I had nothing to eat. Oats in their tongue are called *hlunnh*. This word I pronounced two or three times; for although I had refused them at first, yet upon second thoughts, I considered that I could contrive to make of them a kind of bread, which might be sufficient with milk to keep me alive, till I could make my escape to some other country, and to creatures of my own species. The horse immediately ordered a white mare-servant of his family to bring me a good quantity of oats in a sort of wooden tray. These I heated before the fire as well as I could, and rubbed them till the husks came off, which I made a shift to winnow from the grain; I ground and beat them between two stones, then took water, and made them into a paste or cake, which I toasted at the fire, and eat warm with milk. It was at first a very insipid diet, although common enough in many parts of Europe, but grew tolerable by time; and having been often reduced to hard fare in my life, this was not the first experiment I had made how easily nature is satisfied. And I cannot but observe, that I never had one hour's sickness, while I stayed in this island. It is true, I sometimes made a shift to catch a rabbit, or bird, by springes made of yahoos' hairs, and I often gathered wholesome herbs, which I boiled, or eat as salads with my bread, and now and then, for a rarity, I made a little butter, and drank the whey. I was at first at a great loss for salt; but custom soon reconciled the want of it; and I am confident that the frequent use of salt among us is an effect of luxury, and was first introduced only as a provocative to drink; except where it is necessary for preserving of flesh in long voyages, or in places remote from great markets. For we observe no animal to be fond of it but man: and as to myself, when I left this country, it was a great while before I could endure the taste of it in anything that I eat.

This is enough to say upon the subject of my diet, wherewith other travellers fill their books, as if the readers were personally concerned whether we fared well or ill. However, it was necessary to mention this matter, lest the world should think it impossible that I could find sustenance for three years in such a country, and among such inhabitants.

When it grew towards evening, the master horse ordered a place for me to lodge in; it was but six yards from the house, and separated from the stable of the yahoos. Here I got some straw, and covering myself with my own clothes, slept very sound. But I was in a short time better accommodated, as the reader shall know hereafter, when I come to treat more particularly about my way of living.

Chapter III.

The author studious to learn the language, the Houyhnhnm his master assists in teaching him. The language described. Several Houyhnhnms of quality come out of curiosity to see the author. He gives his master a short account of his voyage.

My principal endeavour was to learn the language, which my master (for so I shall henceforth call him) and his children, and every servant of his house were desirous to teach me. For they looked upon it as a prodigy that a brute animal should discover such marks of a rational creature. I pointed to every thing, and enquired the name of it, which I wrote down in my journal-book when I was alone, and corrected my bad accent, by desiring those of the family to pronounce it often. In this employment, a sorrel nag, one of the under servants, was very ready to assist me.

In speaking, they pronounce through the nose and throat, and their language approaches nearest to the High Dutch or German, of any I know in Europe; but is much more graceful and significant. The Emperor Charles V made almost the same observation, when he said, that if he were to speak to his horse, it should be in High Dutch.

The curiosity and impatience of my master were so great, that he spent many hours of his leisure to instruct me. He was convinced (as he afterwards told me) that I must be a yahoo, but my teachableness, civility and cleanliness astonished him; which were qualities altogether so opposite to those animals. He was most perplexed about my clothes, reasoning sometimes with himself, whether they were a part of my body; for I never pulled them off till the family were asleep, and got them on before they waked in the morning. My master was eager to learn from whence I came, how I acquired those appearances of reason which I discovered in all my actions, and to know my story from my own mouth, which he hoped he should soon do by the great proficiency I made in learning and pronouncing their words and sentences. To help my memory, I formed all I learned into the English alphabet, and writ the words down with the translations. This last, after some time, I ventured to do in my master's presence. It cost me much trouble to explain to him what I was doing; for the inhabitants have not the least idea of books or literature.

In about ten weeks time I was able to understand most of his questions, and in three months could give him some tolerable answers. He was extremely curious to know from what part of the country I came, and how I was taught to imitate a rational creature, because the yahoos (whom he saw I exactly resembled in my head, hands and face, that were only visible), with some appearance of cunning, and the strongest disposition to mischief, were observed to be the most unteachable of all brutes. I answered, that I came over the sea, from a far place, with many others of my own kind, in a great hollow vessel made of the bodies of trees. That my companions forced me to land on this coast, and then left me to shift for myself. It was with some difficulty, and by the help of many signs, that I brought him to understand me. He replied, that I must needs be mistaken, or that I 'said the thing which was not.' (For they have no words in their language to express lying or falsehood.) He knew it was impossible that there could be a country beyond the sea, or that a parcel of brutes could move a wooden vessel whither they pleased upon water. He was sure no Houyhnhnm alive could make such a vessel, or would trust yahoos to manage it.

The word *Houyhnhnm*, in their tongue, signifies a *horse*, and in its etymology, *the perfection of nature*. I told my master, that I was at a loss for expression, but would improve as fast as I could; and hoped in a short time I should be able to tell him wonders: he was pleased to direct his own mare, his colt and foal, and the servants of the family to take all opportunities of instructing me, and every day for two or three hours he was at the same pains himself: several horses and mares of quality in the neighbourhood came often to our house upon the report spread of a wonderful yahoo, that could speak like a Houyhnhnm, and seemed in his words and actions to discover some glimmerings of reason. These delighted to converse with me; they put many questions, and received such answers as I was able to return. By all which advantages, I made so great a progress, that in five months from my arrival I understood whatever was spoke, and could express myself tolerably well.

The Houyhnhnms who came to visit my master, out of a design of seeing and talking with me, could hardly believe me to be a right yahoo, because my body had a different covering from others of my kind. They were astonished to observe me without the usual hair or skin except on my head, face, and hands; but

I discovered that secret to my master, upon an accident, which happened about a fortnight before.

I have already told the reader, that every night, when the family were gone to bed, it was my custom to strip and cover myself with my clothes: it happened one morning early, that my master sent for me, by the sorrel nag, who was his valet; when he came, I was fast asleep, my clothes fallen off on one side, and my shirt above my waist. I awaked at the noise he made, and observed him to deliver his message in some disorder; after which he went to my master, and in a great fright gave him a very confused acount of what he had seen: this I presently discovered; for going, as soon as I was dressed, to pay my attendance upon his Honour, he asked me the meaning of what his servant had reported, that I was not the same thing when I slept as I appeared to be at other times; that his valet assured him, some part of me was white, some yellow, at least not so white, and some brown.

I had hitherto concealed the secret of my dress, in order to distinguish myself as much as possible from that cursed race of yahoos; but now I found it in vain to do so any longer. Besides, I considered that my clothes and shoes would soon wear out, which already were in a declining condition, and must be supplied by some contrivance from the hides of yahoos or other brutes; whereby the whole secret would be known: I therefore told my master, that in the country from whence I came those of my kind always covered their bodies with the hairs of certain animals prepared by art, as well for decency, as to avoid inclemencies of air both hot and cold; of which, as to my own person, I would give him immediate conviction, if he pleased to command me; only desiring his excuse, if I did not expose those parts that nature taught us to conceal. He said my discourse was all very strange, but especially the last part; for he could not understand why nature should teach us to conceal what nature had given. That neither himself nor family were ashamed of any parts of their bodies; but however I might do as I pleased. Whereupon, I first unbuttoned my coat, and pulled it off. I did the same with my waistcoat; I drew off my shoes, stockings, and breeches. I let my shirt down to my waist, and drew up the bottom, fastening it like a girdle about my middle to hide my nakedness.

My master observed the whole performance with great signs of curiosity and admiration. He took up all my clothes in his pastern, one piece after another, and examined them diligently; he then stroked my body very gently and looked round me several times, after which he said, it was plain I must be a perfect yahoo; but that I differed very much from the rest of my species, in the whiteness and smoothness of my skin, my want of hair in several parts of my body, the shape and shortness of my claws behind and before, and my affectation of walking continually on my two hinder feet. He desired to see no more, and gave me leave to put on my clothes again, for I was shuddering with cold.

I expressed my uneasiness at his giving me so often the appellation of *yahoo*, an odious animal, for which I had so utter an hatred and contempt; I begged he would forbear applying that word to me, and take the same order in his family, and among his friends whom he suffered to see me. I requested likewise, that the secret of my having a false covering to my body might be known to none but himself, at least as long as my present clothing should last; for as to what the sorrel nag his valet had observed, his Honour might command him to conceal it.

All this my master very graciously consented to, and thus the secret was kept till my clothes began to wear out, which I was forced to supply by several contrivances, that shall hereafter be mentioned. In the mean time, he desired I would go on with my utmost diligence to learn their language, because he was more astonished at my capacity for speech and reason than at the figure of my body, whether it were covered or no; adding, that he waited with some impatience to hear the wonders which I promised to tell him.

From thenceforward he doubled the pains he had been at to instruct me; he brought me into all company, and made them treat me with civility, because, as he told them privately, this would put me into good humour, and make me more diverting.

Every day when I waited on him, beside the trouble he was at in teaching, he would ask me several questions concerning myself, which I answered as well as I could; and by those means he had already received some general ideas, although very imperfect. It would be tedious to relate the several steps by which I advanced to a more regular conversation: but the first account I gave of myself in any order and length, was to this purpose:

That I came from a very far country, as I already had attempted to tell him, with about fifty more of my own species; that we travelled upon the seas, in a great hollow vessel made of wood, and larger than his Honour's house. I described the ship to him in the best terms I could, and explained by the help of my handkerchief displayed, how it was driven forward by the wind. That upon a quarrel among us, I was set on shore on this coast, where I walked forward without knowing whither, till he delivered me from the persecution of those execrable yahoos. He

asked me, who made the ship, and how it was possible that the
Houyhnhnms of my country would leave it to the management
of brutes? My answer was, that I durst proceed no farther in my
relation, unless he would give me his word and honour that he
would not be offended, and then I would tell him the wonders I
had so often promised. He agreed; and I went on by assuring
him, that the ship was made by creatures like myself, who in all
the countries I had travelled, as well as in my own, were the only
governing, rational animals; and that upon my arrival hither, I
was as much astonished to see the Houyhnhnms act like rational
beings, as he or his friends could be in finding some marks of
reason in a creature he was pleased to call a yahoo, to which I
owned my resemblance in every part, but could not account for
their degenerate and brutal nature. I said farther, that if good
fortune ever restored me to my native country, to relate my
travels hither, as I resolved to do, every body would believe that
I 'said the thing which was not'; that I invented the story out of
my own head; and with all possible respect to himself, his family
and friends, and under his promise of not being offended, our
countrymen would hardly think it probable, that a Houyhnhnm
should be the presiding creature of a nation, and a yahoo the
brute.

CHAPTER IV.

*The Houyhnhnms' notion of truth and falsehood. The author's dis-
course disapproved by his master. The author gives a more particular account of himself, and the accidents of his voyage.*

My master heard me with great appearances of uneasiness in
his countenance, because *doubting* or *not believing*, are so little
known in this country, that the inhabitants cannot tell how to
behave themselves under such circumstances. And I remember
in frequent discourses with my master concerning the nature of
manhood, in other parts of the world, having occasion to talk of
lying and *false representation*, it was with much difficulty that he
comprehended what I meant, although he had otherwise a most
acute judgment. For he argued thus; that the use of speech was
to make us understand one another, and to receive information of
facts; now if any one *said the thing which was not*, these ends
were defeated; because I cannot properly be said to understand
him, and I am so far from receiving information, that he leaves
me worse than in ignorance, for I am led to believe a thing black

when it is white, and short when it is long. And these were all the notions he had concerning that faculty of lying, so perfectly well understood, and so universally practised among human creatures.

To return from this digression; when I asserted that the ya-hoos were the only governing animals in my country, which my master said was altogether past his conception, he desired to know, whether we had Houyhnhnms among us, and what was their employment: I told him, we had great numbers, that in summer they grazed in the fields, and in winter were kept in houses, with hay and oats, where yahoo servants were employed to rub their skins smooth, comb their manes, pick their feet, serve them with food, and make their beds. I understand you well, said my master, it is now very plain, from all you have spoken, that whatever share of reason the yahoos pretend to, the Houyhnhnms are your masters; I heartily wish our yahoos would be so tractable. I begged his Honour would please to excuse me from proceeding any farther, because I was very certain that the account he expected from me would be highly displeasing. But he insisted in commanding me to let him know the best and the worst: I told him, he should be obeyed. I owned, that the Houyhnhnms among us, whom we called horses, were the most generous and comely animal we had, that they excelled in strength and swiftness; and when they belonged to persons of quality, employed in travelling, racing, and drawing chariots, they were treated with much kindness and care, till they fell into diseases, or became foundered in the feet; but then they were sold, and used to all kind of drudgery till they died; after which their skins were stripped and sold for what they were worth, and their bodies left to be devoured by dogs and birds of prey. But the common race of horses had not so good fortune, being kept by farmers and carriers and other mean people, who put them to greater labour, and feed them worse. I described, as well as I could, our way of riding, the shape and use of a bridle, a saddle, a spur, and a whip, of harness and wheels. I added, that we fastened plates of a certain hard substance called 'iron' at the bottom of their feet, to preserve their hoofs from being broken by the stony ways on which we often travelled.

My master, after some expressions of great indignation, won-dered how we dared to venture upon a Houyhnhnm's back, for he was sure that the weakest servant in his house would be able to shake off the strongest yahoo, or by lying down, and rolling upon his back, squeeze the brute to death. I answered, that our horses were trained up from three or four years old to the several uses we intended them for; that if any of them proved intolerably vicious, they were employed for carriages; that they were severely beaten while they were young, for any mischievous tricks; that the males, designed for the common use of riding or draught, were generally castrated about two years after their birth, to take down their spirits, and make them more tame and gentle; that they were indeed sensible of rewards and punishments; but his Honour would please to consider, that they had not the least tincture of reason any more than the yahoos in this country.

It put me to the pains of many circumlocutions to give my master a right idea of what I spoke; for their language doth not abound in variety of words, because their wants and passions are fewer than among us. But it is impossible to express his noble resentment at our savage treatment of the Houyhnhnm race, particularly after I had explained the manner and use of castrating horses among us, to hinder them from propagating their kind, and to render them more servile. He said, if it were possible there could be any country where yahoos alone were endued with reason, they certainly must be the governing animal, because reason will in time always prevail against brutal strength. But, considering the frame of our bodies, and especially of mine, he thought no creature of equal bulk was so ill contrived for employing that reason in the common offices of life; whereupon he desired to know whether those among whom I lived resembled me or the yahoos of his country. I assured him, that I was as well shaped as most of my age: but the younger and the females were much more soft and tender, and the skins of the latter generally as white as milk. He said, I differed indeed from other yahoos, being much more cleanly, and not altogether so deformed, but in point of real advantage he thought I differed for the worse. That my nails were of no use either to my fore or hinder feet; as to my forefeet, he could not properly call them by that name, for he never observed me to walk upon them; that they were too soft to bear the ground; that I generally went with them uncovered, neither was the covering I sometimes wore on them of the same shape or so strong as that on my feet behind. That I could not walk with any security, for if either of my hinder feet slipped, I must inevitably fall. He then began to find fault with other parts of my body, the flatness of my face, the prominence of my nose, my eyes placed directly in front, so that I could not look on either side without turning my head: that I was not able to feed myself without lifting one of my forefeet to my mouth: and therefore nature had placed those joints to answer that necessity. He knew not what could be the use of those several clefts and divisions in my feet behind; that these were too soft to bear the hardness and sharpness of stones without a covering made from the skin of some other brute; that my whole body wanted a fence against heat and cold, which I was forced to put on and off every day with tediousness and trouble. And lastly, that he observed every animal in this country naturally to abhor the yahoos, whom the weaker avoided, and the stronger drove from them. So that supposing us to have the gift of reason, he could not see how it were possible to cure that natural antipathy which every creature discovered against us; nor consequently, how we could tame and render them serviceable. However, he would (as he said) debate the matter no farther, because he was more desirous to know my own story, the country where I was born, and the several actions and events of my life before I came hither.

I assured him how extremely desirous I was that he should be satisfied in every point; but I doubted much, whether it would be possible for me to explain myself on several subjects whereof his Honour could have no conception, because I saw nothing in his country to which I could resemble them. That however, I would do my best, and strive to express myself by similitudes, humbly desiring his assistance when I wanted proper words; which he was pleased to promise me.

I said, my birth was of honest parents, in an island called England, which was remote from this country as many days' journey as the strongest of his Honour's servants could travel in the annual course of the sun. That I was bred a surgeon, whose trade is to cure wounds and hurts in the body, got by accident or violence; that my country was governed by a female man, whom we called *queen*. That I left it to get riches, whereby I might maintain myself and family when I should return. That in my last voyage I was commander of the ship, and had about fifty yahoos under me, many of which died at sea, and I was forced to supply them by others picked out from several nations. That our ship was twice in danger of being sunk; the first time by a great storm, and the second, by striking against a rock. Here my master interposed, by asking me, how I could persuade strangers out of different countries to venture with me, after the losses I had sustained, and the hazards I had run. I said, they were fellows of desperate fortunes, forced to fly from the places of their birth, on account of their poverty or their crimes. Some were undone by lawsuits; others spent all they had in drinking, whoring, and gaming; others fled for treason; many for murder, theft, poisoning, robbery, perjury, forgery, coining false money, for committing rapes or sodomy, for flying from their colours, or deserting to the enemy, and most of them had broken prison; none of these durst return to their native countries for fear of being hanged, or of starving in a jail; and therefore were under a necessity of seeking a livelihood in other places.

During this discourse, my master was pleased often to interrupt me; I had made use of many circumlocutions in describing to him the nature of the several crimes, for which most of our crew had been forced to fly their country. This labour took up several days' conversation before he was able to comprehend me. He was wholly at a loss to know what could be the use or necessity of practising those vices. To clear up which I endeavoured to give him some ideas of the desire of power and riches, of the terrible effects of lust, intemperance, malice and envy. All this I was forced to define and describe by putting of cases, and making suppositions. After which, like one whose imagination was struck with something never seen or heard of before, he would lift up his eyes with amazement and indignation. Power, government, war, law, punishment, and a thousand other things had no terms wherein that language could express them, which made the difficulty almost insuperable to give my master any conception of what I meant. But being of an excellent understanding, much improved by contemplation and converse, he at last arrived at a competent knowledge of what human nature in our parts of the world is capable to perform, and desired I would give him some particular account of that land which we call Europe, especially of my own country.

CHAPTER V.

The author, at his master's commands, informs him of the state of England. The causes of war among the princes of Europe. The author begins to explain the English constitution.

The reader may please to observe, that the following extract of many conversations I had with my master contains a summary of the most material points which were discoursed at several times for above two years; his Honour often desiring fuller satisfaction as I farther improved in the Houyhnhnm tongue. I laid before him, as well as I could, the whole state of Europe; I discoursed of trade and manufactures, of arts and sciences; and the answers I gave to all the questions he made, as they arose upon several subjects, were a fund of conversation not to be exhausted. But I shall here only set down the substance of what passed between us concerning my own country, reducing it into order as well as I can, without any regard to time or other circumstances, while I strictly adhere to truth. My only concern is, that I shall hardly be able to do justice to my master's arguments and expressions, which must needs suffer by my want of capacity, as well as by a translation into our barbarous English.

In obedience therefore to his Honour's commands, I related to him the Revolution under the Prince of Orange; the long war with France entered into by the said prince, and renewed by his successor the present queen, wherein the greatest powers of Christendom were engaged, and which still continued: I computed, at his request, that about a million of yahoos might have been killed in the whole progress of it, and perhaps a hundred or more cities taken, and five times as many ships burnt or sunk.

He asked me what were the usual causes or motives that made one country go to war with another. I answered they were innumerable, but I should only mention a few of the chief. Sometimes the ambition of princes, who never think they have land or people enough to govern: sometimes the corruption of ministers, who engage their master in a war in order to stifle or divert the clamour of the subjects against their evil administration. Difference in opinions hath cost many millions of lives: for instance, whether flesh be bread, or bread be flesh; whether the juice of a certain berry be blood or wine; whether whistling be a vice or a virtue; whether it be better to kiss a post, or throw it into the fire; what is the best colour for a coat, whether black, white, red, or grey; and whether it should be long or short, narrow or wide, dirty or clean, with many more. Neither are any wars so furious and bloody, or of so long continuance, as those occasioned by difference in opinion, especially if it be in things indifferent.

Sometimes the quarrel between two princes is to decide which of them shall dispossess a third of his dominions, where neither of them pretend to any right. Sometimes one prince quarrelleth with another, for fear the other should quarrel with him. Sometimes a war is entered upon, because the enemy is too strong, and sometimes because he is too weak. Sometimes our neighbours want the things which we have, or have the things which we want; and we both fight, till they take ours or give us theirs. It is a very justifiable cause of war to invade a country after the people have been wasted by famine, destroyed by pestilence, or embroiled by factions amongst themselves. It is justifiable to enter into a war against our nearest ally, when one of his towns lies convenient for us, or a territory of land, that would render our dominions round and compact. If a prince send forces into a nation where the people are poor and ignorant, he may lawfully put half of them to death, and make slaves of the rest, in order to civilize and reduce them from their barbarous way of living. It is a very kingly, honourable, and frequent practice, when one prince desires the assistance of another to secure him against an invasion, that the assistant, when he hath driven out the invader, should seize on the dominions himself, and kill, imprison or banish the prince he came to relieve. Alliance by blood or marriage is a sufficient cause of war between princes, and the nearer the kindred is, the greater is their disposition to quarrel: poor nations are hungry, and rich nations are proud, and pride and hunger will ever be at variance. For these reasons, the trade of a soldier is held the most honourable of all others: because a soldier is a yahoo hired to kill in cold blood as many of his own species, who have never offended him, as possibly he can.

There is likewise a kind of beggarly princes in Europe, not able to make war by themselves, who hire out their troops to richer nations, for so much a day to each man; of which they keep three fourths to themselves, and it is the best part of their maintenance; such are those in Germany and many northern parts of Europe.

What you have told me (said my master) upon the subject of war, does indeed discover most admirably the effects of that reason you pretend to: however, it is happy that the shame is greater than the danger; and that nature hath left you utterly uncapable of doing much mischief. For your mouths lying flat with your faces, you can hardly bite each other to any purpose, unless by consent. Then as to the claws upon your feet before and behind, they are so short and tender, that one of our yahoos would drive a dozen of yours before him. And therefore in re-counting the numbers of those who have been killed in battle, I cannot but think that you have *said the thing which is not.*

I could not forbear shaking my head and smiling a little at his ignorance. And being no stranger to the art of war, I gave him a description of cannons, culverins, muskets, carabines, pistols, bullets, powder, swords, bayonets, battles, sieges, retreats, attacks, undermines, countermines, bombardments, sea-fights; ships sunk with a thousand men, twenty thousand killed on each side; dying groans, limbs flying in the air, smoke, noise, confusion, trampling to death under horses' feet; flight, pursuit, victory; fields strewed with carcases left for food to dogs, and wolves, and birds of prey; plundering, stripping, ravishing, burning and destroying. And to set forth the valour of my own dear countrymen, I assured him, that I had seen them blow up a hundred enemies at once in a siege, and as many in a ship, and beheld the dead bodies drop down in pieces from the clouds, to the great diversion of all the spectators.

I was going on to more particulars, when my master commanded me silence. He said, whoever understood the nature of yahoos might easily believe it possible for so vile an animal to be capable of every action I had named, if their strength and cunning equalled their malice. But as my discourse had increased his abhorrence of the whole species, so he found it gave him a disturbance in his mind, to which he was wholly a stranger before. He thought his ears being used to such abominable words, might by degrees admit them with less detestation. That although he hated the yahoos of this country, yet he no more blamed them for their odious qualities, than he did a *gnnayh* (a bird of prey) for its cruelty, or a sharp stone for cutting his hoof. But when a creature pretending to reason could be capable of such enormities, he dreaded lest the corruption of that faculty might be worse than brutality itself. He seemed therefore confident, that instead of reason, we were only possessed of some quality fitted to increase our natural vices; as the reflection from a troubled stream returns the image of an ill-shapen body, not only larger, but more distorted.

He added, that he had heard too much upon the subject of war, both in this and some former discourses. There was another point which a little perplexed him at present. I had said, that some of our crew left their country on account of being ruined by *law;* that I had already explained the meaning of the word; but he was at a loss how it should come to pass, that the *law* which was intended for every man's preservation, should be any man's ruin. Therefore he desired to be farther satisfied what I meant by *law*, and the dispensers thereof according to the present practice in my own country; because he thought nature and reason were sufficient guides for a reasonable animal, as we pretended to be, in showing us what we ought to do, and what to avoid.

I assured his Honour, that law was a science wherein I had not much conversed, further than by employing advocates in vain, upon some injustices that had been done me. However, I would give him all the satisfaction I was able.

I said there was a society of men among us, bred up from their youth in the art of proving by words multiplied for the purpose, that white is black, and black is white, according as they are paid. To this society all the rest of the people are slaves.

For example, if my neighbour hath a mind to my cow, he hires a lawyer to prove that he ought to have my cow from me. I must then hire another to defend my right, it being against all rules of law that any man should be allowed to speak for himself. Now in this case, I who am the true owner lie under two great disadvantages. First, my lawyer, being practiced almost from his cradle in defending falsehood, is quite out of his element when he would be an advocate for justice, which as an office unnatural, he always attempts with great awkwardness, if not with ill will. The second disadvantage is, that my lawyer must proceed with great caution, or else he will be reprimanded by the judges, and abhorred by his brethren, as one who would lessen the practice of the law. And therefore I have but two methods to preserve my cow. The first is to gain over my adversary's lawyer with a double fee, who will then betray his client by insinuating that he hath justice on his side. The second way is for my lawyer to make my cause appear as unjust as he can, by allowing the cow to belong to my adversary; and this if it be skilfully done will certainly bespeak the favour of the bench.

Now, your Honour is to know that these judges are persons appointed to decide all controversies of property, as well as for the trial of criminals, and picked out from the most dextrous lawyers who are grown old or lazy, and having been biassed all their lives against truth and equity, lie under such a fatal necessity of favouring fraud, perjury, and oppression, that I have known several of them refuse a large bribe from the side where justice lay, rather than injure the faculty by doing any thing unbecoming their nature or their office.

It is a maxim among these lawyers, that whatever hath been done before may legally be done again: and therefore they take special care to record all the decisions formerly made against common justice and the general reason of mankind. These, under the name of *precedents*, they produce as authorities, to justify the most iniquitous opinions; and the judges never fail of decreeing accordingly.

In pleading, they studiously avoid entering into the merits of the cause, but are loud, violent, and tedious in dwelling upon all circumstances which are not to the purpose. For instance, in the case already mentioned; they never desire to know what claim or title my adversary hath to my cow, but whether the said cow were red or black, her horns long or short; whether the field I graze her in be round or square, whether she was milked at home or abroad, what diseases she is subject to, and the like; after which they consult precedents, adjourn the cause from time to time, and in ten, twenty, or thirty years come to an issue.

It is likewise to be observed that this society hath a peculiar cant and jargon of their own, that no other mortal can understand, and wherein all their laws are written, which they take special care to multiply; whereby they have wholly confounded the very essence of truth and falsehood, of right and wrong; so that it will take thirty years to decide whether the field left me by my ancestors for six generations belongs to me or to a stranger three hundred miles off.

In the trial of persons accused for crimes against the state the method is much more short and commendable: the judge first sends to sound the disposition of those in power, after which he can easily hang or save the criminal, strictly preserving all due forms of law.

Here my master, interposing, said it was a pity, that creatures endowed with such prodigious abilities of mind as these lawyers, by the description I gave of them, must certainly be, were not rather encouraged to be instructors of others in wisdom and knowledge. In answer to which I assured his Honour, that in all points out of their own trade they were usually the most ignorant and stupid generation among us, the most despicable in common conversation, avowed enemies to all knowledge and learning, and equally disposed to pervert the general reason of mankind in every other subject of discourse, as in that of their own profession.

Chapter VI.

A continuation of the state of England under Queen Anne. The character of a first minister in the courts of Europe.

My master was yet wholly at a loss to understand what motives could incite this race of lawyers to perplex, disquiet, and weary themselves by engaging in a confederacy of injustice, merely for the sake of injuring their fellow-animals; neither could he comprehend what I meant in saying they did it for hire. Whereupon I was at much pains to describe to him the use of money, the materials it was made of, and the value of the metals; that when a yahoo had got a great store of this precious substance, he was able to purchase whatever he had a mind to, the finest clothing, the noblest houses, great tracts of land, the most costly meats and drinks, and have his choice of the most beautiful females. Therefore since money alone was able to perform all these feats, our yahoos thought they could never have enough of it to spend or to save, as they found themselves inclined from their natural bent either to profusion or avarice. That the rich man enjoyed the fruit of the poor man's labour, and the latter were a thousand to one in proportion to the former. That the bulk of our people were forced to live miserably, by labouring every day for small wages to make a few live plentifully. I enlarged myself much on these and many other particulars to the same purpose: but his Honour was still to seek, for he went upon a supposition that all animals had a title to their share in the productions of the earth, and especially those who presided over the rest. Therefore he desired I would let him know what these costly meats were, and how any of us happened to want them. Whereupon I enumerated as many sorts as came into my head, with the various methods of dressing them, which could not be done without sending vessels by sea to every part of the world, as well for liquors to drink, as for sauces, and innumerable other conveniencies. I assured him, that this whole globe of earth must be at least three times gone round, before one of our better female yahoos could get her breakfast, or a cup to put it in. He said, that must needs be a miserable country which cannot furnish food for its own inhabitants. But what he chiefly wondered at was how such vast tracts of ground as I described should be wholly without fresh water, and the people put to the necessity of sending over the sea for drink. I replied, that England (the dear place of my nativity) was computed to produce three times the quantity of food more than its inhabitants are able to consume, as well as liquors extracted from grain, or pressed out of the fruit of certain trees, which made excellent drink, and the same proportion in every other convenience of life. But in order to feed the luxury and intemperance of the males, and the vanity of the females, we sent away the greatest part of our necessary things to other countries, from whence in return we brought the materials of diseases, folly, and vice, to spend among ourselves. Hence it follows of necessity that vast numbers of our people are compelled to seek their livelihood by begging, robbing, stealing, cheating, pimping, forswearing, flattering, suborning, forging, gaming, lying, fawning, hectoring, voting, scribbling, star-gazing, poisoning, whoring, canting, libelling, free-thinking, and the like occupations: every one of which terms, I was at much pains to make him understand.

That wine was not imported among us from foreign countries to supply the want of water or other drinks, but because it was a sort of liquid which made us merry, by putting us out of our senses; diverted all melancholy thoughts, begat wild extravagant imaginations in the brain, raised our hopes, and banished our fears, suspended every office of reason for a time, and deprived us of the use of our limbs, until we fell into a profound sleep; although it must be confessed, that we always awaked sick and dispirited, and that the use of this liquor filled us with diseases, which made our lives uncomfortable and short.

But beside all this, the bulk of our people supported themselves by furnishing the necessities or conveniencies of life to the rich, and to each other. For instance, when I am at home and dressed as I ought to be, I carry on my body the workmanship of an hundred tradesmen; the building and furniture of my house employ as many more, and five times the number to adorn my wife.

I was going on to tell him of another sort of people, who get their livelihood by attending the sick, having upon some occasions informed his Honour that many of my crew had died of diseases. But here it was with the utmost difficulty that I brought him to apprehend what I meant. He could easily conceive that a Houyhnhnm grew weak and heavy a few days before his death, or by some accident might hurt a limb. But that Nature, who works all things to perfection, should suffer any pains to breed in our bodies, he thought impossible, and desired to know the reason of so unaccountable an evil. I told him, we fed on a thousand things which operated contrary to each other; that we eat when we were not hungry, and drank without the provocation of thirst; that we sat whole nights drinking strong liquors without eating a bit, which disposed us to sloth, enflamed our bodies, and precipitated or prevented digestion. That prostitute female yahoos acquired a certain malady, which bred rotteness in the bones of those who fell into their embraces; that this and many other diseases were propagated from father to son, so that great numbers come into the world with complicated maladies upon them; that it would be endless to give him a catalogue of all diseases incident to human bodies; for they could not be fewer than five or six hundred, spread over every limb and joint; in short, every part, external and intestine, having diseases appropriated to each. To remedy which, there was a sort of people bred up among us, in the profession or pretence of curing the sick. And because I had some skill in the faculty, I would, in gratitude to his Honour, let him know the whole mystery and method by which they proceed.

Their fundamental is, that all diseases arise from repletion, from whence they conclude that a great evacuation of the body is necessary, either through the natural passage, or upwards at the mouth. Their next business is, from herbs, minerals, gums, oils, shells, salts, juices, seaweed, excrements, barks of trees, serpents, toads, frogs, spiders, dead men's flesh and bones, birds, beasts and fishes, to form a composition for smell and taste the most abominable, nauseous and detestable that they can possibly contrive, which the stomach immediately rejects with loathing; and this they call a vomit; or else from the same storehouse, with some other poisonous additions, they command us to take in at the orifice above or below (just as the physician then happens to be disposed) a medicine equally annoying and disgustful to the bowels, which, relaxing the belly, drives down all before it, and this they call a purge or a clyster. For nature (as the physicians allege) having intended the superior anterior orifice only for the intromission of solids and liquids, and the inferior posterior for ejection, these artists ingeniously considering that in all diseases Nature is forced out of her seat, therefore to replace her in it, the body must be treated in a manner directly contrary, by interchanging the use of each orifice, forcing solids and liquids in at the anus, and making evacuations at the mouth.

But besides real diseases we are subject to many that are only imaginary, for which the physicians have invented imaginary cures; these have their several names, and so have the drugs that are proper for them, and with these our female yahoos are always infested.

One great excellency in this tribe is their skill at prognostics, wherein they seldom fail; their predictions in real diseases, when they rise to any degree of malignity, generally portending death, which is always in their power, when recovery is not: and therefore, upon any unexpected signs of amendment, after they have pronounced their sentence, rather than be accused as false prophets, they know how to approve their sagacity to the world by a seasonable dose.

They are likewise of special use to husbands and wives who are grown weary of their mates, to eldest sons, to great ministers of state, and often to princes.

I had formerly upon occasion discoursed with my master upon the nature of our government in general, and particularly of our own excellent constitution, deservedly the wonder and envy of the whole world. But having here accidentally mentioned a 'minister of state', he commanded me some time after to inform him, what species of yahoo I particularly meant by that appellation.

I told him that a first or chief minister of state, who was the person I intended to describe, was a creature wholly exempt from joy and grief, love and hatred, pity and anger; at least makes use of no other passions but a violent desire of wealth, power, and titles; that he applies his words to all uses, except to the indication of his mind; that he never tells a truth, but with an intent that you should take it for a lie; nor a lie, but with a design that you should take it for a truth; that those he speaks worst of behind their backs are in the surest way to preferment; and whenever he begins to praise you to others or to yourself, you are from that day forlorn. The worst mark you can receive is a promise, especially when it is confirmed with an oath; after which every wise man retires, and gives over all hopes.

There are three methods by which a man may rise to be chief minister: the first is, by knowing how with prudence to dispose of a wife, a daughter, or a sister: the second, by betraying or undermining his predecessor: and the third is, by a furious zeal in public assemblies against the corruptions of the court. But a wise prince would rather choose to employ those who practise the last of these methods; because such zealots prove always the most obsequious and subservient to the will and passions of their master. That these 'ministers' having all employments at their disposal, preserve themselves in power by bribing the majority of a senate or great council; and at last, by an expedient called an 'act of indemnity' (whereof I described the nature to him) they secure themselves from after reckonings, and retire from the public, laden with the spoils of the nation.

The palace of a chief minister is a seminary to breed up others in his own trade; the pages, lackeys, and porter, by imitating their master, become ministers of state in their several districts, and learn to excel in the three principal ingredients, of insolence, lying, and bribery. Accordingly, they have a subaltern court paid to them by persons of the best rank, and sometimes by the force of dexterity and impudence arrive through several gradations to be successors to their lord.

He is usually governed by a decayed wench or favourite footman, who are the tunnels through which all graces are conveyed, and may properly be called, in the last resort, the governors of the kingdom.

One day my master, having heard me mention the nobility of my country, was pleased to make me a compliment which I could not pretend to deserve: that he was sure I must have been born of some noble family, because I far exceeded in shape, colour, and cleanliness, all the yahoos of his nation, although I seemed to fail in strength and agility, which must be imputed to my different way of living from those other brutes, and besides, I was not only endowed with the faculty of speech, but likewise with some rudiments of reason, to a degree that with all his acquaintance I passed for a prodigy.

He made me observe, that among the Houyhnhnms, the white, the sorrel, and the iron-grey were not so exactly shaped as the bay, the dapple-grey, and the black; nor born with equal talents of the mind, or a capacity to improve them; and therefore continued always in the condition of servants, without ever aspiring to match out of their own race, which in that country would be reckoned monstrous and unnatural.

I made his Honour my most humble acknowledgments for the good opinion he was pleased to conceive of me; but assured him at the same time that my birth was of the lower sort, having been born of plain honest parents, who were just able to give me a tolerable education: that nobility among us was altogether a different thing from the idea he had of it; that our young noblemen are bred from their childhood in idleness and luxury; that as soon as years will permit, they consume their vigor and contract odious diseases among lewd females; and when their fortunes are almost ruined, they marry some woman of mean birth, disagreeable person, and unsound constitution, merely for the sake of money, whom they hate and despise. That the productions of such marriages are generally scrofulous, ricketty, or deformed children, by which means the family seldom continues above three generations, unless the wife takes care to provide a healthy father among her neighbours or domestics, in order to improve and continue the breed. That a weak diseased body, a meager countenance, and sallow complexion are the true marks of noble blood; and a healthy robust appearance is so disgraceful in a man of quality, that the world concludes his real father to have been a groom, or a coachman. The imperfections of his mind run parallel with those of his body, being a composition of spleen, dulness, ignorance, caprice, sensuality, and pride.

Without the consent of this illustrious body no law can be enacted, repealed, or altered, and these nobles have likewise the decision of all our possessions without appeal.

CHAPTER VII.

The author's great love of his native country. His master's observations upon the constitution and administration of England, as described by the author, with parallel cases and comparisons. His master's observations upon human nature.

The reader may be disposed to wonder how I could prevail on myself to give so free a representation of my own species, among a race of mortals who were already too apt to conceive the vilest opinion of human kind from that entire congruity betwixt me and their yahoos. But I must freely confess, that the many virtues of those excellent quadrupeds, placed in opposite view to human corruptions, had so far opened my eyes and enlarged my understanding, that I began to view the actions and passions of man in a very different light, and to think the honour of my own kind not worth managing; which, besides, it was impossible for me to do before a person of so acute a judgment as my master, who daily convinced me of a thousand faults in myself, whereof I had not the least perception before, and which with us would never be numbered even among human infirmities: I had likewise learned from his example an utter detestation of all falsehood or disguise; and truth appeared so amiable to me, that I determined upon sacrificing every thing to it.

Let me deal so candidly with the reader as to confess, that there was yet a much stronger motive for the freedom I took in my representation of things. I had not been a year in this country before I contracted such a love and veneration for the inhabitants, that I entered on a firm resolution never to return to human kind, but to pass the rest of my life among these admirable Houyhnhnms in the contemplation and practice of every virtue; where I could have no example or incitement to vice. But it was decreed by Fortune, my perpetual enemy, that so great a felicity should not fall to my share. However, it is now some comfort to reflect, that in what I said of my countrymen I extenuated their faults as much as I durst before so strict an examiner, and upon every article gave as favourable a turn as the matter would bear. For, indeed, who is there alive that will not be swayed by his bias and partiality to the place of his birth?

I have related the substance of several conversations I had with my master, during the greatest part of the time I had the honour to be in his service, but have indeed for brevity sake omitted much more than is here set down.

When I had answered all his questions, and his curiosity seemed to be fully satisfied, he sent for me one morning early, and commanding me to sit down at some distance (an honour which he had never before conferred upon me), he said he had been very seriously considering my whole story, as far as it related both to myself and my country: that he looked upon us as a sort of animals to whose share, by what accident he could not conjecture, some small pittance of reason had fallen, whereof we made no other use than by its assistance to aggravate our natural corruptions, and to acquire new ones which Nature had not given us. That we disarmed ourselves of the few abilities she had bestowed, had been very successful in multiplying our original wants, and seemed to spend our whole lives in vain endeavours to supply them by our own inventions. That as to myself, it was manifest I had neither the strength or agility of a common yahoo, that I walked infirmly on my hinder feet, had found out a contrivance to make my claws of no use or defence, and to remove the hair from my chin, which was intended as a shelter from the sun and the weather. Lastly, that I could neither run with speed, nor climb trees like my brethren (as he called them) the yahoos in this country.

That our institutions of government and law were plainly owing to our gross defects in reason, and by consequence, in virtue; because reason alone is sufficient to govern a rational creature; which was therefore a character we had no pretence to challenge, even from the account I had given of my own people, although he manifestly perceived, that in order to favour them I had concealed many particulars, and often *said the thing which was not.*

He was the more confirmed in this opinion, because he observed, that as I agreed in every feature of my body with other yahoos, except where it was to my real disadvantage in point of strength, speed, and activity, the shortness of my claws, and some other particulars where nature had no part; so from the representation I had given him of our lives, our manners, and our actions, he found as near a resemblance in the disposition of our minds. He said the yahoos were known to hate one another more than they did any different species of animals; and the reason usually assigned was the odiousness of their own shapes, which all could see in the rest, but not in themselves. He had therefore begun to think it not unwise in us to cover our bodies, and, by that invention, conceal many of our deformities from each other, which would else be hardly supportable. But he now found he had been mistaken, and that the dissensions of those brutes in his country were owing to the same cause with ours, as I had described them. For if (said he) you throw among five yahoos as

much food as would be sufficient for fifty, they will, instead of
eating peaceably, fall together by the ears, each single one
impatient to have all to itself, and therefore a servant was usually
employed to stand by while they were feeding abroad, and those
kept at home were tied at a distance from each other; that if a
cow died of age or accident, before a Houyhnhnm could secure
it for his own yahoos, those in the neighbourhood would come in
herds to seize it, and then would ensue such a battle as I had
described, with terrible wounds made by their claws on both
sides, although they seldom were able to kill one another, for
want of such convenient instruments of death as we had invented. At other times the like battles have been fought between the
yahoos of several neighbourhoods without any visible cause; those
of one district watching all opportunities to surprise the next
before they are prepared. But if they find their project hath
miscarried, they return home, and, for want of enemies, engage in
what I call a civil war among themselves.

That in some fields of his country there are certain shining
stones of several colours, whereof the yahoos are violently fond,
and when part of these stones are fixed in the earth, as it sometimes happeneth, they will dig with their claws for whole days to
get them out, carry them away, and hide them by heaps in their
kennels; but still looking round with great caution, for fear their
comrades should find out their treasure. My master said, he
could never discover the reason of this unnatural appetite, or how
these stones could be of any use to a yahoo; but now he believed
it might proceed from the same principle of avarice which I had
ascribed to mankind; that he had once, by way of experiment,
privately removed a heap of these stones from the place where
one of his yahoos had buried it: whereupon the sordid animal,
missing his treasure, by his loud lamenting brought the whole
herd to the place, there miserably howled, then fell to biting and
tearing the rest, began to pine away, would neither eat, nor sleep,
nor work, till he ordered a servant privately to convey the stones
into the same hole and hide them as before; which when his
yahoo had found, he presently recovered his spirits and good
humour, but took care to remove them to a better hiding-place,
and hath ever since been a very serviceable brute.

My master farther assured me, which I also observed myself,
that in the fields where these shining stones abound, the fiercest
and most frequent battles are fought, occasioned by perpetual
inroads of the neighbouring yahoos.

He said, it was common, when two yahoos discovered such a
stone in a field, and were contending which of them should be

the proprietor, a third would take the advantage, and carry it away from them both; which my master would needs contend to have some resemblance with our suits at law; wherein I thought it for our credit not to undeceive him; since the decision he mentioned was much more equitable than many decrees among us: because the plaintiff and defendant there lost nothing beside the stone they contended for, whereas our courts of equity would never have dismissed the cause while either of them had any thing left.

My master, continuing his discourse, said, there was nothing that rendered the yahoos more odious than their undistinguishing appetite to devour every thing that came in their way, whether herbs, roots, berries, corrupted flesh of animals, or all mingled together: and it was peculiar in their temper, that they were fonder of what they could get by rapine or stealth at a greater distance, than much better food provided for them at home. If their prey held out, they would eat till they were ready to burst, after which Nature had pointed out to them a certain root that gave them a general evacuation.

There was also another kind of root very juicy, but somewhat rare and difficult to be found, which the yahoos sought for with much eagerness, and would suck it with great delight; and it produced in them the same effects that wine hath upon us. It would make them sometimes hug, and sometimes tear one another; they would howl and grin, and chatter, and reel, and tumble, and then fall asleep in the mud.

I did indeed observe, that the yahoos were the only animals in this country subject to any diseases; which, however, were much fewer than horses have among us, and contracted not by any ill treatment they meet with, but by the nastiness and greediness of that sordid brute. Neither has their language any more than a general appellation for those maladies, which is borrowed from the name of the beast, and called *hnea-yahoo*, or the *yahoo's-evil*, and the cure prescribed is a mixture of their own dung and urine forcibly put down the yahoo's throat. This I have since often known to have been taken with success, and do here freely recommend it to my countrymen, for the public good, as an admirable specific against all diseases produced by repletion.

As to learning, government, arts, manufactures, and the like, my master confessed he could find little or no resemblance between the yahoos of that country and those in ours. For he only meant to observe what parity there was in our natures. He had heard indeed some curious Houyhnhnms observe, that in most herds there was a sort of ruling yahoo (as among us there is

generally some leading or principal stag in a park), who was
always more deformed in body, and mischievous in disposition,
than any of the rest. That this leader had usually a favourite as
like himself as he could get, whose employment was to lick his
master's feet and posteriors, and drive the female yahoos to his
kennel; for which he was now and then rewarded with a piece of
ass's flesh. This favourite is hated by the whole herd, and therefore, to protect himself, keeps always near the person of his
leader. He usually continues in office till a worse can be found;
but the very moment he is discarded, his successor, at the head of
all the yahoos in that district, young and old, male and female,
come in a body, and discharge their excrements upon him from
head to foot. But how far this might be applicable to our courts
and favourites, and ministers of state, my master said I could best
determine.

I durst make no return to this malicious insinuation, which de-
based human understanding below the sagacity of a common
hound, who has judgment enough to distinguish and follow the
cry of the ablest dog in the pack, without being ever mistaken.

My master told me, there were some qualities remarkable in
the yahoos, which he had not observed me to mention, or at least
very slightly, in the accounts I had given him of human kind; he
said, those animals, like other brutes, had their females in
common; but in this they differed, that the she-yahoo would
admit the male while she was pregnant, and that the hees would
quarrel and fight with the females as fiercely as with each other.
Both which practices were such degrees of infamous brutality,
that no other sensitive creature ever arrived at.

Another thing he wondered at in the yahoos was their strange
disposition to nastiness and dirt, whereas there appears to be a
natural love of cleanliness in all other animals. As to the two
former accusations, I was glad to let them pass without any reply,
because I had not a word to offer upon them in defence of my
species, which otherwise I certainly had done from my own inclinations. But I could have easily vindicated human kind from
the imputation of singularity upon the last article, if there had
been any swine in that country (as unluckily for me there were
not), which, although it may be a sweeter quadruped than a
yahoo, cannot, I humbly conceive, in justice pretend to more
cleanliness; and so his Honour himself must have owned, if he
had seen their filthy way of feeding, and their custom of wal-
lowing and sleeping in the mud.

My master likewise mentioned another quality which his servants had discovered in several yahoos, and to him was wholly

unaccountable. He said, a fancy would sometimes take a yahoo to retire into a corner, to lie down and howl, and groan, and spurn away all that came near him, although he were young and fat, and wanted neither food nor water; nor did the servants imagine what could possibly ail him. And the only remedy they found was to set him to hard work, after which he would infallibly come to himself. To this I was silent out of partiality to my own kind; yet here I could plainly discover the true seeds of spleen, which only seizeth on the lazy, the luxurious, and the rich; who, if they were forced to undergo the same regimen, I would undertake for the cure.

His Honour had farther observed, that a female yahoo would often stand behind a bank or a bush, to gaze on the young males passing by, and then appear, and hide, using many antic gestures and grimaces, at which time it was observed, that she had a most offensive smell; and when any of the males advanced, would slowly retire, looking often back, and with a counterfeit show of fear, run off into some convenient place where she knew the male would follow her.

At other times if a female stranger came among them, three or four of her own sex would get about her, and stare and chatter, and grin, and smell her all over, and then turn off with gestures that seemed to express contempt and disdain.

Perhaps my master might refine a little in these speculations, which he had drawn from what he observed himself, or had been told him by others: however, I could not reflect without some amazement, and much sorrow, that the rudiments of lewdness, coquetry, censure, and scandal, should have place by instinct in womankind.

I expected every moment that my master would accuse the yahoos of those unnatural appetites in both sexes, so common among us. But Nature, it seems, hath not been so expert a schoolmistress; and these politer pleasures are entirely the productions of art and reason, on our side of the globe.

Chapter VIII.

The author relates several particulars of the yahoos. The great virtues of the Houyhnhnms. The education and exercise of their youth. Their general assembly.

As I ought to have understood human nature much better than I supposed it possible for my master to do, so it was easy to apply the character he gave of the yahoos to myself and my

countrymen, and I believed I could yet make farther discoveries
from my own observation. I therefore often begged his Honour
to let me go among the herds of yahoos in the neighbourhood, to
which he always very graciously consented, being perfectly convinced that the hatred I bore those brutes would never suffer me
to be corrupted by them; and his Honour ordered one of his
servants, a strong sorrel nag, very honest and good-natured, to
be my guard, without whose protection I durst not undertake
such adventures. For I have already told the reader how much
I was pestered by those odious animals upon my first arrival.
And I afterwards failed very narrowly three or four times of falling into their clutches, when I happened to stray at any distance
without my hanger. And I have reason to believe they had some
imagination that I was of their own species, which I often assisted myself, by stripping up my sleeves, and showing my
naked arms and breast in their sight, when my protector was
with me. At which times they would approach as near as they
durst, and imitate my actions after the manner of monkeys, but
ever with great signs of hatred, as a tame jackdaw, with cap and
stockings, is always persecuted by the wild ones, when he happens to be got among them.

They are prodigiously nimble from their infancy; however, I
once caught a young male of three years old, and endeavoured by
all marks of tenderness to make it quiet; but the little imp fell a
squalling, and scratching, and biting with such violence, that
I was forced to let it go, and it was high time, for a whole troop
of old ones came about us at the noise, but finding the cub was
safe (for away it ran), and my sorrel nag being by, they durst not
venture near us. I observed the young animal's flesh to smell
very rank, and the stink was somewhat between a weasel and a
fox, but much more disagreeable. I forgot another circumstance
(and perhaps I might have the reader's pardon if it were wholly
omitted) that while I held the odious vermin in my hands, it
voided its filthy excrements of a yellow liquid substance all over
my clothes; but by good fortune there was a small brook hard
by, where I washed myself as clean as I could, although I durst
not come into my master's presence, until I were sufficiently
aired.

By what I could discover, the yahoos appear to be the most
unteachable of all animals, their capacities never reaching higher
than to draw or carry burthens. Yet I am of opinion this defect
ariseth chiefly from a perverse, restive disposition. For they are
cunning, malicious, treacherous and revengeful. They are
strong and hardy, but of a cowardly spirit, and by consequence

insolent, abject, and cruel. It is observed, that the redhaired of both sexes are more libidinous and mischievous than the rest, whom yet they much exceed in strength and activity.

The Houyhnhnms keep the yahoos for present use in huts not far from the house; but the rest are sent abroad to certain fields, where they dig up roots, eat several kinds of herbs, and search about for carrion, or sometimes catch weasels and *luhimuhs* (a sort of wild rat), which they greedily devour. Nature hath taught them to dig deep holes with their nails on the side of a rising ground, wherein they lie by themselves, only the kennels of the females are larger, sufficient to hold two or three cubs.

They swim from their infancy like frogs, and are able to continue long under water, where they often take fish, which the females carry home to their young. And upon this occasion, I hope the reader will pardon my relating an odd adventure.

Being one day abroad with my protector the sorrel nag, and the weather exceeding hot, I entreated him to let me bathe in a river that was near. He consented, and I immediately stripped myself stark naked, and went down softly into the stream. It happened that a young female yahoo, standing behind a bank, saw the whole proceeding, and inflamed by desire, as the nag and I conjectured, came running with all speed, and leaped into the water within five yards of the place where I bathed. I was never in my life so terribly frighted; the nag was grazing at some distance, not suspecting any harm. She embraced me after a most fulsome manner; I roared as loud as I could, and the nag came galloping towards me, whereupon she quitted her grasp, with the utmost reluctancy, and leaped upon the opposite bank, where she stood gazing and howling all the time I was putting on my clothes.

This was matter of diversion to my master and his family, as well as of mortification to myself. For now I could no longer deny that I was a real yahoo in every limb and feature, since the females had a natural propensity to me as one of their own species: neither was the hair of this brute of a red colour (which might have been some excuse for an appetite a little irregular) but black as a sloe, and her countenance did not make an appearance altogether so hideous as the rest of the kind; for, I think, she could not be above eleven years old.

Having already lived three years in this country, the reader I suppose will expect that I should, like other travellers, give him some account of the manners and customs of its inhabitants, which it was indeed my principal study to learn.

As these noble Houyhnhnms are endowed by nature with a

general disposition to all virtues, and have no conceptions or ideas of what is evil in a rational creature, so their grand maxim is, to cultivate reason, and to be wholly governed by it. Neither is reason among them a point problematical as with us, where men can argue with plausibility on both sides of a question; but strikes you with immediate conviction; as it must needs do where it is not mingled, obscured, or discoloured by passion and interest. I remember it was with extreme difficulty that I could bring my master to understand the meaning of the word *opinion*, or how a point could be disputable; because reason taught us to affirm or deny only where we are certain; and beyond our knowledge we cannot do either. So that controversies, wranglings, disputes, and positiveness in false or dubious propositions are evils unknown among the Houyhnhnms. In the like manner, when I used to explain to him our several systems of natural philosophy, he would laugh that a creature pretending to reason should value itself upon the knowledge of other people's conjectures, and in things where that knowledge, if it were certain, could be of no use. Wherein he agreed entirely with the sentiments of Socrates, as Plato delivers them; which I mention as the highest honour I can do that prince of philosophers. I have often since reflected what destruction such a doctrine would make in the libraries of Europe, and how many paths to fame would be then shut up in the learned world.

Friendship and benevolence are the two principal virtues among the Houyhnhnms, and these not confined to particular objects, but universal to the whole race. For a stranger from the remotest part is equally treated with the nearest neighbour, and wherever he goes, looks upon himself as at home. They preserve decency and civility in the highest degrees, but are altogether ignorant of ceremony. They have no fondness for their colts or foals, but the care they take in educating them proceeds entirely from the dictates of reason. And I observed my master to show the same affection to his neighbour's issue that he had for his own. They will have it that nature teaches them to love the whole species, and it is reason only that maketh a distinction of persons, where there is a superior degree of virtue.

When the matron Houyhnhnms have produced one of each sex, they no longer accompany with their consorts, except they lose one of their issue by some casualty, which very seldom happens: but in such a case they meet again, or when the like accident befalls a person whose wife is past bearing, some other couple bestows on him one of their own colts, and then go together a second time till the mother be pregnant. This caution is necessary to prevent the country from being overburthened with numbers. But the race of inferior Houyhnhnms bred up to be servants is not so strictly limited upon this article; these are allowed to produce three of each sex, to be domestics in the noble families.

In their marriages they are exactly careful to choose such colours as will not make any disagreeable mixture in the breed. Strength is chiefly valued in the male, and comeliness in the female, not upon the account of love, but to preserve the race from degenerating; for where a female happens to excel in strength, a consort is chosen with regard to comeliness. Court-ship, love, presents, jointures, settlements, have no place in their thoughts, or terms whereby to express them in their language. The young couple meet and are joined, merely because it is the determination of their parents and friends: it is what they see done every day, and they look upon it as one of the necessary actions in a reasonable being. But the violation of marriage, or any other unchastity, was never heard of: and the married pair pass their lives with the same friendship and mutual benevolence that they bear to all others of the same species who come in their way; without jealousy, fondness, quarrelling, or discontent.

In educating the youth of both sexes, their method is admira-ble, and highly deserves our imitation. These are not suffered to taste a grain of oats, except upon certain days, till eighteen years old; nor milk, but very rarely; and in summer they graze two hours in the morning, and as many in the evening, which their parents likewise observe, but the servants are not allowed above half that time, and a great part of the grass is brought home, which they eat at the most convenient hours, when they can be best spared from work.

Temperance, industry, exercise and cleanliness, are the lessons equally enjoined to the young ones of both sexes: and my master thought it monstrous in us to give the females a different kind of education from the males, except in some articles of domestic management; whereby, as he truly observed, one half of our natives were good for nothing but bringing children into the world: and to trust the care of their children to such useless ani-mals, he said, was yet a greater instance of brutality.

But the Houyhnhnms train up their youth to strength, speed, and hardiness, by exercising them in running races up and down steep hills, or over hard stony grounds, and when they are all in a sweat, they are ordered to leap over head and ears into a pond or a river. Four times a year the youth of certain districts meet to show their proficiency in running and leaping, and other feats of strength or agility, where the victor is rewarded with a song made in his or her praise. On this festival the servants drive a herd of yahoos into the field, laden with hay, and oats, and milk for a repast to the Houyhnhnms; after which these brutes are immediately driven back again, for fear of being noisome to the assembly.

Every fourth year, at the vernal equinox, there is a representative council of the whole nation, which meets in a plain about twenty miles from our house, and continues about five or six days. Here they inquire into the state and condition of the several districts; whether they abound or be deficient in hay or oats, or cows or yahoos. And wherever there is any want (which is but seldom) it is immediately supplied by unanimous consent and contribution. Here likewise the regulation of children is settled: as for instance, if a Houyhnhnm hath two males, he changeth one of them with another who hath two females: and when a child hath been lost by any casualty, where the mother is past breeding, it is determined what family in the district shall breed another to supply the loss.

Chapter IX.

A grand debate at the general assembly of the Houyhnhnms, and how it was determined. The learning of the Houyhnhnms. Their buildings. Their manner of burials. The defectiveness of their language.

One of these grand assemblies was held in my time, about three months before my departure, whither my master went as the representative of our district. In this council was resumed their old debate, and indeed, the only debate that ever happened in their country; whereof my master after his return gave me a very particular account.

The question to be debated was, whether the yahoos should be exterminated from the face of the earth. One of the members for the affirmative offered several arguments of great strength and weight, alleging, that as the yahoos were the most filthy, noisome, and deformed animal which nature ever produced, so they were the most restive and indocible, mischievous and malicious: they would privately suck the teats of the Houyhnhnms' cows, kill and devour their cats, trample down their oats and grass, if they were not continually watched, and commit a thousand other extravagancies. He took notice of a general tradition, that yahoos had not been always in their country: but that many ages ago two of these brutes appeared together upon a mountain, whether produced by the heat of the sun upon corrupted mud and slime, or from the ooze and froth of the sea, was never known. That these yahoos engendered, and their brood in a short time grew so numerous as to overrun and infest the whole nation. That the Houyhnhnms, to get rid of this evil, made a general hunting, and at last enclosed the whole herd; and destroying the older, every Houyhnhnm kept two young ones in a kennel, and brought them to such a degree of tameness, as an animal so savage by nature can be capable of acquiring; using them for draught and carriage. That there seemed to be much truth in this tradition, and that those creatures could not be *ylnhniamshy* (or *aborigines* of the land) because of the violent hatred the Houyhnhnms, as well as all other animals, bore them; which although their evil disposition sufficiently deserved, could never have arrived at so high a degree, if they had been aborigines, or else they would have long since been rooted out. That the inhabitants taking a fancy to use the service of the yahoos, had very imprudently neglected to cultivate the breed of asses, which were a comely animal, easily kept, more tame and orderly, without any offensive smell, strong enough for labour, although they yield to the other in agility of body; and if their braying be no agreeable sound, it is far preferable to the horrible howlings of the yahoos.

Several others declared their sentiments to the same purpose, when my master proposed an expedient to the assembly, whereof he had indeed borrowed the hint from me. He approved of the tradition, mentioned by the 'honourable member' who spoke before, and affirmed, that the two yahoos said to be first seen among them had been driven thither over the sea; that coming to land, and being forsaken by their companions, they retired to the mountains, and degenerating by degrees, became in process of time much more savage than those of their own species in the country from whence these two originals came. The reason of his assertion was, that he had now in his possession a certain wonderful yahoo (meaning myself) which most of them had heard of, and many of them had seen. He then related to them how he first found me; that my body was all covered with an artificial composure of the skins and hairs of other animals: that I spoke in a language of my own, and had thoroughly learned theirs: that I had related to him the accidents which brought me thither: that when he saw me without my covering, I was an exact yahoo in every part, only of a whiter colour, less hairy, and with shorter claws. He added, how I had endeavoured to persuade him, that in my own and other countries the yahoos acted as the governing, rational animal, and held the Houyhnhnms in servitude: that he observed in me all the qualities of a yahoo, only a little more civilized by some tincture of reason, which however was in a degree as far inferior to the Houyhnhnm race as the yahoos of their country were to me: that, among other things, I mentioned a custom we had of castrating Houyhnhnms when they were young, in order to render them tame; that the operation was easy and safe; that it was no shame to learn wisdom from brutes, as industry is taught by the ant, and building by the swallow. (For so I translate the word *lyhannh*, although it be a much larger fowl.) That this invention might be practised upon the younger yahoos here, which, besides rendering them tractable and fitter for use, would in an age put an end to the whole species without destroying life. That in the mean time the Houyhnhnms should be exhorted to cultivate the breed of asses, which, as they are in all respects more valuable brutes, so they have this advantage, to be fit for service at five years old, which the others are not till twelve.

This was all my master thought fit to tell me at that time of what passed in the grand council. But he was pleased to conceal one particular, which related personally to myself, whereof I soon felt the unhappy effect, as the reader will know in its proper place, and from whence I date all the succeeding misfortunes of my life.

The Houyhnhnms have no letters, and consequently their knowledge is all traditional. But there happening few events of any moment among a people so well united, naturally disposed to every virtue, wholly governed by reason, and cut off from all commerce with other nations, the historical part is easily preserved without burthening their memories. I have already observed, that they are subject to no diseases, and therefore can have no need of physicians. However, they have excellent medicines composed of herbs, to cure accidental bruises and cuts in the pastern or frog of the foot by sharp stones, as well as other maims and hurts in the several parts of the body.

They calculate the year by the revolution of the sun and the moon, but use no subdivisions into weeks. They are well enough acquainted with the motions of those two luminaries, and understand the nature of eclipses; and this is the utmost progress of their astronomy.

In poetry they must be allowed to excel all other mortals; wherein the justness of their similes, and the minuteness, as well as exactness of their descriptions, are indeed inimitable. Their verses abound very much in both of these, and usually contain either some exalted notions of friendship and benevolence, or the praises of those who were victors in races and other bodily exercises. Their buildings, although very rude and simple, are not inconvenient, but well contrived to defend them from all injuries of cold and heat. They have a kind of tree, which at forty years old loosens in the root, and falls with the first storm; it grows very straight, and being pointed like stakes with a sharp stone (for the Houyhnhnms know not the use of iron), they stick them erect in the ground about ten inches asunder, and then weave in oat-straw, or sometimes wattles betwixt them. The roof is made after the same manner, and so are the doors.

The Houyhnhnms use the hollow part between the pastern and the hoof of their forefeet as we do our hands, and this with greater dexterity than I could at first imagine. I have seen a white mare of our family thread a needle (which I lent her on purpose) with that joint. They milk their cows, reap their oats, and do all the work which requires hands, in the same manner. They have a kind of hard flints, which, by grinding against other stones, they form into instruments, that serve instead of wedges, axes, and hammers. With tools made of these flints they likewise cut their hay, and reap their oats, which there groweth naturally in several fields: the yahoos draw home the sheaves in carriages, and the servants tread them in certain covered huts, to get out the grain, which is kept in stores. They make a rude kind of earthen and wooden vessels, and bake the former in the sun.

If they can avoid casualties, they die only of old age, and are buried in the obscurest places that can be found, their friends and relations expressing neither joy nor grief at their departure; nor does the dying person discover the least regret that he is leaving the world, any more than if he were upon returning home from a visit to one of his neighbours; I remember my master having once made an appointment with a friend and his family to come to his house upon some affair of importance; on the day fixed, the mistress and her two children came very late; she made two excuses, first for her husband, who, as she said, happened that very morning to *lhnuwnh*. The word is strongly expressive in their language, but not easily rendered into English; it signifies, 'to retire to his first mother'. Her excuse for not coming sooner was, that her husband dying late in the morning, she was a good while consulting her servants about a convenient place where his body should be laid; and I observed she behaved herself at our house as cheerfully as the rest: she died about three months after.

They live generally to seventy or seventy-five years, very seldom to fourscore: some weeks before their death they feel a gradual decay, but without pain. During this time they are much visited by their friends, because they cannot go abroad with their usual ease and satisfaction. However, about ten days before their death, which they seldom fail in computing, they return the visits that have been made them by those who are nearest in the neighbourhood, being carried in a convenient sledge drawn by yahoos, which vehicle they use, not only upon this occasion, but when they grow old, upon long journeys, or when they are lamed by any accident. And therefore when the dying Houyhnhnms return those visits, they take a solemn leave of their friends, as if they were going to some remote part of the country, where they designed to pass the rest of their lives.

I know not whether it may be worth observing, that the Houyhnhnms have no word in their language to express any thing that is evil, except what they borrow from the deformities or ill qualities of the yahoos. Thus they denote the folly of a servant, an omission of a child, a stone that cuts their feet, a continuance of foul or unseasonable weather, and the like, by adding to each the epithet of *yahoo*. For instance, *hhnm yahoo*, *whnaholm yahoo*, *ynlhnmawihlma yahoo*, and an ill-contrived house *ynholmhnmrohlnw yahoo*.

I could with great pleasure enlarge farther upon the manners and virtues of this excellent people; but intending in a short time to publish a volume by itself expressly upon that subject, I refer the reader thither. And in the mean time, proceed to relate my own sad catastrophe.

Chapter X.

The author's œconomy and happy life among the Houyhnhnms. His great improvement in virtue, by conversing with them. Their conversations. The author has notice given him by his master that he must depart from the country. He falls into a swoon for grief, but submits. He contrives and finishes a canoe, by the help of a fellow-servant, and puts to sea at a venture.

I had settled my little œconomy to my own heart's content. My master had ordered a room to be made for me after their manner, about six yards from the house, the sides and floors of which I plastered with clay, and covered with rush mats of my own contriving; I had beaten hemp, which there grows wild, and made of it a sort of ticking: this I filled with the feathers of several birds I had taken with springes made of yahoos' hairs, and were excellent food. I had worked two chairs with my knife, the sorrel nag helping me in the grosser and more laborious part. When my clothes were worn to rags, I made myself others with the skins of rabbits, and of a certain beautiful animal about the same size, called *nnuhnoh*, the skin of which is covered with a fine down. Of these I likewise made very tolerable stockings. I soled my shoes with wood which I cut from a tree, and fitted to the upper leather, and when this was worn out, I supplied it with the skins of yahoos dried in the sun. I often got honey out of hollow trees, which I mingled with water, or eat it with my bread. No man could more verify the truth of these two maxims, *That nature is very easily satisfied*; and *That necessity is the mother of invention*. I enjoyed perfect health of body and tranquillity of mind; I did not feel the treachery or inconstancy of a friend, nor the injuries of a secret or open enemy. I had no occasion of bribing, flattering or pimping to procure the favour of any great man or of his minion. I wanted no fence against fraud or oppression; here was neither physician to destroy my body, nor lawyer to ruin my fortune; no informer to watch my words and actions, or forge accusations against me for hire: here were no gibers, censurers, backbiters, pickpockets, highwaymen, housebreakers, attorneys, bawds, buffoons, gamesters, politicians, wits, splenetics, tedious talkers, controvertists, ravishers, murderers, robbers, virtuosos: no leaders or followers of party and faction: no encouragers to vice, by seducement or examples: no dungeon, axes, gibbets, whipping-posts, or pillories: no cheating shopkeepers or mechanics: no pride, vanity, or affectation: no fops, bullies, drunkards, strolling whores, or poxes: no ranting, lewd, expensive wives: no stupid, proud pedants: no importunate, overbearing, quarrelsome, noisy, roaring, empty, conceited, swearing companions: no scoundrels, raised from the dust upon the merit of their vices, or nobility thrown into it on account of their virtues: no lords, fiddlers, judges or dancing-masters.

I had the favour of being admitted to several Houyhnhnms, who came to visit or dine with my master; where his Honour graciously suffered me to wait in the room, and listen to their discourse. Both he and his company would often descend to ask me questions, and receive my answers. I had also sometimes the honour of attending my master in his visits to others. I never presumed to speak, except in answer to a question, and then I did it with inward regret, because it was a loss of so much time for improving myself: but I was infinitely delighted with the station of an humble auditor in such conversations, where nothing passed but what was useful, expressed in the fewest and most significant words: where (as I have already said) the greatest decency was observed, without the least degree of ceremony; where no person spoke without being pleased himself, and pleasing his companions; where there was no interruptions, tediousness, heat, or difference of sentiments. They have a notion, that when people are met together, a short silence doth much improve conversation: this I found to be true; for during those little intermissions of talk, new ideas would arise in their minds, which very much enlivened the discourse. Their subjects are generally on friendship and benevolence, or order and œconomy, sometimes upon the visible operations of nature, or ancient traditions, upon the bounds and limits of virtue, upon the unerring rules of reason, or upon some determinations to be taken at the next great assembly, and often upon the various excellencies of poetry. I may add without vanity, that my presence often gave them sufficient matter for discourse, because it afforded my master an occasion of letting his friends into the history of me and my country, upon which they were all pleased to descant in a manner not very advantageous to human kind; and for that reason I shall not repeat what they said: only I may be allowed to observe, that his Honour, to my great admiration, appeared to understand the nature of yahoos much better than myself. He went through all our vices and follies, and discovered many which I had never mentioned to him, by only supposing what qualities a yahoo of their country, with a small proportion of reason, might be capable of exerting; and concluded, with too much probability, how vile as well as miserable such a creature must be.

I freely confess, that all the little knowledge I have of any value was acquired by the lectures I received from my master, and from hearing the discourses of him and his friends; to which I should be prouder to listen, than to dictate to the greatest and wisest assembly in Europe. I admired the strength, comeliness, and speed of the inhabitants; and such a constellation of virtues in such amiable persons produced in me the highest veneration. At first, indeed, I did not feel that natural awe which the yahoos and all other animals bear towards them; but it grew upon me by degrees, much sooner than I imagined, and was mingled with a respectful love and gratitude, that they would condescend to distinguish me from the rest of my species.

When I thought of my family, my friends, my countrymen, or human race in general, I considered them as they really were, yahoos in shape and disposition, only a little more civilized, and qualified with the gift of speech, but making no other use of reason than to improve and multiply those vices whereof their brethren in this country had only the share that nature allotted them. When I happened to behold the reflection of my own form in a lake or fountain, I turned away my face in horror and detestation of myself, and could better endure the sight of a common yahoo, than of my own person. By conversing with the Houyhnhnms, and looking upon them with delight, I fell to imitate their gait and gesture, which is now grown into a habit, and my friends often tell me in a blunt way that I 'trot like a horse'; which, however, I take for a great compliment: neither shall I disown, that in speaking I am apt to fall into the voice and manner of the Houyhnhnms, and hear myself ridiculed on that account without the least mortification.

In the midst of all this happiness, when I looked upon myself to be fully settled for life, my master sent for me one morning a little earlier than his usual hour. I observed by his countenance that he was in some perplexity, and at a loss how to begin what he had to speak. After a short silence, he told me, he did not know how I would take what he was going to say; that in the last general assembly, when the affair of the yahoos was entered upon, the representatives had taken offence at his keeping a yahoo (meaning myself) in his family more like a Houyhnhnm than a brute animal. That he was known frequently to converse with me, as if he could receive some advantage or pleasure in my company: that such a practice was not agreeable to reason or nature, or a thing ever heard of before among them. The assembly did therefore exhort him, either to employ me like the rest of my species, or command me to swim back to the place from whence I came. That the first of these expedients was utterly rejected by all the Houyhnhnms who had ever seen me at his house or their own: for they alleged, that because I had some rudiments of reason, added to the natural pravity of those animals, it was to be feared, I might be able to seduce them into the woody and mountainous parts of the country, and bring them in troops by night to destroy the Houyhnhnms' cattle, as being naturally of the ravenous kind, and averse from labour.

My master added, that he was daily pressed by the Houyhnhnms of the neighbourhood to have the assembly's exhortation executed, which he could not put off much longer. He doubted it would be impossible for me to swim to another country, and therefore wished I would contrive some sort of vehicle resembling those I had described to him, that might carry me on the sea, in which work I should have the assistance of his own servants, as well as those of his neighbours. He concluded, that for his own part he could have been content to keep me in his service as long as I lived, because he found I had cured myself of some bad habits and dispositions, by endeavouring, as far as my inferior nature was capable, to imitate the Houyhnhnms.

I should here observe to the reader, that a decree of the general assembly in this country is expressed by the word *hnhloayn*, which signifies an *exhortation*, as near as I can render it: for they have no conception how a rational creature can be compelled, but only advised or exhorted, because no person can disobey reason, without giving up his claim to be a rational creature.

I was struck with the utmost grief and despair at my master's discourse, and being unable to support the agonies I was under, I fell into a swoon at his feet; when I came to myself he told me that he concluded I had been dead. (For these people are subject to no such imbecilities of nature.) I answered, in a faint voice, that death would have been too great an happiness; that although I could not blame the assembly's exhortation, or the urgency of his friends, yet, in my weak and corrupt judgment, I thought it might consist with reason to have been less rigorous. That I could not swim a league, and probably the nearest land to theirs might be distant above an hundred; that many materials, necessary for making a small vessel to carry me off, were wholly wanting in this country, which, however, I would attempt in obedience and gratitude to his Honour, although I concluded the thing to be impossible, and therefore looked on my self as already devoted to destruction. That the certain prospect of an unnatural death was the least of my evils: for, supposing I should escape with life by some strange adventure, how could I think with temper of passing my days among yahoos, and relapsing into my old corruptions, for want of examples to lead and keep me within the paths of virtue? That I knew too well upon what solid reasons all the determinations of the wise Houyhnhnms were founded, not to be shaken by arguments of mine, a miserable yahoo; and therefore, after presenting him with my humble thanks for the offer of his servants' assistance in making a vessel, and desiring a reasonable time for so difficult a work, I told him I would endeavour to preserve a wretched being; and, if ever I returned to England, was not without hopes of being useful to my own species, by celebrating the praises of the renowned Houyhnhnms, and proposing their virtues to the imitation of mankind.

My master in a few words made me a very gracious reply, allowed me the space of two months to finish my boat; and ordered the sorrel nag, my fellow-servant (for so at this distance I may presume to call him) to follow my instructions, because I told my master, that his help would be sufficient, and I knew he had a tenderness for me.

In his company my first business was to go to that part of the coast where my rebellious crew had ordered me to be set on shore. I got upon a height, and looking on every side into the sea, fancied I saw a small island, towards the northeast: I took out my pocket-glass, and could then clearly distinguish it about five leagues off, as I computed; but it appeared to the sorrel nag to be only a blue cloud: for as he had no conception of any country beside his own, so he could not be as expert in distinguishing remote objects at sea as we who so much converse in that element.

After I had discovered this island, I considered no farther; but resolved it should, if possible, be the first place of my banishment, leaving the consequence to fortune.

I returned home, and consulting with the sorrel nag, we went into a copse at some distance, where I with my knife, and he with a sharp flint fastened very artificially after their manner, to a wooden handle, cut down several oak wattles about the thickness of a walking-staff, and some larger pieces. But I shall not trouble the reader with a particular description of my own mechanics; let it suffice to say that in six weeks' time, with the help of the sorrel nag, who performed the parts that required most labour, I finished a sort of Indian canoe, but much larger, covering it with the skins of yahoos well stitched together, with hempen threads of my own making. My sail was likewise composed of the skins of the same animal; but I made use of the youngest I could get, the older being too tough and thick, and I likewise provided myself with four paddles. I laid in a stock of boiled flesh, of rabbits and fowls, and took with me two vessels, one filled with milk, and the other with water.

I tried my canoe in a large pond near my master's house, and then corrected in it what was amiss; stopping all the chinks with yahoos' tallow, till I found it staunch, and able to bear me and my freight. And when it was as complete as I could possibly make it, I had it drawn on a carriage very gently by yahoos to the seaside, under the conduct of the sorrel nag and another servant.

When all was ready, and the day came for my departure, I took leave of my master and lady, and the whole family, my eyes flowing with tears, and my heart quite sunk with grief. But his Honour, out of curiosity, and perhaps (if I may speak it without vanity) partly out of kindness, was determined to see me in my canoe, and got several of his neighbouring friends to accompany him. I was forced to wait above an hour for the tide, and then observing the wind very fortunately bearing towards the island, to which I intended to steer my course, I took a second leave of my master: but as I was going to prostrate myself to kiss his hoof, he did me the honour to raise it gently to my mouth. I am not ignorant how much I have been censured for mentioning this last particular. Detractors are pleased to think it improbable, that so illustrious a person should descend to give so great a mark of distinction to a creature so inferior as I. Neither have I forgot how apt some travellers are to boast of extraordinary favours they have received. But if these censurers were better acquainted with the noble and courteous disposition of the Houyhnhnms, they would soon change their opinion.

I paid my respects to the rest of the Houyhnhnms in his Honour's company; then getting into my canoe, I pushed off from shore.

Chapter XI.

The author's dangerous voyage. He arrives at New Holland, hoping to settle there. Is wounded with an arrow by one of the natives. Is seized and carried by force into a Portuguese ship. The great civilities of the captain. The author arrives at England.

I began this desperate voyage on February 15, 1714–5, at 9 o'clock in the morning. The wind was very favourable; however, I made use at first only of my paddles, but considering I should soon be weary, and that the wind might probably chop about, I ventured to set up my little sail; and thus with the help of the tide I went at the rate of a league and a half an hour, as near as I could guess. My master and his friends continued on the shore till I was almost out of sight; and I often heard the sorrel nag (who always loved me) crying out, *Hnuy illa nyha maiah yahoo*, Take care of thyself, gentle yahoo.

My design was, if possible, to discover some small island uninhabited, yet sufficient by my labour to furnish me with the necessaries of life, which I would have thought a greater happiness than to be first minister in the politest court of Europe; so horrible was the idea I conceived of returning to live in the society and under the government of yahoos. For in such a solitude as I desired, I could at least enjoy my own thoughts, and reflect with delight on the virtues of those inimitable Houyhnhnms, without any opportunity of degenerating into the vices and corruptions of my own species.

The reader may remember what I related when my crew conspired aginst me, and confined me to my cabin. How I continued there several weeks, without knowing what course we took, and when I was put ashore in the long-boat, how the sailors told me with oaths, whether true or false, that they knew not in what part of the world we were. However, I did then believe us to be about ten degrees southward of the Cape of Good Hope, or about 45 degrees southern latitude, as I gathered from some general words I overheard among them, being I supposed to the southeast in their intended voyage to Madagascar. And although this were but little better than conjecture, yet I resolved to steer my course eastward, hoping to reach the southwest coast of New Holland, and perhaps some such island as I desired, lying westward of it. The wind was full west, and by six in the evening I computed I had gone eastward at least eighteen leagues, when I spied a very small island about half a league off, which I soon reached. It was nothing but a rock, with one creek, naturally arched by the force of tempests. Here I put in my canoe, and climbing a part of the rock, I could plainly discover land to the east, extending from south to north. I lay all night in my canoe, and repeating my voyage early in the morning, I arrived in seven hours to the southeast point of New Holland. This confirmed me in the opinion I have long entertained, that the maps and charts place this country at least three degrees more to the east than it really is; which thought I communicated many years ago to my worthy friend Mr. Herman Moll, and gave him my reasons for it, although he hath rather chosen to follow other authors.

I saw no inhabitants in the place where I landed, and being unarmed, I was afraid of venturing far into the country. I found some shellfish on the shore, and eat them raw, not daring to kindle a fire, for fear of being discovered by the natives. I continued three days feeding on oysters and limpets, to save my own provisions, and I fortunately found a brook of excellent water, which gave me great relief.

On the fourth day, venturing out early a little too far, I saw twenty or thirty natives upon a height, not above five hundred yards from me. They were stark naked, men, women, and children, round a fire, as I could discover by the smoke. One of them spied me, and gave notice to the rest; five of them advanced towards me, leaving the women and children at the fire. I made what haste I could to the shore, and getting into my canoe, shoved off: the savages observing me retreat, ran after me; and before I could get far enough into the sea, discharged an arrow, which wounded me deeply on the inside of my left knee

(I shall carry the mark to my grave). I apprehended the arrow might be poisoned, and paddling out of the reach of their darts (being a calm day), I made a shift to suck the wound, and dress it as well as I could.

I was at a loss what to do, for I durst not return to the same landing-place, but stood to the north, and was forced to paddle; for the wind, although very gentle, was against me, blowing northwest. As I was looking about for a secure landing-place, I saw a sail to the north-northeast, which appearing every minute more visible, I was in some doubt, whether I should wait for them or no; but at last my detestation of the yahoo race prevailed, and turning my canoe, I sailed and paddled together to the south, and got into the same creek from whence I set out in the morning, choosing rather to trust myself among these barbarians, than live with European yahoos. I drew up my canoe as close as I could to the shore, and hid myself behind a stone by the little brook, which, as I have already said, was excellent water.

The ship came within a half a league of this creek, and sent out her long-boat with vessels to take in fresh water (for the place it seems was very well known) but I did not observe it until the boat was almost on shore, and it was too late to seek another hiding-place. The seamen at their landing observed my canoe, and rummaging it all over, easily conjectured that the owner could not be far off. Four of them well armed searched every cranny and lurking-hole, till at last they found me flat on my face behind the stone. They gazed a while in admiration at my strange uncouth dress, my coat made of skins, my wooden-soled shoes, and my furred stockings; from whence, however, they concluded I was not a native of the place, who all go naked. One of the seamen in Portuguese bid me rise, and asked who I was. I understood that language very well, and getting upon my feet, said, I was a poor yahoo, banished from the Houyhnhnms, and desired they would please to let me depart. They admired to hear me answer them in their own tongue, and saw by my complexion I must be an European; but were at loss to know what I meant by yahoos and Houyhnhnms, and at the same time fell a laughing at my strange tone in speaking, which resembled the neighing of a horse. I trembled all the while betwixt fear and hatred: I again desired leave to depart, and was gently moving to my canoe; but they laid hold on me, desiring to know, what country I was of, whence I came, with many other questions. I told them I was born in England, from whence I came about five years ago, and then their country and ours were at peace. I therefore hoped they would not treat me as an enemy, since I meant them no harm, but was a poor yahoo, seeking some desolate place where to pass the remainder of his unfortunate life.

When they began to talk, I thought I never heard or saw any thing so unnatural; for it appeared to me as monstrous as if a dog or a cow should speak in England, or a yahoo in Houyhnhnmland. The honest Portuguese were equally amazed at my strange dress, and the odd manner of delivering my words, which however they understood very well. They spoke to me with great humanity, and said they were sure their captain would carry me *gratis* to Lisbon, from whence I might return to my own country; that two of the seamen would go back to the ship, inform the captain of what they had seen, and receive his orders; in the mean time, unless I would give my solemn oath not to fly, they would secure me by force. I thought it best to comply with their proposal. They were very curious to know my story, but I gave them very little satisfaction; and they all conjectured that my misfortunes had impaired my reason. In two hours the boat, which went loaden with vessels of water, returned with the captain's commands to fetch me on board. I fell on my knees to preserve my liberty; but all was in vain, and the men having tied me with cords, heaved me into the boat, from whence I was taken into the ship, and from thence into the captain's cabin.

His name was Pedro de Mendez; he was a very courteous and generous person; he entreated me to give some account of my self, and desired to know what I would eat or drink; said, I should be used as well as himself, and spoke so many obliging things, that I wondered to find such civilities from a yahoo. However, I remained silent and sullen; I was ready to faint at the very smell of him and his men. At last I desired something to eat out of my own canoe; but he ordered me a chicken and some excellent wine, and then directed that I should be put to bed in a very clean cabin. I would not undress myself, but lay on the bed-clothes, and in half an hour stole out, when I thought the crew was at dinner, and getting to the side of the ship was going to leap into the sea, and swim for my life, rather than continue among yahoos. But one of the seamen prevented me, and having informed the captain, I was chained to my cabin.

After dinner Don Pedro came to me, and desired to know my reason for so desperate an attempt: assured me he only meant to do me all the service he was able, and spoke so very movingly, that at last I descended to treat him like an animal which had some little portion of reason. I gave him a very short relation of my voyage, of the conspiracy against me by my own men, of the country where they set me on shore, and of my three year's residence there. All which he looked upon as if it were a dream or a vision; whereat I took great offence; for I had quite forgot the faculty of lying, so peculiar to yahoos in all countries where they preside, and, consequently, the disposition of suspecting truth in others of their own species. I asked him, whether it were the custom of his country to *say the thing that was not.* I assured him I had almost forgot what he meant by falsehood, and if I had lived a thousand years in Houyhnhnmland, I should never have heard a lie from the meanest servant; that I was altogether indifferent whether he believed me or no; but however, in return for his favours, I would give so much allowance to the corruption of his nature as to answer any objection he would please to make, and he might easily discover the truth.

The captain, a wise man, after many endeavours to catch me tripping in some part of my story, at last began to have a better opinion of my veracity. But he added, that since I professed so inviolable an attachment to truth, I must give him my word of honour to bear him company in this voyage without attempting anything against my life, or else he would continue me a prisoner till we arrived in Lisbon. I gave him the promise he required; but at the same time protested that I would suffer the greatest hardships rather than return to live among yahoos.

Our voyage passed without any considerable accident. In gratitude to the captain I sometimes sat with him at his earnest request, and strove to conceal my antipathy to human kind, although it often broke out, which he suffered to pass without observation. But the greatest part of the day, I confined myself to my cabin, to avoid seeing any of the crew. The captain had often entreated me to strip myself of my savage dress, and offered to lend me the best suit of clothes he had. This I would not be prevailed on to accept, abhorring to cover myself with anything that had been on the back of a yahoo. I only desired he would lend me two clean shirts, which having been washed since he wore them, I believed would not so much defile me. These I changed every second day, and washed them myself.

We arrived at Lisbon, Nov. 5, 1715. At our landing the captain forced me to cover myself with his cloak, to prevent the rabble from crowding about me. I was conveyed to his own house, and, at my earnest request, he led me up to the highest room backwards. I conjured him to conceal from all persons what I had told him of the Houyhnhnms, because the least hint of such a story would not only draw numbers of people to see me, but probably put me in danger of being imprisoned, or burnt by the Inquisition. The captain persuaded me to accept a suit of clothes newly made, but I would not suffer the tailor to take my measure; however, Don Pedro being almost of my size, they fitted me well enough. He accoutred me with other necessaries all new, which I aired for twenty-four hours before I would use them.

The captain had no wife, nor above three servants, none of which were suffered to attend at meals, and his whole deportment was so obliging, added to very good *human* understanding, that I really began to tolerate his company. He gained so far upon me, that I ventured to look out of the back window. By degrees I was brought into another room, from whence I peeped into the street, but drew my head back in a fright. In a week's time he seduced me down to the door. I found my terror gradually lessened, but my hatred and contempt seemed to increase. I was at last bold enough to walk the street in his company, but kept my nose well stopped with rue, or sometimes with tobacco.

In ten days Don Pedro, to whom I had given some account of my domestic affairs, put it upon me as a point of honour and conscience, that I ought to return to my native country, and live at home with my wife and children. He told me, there was an English ship in the port just ready to sail, and he would furnish me with all things necessary. It would be tedious to repeat his arguments, and my contradictions. He said it was altogether impossible to find such a solitary island as I had desired to live in; but I might command in my own house, and pass my time in a manner as recluse as I pleased.

I complied at last, finding I could not do better. I left Lisbon the 24th day of November, in an English merchantman, but who was the master I never inquired. Don Pedro accompanied me to the ship, and lent me twenty pounds. He took kind leave of me, and embraced me at parting, which I bore as well as I could. During this last voyage I had no commerce with the master or any of his men, but pretending I was sick kept close in my cabin. On the fifth of December, 1715, we cast anchor in the Downs about nine in the morning, and at three in the afternoon I got safe to my house at Redriff.

My wife and family received me with great surprise and joy, because they concluded me certainly dead; but I must freely confess the sight of them filled me only with hatred, disgust and contempt, and the more by reflecting on the near alliance I had to them. For although, since my unfortunate exile from the Houyhnhnm country, I had compelled myself to tolerate the sight of yahoos, and to converse with Don Pedro de Mendez, yet my memory and imaginations were perpetually filled with the virtues and ideas of those exalted Houyhnhnms. And when I began to consider, that by copulating with one of the yahoo species I had become a parent of more, it struck me with the utmost shame, confusion, and horror.

As soon as I entered the house, my wife took me in her arms, and kissed me, at which, having not been used to the touch of that odious animal for so many years, I fell in a swoon for almost an hour. At the time I am writing it is five years since my last return to England: during the first year I could not endure my wife or children in my presence, the very smell of them was intolerable, much less could I suffer them to eat in the same room. To this hour they dare not presume to touch my bread, or drink out of the same cup, neither was I ever able to let one of them take me by the hand. The first money I laid out was to buy two young stone-horses, which I keep in a good stable, and next to them the groom is my greatest favourite; for I feel my spirits revived by the smell he contracts in the stable. My horses understand me tolerably well; I converse with them at least four hours every day. They are strangers to bridle or saddle; they live in great amity with me, and friendship to each other.

Chapter XII.

The author's veracity. His design in publishing this work. His censure of those travellers who swerve from the truth. The author clears himself from any sinister ends in writing. An objection answered. The method of planting colonies. His native country commended. The right of the crown to those countries described by the author is justified. The difficulty of conquering them. The author takes his last leave of the reader, proposeth his manner of living for the future, gives good advice, and concludes.

Thus, gentle reader, I have given thee a faithful history of my travels for sixteen years, and above seven months, wherein I have not been so studious of ornament as of truth. I could perhaps like others have astonished thee with strange improbable tales; but I rather chose to relate plain matter of fact in the simplest manner and style, because my principal design was to inform, and not to amuse thee.

It is easy for us who travel into remote countries, which are seldom visited by Englishmen or other Europeans, to form descriptions of wonderful animals both at sea and land. Whereas a traveller's chief aim should be to make men wiser and better,

and to improve their minds by the bad as well as good example
of what they deliver concerning foreign places.

I could heartily wish a law were enacted, that every traveller,
before he were permitted to publish his voyages, should be
obliged to make oath before the Lord High Chancellor that all he
intended to print was absolutely true to the best of his knowledge; for then the world would no longer be deceived as it
usually is, while some writers, to make their works pass the better
upon the public, impose the grossest falsities on the unwary
reader. I have perused several books of travels with great delight
in my younger days; but having since gone over most parts of the
globe, and been able to contradict many fabulous accounts from
my own observation, it hath given me a great disgust against this
part of reading, and some indignation to see the credulity of
mankind so impudently abused. Therefore since my acquaintance were pleased to think my poor endeavours might not be
unacceptable to my country, I imposed on myself as a maxim,
never to be swerved from, that I would *strictly adhere to truth*;
neither indeed can I be ever under the least temptation to vary
from it, while I retain in my mind the lectures and example of my
noble master, and the other illustrious Houyhnhnms, of whom I
had so long the honour to be an humble hearer.

——— Nec si miserum Fortuna Sinonem
Finxit, vanum etiam mendacemque improba finget.

I know very well how little reputation is to be got by writings
which require neither genius nor learning, nor indeed any other
talent, except a good memory or an exact journal. I know likewise, that writers of travels, like dictionary-makers, are sunk into
oblivion by the weight and bulk of those who come after, and
therefore lie uppermost. And it is highly probable, that such
travellers who shall hereafter visit the countries described in this
work of mine, may, by detecting my errors (if there be any),
and adding many new discoveries of their own, jostle me out of
vogue, and stand in my place, making the world forget that ever I
was an author. This indeed would be too great a mortification if
I wrote for fame: but, as my sole intention was the PUBLIC GOOD,
I cannot be altogether disappointed. For who can read of the
virtues I have mentioned in the glorious Houyhnhnms, without
being ashamed of his own vices, when he considers himself as the
reasoning, governing animal of his country? I shall say nothing
of those remote nations where yahoos preside, amongst which the
least corrupted are the Brobdingnagians, whose wise maxims in

morality and government it would be our happiness to observe.
But I forbear descanting further, and rather leave the judicious
reader to his own remarks and applications.

I am not a little pleased that this work of mine can possibly
meet with no censurers: for what objections can be made against
a writer who relates only plain facts that happened in such distant countries, where we have not the least interest with respect
either to trade or negotiations? I have carefully avoided
every fault with which common writers of travels are often too
justly charged. Besides, I meddle not the least with any *party*,
but write without passion, prejudice, or ill-will against any man
or number of men whatsoever. I write for the noblest end, to
inform and instruct mankind, over whom I may, without breach
of modesty, pretend to some superiority from the advantages I
received by conversing so long among the most accomplished
Houyhnhnms. I write without any view towards profit or praise.
I never suffer a word to pass that may look like reflection, or
possibly give the least offence even to those who are most ready
to take it. So that I hope I may with justice pronounce myself
an author perfectly blameless, against whom the tribe of answer-
ers, considerers, observers, reflecters, detecters, remarkers, will
never be able to find matter for exercising their talents.

I confess, it was whispered to me that I was bound in duty, as
a subject of England, to have given in a memorial to a secretary
of state, at my first coming over; because, whatever lands are
discovered by a subject belong to the crown. But I doubt whether
our conquests in the countries I treat of would be as easy as
those of Ferdinando Cortez over the naked Americans. The
Lilliputians, I think, are hardly worth the charge of a fleet and
army to reduce them, and I question whether it might be prudent
or safe to attempt the Brobdingnagians. Or whether an English
army would be much at their ease with the Flying Island over
their heads. The Houyhnhnms, indeed, appear not to be so well
prepared for war, a science to which they are perfect strangers,
and especially against missive weapons. However, supposing
myself to be a minister of state, I could never give my
advice for invading them. Their prudence, unanimity, unac-
quaintedness with fear, and their love of their country would
amply supply all defects in the military art. Imagine twenty
thousand of them breaking into the midst of an European army,
confounding the ranks, overturning the carriages, battering the
warriors' faces into mummy, by terrible yerks from their hinder
hoofs. For they would well deserve the character given to
Augustus; *Recalcitrat undique tutus*. But instead of proposals

for conquering that magnanimous nation, I rather wish they were in a capacity or disposition to send a sufficient number of their inhabitants for civilizing Europe, by teaching us the first principles of honour, justice, truth, temperance, public spirit, fortitude, chastity, friendship, benevolence, and fidelity. The names of all which virtues are still retained among us in most languages, and are to be met with in modern as well as ancient authors; which I am able to assert from my own small reading.

But I had another reason which made me less forward to enlarge his Majesty's dominions by my discoveries. To say the truth, I had conceived a few scruples with relation to the distributive justice of princes upon those occasions. For instance, a crew of pirates are driven by a storm they know not whither, at length a boy discovers land from the topmast, they go on shore to rob and plunder, they see an harmless people, are entertained with kindness, they give the country a new name, they take formal possession of it for the king, they set up a rotten plank or a stone for a memorial, they murder two or three dozen of the natives, bring away a couple more by force for a sample, return home, and get their pardon. Here commences a new dominion acquired with a title by *divine right*. Ships are sent with the first opportunity, the natives driven out or destroyed, their princes tortured to discover their gold, a free license given to all acts of inhumanity and lust, the earth reeking with the blood of its inhabitants: and this execrable crew of butchers employed in so pious an expedition, is a modern colony sent to convert and civilize an idolatrous and barbarous people.

But this description, I confess, doth by no means affect the British nation, who may be an example to the whole world for their wisdom, care, and justice in planting colonies; their liberal endowments for the advancement of religion and learning; their choice of devout and able pastors to propagate Christianity; their caution in stocking their provinces with people of sober lives and conversations from this the mother kingdom; their strict regard to the distribution of justice, in supplying the civil administration through all their colonies with officers of the greatest abilities, utter strangers to corruption; and to crown all, by sending the most vigilant and virtuous governors, who have no other views than the happiness of the people over whom they preside, and the honour of the king their master.

But as those countries which I have described do not appear to have any desire of being conquered, and enslaved, murdered or driven out by colonies, nor abound either in gold, silver, sugar or tobacco; I did humbly conceive they were by no means proper objects of our zeal, our valour, or our interest. However, if those whom it may concern think fit to be of another opinion, I am ready to depose, when I shall be lawfully called, that no European did ever visit these countries before me. I mean, if the inhabitants ought to be believed; unless a dispute may arise about the two yahoos, said to have been seen many ages ago on a mountain in Houyhnhnmland, from whence the opinion is, that the race of those brutes hath descended; and these, for any thing I know, may have been English, which indeed I was apt to suspect from the lineaments of their posterity's countenances, although very much defaced. But, how far that will go to make out a title, I leave to the learned in colony-law.

But as to the formality of taking possession in my sovereign's name, it never came once into my thoughts; and if it had, yet as my affairs then stood, I should perhaps, in point of prudence and self-preservation, have put it off to a better opportunity.

Having thus answered the *only* objection than can ever be raised against me as a traveller, I here take a final leave of my courteous readers, and return to enjoy my own speculations in my little garden at Redriff, to apply those excellent lessons of virtue which I learned among the Houyhnhnms, to instruct the yahoos of my own family as far as I shall find them docible animals, to behold my figure often in a glass, and thus if possible habituate myself by time to tolerate the sight of a human creature; to lament the brutality of Houyhnhnms in my own country, but always treat their persons with respect, for the sake of my noble master, his family, his friends, and the whole Houyhnhnm race, whom these of ours have the honour to resemble in all their lineaments, however their intellectuals came to degenerate.

I began last week to permit my wife to sit at dinner with me, at the farthest end of a long table, and to answer (but with the utmost brevity) the few questions I ask her. Yet the smell of a yahoo continuing very offensive, I always keep my nose well stopped with rue, lavender, or tobacco leaves. And although it be hard for a man late in life to remove old habits, I am not altogether out of hopes in some time to suffer a neighbour yahoo in my company without the apprehensions I am yet under of his teeth or his claws.

My reconcilement to the yahoo-kind in general might not be so difficult if they would be content with those vices and follies only which nature hath entitled them to. I am not in the least provoked at the sight of a lawyer, a pickpocket, a colonel, a fool, a lord, a gamester, a politician, a whoremonger, a physician, an evidence, a suborner, an attorney, a traitor, or the like; this is all according to the due course of things: but when I behold a lump of deformity and diseases both in body and mind, smitten with pride, it immediately breaks all the measures of my patience; neither shall I be ever able to comprehend how such an animal and such a vice could tally together. The wise and virtuous Houyhnhnms, who abound in all excellencies that can adorn a rational creature, have no name for this vice in their language, which hath no terms to express any thing that is evil, except those whereby they describe the detestable qualities of their yahoos, among which they were not able to distinguish this of pride, for want of thoroughly understanding human nature, as it showeth itself in other countries, where that animal presides. But I, who had more experience, could plainly observe some rudiments of it among the wild yahoos.

But the Houyhnhnms, who live under the government of reason, are no more proud of the good qualities they possess, than I should be for not wanting a leg or an arm, which no man in his wits would boast of, although he must be miserable without them. I dwell the longer upon this subject from the desire I have to make the society of an English yahoo by any means not insupportable, and therefore I here entreat those who have any tincture of this absurd vice, that they will not presume to appear in my sight.

FINIS

NOTES

THE TITLE. It may come as a surprise that the title of the work referred to as *Gulliver's Travels* is in fact *Travels into Several Remote Nations of the World*. The name of the author as given on the title page when the book was published was Lemuel Gulliver, not Jonathan Swift. Curiously, the name *Gulliver* does not appear in the actual text, but merely on the title page, underneath an engraved portrait used as a frontispiece, and in two preliminary pieces, one of which was not printed until 1735. Swift, as well as the few friends who knew the work was in progress, referred to it as the *Travels*, and it is possible, as Professor Frederick Bracher has suggested, that "Lemuel Gulliver" himself did not come into existence until the book was ready for the printer. Any hypothesis about the origin of the name or its meaning must be viewed with scepticism, including the significance attached to the first four letters.

"A Letter . . . to his Cousin Sympson": This letter, though dated 1727, was first printed as a preface to *Gulliver's Travels* in 1735, in the Dublin edition of Swift's *Works*. The date of its composition is a matter of controversy. Gulliver's cousin was possibly named Sympson to suggest a family connection with William Symson, author of *A New Voyage to the East-Indies* (1715). But Swift may have had in mind Richard Simpson, publisher of some of Sir William Temple's works.

3. 6 "Dampier": William Dampier (1652–1715), a famous buccaneer and explorer. He wrote extensively of his voyages and was widely read.

3. 23–25 "omitted . . . changed . . . I do hardly know my own work": After the first publication of *Gulliver's Travels* Swift complained bitterly that portions of his manuscript had been tampered with, that some passages had been blotted out, others changed and mangled. He endeavored to insure corrections and alterations in subsequent editions.

4. 17 "Smithfield": a locality in London, site of a cattle market for several centuries and a place where a number of martyrs and heretics had been put to the flame.

4. 32 "keys . . . second parts": Gulliveriana began to appear at once, e.g., *A Key, being Observations and Explanatory Notes upon*

the Travels of Lemuel Gulliver, by Signor Corolini (1726) and *Travels into several Remote Nations of the World, by Captain Lemuel Gulliver, vol. III* (1727). This latter work contained "A Second Voyage to Brobdingnag".

4. 38–39 "author . . . stranger": In the course of his life (and even afterwards) many works in which Swift had no hand were attributed to him, some actually published under his name or initials. His own works, except two, were published anonymously or with pseudonyms.

4. 40–41 "confound the times, and . . . dates": Swift apparently attempted to achieve accuracy in the time-scheme and dates of Gulliver's voyages, and to obtain a realistic geography within the limits of his fantasy, but either slips by the printer or himself or both have caused some confusion. There is no evidence that Swift was responsible for the maps. The geography and chronology of the *Travels* are discussed by Professor Arthur Case in his *Four Essays on "Gulliver's Travels"* (1945).

15. 3 "at fourteen years old": Students commonly attended the universities at earlier ages in Swift's day. He was himself 14 when he entered Trinity College, Dublin.

15. 15 "physic": Gulliver studied "physic" (i.e., medicine) at the famous center of medical studies, the University of Leyden in Holland.

15. 20 "Levant": the eastern Mediterranean, particularly the coastal areas and adjacent regions.

15. 24 "Old Jury": i.e., Old Jewry, a street in the old City of London, the Jewish quarter of medieval London.

15. 25 "Mrs.": In Swift's day this title (Mistress) was applied to adult women whether married or single.

16. 26–27 "Van Diemen's Land": Tasmania, then believed to be part of the Australian mainland.

17. 26 "six inches high": The sizes of things are reduced roughly to a twelfth in Lilliput and multiplied by twelve in Brobdingnag. Much has been made of Swift's accuracy in keeping to his scale, not only in linear measurements but also in areas and solids (see, for example, William A. Eddy, *Gulliver's Travels: A Critical Study*, 1923, pp. 92 ff.).

17. 34–35 "admiration": i.e., wonderment.

17. 35 "*Hekinah degul*": The languages of the various lands visited by Gulliver have been analyzed by several commentators, who believe that Swift constructed these languages carefully according to certain logical, ascertainable principles (see, for example, Paul Odell Clark, "A *Gulliver* Dictionary," *Studies in Philology*, L [1953], 592 ff.). The more traditional view is that these languages are merely nonsense, revealing Swift's characteristic verbal playfulness, so often exhibited in his puns, anagrams, and other verbal games, such as he and his friends delighted in. For aspects of Swift's interest in language, see his contribution to *The Tatler*, No. 230, and his Letter to Harley, *A Proposal for Correcting . . . the English Tongue*, 1712.

18. 13 "buff jerkin": a close-fitting leather jacket.

21. 26 "engines": mechanical contrivances.

22. 21–22 "an ancient temple": apparently intended to suggest Westminster Hall, in which Charles I had been condemned to death. For Swift's attitude towards Charles I and the political and religious implications of the beheading of that monarch, see his *Sermon Upon the Martyrdom of K. Charles I*, 1726.

23. 13 "stang": a rood or one-fourth of an acre.

23. 34 "in point of cleanliness": These lines reflect what Middleton Murry, in a rather foolish and misleading chapter, has referred to as Swift's "excremental vision" (see his *Jonathan Swift: A Critical Biography*, 1954). Swift's use of naturalistic detail in both prose and poetry (in such poems as "A Beautiful Young Nymph Going to Bed" and "The Lady's Dressing Room") has excited considerable comment, much of it unacceptable, as in Aldous Huxley's essay on Swift in *Do What You Will*, 1929. For a refutation, see the Introduction, p. xii. An intelligent approach to the matter may be found in Maurice Johnson, *The Sin of Wit: Jonathan Swift as a Poet*, 1950, and in Irvin Ehrenpreis, *The Personality of Swift*, 1958, as well as in works by other Swift scholars, such as Professor Herbert Davis and Sir Harold Williams. The latter's edition of Swift's *Poems* is authoritative.

24. 4 "The Emperor": In the political allegory the Emperor represents George I, though the descriptive details are not accurate. As Professor Arthur Case remarks, Swift is either being ironical in these details about the Emperor or guarding against prosecution, or both. The political allegory in Part I reflects some of the circumstances of the last years of Queen Anne when Swift was an active journalist in the Tory cause (see the Introduction, p. xvi), and some of the events of the early part of George I's reign. This was the period just after the close of the War of the Spanish Succession, ended by the Treaty of Utrecht in 1713.

25. 9 "High and Low Dutch": i.e., German and Dutch.

25. 9–10 "Lingua Franca": a mixed jargon or language used by traders in the Mediterranean ports.

27. 12 "to search me": The search and the inventory which follow are generally interpreted as Swift's allegorical treatment of The Committee of Secrecy formed in 1715 by the triumphant Whigs to investigate members of Queen Anne's last ministry. The leaders of that ministry, Robert Harley and Viscount Bolingbroke, were Swift's close friends, and he himself was under suspicion. The charges were sympathy with the Jacobites and betrayal of the nation by making peace with France. In Part I, Gulliver in the political allegory stands for a composite figure, Swift, Harley, and Bolingbroke.

31. 25 "Flimnap . . . is allowed to cut a caper": Flimnap represents the famous Whig statesman, Sir Robert Walpole, head of the government from 1715 to 1717 and from 1721 to 1742. His political dexterity is here satirized. Swift disliked him both as a man and a politician. See the references to him in Swift's *Verses on the Death of Dr. Swift*, 1739.

31. 29 "Reldresal": possibly Lord Carteret, Secretary of State in 1721 and later Lord-Lieutenant of Ireland, a good friend of Swift's who nevertheless in his official capacity offered a reward for the discovery of the Drapier (i.e., Swift) in 1724 (see Swift's amusing essay, *A Vindication of His Excellency John, Lord Carteret, from the Charge of Favouring None but Tories, High-Churchmen and Jacobites*, 1730). Also suggested as Reldresal: Lord Townshend, Secretary of State and a chief ally of Walpole.

31. 41 "one of the King's cushions": the Duchess of Kendal, a mistress of George I, by whose influence it was believed Walpole was restored to power in 1721. He had resigned his offices in 1717.

32. 2 "blue . . . red . . . green": the colors of the ribbons of the Orders of the Garter, the Bath, and the Thistle (see Swift's *Verses on the Revival of the Order of the Bath*, written against Walpole).

33. 9 "close chair": sedan chair.

34. 29 "Skyresh Bolgolam": the Earl of Nottingham, whom Swift had lampooned as "Dismal" and who is reported to have referred in Parliament to Swift as "a certain Divine . . . hardly suspected of being a Christian [yet] is in a fair way of being a Bishop". He was First Lord of the Admiralty from 1680 to 1684. Although a Tory, he opposed Harley and the Tory ministry at times and thus came under Swift's indictment.

35. 7 "most mighty Emperor": The pretentious titles accorded to the Emperor of Lilliput presumably parody the manner of glorifying oriental rulers in popular travel books.

37. 7 "sideling": sideways.

38. 40 *"Tramecksan and Slamecksan"*: Tory and Whig or High Church and Low Church.

39. 2–3 "imperial heels are lower": George I favored the Whigs and Low Churchmen throughout his reign.

39. 11 "hobble in his gait": The Prince of Wales, later George II, cultivated friends among Whigs and Tories. Hence the hobble in his gait. He surrounded himself with men who opposed his father and Walpole, but to the disappointment of Swift and his friends, the prince retained Walpole in office after coming to the throne.

39. 13 "Blefuscu": France.

39. 26 "primitive way of breaking eggs": The Big-Endians and the Little-Endians represent Catholics and Protestants, whose controversies are here adumbrated. Swift's brief allegorical treatment of the religious struggles seems to include Henry VIII (who broke from the Pope, i.e., commanded his subjects to eat their eggs at the small end), Charles I (who lost his life), and James II (who lost his throne). France (Blefuscu) as a center of Catholicism fomented rebellions in England (Lilliput). Swift has not attempted, apparently, to achieve historical exactitude.

39. 41–43 "Big-Endians . . . incapable by law of holding employments": a reference to the Test Act passed by the English Parliament after the Restoration, which prevented Catholics and nonconformists from holding civil and military offices unless they received the sacrament according to the rites of the Anglican Church. Swift strongly supported this policy.

42. 17 "arrived safe at the royal port of Lilliput": Gulliver's destruction of the Blefuscudian fleet appears to represent the presumed destruction of French naval power in the War of the Spanish Succession, 1701–1713. The Tory ministry of Harley and Bolingbroke laid claim to this achievement. Professor Case suggests that Swift symbolized the culmination of the War by a *naval* victory to offset the Whig claims for the exploits of their great general, the Duke of Marlborough. For Swift on the subject of Marlborough, see *The Examiner*, No. 16 and *A Satirical Elegy on the Death of a Late Famous General* (1722).

43. 14 "a peace": The Treaty of Utrecht, signed April 11, 1713, brought the War to a close but left Whigs and Tories a heritage of bitter conflicts, as Gulliver's involvements reveal.

45. 20–22 "it is capital . . . to make water within the precincts of the palace": The Queen's resentment of Gulliver's method of putting out the fire is generally thought to refer to Queen Anne's dislike of *A Tale of a Tub* for its coarseness and presumed profaneness. She resisted endeavors to make him a dean or a bishop in the Church of England. Swift referred to the Queen as "A Royal Prude" in his poem, *The Author Upon Himself* (1714).

46. 16 "manner of writing is very peculiar": Professor R. W. Frantz suggests that Swift has modeled this paragraph on a passage in William Symson's *New Voyage to the East-Indies*, 1715.

46. 19 "The Cascagians": possibly invented by Swift.

50. 41 "domestic": i.e., household.

52. 5–6 "white staff": the symbol of office of the Lord Treasurer.

52. 23 "jealous of his wife": Flimnap's jealousy, Sir Charles Firth supposes, is "an ironical hit at Walpole, whose first wife, Catherine

Shorter, was not above suspicion, while Walpole's indifference to her levities was notorious."

54. 20 "articles of impeachment": The political allegory is still concerned with events rising out of the Treaty of Utrecht. The Committee of Secrecy with Walpole as its chairman (see note to p. 27, l. 12) made its report, and both Oxford and Bolingbroke were impeached for high treason. Swift is here satirizing the charges brought against the ousted Tory ministers.

56. 21 "to put out both your eyes": a reference, possibly, to the proposal in Parliament that Oxford and Bolingbroke be impeached for a lesser crime than high treason, in which instance they would forfeit their property and civil rights but not their lives.

58. 17 "great lenity and tenderness": perhaps an ironic comment on an Address to the King by the House of Lords in 1716, praising him for his "endearing tenderness and clemency." Soon afterwards some distinguished Jacobites were executed despite the pleas of "the mercy men."

59. 17–18 "arrived at . . . Blefuscu": Gulliver's escape parallels Bolingbroke's flight to France just before his trial. The charges against Harley, who did not flee, were dropped after two years.

61. 23 "sent back to Lilliput": The English made diplomatic protests to the French for harboring fleeing Jacobites.

63. 17 "ancient": i.e., ensign or flag.

63. 25–26 "North and South Seas": i.e., North and South Pacific.

63. 44 "the Downs": a roadstead in the English Channel, off the coast of Kent — the approach to England.

64. 25 "upon the parish": i.e., impoverished and dependent upon the charity of the parish.

67. 25 "to overblow": Swift parodies the excessive use of nautical terms. The passage is taken, almost verbatim, from Samuel Sturmy's *Mariners Magazine*, 1669.

68. 30 "Great Tartary . . . frozen sea": i.e., Siberia and the Arctic Ocean.

70. 28 "great or little . . . comparison": Among the philosophers known to Swift who discussed the relativity of size and vision was George Berkeley, in his *New Theory of Vision*, 1709.

77. 1 "baby": i.e., her doll.

77. 20 "*nanunculus* . . . *homunceletino*": apparently Swift's own coinages.

78. 28–29 "ignominy of being carried about for a monster": The public exhibition of Gulliver reflects the common practice of the times in displaying (for a small sum) human oddities, such as dwarfs, and various animal monstrosities. Swift refers to these "monstermongers" in *A Tale of a Tub* (see Aline M. Taylor, "Sights and Monsters and Gulliver's Voyage to Brobdingnag," in *Tulane Studies in English*, vol. vii, pp. 29 ff., 1957).

79. 36 "pumpion": pumpkin.

81. 7 "Sanson's *Atlas*": Sanson was a famous French map-maker of the seventeenth century.

83. 12 "philosophy": in our terminology, science.

84. 7 *"lusus naturæ"*: a sport or freak of nature.

84. 10 "followers of Aristotle": Note that the indictment is of the *followers* of Aristotle, not Aristotle himself (see Pt. III, ch. viii, pp. 159–60.

86. 21 *"Royal Sovereign"*: one of the largest ships of the English navy in the seventeenth century.

86. 40 "birthday clothes": Custom decreed new finery for royal birthdays. Cf. Pope's "Youth more glitt'ring than a *Birthnight Beau*" in *The Rape of the Lock*, Canto I, l. 23.

89. 3 "Gresham College": the home of the Royal Society of London for Improving Natural Knowledge, usually referred to as the Royal Society, or the Royal Society of Scientists.

90. 31 "a square of Westminster Hall": i.e., a square of the same area as Westminster Hall. The Great Hall was used as a court of justice and on state occasions.

90. 44 "through a microscope": The world revealed by the microscope fascinated contemporaries. See the excellent study by Marjorie H. Nicolson, "The Microscope and English Imagination," in *Science and Imagination*, 1956.

92. 6 "Salisbury steeple": The spire of Salisbury Cathedral is over 400 feet high.

92. 21 "cupola at St. Paul's": The dome of St. Paul's Cathedral is well over 100 feet in diameter.

94. 24 "stoop": swoop.

95. 11 "maids of honour": Soon after the appearance of *Gulliver's Travels* Gay and Pope wrote an amusing letter to Swift about its reception in London. They reported to him that "among lady critics, some have found that Mr. Gulliver had a particular malice to maids of honour" (see F. Elrington Ball, *The Correspondence of Jonathan Swift*, III, 358–61). In 1711 Dr. John Arbuthnot and Swift had engaged in a hoax at the Court of Queen Anne. They circulated an announcement among the maids of honor of a forthcoming book entitled *A History of the Maids of Honour since Harry the Eighth*, for which the deceived maids of honor paid in advance (see the *Journal to Stella*, Sept. 19, 21, 23, 1711).

96. 21–22 *"jet d'eau* at Versailles": The largest fountain in the Gardens of Versailles threw its water over 70 feet in the air. Executions were popular public spectacles in Swift's day.

97. 15 "closet": small private room.

100. 23 "levee": It was customary in the period for people of distinction to receive visitors on rising from bed. Though Swift pretended to scorn levees, he sometimes appeared at Harley's.

103. 3 "plantations": colonies.

103. 12 "highest court of judicature": i.e., the House of Lords, in Swift's day the final court of appeal in legal cases.

103. 19 "holy persons": Bishops are members of the House of Lords as spiritual peers.

104. 9–10 "cultivate . . . our young nobility": for Swift's view of the education of the nobility, see his essay, *The Intelligencer*, No. IX.

104. 26–27 "prostitute chaplains to some nobleman": Dignities in the Church of England (deans and bishops) were as often as not considered political appointments. Swift was bitter over the excessive number of Low-Churchmen appointed to bishoprics by George I. He particularly showed his disrespect for the bishops of the Church of Ireland.

105. 36 "generals . . . richer than our kings": an obvious reflection on Marlborough, who profited greatly by the War of the Spanish Succession (see *The Examiner*, No. 16).

105. 39–40 "mercenary standing army . . . peace": proscribed by the Bill of Rights (1689) except with the consent of Parliament, and generally opposed by the Tories.

107. 26–27 "Dionysius Halicarnassensis": A Greek writer who lived in Rome in the days of Augustus. His *Archaeologia* is designed to show the true greatness of Rome.

108. 12 "a certain powder": In the controversy between the Ancients and the Moderns, which preoccupies Swift in *A Tale of a Tub* and *The Battle of the Books*, the Moderns boasted of the perfection of gunpowder as one of their achievements. It had led, they maintained, to the conquest of colonies and thus to the extension of Christianity, trade, and knowledge. If Gulliver's defence of gunpowder is placed in the context of the Ancient-Modern controversy, Swift's irony takes on added sharpness and meaning, as an indictment of the Moderns.

110. 2–3 "entities . . . transcendentals": Swift reacted strongly against so-called "terms of art," that is, the jargon of philosophy, science, and theology, which obscured meaning rather than clarified it (see his *Letter to a Young Gentleman lately entered into Holy Orders*, 1720).

110. 13 "art of printing": Swift is possibly reflecting an aspect of the Ancient-Modern controversy in limiting the king's library to not above a thousand volumes. The Moderns maintained that they had a distinct advantage in knowledge by virtue of the art of printing. Sir William Temple, in defence of the Ancients, remarked that the spread of learning is not dependent on books, that in certain countries tradition has been a better preserver of history and knowledge. He argued also that the invention of printing has not necessarily multiplied books, only copies of them, i.e., that *numbers* of volumes are not a measure of learning.

110. 34 "style . . . not florid": A plain style had become an ideal by Swift's day.

111. 6–7 "nature was degenerated": The idea of the decay of nature was pervasive in seventeenth-century thought. It held that both man and civilization had declined from their earlier excellence, that just as man passes through a cycle of youth, old age, and death, so do nature and human culture in all of their aspects. This concept of universal decay came under attack as the idea of progress developed. The two chief antagonists of the controversy before 1650 were Godfrey Goodman and George Hakewell, both of whom influenced later writers. Swift's reference to the abortive births of these later times as contrasted with the giants of former ages can be found in Goodman's *The Fall of Man*, 1616, where he maintains that men of the past were stronger and larger, demonstrably so from the discovery of the large bones and weapons of early times. The two opposed concepts — the decay of nature and the idea of progress — were fundamental ones in the Ancient-Modern controversy, the first for the Ancients, the second for the Moderns.

111. 31 "tradesmen . . . farmers": Observe that the army in Brobdingnag is a citizens' militia, not the type of professional standing army that the Tories opposed.

112. 26 "tumbril": cart.

120. 21 "conceit": a witty thought or turn of expression.

120. 22 "Tonquin": Tongking, a port in French Indo-China.

120. 26 "coasting New Holland": sailing along the coast-line of Australia.

120. 34 "freight": passage.

123. 26–27 "Fort St. George": established by the East India Company; the area grew into Madras.

124. 29–30 "countries in strict alliance": At this time England and Holland were joined in the Grand Alliance and were at war with France. They were, nevertheless, strong commercial rivals. For Swift's attitude towards the Dutch, see the note to p. 175, ll. 8–9.

126. 26 "an island in the air": As in earlier ages so in Swift's day, there was great interest in the possibility of flying machines. Many parallels to Swift's Laputa have been noted, from Lucian's *True*

History to Defoe's *The Consolidator.*

127. 32 "fiddles, flutes . . .": Swift's satire of the Laputans (who are the English of the reign of George I) reflects the current enthusiasm for abstract science and the theory of music, and the tendency (particularly among scientists) to find analogies between music and mathematics. The main point of the satire, as Professor Marjorie Nicolson points out, is "that the Laputans are concerned with the theory, not with the application, of both mathematics and music" (*Science and Imagination*, p. 121).

128. 21 "kennel": gutter.

128. 33 "the King": George I, a patron of music and, to a lesser extent, of science, but he was not credited with much personal knowledge of or interest in either.

129. 12 "hospitality to strangers": a thrust at George I, much criticized for partiality to Hanoverians who had followed him to England.

129. 20 "hautboys": oboes.

130. 4–5 "the true etymology": Swift here mocks contemporary philology.

130. 20–21 "mistake a figure in the calculation": This is usually considered a reference to an error in one of Newton's publications made by the printer, who had added a cipher to Newton's calculation of the sun's distance from the earth. Swift's attitude towards Newton and Newtonian science is complex. In 1724 he had occasion to be displeased with Newton, who, as Comptroller of the Mint, had made a favorable report on Wood's copper coinage. Swift's second *Drapier's Letter* comments on Newton's assay of the controversial copper coins.

132. 12–14 "earth . . . swallowed up": The Laputans believe, pessimistically, in some of the implications of Newtonian science. Newton's analysis of planetary motion recognized at least the possibility that the earth might after "an immense tract of time" fall into the sun. (This and other notes on the scientific aspects of Pt. III are based on the brilliant article by Marjorie Nicolson and Nora Mohler, "The Scientific Background of Swift's *Voyage to Laputa*," reprinted in Professor Nicolson's *Science and Imagination*, 1956).

132. 14–15 "sun . . . effluvia": a reference to contemporary discussions concerning sun-spots.

132. 38 "avoid the stroke of the approaching comet": an allusion to Halley's comet, due to appear again in 1758. Halley and others had considered the possibility that the earth might be struck and "reduced into its ancient chaos."

134. 4–5 "a philosophical account": The "factual and learned" description which follows mimics the manner of the scientific papers contributed to the *Transactions of the Royal Society*. Swift's use of magnetism as the propelling power of the Flying Island reflects scientific interests of the day, stemming from William Gilbert's *De Magnete*, 1600.

138. 7–8 "deprive them of . . . sun and the rain": Swift is almost certainly thinking here of England's oppressive laws in restraint of Irish trade.

138. 43 "About three years": The account which follows is an allegory of Ireland's resistance to Wood's copper coinage. Swift played an important part in the controversy with his *Drapier's Letters* (1724). Lindalino is Dublin.

140. 11–12 "forced . . . their own conditions": The English government under pressure cancelled Wood's patent.

140. 18 "to leave the island": A clause in the Act of Settlement (1701) provided that the king could leave the country only with the consent of Parliament. George I secured the repeal of this clause. Swift is here glancing at the repeated visits of the king to Hanover, the first of which, in 1716, lasted for six months.

141. 5 "great lord at court": possibly the Prince of Wales, later George II, who was indifferent to the arts and learning. He did, however, become a patron of the famous composer, Handel.

141. 44 "Munodi": variously identified as Bolingbroke, who ostensibly went into rural retirement on his return from exile in 1723, or as Harley, who similarly retired into the country and abstained from public life after charges of treason were dropped in 1717.

143. 37–38 "all arts, sciences . . . upon a new foot": Swift's bias against innovations and the Moderns is reflected in the treatment of Munodi and his estate. The "new rules and methods of agriculture" may be an allusion to the changes in cultivation, manuring, and crop rotation then being introduced.

143. 39 "an academy of Projectors in Lagado": The Grand Academy of Lagado is Swift's satiric representation of the Royal Society, given a royal charter in 1662. The experiments presented in the following pages are in some instances based upon actual experiments of the times, distorted by Swift to achieve his comic intentions (see Marjorie Nicolson, *Science and Imagination*, pp. 110 ff.). The word "projector" in the period meant one addicted to impractical or speculative activities. Professor Case thinks that the foolish experiments of the academicians of Lagado satirize the impractical political and economic schemes of the Whig administration as well as contemporary scientists. Swift is following a well-established tradition in English literature of satirizing the excesses and corruptions of scientific learning.

145. 9 "I was received": Swift himself visited Gresham College, home of the Royal Society, in 1710. In a letter to Stella (Dec. 13) he reports a day's activity which included a visit to the Tower of London, Bedlam, Gresham College, and a puppet-show — an odd mixture, perhaps inspired in some way by "the rainiest day that ever dript" (so he remarked of it).

146. 15–17 "colours . . . by feeling and smelling": The Great Scriblerus "first found out the palpability of colours" — so we are told in *The Memoirs of Scriblerus* (ch. viii), a satiric work in which Swift had a hand, along with Pope, Gay, Dr. Arbuthnot, and others (see the excellent edition of *The Memoirs*, edited by Charles Kerby-Miller, 1950, with valuable notes). A story of a blind man who could distinguish colors is related by the great scientist Robert Boyle, in his "Experiments and Observations upon Colour."

147. 35–36 "the universal artist": possibly an allusion to Robert Boyle, whose experiments touched many fields; but it may reflect, more generally, the pretensions of some contemporaries in the spirit of Bacon, to take all knowledge for their province. The Baconian spirit was strong among scientists.

148. 19–20 "how laborious the usual method": Compare this painless way of achieving learning with that attributed to the Moderns in *A Tale of A Tub*, sec. vii — "without the fatigue of reading or thinking."

150. 26 "school of languages": Swift gibes at the many suggestions, from scientists and others, for the formation of a philosophical or universal language. Comenius and John Wilkins, both influenced by Bacon, were perhaps the most influential of those who wrote on the subject, Wilkins's *Essay Towards a Real Character and a Philosophical Language* being published by the Royal Society in 1668. One of the ideals was that the *name* of a thing should in itself disclose the *nature* of the thing. Swift laughs at this notion by eliminating names altogether, reducing "language" to things.

155. 5 "at stool": thought to be a reference to papers found in Bishop Atterbury's close-stool and presented at his trial for Jacobite intrigues in 1722. Francis Atterbury, Bishop of Rochester and a good friend of Swift's, was found guilty of treason and fled to France. Like Swift, he was a Tory High-Churchman; but, unlike Swift, he actively supported the Pretender.

155. 18–19 "Tribnia . . . Langden": anagrams of "Britain" and "England."

155. 34 "mysterious meanings of . . . letters": Swift, who never believed Atterbury guilty, ridicules here the evidence against the bishop, particularly the endeavor to extract secret meanings from his correspondence. See note to p. 155, l. 5.

158. 37 "he was not poisoned": Plutarch in his *Lives* denies the story that Alexander the Great was poisoned by his cup-bearer. He died of a fever at Babylon in 323 B.C., at the age of 32.

158. 39–40 "Hannibal . . . vinegar in his camp": The progress of Hannibal's army over the Alps in Italy was blocked by a rock. The rock was heated, saturated with vinegar, and then easily cut. The story comes from Livy, Bk. XXI, ch. 37.

158. 44 "a modern representative": i.e., the British parliament.

160. 6 "Didymus and Eustathius": an Alexandrian (fl. 10 A.D.) and a Byzantine (12th century) who wrote commentaries on Homer.

160. 10 "Scotus and Ramus": Duns Scotus, from whose name the word "dunce" originated, was a leading scholastic philosopher (d. 1308) and author of a commentary on Aristotle. Pierre de la Ramée, an influential thinker of the sixteenth century, was a critic of Aristotle.

160. 17–18 "Gassendi . . . made Epicurus . . . palatable": Pierre Gassendi (1592–1655) supported Epicurean physics against Aristotelian and Cartesian physics. Although Epicurean ethics found defenders in the seventeenth and eighteenth centuries, the Epicurean system of physics was much attacked as atheistic and materialistic. In *A Tale of A Tub*, sec. ix, Swift uses Epicurean ideas for satiric purposes.

160. 19 "the *vortices* of Descartes": The physical theories of the great French philosopher and mathematician, René Descartes (1596–1650) were highly controversial in England in the late seventeenth and early eighteenth centuries. Particularly his theory of vortices, basic in his physics, came under fire. Swift refers to it in *A Tale of a Tub*, sec. ix, as a "romantick system."

160. 20 "*attraction*": i.e., Newton's theory of gravitation.

160. 23 "pretend to demonstrate them from mathematical principles": These words reflect the struggle between the natural philosophers (scientists) and the moral philosophers (humanists) in the period. Gulliver as Swift's spokesman expresses the scepticism of the moral philosophers over the claims of the scientists that mathematics, or the sciences founded on it, could arrive at certitude or ultimate truths. The humanists insisted that the most valuable knowledge was the knowledge of man, not of nature. The struggle between these two groups is one of the organizing principles of eighteenth-century thought.

160. 25 "determined": concluded.

160. 28 "Eliogabalus's cooks": Heliogabalus, Roman Emperor of the third century A.D., whose gluttony is proverbial.

161. 8 "Polydore Virgil": an Italian cleric of the sixteenth century who lived in England and wrote a history of England in Latin.

161. 17 "disgusted with modern history": Swift refers to the modern historians in *The Battle of the Books* as "mercenaries." His disgust with historical writers who have falsified the past can be better understood if we keep in mind the idealistic Ciceronian conception of history which prevailed, history as the mistress of man's life, time's witness, the herald of antiquity, the light of truth, and life of memory. The exposure of "prostitute writers" at this point in *Gulliver* recalls Voltaire's remark that "history is only a pack of lies we play on the dead."

164. 27–28 "Dutch . . . the only Europeans permitted": After anti-Christian uprisings in 1638, some Dutch and Chinese traders remained as Japan's sole contact with the outside world. See below, note to p. 175, ll. 2–3.

167. 9–10 "*struldbruggs* or *immortals*": Cf. Swift's remark in his *Thoughts on Various Subjects:* "Every man desires to live long, but no man would be old."

169. 39–40 "revolutions of states and empires": In this paragraph Swift puts into Gulliver's mouth the prevalent conception of cyclical history, the view that nations, letters, the arts, knowledge in general, rise, flourish, languish, and die, only to begin a new cycle in another part of the world. This philosophy of history was opposed to two other theories of history also prevalent, one embodied in the phrase "decay of nature" and the other in the phrase "the idea of progress" (see above, note to p. 111, ll. 6–7). In his *Essay upon the Ancient and Modern Learning* Swift's patron, Sir William Temple, used the cyclical theory to counter the Moderns, who argued that civilization has maintained a steady and cumulative progress from ancient to modern times. The cyclical view of history reaches back to ancient Greece and Rome, and even beyond.

170. 2 "discovery of the longitude": Many attempts were made in the period to discover a simple, accurate method of determining the longitude at sea. The stimulus came in part from a large sum offered by parliament at the close of Anne's reign. "I am told," Swift wrote to Archbishop King in 1712, "it is a thing as improbable as the philosopher's stone, or perpetual motion." Some of the foolish proposals were satirized in Swift's circle.

170. 2–3 "perpetual motion": The idea of a perpetual motion machine had teased the imagination of scientists and others in England from the time of Bacon, who had included such machines in Solomon's House in *The New Atlantis*, 1627. By the time of *Gulliver* they were the subject of satire. Some scientists still toyed seriously with the idea; others felt that, given the laws of matter and motion, the construction of such a machine was impossible.

170. 3 "the universal medicine": another name for the elixir of life, which the alchemists maintained would prolong life indefinitely. In *A Tale of a Tub* Swift refers to Artephius, an alchemist who is reputed to have lived a thousand years or more by virtue of the *elixir vitae*. The editor of this volume does not know the elixir used by

Artephius. He offers the following as a substitute: "Take ten parts of celestial slime; separate the male from the female, and each afterwards from its earth, but physically, mark you, and with no violence. Conjoin after separation in due harmonic, vital proportion. Straightway the soul, descending from the pyroplastic sphere, shall restore, by a vivific embrace, its dead and deserted body. The conjoined substances shall be warmed by a natural fire in a perfect marriage of spirit and body. Proceed according to the Vulcanico-magical theory till they are exalted into the fifth metaphysical rota. This is that world-renowned medicine of which so many have scribbled, and yet so few have known" (from A. E. Wait, *The Hermetic and Alchemical Writings of Aureolus Philippus Theophrastus Bombast, of Hohenheim, called Paracelsus the Great*, 1894, II, 384).

170. 9–10 "desire of endless life": As a divine, Swift could hardly have been unaware that the concept of an earthly immortality ran counter to the Christian view of death as coming in with the Fall and being the inevitable lot of man.

170. 40–41 "disadvantages which old age brings": The subject of old age, with its attendant physical and moral deterioration, had been a convention in literature from the time of the ancients. Cicero in *De Senectute* (c. 44. B.C.) depicted the compensations and consolations of age, but perhaps the preponderance of literature up to Swift's day had been less favorably disposed. Swift should be seen in the latter tradition, very strong in his time.

174. 20 "Yedo": Tokyo.

175. 2–3 *"trampling upon the crucifix"*: the *Jefumi* or "figure treading" was a test apparently used in certain localities to detect Japanese suspected of being converts to Christianity. There is no evidence that it was applied to the Dutch, as Swift indicates.

175. 8–9 "suspected I must be a Christian": Swift's bias against the Dutch resulted in part from the commercial rivalry between England and Holland and in part from the danger to the established Church in England from Holland as a symbol of a nation where religious toleration prevailed, to the benefit of domestic tranquility and commercial prosperity. Holland was also politically anathema as a republic and as an obstructive ally in the Grand Alliance against France.

175. 23 *"Amboyna"*: As Mr. William Brown points out, Swift did not innocently choose the name of this ship. He is trying to keep alive English belief in the cruelty of the Dutch, who had tortured some Englishmen at Amboyna, in the East Indies in 1623. Dryden had revived memories of the Amboyna massacre in a play in 1673.

175. 39 "skipper": seaman.

179. 11 "Tenariff": Teneriffe, largest of the Canary Islands.

179. 12 "Campechy": on the coast of Yucatan. The logwoods, called campeachy wood, brought in from that area were used for making dyes.

181. 6–7 "shape . . . singular, and deformed": Swift's description of the Yahoos may have been suggested, according to Professor R. W. Frantz, by the accounts of large apes or of the Hottentots to be found in contemporary voyage literature. The word "Yahoo" derives, possibly, from two common expressions of disgust in the period, "yah" and "ugh" (Morley).

183. 12–13 "coat . . . wonder": The antithesis between nature and art, the natural and the artificial, a dominant theme in Pt. IV, is thus suggested early, when the Houyhnhnms who discover Gulliver are bewildered by his clothes, an artifice which does not exist among those who live according to nature. See below, note to p. 190, l. 2.

184. 14 "*Houyhnhnm*": generally accepted as an imitation of the whinny of a horse.

186. 14–15 "in this abominable animal a perfect human figure": Swift's denigration here, and elsewhere in Pt. IV, of the human body may be a satirical reaction to the physico-theologists of the times, who were lyrical in praising the body's perfection as evidence of God's handiwork and of design in the universe.

188. 19–20 "insipid diet": Gulliver's remarks on his simple diet and the good health which resulted contain more than meets the eye. It touches Swift personally in that he experimented much with diets for reasons of health, but it is also a reflection of contemporary primitivistic thought. The simple, health-giving diet of peoples living in a state of nature was often contrasted with the rich, harmful food of people in artificial societies. Furthermore, the passage reflects medical and theological tradition, particularly with respect to the concept of temperance, a virtue that man lost in the Fall. It was believed that disease (a result of repletion) and sin (as gluttony: intemperance in diet) went hand in hand. The diet of the Houyhnhnms, the very essence of temperance, is part and parcel of their rational behavior and moral perfection, in sharp contrast to the diet of the Yahoos, which is immoderate and in good part proscribed under the Levitical code of the Old Testament.

188. 29 "salt": Many commentators have noted the inaccuracy of Gulliver's remark that no animal except man is fond of salt.

189. 14–15 "speak to his horse . . . in High Dutch": i.e., German. Charles V is credited with the remark that he would address his God in Spanish, his mistress in Italian, and his horse in German.

190. 2 "not the least idea of books": Like clothes, books have no place in a "natural" society. Here again the Houyhnhnms reflect the primitivistic strain in eighteenth-century thought. See above, the note to p. 183, ll. 12–13.

195. 39–40 "find fault with . . . my body": See above, note to p. 186, ll. 14–15.

198. 24 "difference in opinions": There follow four references to contemporary religious controversies — over the consecrated elements of bread and wine in the Eucharist, the use of music in church services, the veneration of the Crucifix, and the nature of ecclesiastical vestments. Cf. the controversy in Pt. I between the Big and Little Endians. In *A Tale of a Tub* Swift gives elaborate treatment to sectarian differences.

199. 19–20 "beggarly princes . . . hire out their troops": an allusion to the mercenaries of George I when Elector of Hanover.

199. 37–38 "a description of cannons": See Pt. II, ch. vii, p. 108 and note.

201. 30 "faculty": the profession.

202. 34–35 "the use of money": For a contemporary comment on the power of money, see Bernard Mandeville's *Fable of the Bees*, Part II, Sixth Dialogue, where Cleomenes remarks that "nothing is more universally charming than Money."

203. 14–15 "especially those who presided over the rest": The ambiguity of this statement has been noted. Case suggests persuasively that it means "especially that species which presided over the rest."

203. 23 "female yahoos . . . breakfast": In this passage Swift reflects the contemporary mercantilist animus against imports, especially of luxuries. He complained that Ireland imported tea, coffee, and chocolate at an annual cost of £150,000; and he agreed with Bishop Berkeley that an Irish woman of fashion dressed in imported clothes is a public enemy.

204. 1 "wine": In 1729 Swift argued amusingly against Ireland's increasing the duty on the importation of wine "because there is no nation yet known, in either hemisphere, where the people of all conditions are more in want of some cordial, to keep up their spirits, than this of ours" (*A Proposal that all the Ladies . . . of Ireland should appear constantly in Irish Manufactures*, 1729).

213. 8–9 "seeds of spleen": Spleen was the fashionable malady of the early eighteenth century, all the more socially acceptable because Queen Anne suffered from it. The term was used rather loosely to describe vapors, hypochondria, ennui, lowness of spirits, and particularly melancholy, which was thought by both Englishmen and foreigners to be a special characteristic of the English — "a kind of demon that haunts the island" — so Addison remarked (*Spectator*, No. 387; see also Pope's Cave of Spleen in *The Rape of the Lock*). For an excellent study consult "The English Malady," in Cecil A. Moore's *Backgrounds of English Literature, 1700–1760*, 1953.

216. 20 "as Plato delivers them": an allusion, possibly, to *The*

Republic (bk. v), where *opinion* and *real knowledge* are distinguished.

216. 31 "fondness": foolish doting.

226. 26 "devoted": doomed.

226. 29 "temper": calmness.

227. 19 "artificially": skilfully.

228. 17 "February 15, 1714–15": i.e., 1715 in our reckoning. In Swift's day the English New Year began not on Jan. 1, but on March 25.

229. 26 "Mr. Herman Moll": a famous map-maker of the period.

232. 40 "backwards": situated at the rear.

234. 15 "stone-horses": stallions.

235. 23–24 *"Nec . . . finget"*: Although vile Fortune has made Sinon wretched, she has not made him false and a liar (Virgil, *Aeneid*, II, 79–80).

236. 44 *"Recalcitrat . . . tutus"*: He kicks backward, secure on every side (Horace, *Satires*, II, i, 20).

THE TEXT. The collected edition of Swift's *Works*, Dublin, 1735, published by George Faulkner, with Swift's approval and containing his own corrections, revisions, and suggestions to improve the editions printed by Motte in 1726 and 1727. Some readings have been adopted from the Motte editions and from the various corrections and additions made by Swift's friend, Charles Ford, at the time of the first publication of *Gulliver* in 1726. Faulkner's italics, spelling, capitalization, and punctuation have been normalized amply enough, I trust, so that the text should present no difficulty to the student from "accidentals."

RIVERSIDE EDITIONS

° In preparation